Panicking, Jaci stabbed the key at the lock, got it into the hole on the third try, and unlocked the door. She pulled the key out, darted inside, and locked the door again. Draping the pendant chain back around her neck, she ran across the room to the grandfather clock. *Please, please let this work!*

She held the lantern up close to the glass front. The glass seemed dark, shadowed, with faint long lines tracing upward at an angle from the bottom to most of the way up to the top of the left side of the glass, as if some long, thin things leaned against a wall. Something bulky and darker filled the right side of the glass. *Yes!* There was an etching. But what in the world was it?

Thud! A shoulder crashed into the door.

Jaci whirled, just managing to swallow her shriek.

"Break it down!" the castellan ordered.

Another thud. The hinges groaned, but held.

Jaci turned back to the clock and whispered, "*Saelarin.*"

The familiar electrical charge zinged the air around the clock. With a sob of relief, Jaci pressed the release mechanism, and the back of the clock opened. Shuttering the lantern and clutching it to her, she crammed herself into the tiny space and pulled the back shut.

Thud! She felt the room shudder, heard the chamber door crack. Then silence.

Also by Lori L. MacLaughlin:

LADY, THY NAME IS TROUBLE

TROUBLE BY ANY OTHER NAME

THE ROAD ONCE TAKEN

Lori L. MacLaughlin

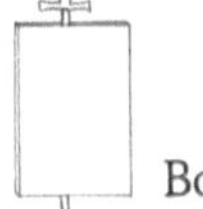
Book and Sword Publishing

Lori L. MacLaughlin/Book and Sword Publishing, LLC
Milton, Vermont, USA
www.bookandswordpublishing.com

Publisher's Note: This is a work of fiction. Names, characters, places, and incidents are a product of the author's imagination. Locales and public names are sometimes used for atmospheric purposes. Any resemblance to actual people, living or dead, or to businesses, companies, events, institutions, or locales is completely coincidental.

Cover Design: Lori L. MacLaughlin and Forward Authority Design
Cover Art: © iStock/mppriv; iStock/lolostock; iStock/Ryan J. Lane
Book Layout © 2014 BookDesignTemplates.com
Map: © 2018 Lori L. MacLaughlin

The Road Once Taken / Lori L. MacLaughlin. -- 1st ed.
ISBN 978-1-942015-04-8

Library of Congress Control Number: 2018904333

Book and Sword Publishing

ACKNOWLEDGEMENTS

Book #3 has finally reached publication! As always, many thanks go to my writing group, the ELFS: Kari Jo Spear and Jody Wood; to copy editor and wordsmith extraordinaire Sue Archer; to designer Carrie Butler of Forward Authority Design, who again worked her magic on the cover; and to the always inspirational League of Vermont Writers.

I would especially like to thank my wonderful family and friends for their unfailing support while I worked on this book in my scarce moments of free time during the past year. Your patience and understanding of my need to finish it is truly appreciated.

For My Children

*Whose imaginations take flight
as often as mine does...*

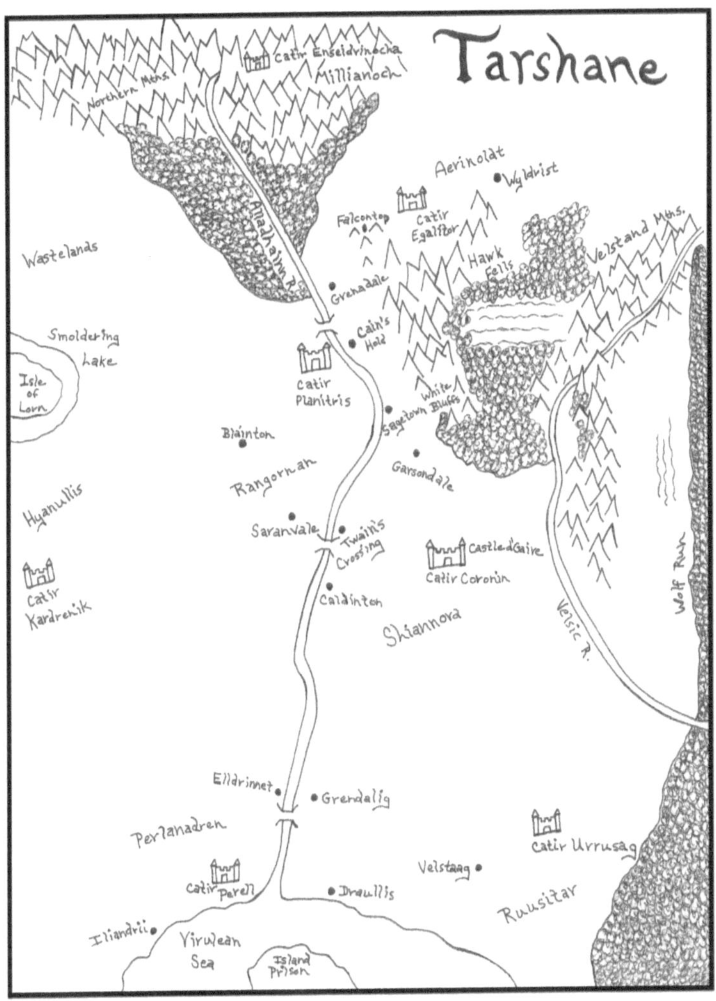

Tarshane
Northern Mths.
Catir Enseidvinocha
Millianoch
Wastelands
Aerinolat
Wyldvist
Falcontop
Catir Egalflor
Hawk Fells
Velstand Mths.
Smoldering Lake
Isle of Lorn
Alladhainn R.
Grenadale
Cain's Hold
Catir Planitris
White Bluffs
Sagetown
Hyanullis
Blainton
Rangornan
Garsondale
Catir Kardrenik
Saranvale
Twain's Crossing
Castle d'Gaive
Catir Coronin
Caldinton
Shiannova
Velsic R.
Wolf Run
Elldrinnet
Grendalig
Perlanadren
Catir Urrusag
Velstaag
Catir Parell
Draullis
Ruusitar
Iliandrii
Virulean Sea
Island Prison

THE
ROAD
ONCE
TAKEN

CHAPTER 1

Jacinda Harper jammed on the brakes and, swerving a bit on the rain-slicked pavement, brought her bright blue Porsche to a screeching halt by the side of the empty highway.

"A road sign! It's about time," she said out loud, though she was alone in the car.

Powering down her window, Jaci squinted into the early evening rain. "Marston, five miles." She buzzed her window back up and grabbed the unfolded Vermont map that lay strewn over the passenger seat. "Where on God's green earth is Marston?"

As she scoured the northern portion of the map, a car whizzed by her from behind, the sudden growl and whine of its engine harsh against the patter of rain. She jumped, startled, and whacked her elbow on the steering wheel.

"Ow!" She rubbed her sore elbow as she watched the car's taillights disappear around a bend. "And they say I drive fast."

She looked back at the map, wishing for the hundredth time she hadn't forgotten her GPS. After a few moments, she found the dot that represented the small town of Marston. She scowled. "Great. That's nowhere near where I'm supposed to be." She glanced at the time on the dashboard. Six o'clock. She should have been at Courtney's an hour ago. Courtney was probably getting worried. She'd always been a worrier, even when they were kids. Now that Courtney had a week-old infant, she was even more prone to anxiety. If only Courtney had stayed in White Plains. It would have made visiting her so much easier.

Jaci shoved back her unruly dark curls in annoyance, then tossed the map onto the passenger seat. She'd have to call Courtney and let her know she'd gotten lost. She dug her cell phone out of her purse, glared at it in disgust, and threw it back in. Still no service. Marston better have a phone she could use. Her stomach growled audibly. And a restaurant. She was starving. She hadn't eaten since breakfast. Flooring the accelerator, she peeled out onto the wet road.

She hadn't gone far when she noticed two shafts of light pointing upward into the rain from the side of the road up ahead.

"What on earth...?" She stepped on the brakes more carefully this time as she took in the bent sign indicating a sharp corner. Then she spotted the sliding tire tracks going off the road and down over the bank. Apprehension chilled her as she remembered the car that had sped by her earlier.

She pulled over to the side of the road and punched on her four-ways. Goosebumps crawled over her skin as she climbed out of her car and jogged through the rain to where the tracks went off the road. Headlights beamed up at her from the twisted frame of a small car lying upside down in the gully below.

"Oh, no," she whispered.

A weak cry rose from the wreckage. "H—help me..." The voice died away.

Jaci looked frantically up and down the road, but no headlights approached from either direction. Taking a deep breath to steady herself, she half-climbed, half-skidded down the steep bank to the wreck.

"Hello!" she called out, circling carefully around the crumpled car. The whole area stank of gasoline. When she reached the driver's side, she stopped and sucked in her breath.

A woman lay pinned beneath the car. It looked as if she'd been partially thrown through the side window. She lay face up, her head and shoulders barely visible in the shadow of the flattened car, the rest of her body buried beneath the wreckage.

The woman moaned and turned her head. Blood mixed with rainwater matted her hair and streaked down the side of her face.

Jaci hurried forward and crouched beside her. She reached toward her, then hesitated, unsure what to do. With shaking fingers, she took off her jacket and hooked it over the wreckage.

"Help me," the woman rasped, as Jaci grabbed a stick and propped her jacket up so that it kept the rain out of the woman's face. The woman coughed, and blood foamed on her lips. "Can't breathe..."

"Hang on, I'll get help!" Jaci leaped to her feet.

"No! Come back! Must listen! Please..." The woman's words ended in a ragged sob.

Jaci bent down again. "I can't get you out by myself. I have to go get someone." She cursed her small size. At five-foot-two and 110 pounds, there was no way she was going to budge that car.

The woman moved her head. "Listen."

Hunching her shoulders against the cold rain, Jaci leaned close.

The woman's voice was barely a whisper now. "Go... my house... Brunswick place... clock... inside it... must go tonight..." She coughed again, her breathing loud and labored. "Tonight... must... take the key back..." Her eyes closed. She gasped for breath.

Jaci scrambled up the bank and ran for her car, looking for approaching headlights in hopes of finding someone who could help. Nothing. The road trailed away into darkness. She swung into her car and roared toward Marston.

Two minutes later she passed the "Welcome to Marston" sign. Just beyond it, she spied an open gas station. She veered into the station and pulled up to the front door, honking her horn. A young man with a black ponytail hustled out of the station, wiping his hands on an oily rag. Snatching up her purse, she flung open her door and jumped out.

"There's been an accident! A car went off the road back there." Jaci pointed back the way she'd come. "A woman's pinned under her car. Call the fire department or rescue squad or whatever you have out here!"

"An accident?" The attendant looked in the direction she'd pointed. "Where?"

"A couple of miles down the road." Jaci pushed the young man toward the station door. "Where's the phone... Tom?" she added, reading the name on his shirt. "I would have used my cell, but there's no service."

"There's a phone in here." Tom hastened inside with Jaci right behind him. "I'd better call Charlie."

"You do that." Jaci urged him forward.

Tom made the call, and within five minutes two fire trucks, an ambulance, and a lone police car raced by the gas station, sirens blaring.

Another police car with its lights flashing pulled into the station. A large man got out, crunched down his hat against the rain, and lumbered inside.

Jaci noted his gun belt and the deputy sheriff's badge pinned to his brown jacket. Something about the narrow set of his eyes and the thickness of his hunched shoulders reminded her of an angry bear. His gaze was definitely not friendly.

The deputy shook the rain from his hat and wiped his nose on his sleeve. Taking a notebook out of his pocket, he frowned at Tom.

Tom paled and disappeared into one of the connecting garage bays.

What was that about? Jaci wondered. She clutched her purse and forced herself to hold her ground as the brutish lawman came toward her. He might be unfriendly, but he was still a police officer, and this was the real world, not one of the mystery thriller novels she loved where corrupt policemen ran rampant. Still, her mind went into self-defense mode. She darted glances around the station, looking for possible escape routes and things that could be used as weapons. At least she had pepper spray in her purse. *Stop it right now!* she scolded herself. *He's not going to attack you.*

The deputy towered over her, but maintained an appropriate distance. He gave her a peculiar look and grunted a few questions about the time and location of the accident. Jaci answered as best she could. When he finished, he glanced toward the silent garage bays, then swept her with another odd look before heading out to his car. The screech of the siren grated on Jaci's raw nerves as he sped out of the parking lot toward the scene of the accident.

As the harsh sound of the siren faded in the distance, Jaci suddenly felt weak. She sagged against the counter, her fingers seeking her jewel pendant, a two-inch-long teardrop of milky opalescence she always wore on a long chain beneath her shirt. Her mother had given it to her two years ago, right before she died. She'd told Jaci it was magical. Jaci had never believed in magic or any of that hocus-pocus stuff, but she had to admit that just touching its smoothness, even through her shirt, had a strange way of soothing her, and she'd gotten into the habit of reaching for it when she felt scared or agitated.

"Are you all right, miss?"

Jaci jumped, startled.

Tom was standing three steps away, still fidgeting with the oily rag. "Can I get you a cup of coffee or something?"

"Coffee would be nice, thank you." Jaci gave him a tense smile. "Do you mind if I use your phone?"

"No, ma'am. Go right ahead." He hurried off to get the coffee.

Digging her cell phone out of her purse, she looked up Courtney's phone number. Still no service. Gingerly, she picked up the dirty handset from the landline phone on the counter and punched in the number.

"Hi, Courtney?" she said when her friend picked up.

"Jaci. Thank God! I was worried. Where are you?"

"I'm in Marston."

"Marston! What are you doing way out there?"

"I took a wrong turn somewhere. Look, I'm going to stay at a motel or something here in Marston and drive out to your place tomorrow. I've just had a horrible experience, and I don't feel like driving any more tonight."

"Why? What happened?"

"There was an accident —"

"Oh, no! Are you hurt?"

"No, no, I wasn't in the accident," Jaci said hastily. "I came along after it happened. It was terrible. There was a woman pinned under her car."

"How awful!"

"Yes, it was. So I'm going somewhere quiet to get something to eat and take a hot bath and try to relax. I'll see you tomorrow."

"Okay. Get some sleep and don't worry about getting here early. Come when you're rested. Drive carefully! And thanks for calling me. Bye."

"Bye." Jaci hung up the phone.

Tom appeared with a cup of dark coffee. "Here you go, miss... er... ma'am." He handed her the cup.

Jaci accepted the cup gratefully. "Thanks, Tom. Say, do you know where I could get some dinner and a room for the night?"

"There's an inn just up the road on the left, ma'am."

"Wonderful." She leaned back against the counter and sipped the coffee.

Tom hovered around, tidying shelves of bottled motor oil and other automobile necessities, then he snapped on a radio scanner.

"Is that the police band?" Jaci asked.

He nodded and fiddled with the knobs until the voices came in clearly.

"10-23 — MVA located — 20f — FD and EMU on scene. One pinned. FD extracted. Enroute to County Hospital. ETA 10 minutes."

"10-4."

Jaci nearly spilled her coffee. She knew those codes. One of her friends was a police sergeant. Code 20f meant "car accident with fatality." She looked at Tom. "Was that my accident?"

"Must've been." Tom twisted the rag in his hand. He wouldn't quite meet her eyes. "Can I get you a chair or something?"

"Yes, please." She set the coffee cup down and gripped the counter to keep her hands from shaking. The woman had died. Was it her fault for taking too long to get help? But the woman had insisted she stay and listen. The woman's words came back to her — a house, the Brunswick place, something about a clock... no, it was something about the inside of a clock, and a key, something that had to be done tonight. The words made no sense, but the urgency in the woman's voice had been unmistakable.

Tom hurried back with a folding chair. "Here you are, miss. Want me to call the inn for you?"

"Not just yet, Tom, thanks." She picked up her coffee and sat down. "Do you know where the Brunswick place is?"

Tom looked at her sharply before he answered. "The old Brunswick place's about two miles north of town."

"Who lives there?"

"Mr. Brunswick and the Missus lived there until about a month ago. They died in a car crash. Now their niece lives there. Deirdre." He looked at her closely. "Are you a cousin or something?"

Jaci felt the hairs lifting on the back of her neck. "No. Why do you ask?"

"No reason." He began straightening the already neat shelves again. "You just look a lot like her."

Jaci swallowed the rest of her coffee in one gulp and rose to her feet. "Thanks so much for the coffee. How much do I owe you?"

"Forget it. It's on the house." Tom put down his rag and came toward her. "Can I drive you to the inn?"

Jaci caught up her purse and headed for the door. "No thanks. I'll find it. It's on the left, you said."

"Yeah." He stopped in the doorway and watched her get into her car.

"Thanks again!" she called and quickly climbed in and locked her door. "You're giving me the creeps," she muttered as she drove away from the station.

It was still raining when Jaci found the inn and pulled into the empty parking lot. "That's strange," she said as she shut off the car. It was October, the height of the foliage season, and this was northern Vermont, a tourist mecca at this time of the year. So where were all the guests?

Only one light shone through a shade-covered window on the ground floor of the inn. All the other windows were dark. It didn't look very appealing, but the thought of a warm meal and a hot bath drew Jaci in spite of her misgivings. She reached for the car door, then hesitated as the dead woman's — Deirdre's — urgent plea played through her mind.

Her conscience berated her. If only she hadn't taken the time to listen, poor Deirdre might still be alive. But she was so insistent... A tear trickled down Jaci's cheek, with more threatening to follow. She wiped her eyes and sat for a moment, undecided. Her empty stomach growled loudly. She could check in and order a quick bite to eat to settle her nerves, then go find the Brunswick house. A change of clothes would be nice, too, since the rain had soaked through her thin sweater.

Her conscience stung her again. Taking the time might make her too late. Would another catastrophe happen as a result?

She grabbed her purse and pawed through it until she found a stick of spearmint gum. Popping it into her mouth, she started the car and sped off down the road, heading north.

She found the Brunswick place two miles north of town, just as Tom had said. A large mailbox in front of the solitary, gothic-style mansion proclaimed the Brunswick name in bold lettering.

Jaci turned into the circular driveway, car tires crunching on the gravel. She stared at the imposing manor house.

Silent and somber in the glare of the headlights, the house rose a full three stories with a gabled roof and many windows, some of them broken and boarded up from the inside. Black shutters gleamed dully in the rain. Dark red paint covered the clapboard front. The words "loony" and "freak" along with several other more nasty epithets were spray-painted across the crimson facade. Half a dozen steps led up to a wide wraparound porch, its depths lost in sullen shadow.

Jaci's stomach clenched as she read the hateful words marring the walls around the large front door. Who had done this? And why? She thought of Deirdre and wondered what the woman could have done to cause such hatred. Or was she an innocent victim of some kind of backwoods prejudice?

A cold thought crept into Jaci's mind. What if the people who had written these things were the same people who had responded to the accident call? That bear of a deputy and Tom the attendant had both acted strangely. What if the people sent to rescue Deirdre had actually killed her?

Jaci shivered and shoved the thought out of her head. She'd definitely been reading too many mystery novels. Gathering her resolve, she opened the glove compartment and took out a pocket flashlight. She flipped the switch and a beam of light struck the dashboard. She spit her gum into a small trash bag, then shut off the car and climbed out.

Without the headlights, the evening darkness closed in around her. *What a lonely place,* she thought, as she ducked her head and darted through the rain to the wet porch.

The floorboards creaked like old joints as she walked across them. The incessant beating of the rain against the house and gravel drive thudded against her consciousness, straining her already taut nerves. She tried the door, but it was locked. She glanced around. There were no mats on the porch or any other likely places nearby where anyone might have hidden a spare key.

Gripping her tiny flashlight, she crept along the veranda to her right. She stopped at the corner and peered around it. The porch continued on toward the back of the house. Her flashlight barely penetrated the thick darkness, revealing only three or four feet of the wet floorboards. She forced herself to keep walking until she reached the end of the porch at the back corner of the house. Leaning over the edge of the waist-high railing, she held the little light out as far as she could, aiming it toward the back wall. More graffiti curses and venomous names showed dimly in the flickering light, then disappeared as the flashlight suddenly went out. Jaci gasped and whacked the flashlight with her hand. The narrow beam shone again.

Shaking, Jaci leaned on the railing and caught her breath. She felt like a character in a horror movie. Images from some of the gory movies she'd seen began to seep into her mind. Panicking, she ran back around to the front of the house. Her car sat in the driveway, ready to whisk her back to the inn.

Help me... The memory of the desperate plea rang in Jaci's head. Deirdre's face appeared in her mind, replacing the knife-wielding maniacs her imagination had conjured. Her conscience rebuked her. How could she ignore the woman's last request?

Jaci's fingers curled around the pendant through her shirt, and the familiar calmness suffused her body like the warmth and light of a candle glow. She could do this. She forced her mind back to the problem at hand. How to get into a locked house. Perhaps she could climb in a window. She examined the windows beside her. They, too, were locked.

She hesitated. She'd never broken the law before — well, except for speed limits. The thought of facing that brutish deputy on a breaking-and-entering charge was not a pleasant prospect. But how else could she get in?

She took a deep breath, her decision made. Using the handle of the flashlight, she smashed a small pane of glass to expose the locking mechanism. She unlocked the window and levered it open, then looked back toward the road. No headlights, nothing. She wished there were a better place to park. Anyone driving by would see her car in the open driveway, and there were no garages or trees or shrubs to hide it behind. But it couldn't be helped.

She turned back to the window and climbed through into the house. Broken glass crackled under her sneakers. The room was black and stuffy like a closet, and the glow of the flashlight chased weird shadows across the hardwood floor. Jaci glanced around. Bookshelves filled to overflowing lined the walls from floor to ceiling. A large fireplace took up the middle third of the wall facing her. Two easy chairs and a sofa sat cozily around it, framing an Oriental rug. A library, by the looks of things.

A high-pitched "ku-coo" shattered the silence.

Jaci cried out, then clapped her hand over her mouth. She shone her light high up on the wall, revealing a small cuckoo clock. The little bird chirped impudently, six more "ku-coos" before retreating behind a tiny door.

Jaci began breathing again. Well, she'd found a clock, but there was no way she could reach it. What had Deirdre said, something about the inside of a clock? There were probably several clocks in the house. Which one was she supposed to find?

A low bong sounded somewhere else in the house as another clock struck the hour. Following the sound, Jaci hurried to the open library door and stepped out into a long, wide entrance hall. Shadows slid across the walls and furniture like live creatures as Jaci searched for the source of the bonging. Before her, a grand staircase rose up to a balconied second floor. Her small flashlight barely illuminated the top step. The sound was emanating from somewhere upstairs.

Clutching the smooth banister, Jaci started up the steps. The clock continued to strike slowly — five, six, seven. Then silence fell once more.

Reaching the top, Jaci turned to her left. Straight ahead at the end of the balcony stood a huge, ornate grandfather clock. Its pendulum swung rhythmically, marking the inexorable passage of time. Jaci crossed the balcony and stopped in front of the massive clock.

The clock stood about eight feet tall. It was made of rich ebony wood inlaid with gold. Roman numerals adorned its gold face, and a pane of etched glass protected the swinging gold pendulum. The tick-tock of the counted seconds was strangely soft, a soothing sound.

A slight movement — or was it? — caught Jaci's eye, drawing her gaze to the scene etched into the glass front. Three men on horseback rode along a hillside surrounded by forest, the sharp spike of a mountain stabbing the sky in the distance. She frowned. The figures in the etching seemed to move, and yet they did not. She closed her eyes for a moment, then looked again. The scene appeared the same, yet... no. She blinked. A large hawk floated high above the riders.

That bird had definitely not been there before.

Shaken, she stepped back a few paces. She had to be imagining things. The creepiness of the place and the strain of the night's events were getting to her. She shone her light along the balconied hall, illuminating four doors, all closed. There could be clocks in those rooms also. She should check them. But somehow she couldn't move. Her gaze slid back to the massive grandfather clock, ticking, ticking hypnotically. It almost seemed as if the ticking matched her heartbeat. She looked at the glass again. Her breath caught. Two horsemen now rode along the hillside. The lead rider had ridden beyond the bounds of the glass and was out of sight.

"Impossible," Jaci muttered, her eyes searching the glass. Nothing moved.

Deirdre's urgent plea slipped unbidden into her mind. *The clock... inside it... you must go... tonight.*

With a knot the size of a bowling ball in her stomach, Jaci approached the clock again. The image in the glass remained frozen. She moved to within arm's length. Tentatively, she touched the wood frame with her fingertips. The dark wood was cool and smooth, vibrating faintly to the pendulum's beat. She touched the glass, her fingers sliding down the neck of one of the horses. She couldn't bring herself to touch the men. The glass, too, was cool and smooth as any window pane. She couldn't feel the etch marks. Carefully, she examined both sides of the clock. Nothing unusual leaped out at her.

She moved around to the back. The huge clock stood away from the wall about eighteen inches. Bracing herself gingerly on the back corner of the clock, she leaned into the narrow space. Her light drove away the shadows, revealing only a few feathery cobwebs. She leaned farther in and looked toward the top. Her hand slipped off the back of the clock. With a cry she fell forward, bumping against the back panel of the clock. The panel popped outward.

Regaining her balance, she shone her flashlight into the musty space. Inside on the floor of the clock lay a small book, a pocket calendar, and a key.

CHAPTER 2

After a moment's hesitation, Jaci reached into the clock and picked up the calendar. It lay open to the month of October. Today's date, October 1st, was circled in black marker. The word *saelarin* was written in stilted script beneath the date.

"*Saelarin.* What does that mean?" Jaci asked softly.

She felt a sudden charge in the air around her, as if the house had been struck by lightning. The back of her neck prickled. She cast a nervous eye upward, expecting to hear a crack of thunder, but none came. Shivering, she put down the calendar and picked up the small dark-blue leather-bound book. Its grainy cover had been worn smooth in places from much use. A small strap with a locking mechanism held the book closed. She pushed the tiny button sideways, and with a faint click, the strap pulled out of the metal bracket. She opened the cover.

Deirdre Brunswick.

Jaci's hands shook as she read the name scrawled on the inside cover in childish handwriting. Swallowing hard, she turned the page. More writing in the same young hand, with a date at the top.

March 1 — she looked at the year, then subtracted quickly in her head — nineteen years ago.

A diary. Jaci closed the book. Reading someone's private thoughts made her uncomfortable enough, but to read the words of someone who had just died was ghastly. Yet, what else could she do? Deirdre had begged her to come to this house and find what was in the clock. Biting her lip, Jaci opened the book once more.

Today we had a test in Mathematics on multiplying great numbers. I failed. Uncle William and Aunt Meredith yelled at me. They said I did not study hard enough. I did try but I just cannot do it. It is not like any ciphering I have ever seen or can remember.

Water stains marred the page. Were they tears? Jaci felt sorry for the girl.

She skimmed through several more pages, scanning the entries. Sparse descriptions of days at school and evenings spent with either a nanny or a tutor. The words seemed stilted, the language formal, yet the handwriting was definitely no more than fourth or fifth grade level. That would make Deirdre — what... ten or eleven years old? *The same age I was back then,* Jaci suddenly realized.

Jaci skipped ahead to the middle of the book. The daily entries continued up through December 12th , then stopped. Jaci thumbed through several blank pages. The next entry was dated September 10th of this year — less than a month ago.

Free! I am finally free of that horrible place. Nineteen years of my life wasted, stolen by my aunt and uncle and those monsters who call themselves Doctors of Psychiatry. I must go back to Tarshane. I understand the drawings now. I know how to get through. And I have remembered another name — Galenock. When I return to Tarshane, I will find him. Perhaps he will help me to remember who I am and what this key unlocks. I'm sure the key is of vital importance. I must take it back.

Who was Galenock, and what was Tarshane? And what did Deirdre mean — "get through?" Jaci shook her head. It made no sense. She looked down at the key still lying inside the clock. Marking her place in the diary with her finger, she lifted the key and studied it under the flashlight's beam. It looked like an old skeleton key, the kind her grandparents had used to unlock the doors in their 150-year-old farmhouse, except that it was only about three inches long and was made of some kind of copper-colored metal instead of silver. A thin ribbon of black metal curled around the circular end of the key and twisted down the shaft.

Jaci turned her attention back to the diary, thumbing back through the blank pages to the final December entry from nineteen years past.

Last night I had another dream. Aunt Meredith and Uncle William said I screamed and screamed and hit them when they tried to wake me. Again, I do not remember. They said I have the dreams every night now. They talked about sending me away to a place where someone called Doctor could help me. I am frightened.

Jaci shivered again. The rain pounded hard on the roof as if it would drive through the shingles and drown her. She glanced up, hoping the old roof would hold. Looking back at the diary, she flipped randomly through a few more pages, then threw her hands up.

"What am I supposed to do with this?" she whispered into the darkness. Only the driving rain answered.

Shoving her hair back, Jaci skipped ahead to the final entry: October 1st. Today.

Jaci's skin crawled. Deirdre had written in this diary today. An image of the dying woman crushed under a wreck of twisted metal flashed into her mind, and she nearly dropped the book.

"I can't do this," she whispered.

Muffled by the drumming rain, a single "ku-coo" sounded from the library downstairs. Seven-thirty. Jaci bit her lip again. She must be insane.

A loud bong reverberated through the darkened house as the grandfather clock struck the half hour. Jaci leaped in fright.

"All right. That's it." She stuffed the diary and key in the front pocket of her jeans and scooped up the calendar. She could look at these things in the safety of her own room at the inn and still fulfill Deirdre's request.

Thunder boomed outside. Jaci froze. No, it wasn't thunder. Tires were crunching on the gravel driveway. Two sets of headlights beamed in the first floor windows. Shouts and voices sounded outside as heavy feet thudded up onto the porch.

"Oh, no," she breathed.

Something crashed against the front door. Another bang, and the hinges groaned, gave way.

Clutching the calendar to her, Jaci scrambled into the clock. She scrunched her small body into the narrow space and drew the back panel shut. Her fingers trembled so badly she dropped the flashlight, which clattered on the floor of the clock and winked out. Darkness swallowed her, claustrophobic, suffocating.

"She's here somewhere!" yelled a rough voice. "Find her!"

Footsteps stomped through the house, up the stairs. The clamor of slamming doors and sliding furniture beat against the high ceiling like panicked birds.

Jaci cringed and clamped her hands over her ears. Her eyes screwed shut.

All at once, the racket ceased. Cool, fresh air brushed her cheek. The harsh caw of a crow sounded in the distance. She smelled grass, heard it whisper in the breeze.

Cautiously, she squinted one eye open. Waves of waist-high, greenish-brown grass surrounded her. Thin white clouds drifted in a purplish twilight sky. Still gripping the calendar, she opened both eyes and looked around in confusion. A vast meadow spread out before her, rolling into grassy hills. Dark forest loomed behind. And high in the evening sky, a huge hawk circled, its lonely cry carrying on the wind.

CHAPTER 3

Dazed, Jaci looked around her. Where on God's green earth was she? Where was the Brunswick house and the clock? The dull grass surrounding her waved stiffly in the breeze, brittle as if it had survived a hard frost. The air grew cooler. Dusk was falling rapidly.

Jaci shivered and wrapped her arms around herself for warmth. Her clothes were still damp from the time she'd spent at the accident site. She wished she hadn't left her jacket behind. But at that point, Deirdre had needed it more than she did. Jaci glanced up at the swiftly darkening sky. At least it wasn't raining here — wherever here was.

Shoving back her tangled hair, she looked around again, at a loss. The meadow of waist-high grass stretched out before her. Evening shadows obscured the hills at the far end. Close behind her stood a silent forest. The tips of the lofty trees blurred into the gloaming. A deep, forbidding blackness lurked between the massive, close-set trunks. The forest curved around her, both right and left, bordering the meadow until lost from sight.

A rhythmic drumming rose on the wind, blowing toward her from the dusk-cloaked hills. A flock of crows squawked in alarm and launched into the sky at the far end of the meadow. High above, the hawk shrieked. The pounding beat grew louder.

Jaci dropped into the grass and peered through it in the direction of the approaching sound. Three horsemen galloped into view, racing hard across the meadow. Veering away from the forest, they passed about thirty yards from where Jaci crouched and continued on down the meadow to her right. She heard the horses' labored grunts as they sped by.

Moments later, a thunderous clamor drowned out the sound of retreating hoofbeats. Twenty or so red-cloaked riders pounded out of the darkened hills, following the trail of the three horsemen. A red flag divided by a black cross streamed out above them, carried by one of the front-runners. Gilded scabbards hung from their belts.

Jaci stared through the tall grass in shock. Riders with swords? *What* was going on?

The riders galloped on in pursuit of the three horsemen and disappeared into the night.

After ten minutes of silence, Jaci cautiously stood up. Darkness had settled so that she could barely distinguish the massive tree trunks edging the forest. There was no sign of the three horsemen or the pursuing riders. Perhaps in the morning she could follow their trail and find a town or a village, something that would tell her where she was. She wished she had her can of pepper spray. Unfortunately, it was in her purse, along with her cell phone, on the front seat of her car. A lot of good it would do her there.

She looked back and forth between the meadow and the forest. Deciding a tree would probably be the safest place to spend the night, she unclenched her fingers from around the now crumpled calendar and slipped it into her back pocket. After making sure she still had the diary and the key, she jogged through the tall grass toward the woods. Her breath puffed out around her in frosty clouds as she ran.

Just as she reached the trees, the blood-freezing howl of a wolf ghosted through the air, coming from the left sweep of forest. A chorus of howls answered from across the meadow.

"Oh, no," Jaci whispered. She stumbled through the trees, clutching at the trunks until she found one that had low branches. Pine-like needles covered the limbs. The spicy odor of evergreens floated around her, released from the needles crushed by her scrambling feet as she clambered up into the tree.

Something leaped at her and snapped. Pain seared her ankle, and her pantleg was jerked downward. She screamed and kicked as the teeth of a huge beast ripped through the leg of her jeans. The fabric tore. The beast fell back with a snarl.

Gasping, Jaci pulled herself higher into the tree. The beast lunged again. Claws scrabbled against the branches, but did not catch hold. Jaci looked down. Several pairs of golden eyes stared up at her. Growls and barks surrounded the base of the tree. Jaci climbed until the branches grew too thin to bear her weight.

A screech rent the night air. Jaci heard the whisper of wings not far above her head. The hawk's cry sounded again, close. Unnerved, Jaci shrank back against the trunk of the tree, pulling branches around her to shield her from attack.

Angry howls rose from the beasts below, and then the golden eyes disappeared. Jaci looked downward but could see nothing in the blackness below. Then she heard the sound of muffled hoof-beats. And a male voice.

"I'm telling you I heard a scream. It sounded like a woman."

"That's because all you think about is women," said another male voice.

"Quiet," commanded a third, his voice deeper-toned than the others. "Sharrow agrees someone is here, and so do the wolves. Keep watch."

All three spoke with an accent that sounded Gaelic — not quite Scottish, but not like any Irish she'd ever heard, either.

The hoofbeats stopped. Leather creaked as one of the men dismounted. He entered the forest, threading quietly through the trees.

Jaci held her breath as the sounds drew nearer.

"Helloooo," he called softly.

Jaci recognized the deeper voice of the third man. He'd sounded like the leader of the group.

"We'll not harm you." The footsteps moved away, came near again.

Jaci bit her lip. The deep voice sounded strong and strangely trustworthy. Having lived in the outskirts of New York City for several years, Jaci had learned to judge people by both face and voice. Her assessments were usually close to the mark.

"If you prefer to spend the night with the wolves, that is, of course, your choice." The footsteps receded.

A long, low howl rose from the forest, frighteningly near.

"Wait!" Jaci released the branches she was holding in front of her. They swished back into place. "Please."

The man stopped, came slowly back toward her. "Where are you?"

"Up here, in the tree."

"Can you get down?"

"I'm... not sure." She looked toward the forest floor and swallowed hard. It was a long way down. "I guess we'll find out," she muttered to herself.

Slowly, she climbed down out of the tree, lowering herself blindly from branch to branch. Pain stabbed her ankle with each step. Her arms ached. The rough branches scraped and bruised her hands and shins.

She had nearly reached the bottom when, with a loud crack, the limb on which she was balancing snapped. She fell a short distance, landing on her feet. Pain shot up her leg. She cried out as she sank to the ground. Touching her swollen ankle, she felt a warm wetness.

"You're hurt?" The strong voice was beside her. She smelled the musky scent of horses, sweat, and the wild outdoors.

"My ankle."

A hand touched her lower calf, slid down to her ankle. "A wolf did this?"

"Yes."

"Hold still." He produced a length of cloth from somewhere and gently wrapped it around her ankle. "Can you walk?"

"I think so."

"Give me your hand."

Jaci held out her hand and felt calloused fingers, then a strong clasp.

He helped her to her feet. "Neither I, nor my men, will hurt you. You have my word. Come."

Limping slightly, Jaci followed. "Thank you."

The man led her back to the edge of the meadow, where two men on horseback stood guard nearby. In the dim light, she thought she recognized the men she had seen being chased earlier. Effortlessly, the man lifted Jaci onto his horse, then swung up behind her. A large bird launched into the air from the edge of the trees, rising upward in ever-widening spirals. The three horsemen turned their mounts and, skirting the forest, rode away from the hills, following the trampled trail they had created earlier in their headlong flight from the red-cloaked riders.

CHAPTER 4

The horsemen rode in single file, with Jaci and her rescuer in the lead. The clinging darkness kept them to a steady walk.

In spite of her precarious situation, Jaci felt herself relaxing. The body of the man behind her was warm, his chest hard yet comfortable. The arm about her waist held her firmly, but without intimacy or threat. She felt safe with him, though she knew nothing about him. She tried to imagine his face from the voice she had heard, but soon gave up the effort. She was too exhausted.

To keep from being lulled to sleep by the horse's even gait, Jaci tried to focus on where they were going. The barest sliver of a moon had risen, but it shed very little light on their path. Jaci sensed the forest close on her right. She could still hear the wolves howling somewhere behind her and wished the horsemen would move farther away from the trees. Crickets chirped all around them, vibrant drops of sound, falling silent as they passed, then resuming their chorus. Saddle leather creaked, the metal rings on the bridles jingling softly with the horses' movements.

What had happened to the posse of red-cloaked riders? Jaci wondered. *And why were they chasing these men?* She thought about the riders she had seen in the etched glass door of the grandfather clock.

There had been three of them. And a hawk. They couldn't be the same ones... could they? She closed her eyes for a moment, trying to make sense of the situation, but she couldn't. What had happened defied logic. She suddenly remembered Deirdre's diary and the key. Deirdre had said she needed to return to — where was it? Tar... something. Tarsheen, Tarshane — Tarshane, that was it, and find someone named Galenock, who could help her remember who she was and what the key unlocked. Jaci looked around into the darkness. Was that where she was? In Tarshane?

Her rescuer pulled their mount up sharply. "The forest, quickly."

The riders ducked into the edge of the woods.

A short distance beyond the tree line, Jaci heard hoofbeats and the swish of tall grass. Two or three horses trotted by, heading up the meadow in the direction from which Jaci and the others had come. Jaci wondered how they could see where they were going.

"They must have camped on the flat," whispered one of the horsemen.

"Yes," the man behind her agreed. "We'll cut across the valley."

They waited inside the edge of the woods for several more minutes, then moved out into the meadow.

Urging their horses into a canter, they put their backs to the forest and rode out across the field. Jaci adjusted easily to the smooth gait. She'd always loved horseback riding, though it had been a while since she'd ridden.

They left the valley, slowing as they entered rough marshland. Jaci dug her fingers under the edge of the flat leather saddle, damp against the horse's sweaty withers, to keep her balance. She twisted her other hand in the horse's mane. The man behind pulled her closer against him, steadying her. His masculine scent, mingled with horse and leather, surrounded her, and she inhaled the smells deeply. A strange inner warmth seeped into her blood, and a tingling sensation spread through her body as if she'd been plugged into a wall socket.

All at once she felt... *alive.* Her exhaustion disappeared as the blackness of the night lightened to gray. She could see the marshland knotted with patches of brush.

Scents grew sharper. The stagnant odor of the marsh carried on the breeze, mixed with animal scents she couldn't identify and the pungent evergreen of the forest they'd left behind. Sounds, too, seemed clearer, more distinct. She could almost hear words in the crickets' songs, in the whisper of the grasses, the whistle of the wind — an unknown language of such exquisite beauty... She closed her eyes and let it flow into her soul.

Just then, the ground evened out, and her rescuer sat back, resuming his impersonal hold around her waist. The tingling sensation faded to a barely perceptible level. Her awareness dimmed; the wild song slipped away. The night darkened to black.

Jaci nearly cried out at the loss. Tears filled her eyes as exhaustion reclaimed her body. She blinked back the tears, shivering as the chill of the night bit into her skin, raising goosebumps.

"*Mirochnae.* Try to sleep," he whispered.

She felt her tired eyes closing in spite of her efforts to stay awake.

"You are safe with me."

The words echoed in her consciousness as she drifted off.

* * * * *

Wrapped in warmth and softness, Jaci slowly rose through shifting layers of haze into wakefulness. She pushed back the blankets covering her and opened her eyes. She froze. This was not her bed in White Plains, or even a bed at an inn. Scrub grass and small boulders covered the floor of the ravine in which she lay. A bright yellow sun beat down from a piercingly blue sky.

The happenings of the day before snapped back to her like a stinging blow.

A shadow fell across her. She gasped.

A huge man stood beside her. He had to be close to seven feet tall with wide shoulders and a body like a redwood, topped by a roughhewn face sprouting a thick beard and bristly eyebrows that matched his shoulder length shaggy black hair. Vivid blue eyes stared down at her. In one hand, he held a steaming bowl.

Jaci gulped and began to edge backward. The man held up his free hand and shook his head. Wordlessly, he pointed along the ravine and shook his head. Then he pointed to a rope lying nearby and pointed to her.

Jaci's mind began to function again.

"Um... if I try to run away, you'll tie me up, is that it?"

He nodded.

"And if I don't, you won't."

He nodded again.

"Uh huh. Great," Jaci muttered.

He held out the bowl and pointed to his mouth.

Jaci watched him warily, but didn't move.

He stepped closer, squatted down, and held the bowl within arm's reach. The savory odor of some kind of meat stew filled Jaci's nostrils, and her stomach growled like a lion that had missed a few meals.

Cautiously, Jaci accepted the bowl.

The giant backed away, returning a moment later with a tin cup brimming with water.

"Thank you," Jaci said as she took the cup.

He nodded.

As he turned away, Jaci asked, "Do you speak?"

He looked back at her, shook his head once, then went over and sat down on a rock. He picked up a whetstone and began sharpening a very long knife.

Jaci tasted the stew. It was delicious, and she had to force herself not to gobble it down. She watched her guardian furtively while she ate. He was definitely not the man who had ridden behind her last night. Besides the fact that he couldn't speak, this man was much bigger, and his scent was different, though not unpleasant. He wore a forest-green shirt and leggings, a sturdy brown leather jerkin, scuffed black boots, and a heavy black cloak. A two-handed sword that resembled a blade she'd seen in a movie about the Scots hung from a swordbelt girding his waist. He looked like he hadn't combed his hair in weeks, but other than that, he was not unkempt.

She was pretty sure he wasn't one of the other two riders, either, and she wondered where they all had gone. Had they abandoned her?

Jaci finished the stew. She could have eaten more, but decided against asking for seconds. She set the bowl down and sipped the water. Before, she'd felt like a damsel in distress. Now, she felt like a prisoner. Should she try to get away? Looking around, she studied her surroundings. The ravine measured about twenty feet across, stretching away on both sides of her until curving out of sight. A tiny stream flowed down the middle. The steeply angled banks rose seven or eight feet from the floor of the streambed. Clumps of coarse grass and brush grew here and there in between smooth, rounded boulders strewn haphazardly by past floods.

If she were to take off and run, she probably wouldn't get very far. Especially with her sore ankle. Mr. Redwood would catch her before she reached the end of the ravine. Then he would tie her up, which would seriously hamper any other attempt at escape. Even if she distracted him first, she wasn't likely to get away. Scenarios she'd practiced in the self-defense martial arts classes she'd taken played through her mind, and she considered possible weapons she might use to protect herself. All she had right now were the bowl and the cup, which wouldn't be of much use on someone that size. Well, she could feign compliance, then bash him over the head with one of the many rocks scattered throughout the streambed...

She shot a sidelong glance at the behemoth, who was still sharpening his knife, and sighed with resignation. No, she couldn't quite bring herself to do that. He might be scary looking, but he'd done nothing to harm her and he'd given her food and water. She wouldn't know where to go anyway, even if she did escape. She would just have to wait and see what happened when her rescuer from last night came back — assuming, of course, that he did come back.

She swallowed the last of the water, then set the cup down and rose gingerly to her feet. She took a few steps to test her ankle and found it much improved from the night before. When she looked up, she saw the giant watching her.

"I need to — you know." She blushed.

He gestured to a large bush in the middle of the ravine.

"I see." Jaci limped over to the bush, making certain he couldn't see her before squatting down.

When she was through, she washed her hands in the stream, then retreated to the spot where she'd awakened and sat down on the blankets. She examined her ankle and found it had been wrapped in a clean bandage with some sort of herbal ointment or salve that smelled like liniment. The swelling had gone down, and the ankle hardly hurt at all.

Her captor had finished with his knife and was working on a nasty-looking axe. He seemed to be paying no attention to her. Turning on her side away from him as if she were sleeping, she pulled the calendar out of her pocket and opened it. October 1ˢᵗ was circled in black marker. Under the date was a solid black circle, the moon phase. The words 'new moon' had been underlined, along with the word she'd read before, *saelarin*. She skimmed through the calendar. Nothing else had been written in October or any other month. She scowled. That was no help. She needed to find a way to get home. She stuffed the calendar back into her pocket.

The sun beat down warmly for what appeared to be an autumn day. No breeze stirred even the dust along the floor of the ravine. Wiping the sweat from her brow, Jaci slid the blankets backward into the relative shade of a leafless brown bush and lay down. The giant continued to ignore her. Keeping her back to him, she slipped the diary out of her other pocket. There had to be a clue in it somewhere, something to explain what had happened.

She flipped back to the December 12ᵗʰ entry and reread the childish script.

Last night I had another dream.

Deirdre had been plagued by nightmares. Her aunt and uncle were going to send her away somewhere to a doctor who could help her, and the prospect had frightened her. Strange, how she wrote *someone called Doctor* as if she didn't know what a doctor was. How could she not know?

Jaci reread the next entry, dated September 10ᵗʰ of this year.

Free! I am finally free of that horrible place.

"Poor girl," Jaci whispered. Deirdre must have been sent to a psychiatric institution. For nineteen years she had been locked away.

I must go back to Tarshane. I understand the drawings now. I know how to get through. And I have remembered another name — Galenock. When I return to Tarshane, I will find him. Perhaps he will help me remember who I am and what this key unlocks.

Jaci frowned. What drawings? She flipped through the diary but found no markings other than script. Going more carefully, she searched the pages again. Nothing. What was Deirdre referring to?

Then she noticed a tiny yellowish-white speck against the dark blue of the inside back cover. She ran her thumb over it, and a small piece of paper emerged from a hidden pocket. Yellowish and wrinkled like parchment, the paper unfolded into a small three-by-four-inch rectangle. The words *ne*, *ris*, *ful*, and *set* were written down the left side of the paper in faded reddish-brown ink. Across from the letters were rough sketches of trees and grass, a solid red-brown square, a clock face, and what looked like mountains. Along the bottom in delicate script was that same word — *saelarin*. What could it mean?

The clatter of hoofbeats interrupted her thoughts.

Hastily, she refolded the parchment and slipped it back into its hiding place. She shoved the diary into the pocket of her jeans and made sure the key was still secure in her watch pocket. Sucking in deep breaths to calm herself, she sat up and looked toward the approaching sound.

A short distance away, her giant captor squatted beside a brown pack, stuffing utensils into it. Farther up the ravine, three horsemen galloped into view, the horses' hooves ringing on the hard ground. The riders cantered up the gully and reined in beside her guardian. They conferred a moment in some sort of sign language, then the giant motioned for her to come forward.

She stood, suddenly realizing what a sight she must look — dirty and disheveled, her hair uncombed. She ran her hand through her tangled dark curls and smoothed her clothing.

"This should be interesting," she muttered as she walked toward them. She advanced to within a few feet, then stopped.

"Great gods," breathed one of them. Stocky and wide-shouldered, with short blond hair and blue eyes, the horseman stared at her with an expression of complete shock. "She looks like —"

"Solon," the leader snapped, cutting him off, his deep-toned voice cold and harsh as a frozen plain of ice.

Jaci instantly recognized the accented voice as belonging to the man who had rescued her the night before. Her eyes flew to his face, taking in his rugged features. He had short black hair with a few days' growth of beard and dark, dark eyes. He, too, looked shocked to the very core.

But it was the pain, the gut-wrenching anguish ripping through his heart that seized her and tore at her own heart until she felt stricken by the loss of something deemed more precious than life. She gasped, stunned by the sudden violent upheaval of emotion inside her.

Her rescuer's face became a stony mask.

"Bring her." He wheeled his horse and galloped back up the ravine.

The remaining horsemen looked at each other, then at the giant tree-man.

He shrugged.

Solon, the blond rider who had spoken first, urged his mount forward. Stopping in front of Jaci, he leaned down and held out his hand.

"You will ride with me. Give me the blankets."

Still reeling, Jaci handed him the bedding, bowl, and cup, which he stuffed into his saddlebags, then she took his arm and swung up behind him. The giant whistled softly, and a great chestnut horse, already saddled and bridled, trotted up to him from around the bend in the gully. The big man stroked the horse's head and neck, then climbed onto its back.

They kicked their horses into a canter and headed up the gully.

CHAPTER 5

All afternoon they rode, and on into the twilight. The sky remained clear. The streambed had given way to hilly scrub land
cluttered with rocks and brush. Scattered clumps of juniper-like
evergreens clung to the stony soil, the stunted trees clustered together like nervous people.

The horsemen seemed uneasy. Their eyes swept the passing
hills and surrounding brush like the red-brown hawk who soared
on the wind currents above them. They stopped only once, near
sunset, to eat a meager meal and rest the horses. No one spoke. The
horsemen communicated through gestures. Jaci tried to ask her
riding companion where they were going, but Solon shushed and
then ignored her.

The pace varied from an easy lope to a fast gallop to a slow walk
as their path climbed upward onto mountainous ridges. The slate-
colored rock rose around them, jagged edges against the darkening
sky. The temperature dropped with the sun. Jaci clenched her teeth
to keep them from chattering. Her back and thighs ached from the
constant riding.

As they topped the rise, a stiff breeze buffeted them, blowing
through Jaci's thin sweater and shirt with a bone-numbing chill.

"It's freezing up here." She shook back her windblown hair and shrank against the warmth of Solon's body in front of her, tightening her arms around his waist.

Solon said nothing. He guided his mount higher onto the ridge, following the others.

Jaci cringed as another gust of wind sent icicles down her back. Her fingers and toes began to grow numb. She stretched herself up until her lips were level with Solon's ear. The wind blew his blond hair into her face. She brushed it aside. "How much farther do we have to go?"

"Not far," he said without turning.

"That's real specific," Jaci grumbled. "Oh, wait a minute — blankets." She had slept in blankets earlier. She looked down at the worn saddlebag hanging just behind her left knee. The horseman hadn't buckled the saddlebag after shoving her bedding into it. She leaned over, raised the leather flap, and tugged on the blankets.

The horse stumbled on a loose rock. Jaci lurched sideways. She clutched at Solon's cloak and nearly pulled him out of the saddle. With a startled oath, he caught himself and recovered his seat. Jaci hauled herself back up behind him as he reined in his mount.

He turned in the saddle and glared at her. "What are you doing?"

She glared back. "I'm cold. I want a blanket." She pointed down at the saddlebag. A blast of freezing wind made her eyes water.

His look softened. "I'm sorry. I had forgotten you had no cloak."

"Solon, what's wrong?" The lead horseman appeared beside them.

"The lady is cold."

"And she could use some rest and something to eat," Jaci added, rubbing her aching thighs.

The leader of the horsemen didn't look at her.

"We will use the cave."

Solon nodded.

Jaci's rescuer turned his mount and headed back up the dusk-shadowed path.

A few minutes later, the horsemen halted in front of a steep rocky cliff. The knife-like wind whistled through the thick brush growing at its base.

Hunched against the cold, the horsemen dismounted. The leader and the tree-man began pulling the brush out away from the rugged cliff face. A gaping maw of blackness appeared. The third horseman, a tall, slim man with a blond ponytail, led their mounts inside. He had a bow and a quiver full of arrows slung across his back.

Jaci waited as Solon swung his leg over their horse's drooping neck and slid to the ground. He turned as if to offer help, but Jaci jumped down before he could get the words out. He glanced at her with raised eyebrows, then moved to the saddlebags and pulled out the blankets she had been trying to reach earlier. She snatched them out of his hand and waddled toward the cave. The other horsemen had already disappeared inside.

As she stepped through the opening in the brush, something squawked in her ear. Jaci squealed and ducked as a large bird whooshed by her into the cave, its wings brushing her hair.

A snort of laughter came from somewhere just ahead of her. She focused on the sound. Torchlight flared along the walls of the cave, illuminating the speaker. The man with the blond ponytail chuckled as he regarded the hawk gripping his gloved arm.

"Sharrow, you have no manners."

Jaci glared at him. "It's *not* funny."

He laughed again, then gave her a disarming smile. "Forgive me. It seems I have forgotten my manners as well."

"You never had any," said Solon. He had brought his horse inside, and he and the giant were pulling the brush back into place to block off the entrance to the cave mouth.

"I would not have made the lady carry her bedding."

"No. You would have brought her to your own bed."

Jaci looked from one to the other. They both had blond hair and the same wide blue eyes and straight noses. They had to be brothers. But where the man she had ridden with was broader of face and body, the man laughing at her was slimmer, his face thinner, more handsome. He seemed younger, and Jaci guessed him to be in his early thirties, while Solon was in his late thirties.

The leader of the horsemen, who had stayed silent, lit the last wall torch, then stepped over to the man with the hawk and took the bird onto his own gloved wrist. "Would you see to the horses." It was a statement, not a question.

The younger man frowned. "Why must I always take care of the horses?"

"Because you are always causing trouble," retorted Solon.

Grumbling, the younger man gathered up the reins of the four horses and led them deeper into the dimly lit cave.

Jaci wondered again at their accents, so similar, yet different than any Scottish or Irish she'd heard.

Her rescuer faced her. The hawk fluffed its feathers and gave a soft cry, then hopped onto a nearby boulder and preened.

The man smiled faintly. "She apologizes."

"So do I," floated a voice from somewhere deep in the cave. A horse snorted and stamped. "Ow! Stop that, you miserable pack beast."

"Perhaps I should assist my brother," said Solon. He disappeared into the depths of the cave.

Jaci and her rescuer stared at each other in the torchlight. She had to crane her neck, as the man stood head and shoulders above her. *Such a stern face,* she thought. Not really handsome, yet striking. Jaci estimated him to be about the same age as the elder of the two brothers.

Growing uncomfortable under his searching gaze, she drew herself up to her full height. "Will you please stop staring at me?"

He blinked as if his mind had been elsewhere. "I'm sorry. What is your name?"

Jaci hesitated. This could get sticky. If she made up a name, would she remember to answer to it? Probably not. Better to at least keep that detail the same. "My name is Jacinda. Who are you?"

Just then, the younger of the blond brothers strode in from the back of the cave. He threw his hands up in disgust. "He said I wasn't doing it right." He shook his head. "Solon must have everything a particular way and no other. *Every* time. He does not understand that a man needs variety, else he will grow bored and find alternate and often unhealthy sources of amusement." He stopped before Jaci. "Allow me to introduce myself." He swept into a low bow. "My name is Nickalonis."

"Nick who?" Jaci asked.

"Nickalonis," he repeated, more slowly this time. "Nickalonis d'Camran. And what name adorns such a lovely creature as yourself?"

Jaci rolled her eyes. Apparently men were men no matter what world they were in. "You can't be serious."

"Serious about what?" He looked confused.

"My name is Jacinda — Jaci — Harper."

"So you're a bard, then?"

"A bard?" It was Jaci's turn to look confused.

"A bard — singer of songs, purveyor of poetry —"

"I know what a bard is," Jaci cut in. "Why do you think I'm a bard?"

"Your surname, of course — Harper. Do you not play the harp?"

Jaci stifled a laugh at the mental image of her strumming a harp and singing. Musically inclined she was not. "Um... no, I don't."

"Too bad. A song or two would have been a pleasant diversion. Just imagine it — you and I in a sweet duet. Ah, well. Jaci, it is. What a perfect name. Very beautiful and very... short..."

Jaci bristled. "If you say 'like me,' I'll kick you so hard your balls will come out your nose."

The two men stared at her, surprise on their faces.

Jaci heard a grunting noise and looked toward the front of the cave. The giant who had watched over her that morning had dropped the pack of provisions and was sitting on a rock shaking with laughter.

The leader of the horsemen cracked a smile, then gave in to the mirth. Nickalonis began to chuckle. Jaci giggled in spite of herself. The giant doubled over with glee and fell off the rock.

Solon strode in from where they had stabled the horses. "Great gods! What is the matter with you all?"

Jaci and the others laughed harder.

"What is so funny?" he demanded.

The leader of the horsemen recovered first. "Solon, your brother has been put in his place."

Solon scowled. "And I missed it. You must tell me."

"I will let the lady tell you." He wiped the corner of his eye. "Barayan, where is our supper?"

The giant picked himself up and retrieved the pack. He brought it over to the right side of the cave where a spring bubbled up through the rock. The constant flow of water had carved a shallow pool that trickled into a tiny stream that flowed toward the back of the cave and disappeared into a crack in the floor.

The leader of the horsemen stepped across to the stream and washed his hands and splashed water on his face. Nickalonis did the same, followed by the giant, who then handed out scant provisions of bread, cheese, and dried meat.

Ignoring Solon's curiosity, Jaci set her blankets on the floor near the pool and scrubbed her hands in the icy water. Her teeth chattered again as she accepted her portion and sat down.

Solon washed hurriedly. Meal in hand, he sat down in front of Jaci. "What did you say to him?"

"She threatened to unman me," said Nickalonis with a sheepish grin.

"That wouldn't take much." He addressed Jaci again. "Come. I must know what you said."

Jaci flushed. "Your brother was going to make another joke at my expense, so I told him what would happen if he did."

"Yes, yes, what did you say?" demanded Solon.

Jaci shifted uncomfortably, then repeated what she had said.

Solon roared.

"I'm glad you find it so enjoyable, brother," said Nickalonis. "You should have something to eat so you can choke on it."

Solon rubbed his eyes with his sleeve. "I will remember that one."

Jaci pulled one of the blankets up around her shoulders and wrapped it around her legs. The giant, Barayan, had built a small fire, and warmth began to penetrate her aching limbs. The smoke was drawn up and back into the depths of the cave by faintly perceptible air currents, as was the smoke from the torches.

They ate in silence, washing down the dry meal with cold water from the spring. Jaci was so hungry she could have eaten all their portions with room to spare. She wondered how they survived on such small rations.

Her rescuer tore off a few thin strips of meat and fed them to the hawk. Jaci was surprised the bird ate them. She'd thought birds of prey would only eat fresh meat.

As she finished her meal and wiped the crumbs from her hands, she looked up and found her rescuer watching her, his dark eyes studying her face as if tracing every line. She felt an edge of pain, a touch of the anguish she had felt earlier.

"Lady, I must know who you are, and how you came to be in Wolf Run."

Jaci's stomach clenched. "I'm... not sure how I got to... where I was." Her mind reached for a plausible explanation, or at least, one he would believe. She didn't dare tell the truth. They'd think she was crazy. Seizing on an idea that might buy her some time, she frowned and rubbed the back of her head. "I remember falling... off a horse maybe... and hitting my head. I don't remember anything after that. I know my name, but that's all I know. That, and the fact I'm not a bard," she added, half to herself.

She looked from one horseman to another. Their faces revealed nothing, their expressions blank as the stone wall of the cave. The playfulness of a moment ago was gone.

"I have never seen clothing such as yours." The leader of the horsemen looked down at his own brown leather tunic and leggings and then looked back at her. "And your accent and manner of speech is like none I have heard."

Jaci fingered the material of her jeans. "I'm sorry. I don't know. I can't remember..." Their eyes met and held. Jaci felt again the deep fathomless ache in her soul — in his soul. "Why are you in such pain?" she murmured.

He looked startled, then his expression grew as cold as the wind outside. "Get some sleep. We ride out early." He rose and crossed to the back of the cave, disappearing into the darkness. One of the horses nickered softly.

The two brothers began unpacking their bedrolls. Without undressing, they lay down and within minutes were snoring quietly.

Jaci looked over at the giant tree-man — Barayan, they'd called him. He had rechecked the brush covering the cave mouth and was now sitting cross-legged on the ground sharpening a sword blade.

"Looks like it's you and me again," said Jaci.

He glanced at her, one bushy eyebrow raised a fraction, then went back to his work.

Tired beyond measure, Jaci wrapped herself in her blankets, pillowed her head on her arm, and slept.

CHAPTER 6

Jaci started awake as a rough hand shook her shoulder. A hairy face with bushy black eyebrows looked down at her and grunted. She jerked back with a screech, then caught herself.

The tree-man looked amused.

Nickalonis appeared beside him, grinning. He slapped Barayan on the back. "Leave her alone, you big oaf. Can't you see you're scaring her?"

Barayan snorted and started packing up their gear.

Nickalonis held out his hand to Jaci and helped her up. "You need not fear our hirsute friend. He may be twice as tall as you, but he is quite harmless."

"Oh, yes, he really looks harmless," Jaci said as she brushed off her clothes. "And thank you, once again, for pointing out how short I am."

Nickalonis laughed. "You shouldn't be so sensitive about your size." He slid his arm around her shoulders. "I like ... um ... delicate women."

"I'll show you delicate." Using a maneuver she'd practiced many times in her martial arts classes, Jaci grabbed his arm, braced herself, and flipped him over her shoulder. He landed flat on his back with a *whoompf.*

Hearty applause echoed through the cave. Jaci turned to see Solon laughing and clapping enthusiastically. "Well done, my lady. Well done."

Barayan grunted and nodded in agreement, a wide grin on his face.

Jaci blushed. "I guess I lost my temper." She looked at Nickalonis, who lay sucking in air. She noticed a white patch of cloth on his lower left side where his disheveled shirt had ridden up from his waist. "Is that a bandage? I'm sorry if I —"

"Don't worry about him," Solon said. "It is an old wound. He'll recover soon enough."

Nickalonis sat up slowly and smiled at Jaci. "I give you this battle, my lady, but the war continues."

Solon beckoned to Jaci. "Come. Bring your things. I think you'd best ride with me."

Jaci gathered up her blankets and followed after him.

They emerged from the cave into darkness. Dawn was barely a glimmer on the horizon, and bright stars glinted in the deep violet-black sky. The surrounding rocks stood dark and silent, not yet roused from slumber. Thick frost covered the sparse vegetation. Jaci shivered as the penetrating cold dug into her skin.

The horses had already been saddled. Clutching the blankets more closely for warmth, Jaci watched Barayan load the gear and strap it down, then jumped as the leader of the horsemen suddenly appeared from the dense blackness between two tall boulders. Sharrow flew out of the rocks and landed on his outstretched wrist. He whispered to her and stroked her smooth feathers. With a soft cry, she launched into the air, climbing in tight spirals until she was lost from sight. The leader looked at Solon, who nodded. The horsemen began to mount up. Jaci mounted behind Solon, and they started off across the ridge.

They moved slowly over the rough ground, her rescuer in the lead. Jaci squinted into the fading starlight, but she could see very little. Their path wound down off the ridge, over treacherous shale-like rock. The horses slipped and stumbled as the rock crumbled under them but managed to keep their footing. Jaci's arms and legs ached from gripping Solon and the horse, but she didn't dare loosen her hold.

Soon they left the ridge behind. The trail led downward through treeless hills, barren rock-strewn valleys, and gorse-choked ravines. The air was still, the sky cloaked in varying shades of mauve as dawn approached.

Jaci adjusted her blankets and leaned forward, trying to absorb some warmth from Solon's back. Her sore legs complained with every movement of the rough-gaited horse. She wished she could have ridden with the leader. His steed out-classed Solon's by far. Having grown up around horses, Jaci had ridden enough clunkers to appreciate a good mount. Her rescuer, however, had not spoken to her or even looked at her since he had disappeared into the back of the cave the night before. He seemed to be avoiding her, and she thought she knew why. She had pried into his pain. What could possibly have hurt him so? Earlier, Solon had started to say that she looked like someone. Who? Some woman who had broken his heart? Was that why he hurt so much?

Jaci frowned. Why did she care? Yes, he had rescued her, but he might have done so for anyone else in her position. He could be an escaped murderer for all she knew. He and the others were obviously running from something. She didn't even know his name.

Stop thinking about him, she told herself sternly. *You don't want to get mixed up any further in whatever trouble he's in.* Yet she couldn't help but wonder why she was so strongly affected by his pain. Was it possible for one person to experience another's torment? The tumult of emotions that had run through her — agonizing grief, horror, guilt, yearning — had stunned her. His wound ran deep, had festered for a long time. It was slowly bleeding the life out of him. She didn't know how she knew that. She should be frightened, but she wasn't.

And why did she feel so drawn to him? She wanted to touch him and see if she felt again that sense of aliveness that had zinged her like an electric shock when she'd ridden with him. She needed to prove to herself that it hadn't been a figment of her imagination, born of exhaustion. Such a strange experience…

Stop it right now! What was the matter with her? She should be thinking about how to get home. She would never be able to find the meadow again — they had ridden too far, and she'd been asleep part of the time. If only she could get a few minutes to herself to finish reading the diary. So far, she had nothing to go on but the name Galenock.

She would have to start asking questions. After all, she had amnesia. She should be expected to ask questions. She had the feeling, though, that the horsemen wouldn't be very forthcoming with answers.

Solon's horse stumbled, derailing her train of thought. She winced and gritted her teeth. She wished they would get to wherever they were going, and soon.

They picked their way down the tortuous trail, descending into a long narrow valley sided with thick evergreens and carpeted with frost-browned grass. Dewdrops glistened in the rays of the rising sun. A shallow stream burbled down the valley's center. The tang of cedar and the musty smell of the trampled grass filled the air. Sharrow flew silently overhead, her shadow gliding over the valley floor.

They rode on down the valley without stopping. The bright sun climbed higher, warming the air until Jaci felt sweat trickling down her back. Her stomach growled and cramped. She put her hand over her belly as if it would quiet the sound. She couldn't remember ever being so hungry.

She leaned forward. "Will we be stopping to eat soon?"

Solon glanced back at her. "We will likely stop at the far end of the valley."

Jaci sat back. "I hope so. The few bites we had last night would hardly sustain a fly."

"You should be grateful for food so generously shared," he replied, not unkindly.

Jaci closed her mouth on what she'd been about to say. He had a point. They didn't have to share their rations with her at all. They could have left her to the wolves.

"You're right," she said. "I'm sorry."

"No offense taken, my lady."

As Solon had predicted, they pulled up near the trees at the end of the valley. This time Jaci allowed Solon to help her down.

"Oh, my legs," she groaned as she hit the ground and straightened up.

"You haven't done much riding, have you?" Solon asked as he loosened the tack.

"Actually, I've ridden quite a bit." Jaci stuffed her blankets into the saddlebag. "Just not lately."

"Then it's not likely you hit your head by falling off a horse."

Jaci froze, remembering the story she had given them last night. She would have to be more careful. She finished packing the saddlebag, then turned to face him, hoping she looked sufficiently confused.

"No, it isn't." She rubbed the back of her head. "How else could it have happened?"

"Yes. How else?" Solon repeated, his expression neutral.

He was giving her the benefit of the doubt — a chance to explain herself... a chance she dared not take.

"I don't know," she said. "But since I remember that I haven't ridden in a while, maybe more memories will come back to me."

Solon's face remained devoid of expression. "That would be prudent." He caught up the horse's reins and led the animal to the stream, where her rescuer was already watering his mount. They talked quietly.

Jaci took a deep breath to calm herself. She would definitely have to watch what she said. These men acted friendly, but maybe they were just trying to lull her into a false sense of security, waiting for her to make a mistake that would reveal who she was. She wondered why Solon hadn't questioned her more closely. Perhaps that job would fall to her rescuer.

She glanced at the two men surreptitiously as she hurried to the stream and washed her hands and face, wishing she could read lips.

Barayan had divided up the last of their rations and was handing them out. Jaci accepted the chunk of bread and strip of dried meat gratefully. She sat near the edge of the stream and gobbled them down. Solon handed her a water flask he had taken from his saddlebag.

"You can fill it from the brook when you are through with it," he said, and went to get his portion from Barayan.

"Thanks," Jaci said. She drank deeply. Then she leaned over the stream and refilled the flask. As she straightened up, she caught Nickalonis staring at her with an unusual intensity. Their eyes locked. Jaci stopped in mid-motion, startled by the cold, calculating maliciousness reflected in the brown depths.

"If you are through with the flask, I will take it back."

Jaci jumped at Solon's nearness and dropped the flask into the brook.

Solon leaped into the shallow water, grabbing the flask before it washed downstream. "Great gods, woman!" he sputtered as he clambered back onto the bank. "What is the matter with you?"

Jaci gathered her scattered wits. "I'm sorry. You startled me. You should know better than to sneak up on people like that."

He looked at her more closely. "Your face is as white as Brackan's shroud. Are you ill?"

"No," she said, glancing over to where Nickalonis had been sitting. "I—I'm fine." He had finished eating and was standing beside his horse with his back to her, cinching up his saddle.

"We will be leaving in a few minutes." Solon turned to go.

"Solon..."

"Yes?"

"Your brother... he has blue eyes, doesn't he?"

Solon frowned, his expression faintly disapproving. "Yes. Why do you ask?"

"No reason," she said quickly. "I was just... thinking about it."

"You would do well not to think about him, my lady." Solon went to retrieve his mount.

Jaci rose and stood for a moment, brushing the grass and crumbs from her jeans. A chill shivered down her back. Nickalonis had looked at her with such hatred. And his eyes had definitely been brown.

She looked up to find Nickalonis walking toward her. She stiffened.

He gave her an easy smile. "I overheard you asking about me. I'm flattered." He winked and smiled again.

Jaci searched his eyes. They appeared friendly and guileless — and very blue.

"Don't let it go to your head," she said and brushed past him.

He caught up with her as she hurried toward the horses. "You ride with me this time." He linked his arm in hers.

She stopped in dismay, but he pulled her along, either oblivious to or ignoring her rigidity.

Catching up the reins of his steed, he waited for her to mount.

She hesitated. The others had already mounted and were moving toward the woods at the valley's edge.

"Up you go," Nickalonis said, and boosted her up into the saddle. He swung up behind and settled in close.

She sat forward as his arm wrapped around her waist. Then his hand brushed her breast.

She slapped his hand away. "I'll thank you to keep your hands to yourself."

"Sorry," he said with a chuckle. "I'll try to be more careful."

They caught up with the others at the edge of the forest. Her rescuer led the way in, following what looked like an animal trail that wove through the thin undergrowth. Pine needles covered the forest floor. The midday sun filtered through the canopy of interlaced branches, dappling their path with patches of gold. Cool air, scented with pine, drifted past, the breath of the living forest. Small brown birds Jaci didn't recognize flitted among the trees.

An hour later, they emerged from the thinning woods onto rolling grassland. Not far in the distance rose another stand of forest, and the horses broke into a canter as if scenting home.

Halfway across the grassland, the leader reined in, his progress impeded by a wide, slow-flowing river. As the others pulled up beside him, he urged his mount down the short, steep bank into the river. Water swirled up around the horse's legs, not quite reaching its belly. Solon followed.

"Hold on," Nickalonis said.

Jaci snagged the front of the saddle and her mount's mane again. He kicked his horse forward into the river, his arm rising and wrapping around her chest.

She let go of the saddle and pried at his arm. "I told you not to do that."

His grip tightened. "Relax. Most women enjoy a good cuddle with a handsome man."

"I'm not most women!" She grabbed his thumb and twisted it backward.

With a cry of pain, he let go. "You little minx!"

Before he could do anything else to her, she bit his hand hard.

He yelped and snatched it away.

She spat into the river. "And you're not handsome, either."

Dropping the reins, he caught her shoulders and twisted her around in the saddle. His blue eyes gleamed. "You owe me for that one." He bent to kiss her.

She punched him in the solar plexus.

He gasped, his arms falling away.

She elbowed him hard in the gut, then shoved him backward. With an "oof," Nickalonis tumbled over the horse's tail and splashed into the river.

The horse shied and lunged sideways, throwing Jaci out of the saddle. She caught the saddle with one hand and the horse's mane with the other and hung on, her legs dragging in the water.

Solon, who hadn't yet ascended the far bank, swung his horse around and intercepted the runaway steed. Jaci got her foot in the stirrup and heaved herself back into the saddle. Turning, she saw that Barayan had fished Nickalonis out of the river and was bringing him across. Nickalonis looked like he was in serious pain, more than he should have been for what she'd done to him. Then she remembered the bandage she had seen. His wound had been right where she'd elbowed him. Apprehension knotted her stomach. What if she'd really hurt him?

Her horse, pulled along by Solon, reached the opposite bank and climbed up out of the river beside the leader. Jaci avoided his gaze, frightened by the grim fury in his eyes. He'd said neither he nor his men would harm her, but at the moment, he looked ready to kill. Would he change his mind? Or would he instead abandon her, here in the middle of nowhere? What would she do? Where would she go?

The shriek of a hawk directly overhead startled her already skittish horse and sent it plunging along the bank. Jaci could only hold on, since Solon still held the reins. Cursing roundly, Solon jerked her mount up short.

Sharrow screamed again and flew in a swift, straight line back toward the woods they had just traversed.

The leader mouthed an oath, his steed prancing under him. "Barayan, hurry! Solon, go!"

"How did they find us?" Solon muttered. He rein-whipped his horse into a run, pulling Jaci's mount along behind.

Jaci lay low and clung to the grunting animal. In the moment before Solon had whirled her around, she'd seen at least a dozen red-cloaked horsemen break from the trees behind them.

CHAPTER 7

Jaci reined in her sweating horse and sagged with relief for the few moments' rest. Just ahead of her, at the edge of yet another forest they'd barreled through, Solon had halted, eyes trained on an open meadow that led up into a series of rocky hills.

In their flight from the red-cloaked riders, the group had split up. Solon had slowed only long enough to toss her the reins with a gruff "Follow me." Then he had raced cross-country, careening through forests, hard-packed canyons and brush-strewn ravines, splashing down streambeds, even stampeding a couple of herds of range cattle — anything to cover their tracks and throw off the tenacious pursuit.

She pulled up beside Solon, shifting in the saddle to ease her aching legs. If she hadn't been so scared and sore, she would have relished the challenging ride. Nickalonis' horse had a much smoother gait than Solon's, similar to her rescuer's horse, and it had flown over the fallen trees like a winged beast. Both mounts had surprising speed and stamina. She hadn't seen or heard the red-cloaked riders for some time, and Jaci thought they must have finally lost them. But what of the others? Her rescuer had ridden off to the right, upriver, while Barayan, with Nickalonis, had headed in the opposite direction, their horses running at top speed. The red-cloaked riders had split then as well, pursuing all of them. She hoped the others had managed to escape.

Wordlessly, Solon urged his mount into the meadow. Jaci followed, and they cantered across, Solon's gaze sweeping around them constantly like a deer fearing the hunter. They rode up into the rocky hills, slowing to let the horses pick their way.

They reined in again at the top of a low rise, and Jaci caught her breath in surprise. In the half-wooded, half-grassy glen below sprawled the ruins of an ancient castle. Ragged gray stone walls rose forty feet in some places, and crumbled towers shared space with massive trees. Grass and wildflowers grew along the tops of the walls, with curtains of vines clinging to the sides. Moss-covered rocks, remnants of some of the walls and towers, lay strewn across the glen floor as if hurled by an explosive force.

"Is that where we're going?" Jaci asked. Two thoughts had struck her at the same time: *How beautiful!* and *No plumbing.* She had never been fond of camping. She liked hiking and appreciated the beauty of the wilderness, but when she was done enjoying scenic areas, she wanted to return to the comforts of a solid roof over her head, a soft bed to sleep in, and flush toilets.

Solon shot her a troubled glance but didn't answer. He raised his hands to his mouth and trilled some kind of bird call. An answering call sounded in the trees to their left. He studied the landscape behind them for a few more long moments, then descended into the glen.

Jaci followed, pondering the expression he had given her. He'd seemed worried. *Well, of course,* she thought. *He's worried about his brother and the others.* But somehow, she didn't think that was it. Her intuition told her there was some other reason for his concern. Did he think their pursuers might still find them?

They were met at the edge of the ruins by three men in forest-colored clothing, who had slipped out from behind one of the high walls. All were armed with swords and daggers. Solon dismounted and spoke to them with gestures rather than words. They nodded once, then shook their heads, replying in kind. Jaci watched, baffled. She had no idea what they were saying. She dismounted slowly, her muscles groaning with every movement. The men eyed her suspiciously, then disappeared behind the wall. Moments later, the ruins swarmed with activity. She saw dozens of men rushing around, packing up supplies, conversing either in low tones or sign language. They appeared to be preparing to move out.

"Come. Bring your horse," Solon said to her, and led the way around the high walls.

Jaci fell in behind him, her eyes lifting to the tops of the walls. She wondered how many centuries ago the castle had been built. And what had destroyed it.

They handed off their horses to another forest-colored man near the rear of the castle, then Solon hurried toward the remains of the inner keep. Jaci cursed her short legs. She almost had to jog to keep up with him. He stopped before an opening to a small room that measured about eight by ten feet across. Most of the ceiling had long since fallen in, but the windowless walls were solid, rising a few feet above her head before opening to the late afternoon sky.

He pointed to the room. "Stay there. Do not leave the room. I must talk with my brother."

"He's here?" Her heart rate quickened, fueled by both relief and dread. "With Barayan?"

"Yes."

"What about —?" She stopped, realizing she still didn't know her rescuer's name.

"No." He gestured toward the room again.

Reluctantly, she stepped through the opening into the small room. Solon waved to one of the other men in the courtyard, a muscular fellow with a strip of solid black cloth like a bandanna knotted around his upper left arm. One look at his bulging biceps and hard face told Jaci she did not want to tangle with him. The man crossed the courtyard and stood silently as Solon signed instructions, including a jerk of his thumb in her direction. She saw again the worry in Solon's eyes, the tension in his jaw.

The man with the black bandanna gave Jaci a cold, appraising glance, then planted himself beside the doorway, outside, with his back to the wall. He fidgeted with the knife at his belt, as if his fingers itched to use it. Solon hastened away, out of sight.

Jaci backed further into the room. She didn't want to be anywhere near that nervously twitching knife. She wished Solon hadn't left her there. She glanced about the room — empty, save for grass-covered lumps she took to be rock from the collapsed ceiling. She wanted to sit and rest her aching legs, but she knew it would be hard to get up again if she did, so she paced the back of the room, thinking.

So Solon had set a guard on her. Obviously, he didn't trust her, and didn't want her to overhear his conversation with his brother. But then, why should he trust her? He knew even less about her than she knew about him. And actually, it was probably just as well. She had no desire to see Nickalonis after the episode at the river. Yet she was glad he and Barayan had escaped the red-cloaked riders. Her thoughts slipped to the leader of the group, and worry gnawed at her. What if the riders had caught him? What would happen to him? She had the feeling it wouldn't be good.

She shoved her hair back away from her face impatiently. What she needed was information — an opportunity to ask questions.

But there hadn't been one. The horsemen had insisted on riding silently through the day. Why all the secrecy?

A cold thought crept into her mind, momentarily stopped her in her tracks. What if the horsemen were outlaws? What if they were the bad guys, and the red-cloaked riders were good? It wouldn't take much stretch of the imagination to see Twitchy Knife as a villain. She could be in a lot more trouble than she'd thought. Fear shivered through her, weakened her legs. She sat on one of the grassy lumps and clenched her mother's pendant through her shirt. The paralyzing tumult of thoughts and emotions eased, and she took a deep breath. She had to keep her wits about her. She needed a plan of action.

Well, if she couldn't get information from the horsemen right now, at least she could read more of the diary and maybe find something useful.

She glanced at the open doorway. All she could see of the guard was his elbow. Carefully, she pulled the diary out of her pocket. There were some entries between September 10th, when Deirdre had been released from the institution, and the final entry of October 1st, that Jaci hadn't had time to read.

Turning so that the slanting rays of the late afternoon sun shone on the diary, she found the page she wanted and scanned the first few entries. Deirdre expressed sorrow for the loss of her aunt and uncle, who had died in a car accident. Jaci recalled the man at the garage — Tom — mentioning their recent deaths. Apparently Deirdre had been released from the institution because no more checks came to pay for her to be there. She wrote of her confusion in dealing with the haughty lawyer who had come to get her and her difficulties in dealing with life outside the institution. Her aunt and uncle had left her the house and all they had, but she didn't know how to take care of a house or use money. She'd never had to buy her own food or clothes. She taught herself to drive her uncle's car and had ventured as far as the local grocery for food, but the people of Marston had been mean to her and wouldn't help her. They'd laughed at her and taken advantage of her helplessness.

"What monsters!" Jaci fumed, then gulped and glanced at the doorway to see if the guard had heard her. He didn't look in at her, so she turned back to the diary, flipping to the next page, dated September 22nd.

I dreamed of Tarshane again. I saw two men fighting in the Great Room of a castle. One had gray-streaked dark hair, and the other, short reddish-blond hair and a beard. They fought with magic, and all around them, blue fire burned. I think one of them is Galenock, but I don't know which. I believe, now, that they are not really dreams, but memories coming back to me from a childhood that somehow so traumatized me that my mind tried to lock everything away.

That poor girl. What had happened to her, so long ago? Jaci had read that it was possible for the mind to block out traumatic events. Men fighting with magic — could it really be? What were they fighting about? And Galenock — that name again. She must ask about him the first chance she had.

I don't belong here in this world. I belong in Tarshane. I must find my real family and discover who I am. Only eleven more days...

Did that mean the Brunswicks weren't really Deirdre's blood relatives? Had she been adopted? Jaci turned the page — September 26th. Her heartbeat sped up as she noted the many tear stains blurring the words.

I can hardly bear to write of this dream. It is horrible beyond measure. I am hiding in a tiny black space. A soft thump, thump, thumping matches my heartbeat. Outside the space, I hear many heavy footsteps, then I hear a girl screaming in terror as she is taken away. I close my eyes and cover my ears. I don't remember her name, but I know she was my sister.

Jaci held her breath, her heart pounding. Tiny black space... heartbeat-like thumping — the clock! Could there be a similar clock, here in this world, that Deirdre had hidden in and unexpectedly been transported to Jaci's world? If Jaci could find it, she could go home!

Jaci reread the entry, her eyes filling with tears as she imagined the horror of Deirdre's experience. Had her sister lived? Who had taken her away? And why?

Only two more entries — September 29th and October 1st. Jaci read on.

I finally slept last night, after three nights of wakefulness caused by the dream of my sister's death. I did not see her die in the dream, but I know in my heart that she is dead. I dreamed of her again last night. She was arguing with a dark-haired young man — Talan — that was his name. I remembered! His anger filled the room like a black cloud. He is dangerous. I don't know what they were fighting about. I could not hear their words. It was as if I was watching through a distant peephole. He stormed out of the room, and my sister cried.

So Deirdre's sister hadn't survived. How terribly sad. Was this Talan involved in her death? Jaci should ask about him, too, though the part about him being dangerous made her nervous. She'd broach the subject of Galenock first — not that that was likely any better. He supposedly had been battling with magic. And was he fighting on the good side, or the bad? For that matter, maybe all of them were bad... No, she wouldn't go there — that would be too frightening to contemplate.

One more entry — October 1st. The day Deirdre had died, and Jaci had been transported to this world. Jaci shivered. Only two days had passed since then, but it seemed a lifetime.

The lawyer called me on the telephone. He said there was some paper related to the Brunswick estate that should have been signed when the will was read, but was missed somehow, and that I must sign it immediately. He spoke like it was my fault the paper didn't get signed and insisted I meet him at an airport in the city, because he was going away on vacation and would be gone for a while. I asked why it had to be signed so quickly, and he explained in such a way that I didn't really understand — something about losing the house and the money. I don't know if what he says is truthful or not, but there is no one I can ask. I don't know what to do. I don't care about the house or the money and will not need either if I can get back to Tarshane, but if my plan tonight doesn't work... if I have misinterpreted the drawings or can't work the magic... Why did it have to be today of all days? I will go and try and find the city and the airport. I think I remember the way to the city from before. As long as I am back by nightfall, everything should be all right.

Jaci felt a lump in her throat. Deirdre hadn't made it back. What a tragic, wasted life she'd had. If not for the accident, Deirdre would be here in this world, instead of Jaci, and Jaci would be at Courtney's house, oohing and aahing over her friend's new baby. How strange it was, the turn of events. If only she'd remembered her GPS, she wouldn't have gotten lost, and she wouldn't have somehow ended up in some meadow, who knows where... Wait a minute. If there was another clock here somewhere, why did she end up in the meadow?

She slipped the small rectangle of paper out of its hiding place in the back cover of the diary and studied it again. Four words — *ne, ris, ful,* and *set* — corresponded with four drawings — trees and grass, a red-brown square, a clock face, and mountains. October 1st, the date that she had been transported to this world, had been circled on the calendar, and the words "new moon" had been underlined. Could *ne* mean new moon? If the words corresponded to the moon phases, that might explain why she ended up in a meadow near a forest — trees and grass. But how did it work?

Deirdre had said if she couldn't work the magic... Jaci considered. Could magic really exist? Skepticism warred with curiosity. And yet, how else could she explain how she'd gotten here? Then her eyes caught the word at the bottom of the page — *saelarin*. Could that be some kind of magic word? She gasped. She'd said that word aloud when she'd been standing by the clock in Deirdre's house. It had been written on the calendar. She remembered feeling an electrical charge in the air and thought the house had been struck by lightning. By speaking the word, could she have unwittingly opened some sort of magic portal between the two worlds?

She struggled to comprehend the enormity of the idea. Then another thought struck her. The electrical charge she'd felt when riding with her rescuer — all those sensations — were they... was he... magical, too? She clasped her pendant to calm herself. Better not to think about him right now. His fury had frightened her, and the thought of his being magical made him seem like an alien from another planet. In fact, this whole situation was like something out of a science fiction movie.

She looked back at the paper. *Saelarin.* What if she said the word now? After a moment's hesitation, she whispered the word aloud. Nothing. She waited tensely, but no electrical charge zinged the air. She slumped. If magic existed in this world, why hadn't it worked? She sat up straighter. Maybe she just wasn't in the right place. Maybe the word took effect only in certain spots. And only at certain times. But if that were the case, how would she ever get home? Not only would she have to find the right spot, but she'd have to be there at the right phase of the moon. And that was only if her theory was correct — a very big "if."

A shuffling footstep near the doorway startled her. Solon had returned and was conversing silently with the man guarding her. She slid the paper into the back cover and stuffed the diary in her pocket. The man gave a final nod and jogged away. She rose stiffly, gritting her teeth to keep from groaning.

Solon beckoned her forward and handed her a small burlap sack containing bread and cheese. "You can eat while we walk," he said as he headed across the courtyard.

"Thanks." Jaci hurried to catch up with him. She pulled out the bread and ate hungrily.

The ruins now stood empty. All the men — about fifty of them, she estimated — had gathered with their horses just beyond the far end of the castle and were either mounted and ready to go or settling packs and preparing to mount. About one-third of them had black bandannas tied around their left arms, like the man with the twitchy knife who had guarded her. Jaci wondered what the bandanna signified.

She spotted Barayan on his huge chestnut, with Nickalonis nearby, not yet mounted, adjusting his horse's saddle girth. Solon's horse stood quietly beside him. She couldn't see her rescuer anywhere. Were they just going to leave without him? Well, what if they were? That was their business, not hers. And maybe that was best, for her. She didn't want to see him anyway. Well, not really. Did she? She'd never had such confusing feelings about a man. A sober thought chilled her. Maybe they'd given him up for dead. She glanced at Solon, but didn't quite dare ask.

Solon walked straight toward his brother.

"Oh, great," she muttered under her breath. She certainly didn't want to see him.

By the time they reached Nickalonis, Jaci had finished her meal and handed the sack back to Solon.

"You ride with Barayan," Solon said, and caught up the reins of his horse.

She gave an inward sigh of relief and looked up at Barayan. At least she could ride in peace. Wherever they were going.

Nickalonis blocked her path. He grinned roguishly. "I owe you for two, now."

She glared at him. "If you do anything like that again, you'll get more of the same. Now get out of my way."

He laughed and started to reply, but Solon cuffed him aside.

"What?" asked Nickalonis with hurt innocence.

"Leave her alone," Solon warned.

Jaci grasped the hand Barayan held out to her. She had a hard time stretching to reach the stirrup, his horse was so tall, but she managed and climbed up behind him.

Nickalonis scowled at his brother. "You are no fun at all." He mounted gingerly and eased his horse forward, his wound obviously still bothering him.

Well, he deserved it, Jaci thought, not sorry for what she had done to him. And she'd meant what she'd said. She'd do it again if he didn't keep his hands to himself.

Solon and Nickalonis rode to the front of the group and led them out of the glen at a canter. Barayan kept to the rear.

Seeing all those men in front of her — there were no women in the group — Jaci was suddenly very glad she had invested the time and money in her martial arts classes. She might very well need to defend herself again before she got home. If she got home...

CHAPTER 8

All through the evening they rode, and long into the night. By the time they stopped, Jaci was so exhausted she fell asleep the moment she pillowed her head on a saddlebag.

Voices woke her — familiar voices, sort of. Who were they? She tried to get her sleep-fogged mind to think.

"She rides well, that's for certain. In fact, she handled your horse better than you do."

Solon, her mind registered, as the full measure of her plight doused her like a bucket of cold water.

"Hmmph," groused another voice. "She's a little minx, that one." Nickalonis.

"If you touch her like that again, you will answer to me," said a deeper voice, cold with tightly reined anger.

She froze. She'd know that voice anywhere. Her rescuer had returned.

She rolled over and looked around, but saw nothing in the chill dawn light other than rows of sleeping men scattered across the clearing in the forest where they'd stopped for the night. The voices had passed out of hearing. Several men stood on guard along the perimeter of the camp. The only one close to her was the man with the twitchy knife.

Great. She settled back against her saddlebag pillow, suddenly noticing that someone had thrown blankets over her while she'd slept. She hadn't had them when she'd dismounted, or rather collapsed, off Barayan's horse when they'd finally halted for a rest. She wondered who had done it. She appreciated their thoughtfulness, for the air was quite cold.

She smiled to herself. Solon had been impressed with her riding skills. She wished she knew what else they were saying. Part of her was irrationally glad that her rescuer had returned safely, while another part was scared to death by his reappearance.

She glanced around again, but still couldn't see or hear the three of them. Well, at least she didn't have to worry about dealing with her rescuer right now. She knew she should take advantage of the rest time and go back to sleep, but his voice had keyed her nerves, and she also really needed a toilet. *A real one*, she grumped to herself. She looked back at Twitchy Knife. Why did it have to be him?

Gathering her courage, she rose and approached him. He watched her narrowly, his fingers itching over the knife hilt.

"Um... I need to use the bushes." She pointed toward the trees.

He jerked his head in the direction she'd pointed, which she interpreted as a nod of assent.

She hurried through the trees until she found a thicket she could climb into and be completely hidden. Afterward, she washed her hands on a patch of dewy grass. What she wouldn't give for a hot shower and soap. She turned back toward the campsite, then stopped, hearing voices again, this time off to her left. She hesitated. Should she? What if Twitchy Knife came looking for her? Curiosity won out, and she crept toward the sounds.

Not far ahead, she saw them — Solon, Nickalonis, and her rescuer — talking heatedly. She crouched behind a tangle of berry briars, close enough to hear what they were saying.

"But what if she *is* a spy?" Solon asked. "The Riders keep finding us."

"The Riders found us twice *before* we discovered her in Wolf Run," Nickalonis argued. "I think it's just coincidence."

Jaci caught her breath. So that was why Solon had given her that worried look, back at the ruins. He thought he might be bringing a spy into their hideout. A spy for whom?

"Coincidence or not, it does not explain how she came to be there, or her strange clothes and speech," said her rescuer, his eyes searching the trees around them.

"No, it doesn't," Nickalonis admitted, "nor does it explain her resemblance to —" He bit off what he'd been about to say after Solon surreptitiously elbowed him.

Jaci held her breath as her rescuer's roving gaze stopped. He seemed to be staring right at her through the intervening briars.

Sensing a movement behind her, she whirled just as Twitchy Knife lunged at her. A shriek of fright escaped her as he seized her arm, hauled her to her feet, and dragged her into the open. Solon stared at her in dismay, convinced now, she could see, that she was a spy as he had feared. Nickalonis looked surprised, but nothing more.

Her rescuer's face was coldly impassive. "Thank you, Katar. You can return to your post. We will see to her."

Katar nodded once, sheathed the knife that had found its way into his other hand, and melted into the trees, toward the camp.

Shivering with apprehension, Jaci faced the three men.

"Why were you spying on us?" her rescuer asked.

"I wasn't spying on you," Jaci said, trying to keep the nervousness out of her voice, "at least, not intentionally. I had to use the bushes, and I heard someone talking, and my curiosity got the better of me."

"But you were hiding," Solon said harshly. "If you weren't spying, you would have come out and spoken with us, instead of listening without our knowledge."

"If I had come out, you would have stopped talking, and I wouldn't have learned anything —" She stopped, realizing how that sounded. She raked her hand through her hair, disgusted with herself. She had to *think* before she spoke. "What I meant was, I had the feeling you wouldn't say the same things in front of me that you would say in private, and I hoped to hear something that might jog my memory."

Her rescuer stepped toward her, and she instinctively stepped back.

He halted, lifting his hands in a gesture of peace. "As I said before, I will not hurt you."

Jaci forced herself to stand still. "I was afraid you might have changed your mind."

He pointed to her waist. "What is that?"

She looked down and sucked in a sharp breath. Deirdre's diary had slipped a third of the way out of her pocket. It must have happened when Twitchy Knife — Katar — had dragged her out from behind the briars. Her heart sank. So much for the amnesia defense. She'd have to come clean.

She pulled the small book out of her pocket. "It's a diary. Not mine. And no, I didn't steal it," she added.

Her rescuer moved closer and held out his hand.

She gave him the diary, then slid the calendar out of her back pocket and gave him that, too. "I'll try to explain." *But you're going to think I'm nuts*, she added silently. Then the irony of her predicament struck her. In Jaci's world, they'd thought Deirdre was crazy and had institutionalized her. Would the same happen to Jaci in Deirdre's world?

Her rescuer opened the cover of the diary and drew a sharp breath. "Deirdre," he whispered hoarsely.

"What?" Solon gasped. He rushed to her rescuer's side. "Deirdre Brunswick." They looked at each other, faces pale, appearing as shocked as they'd been when they'd first seen Jaci. "It couldn't be the same..."

They turned to Jaci.

"The same what?" she asked.

"The age is about right," Solon said to her rescuer, still in a tone of disbelief. "And if she really does have amnesia..." He turned back to Jaci. "Are you... Deirdre?"

"No," Jaci answered, stunned by the question. She wasn't sure which surprised her more — that these men seemed to know who Deirdre was or that they thought she and Deirdre were the same person. "I —" Her breath caught in her throat. Nickalonis was staring at her with eyes as deep brown as hers. Such hatred radiated from him, she felt sure that if he'd had a weapon in his hand, he'd have killed her on the spot. She backed away rapidly and bumped into a tree.

Her rescuer was beside her instantly. "What's wrong?"

She pointed weakly at Nickalonis. "His... his eyes..."

Nickalonis blinked, his eyes now blue as an autumn sky, the murderous intent gone.

Her rescuer and Solon turned as one toward Nickalonis.

"Why are you all staring at me?" Nickalonis asked in confusion.

Her rescuer turned back to Jaci. "What about his eyes?"

"They — they were brown again," she stammered. "He looked like he wanted to kill me."

"What is she talking about?" Nickalonis demanded.

"Look at him. His eyes are blue," Solon said with a frown. "She is trying to distract us —"

Her rescuer held up his hand for silence, and Solon closed his mouth in a grim line.

"What did you mean — 'again'?" her rescuer asked.

Jaci took a deep breath and tried to stop shaking. "It happened once before — yesterday, when we stopped to eat, where I dropped the water flask into the stream." She turned to Solon. "You remember, don't you? I asked you then if his eyes were blue, and you said yes and that I shouldn't be thinking about him. That was why I asked — because I'd caught him looking at me, and his eyes were brown. Then you startled me, and I dropped the flask, and when I looked back, his eyes were blue again."

Solon said nothing, his expression a mix of anger, disbelief, and uncertainty.

Her rescuer eyed him. "Did this happen, or did it not?"

"She did drop the flask, and she did ask me the question," Solon said flatly, "but I have never known my brother's eyes to be anything other than blue."

Her rescuer's gaze shifted to Nickalonis, his eyes narrowing speculatively.

"Are you calling me a traitor?" Nickalonis asked, incredulously.

Solon took a step toward her rescuer. "Talan, you can't think —"

Jaci gasped and would have backed farther away from her rescuer if she hadn't been up against a tree. "You are Talan?" *He is dangerous.* Deirdre's written words repeated themselves in her mind.

He turned sharply. "How do you know me?"

His anger filled the room like a black cloud. She shrank back. "Your name is in the diary — at the end."

His attention swung back to the book. Jaci edged away around the tree trunk. *He stormed out of the room, and my sister cried …I know in my heart that she is dead.*

A twang split the stillness, and an arrow whizzed past Solon's ear to lodge in the tree behind him. With a startled oath, Solon jumped sideways, and he and Nickalonis hit the dirt. Jaci blinked in confusion. What was happening? Talan snatched her by the shoulders and pulled her to the ground, covering her with his body as more twangs sounded and more arrows flew past.

Cries of "Riders!" and "Ambush!" swept through Talan's men, then all was chaos as the red-cloaked Riders came crashing through the woods around them, their swords already dripping blood.

Frightened, Jaci scrunched into as small a shape as she could. Faint tingles of sizzling warmth tickled her skin wherever Talan's body touched hers.

Talan rose to a crouch and caught her hand. "Stay low." He pulled her across to Solon's side. "Are you all right?" he asked Solon.

"Yes." Solon scrambled to a crouch.

Nickalonis rose more slowly, favoring his wounded side.

Barayan appeared through the trees. He unhorsed one of the Riders and clubbed him to the ground, then rushed across to them.

Talan thrust Jaci toward Barayan. "Get her away from here —" He stopped, eyes widening, his face growing even paler as he stared at her.

Another bolt of fear shot through her. "Why are you looking at me like that?"

"Great gods in the heavens," whispered Solon, his and Nickalonis' expressions mirroring their leader's.

A spark of light caught Jaci's eye, a flash of brilliance emanating from her shirt front. She looked down and realized her pendant had slipped out from beneath her shirt. Its smooth iridescence shimmered in the light of the rising sun breaking through the trees.

An arrow thunked into her rescuer's left arm. He hissed in a breath and staggered.

"Talan!" Solon cried.

Three red-cloaked Riders charged into their midst, swinging their bloody swords.

Before Jaci could move, Barayan swept her up and swung her over his shoulder like a sack of potatoes. The three horsemen drew swords and attacked the Riders. Dodging the slashing blades, Barayan plunged into the forest, carrying her away from the battle.

Jaci thumped him on the back. "Hey, put me down! I can run."

One of the Riders bore down on them, and Jaci heard another twang just before an arrow sank into the back of Barayan's thigh. He grunted and fell, rolling onto his side in an effort not to crush her. A few paces away, the Rider reined in his horse and leaped to the ground. Jaci disentangled herself from Barayan, snatched up a fist-sized rock, and threw it at the Rider, hitting him in the chest. The rock bounced off his leather armor.

"Aaaargh! Wench! I'll cut off your ear for that —"

The second rock took him square in the forehead, and he dropped, senseless.

Jaci turned back to Barayan and helped him to his feet. "Can you run?"

He pushed her away and jabbed his finger repeatedly toward a denser part of the forest. He wanted her to run.

"But —"

Hoofbeats pounded toward them. Barayan shoved her forward, then hop-shuffled in the other direction, dragging his wounded leg.

Jaci swallowed a sob and raced toward the thicket he'd indicated. She knew he was trying to distract the Riders and lead them away from her, but it hurt to leave him. *The Riders will kill him, and it's my fault,* she thought with a catch in her throat. *If he hadn't been trying to save me...* She swiped the back of her hand across her eyes to clear the tears.

She ducked into the thicket and kept running. Hoofbeats sounded behind her. She shoved her pendant back inside her shirt, then veered to the right through another thick stand of trees. Red-cloaked Riders filled the woods around her, cutting off her escape. She darted this way and that, but soon found herself surrounded.

She put her back to a tree as they closed in and tried to follow her martial arts lessons by emptying her mind of her terror. If they wanted a fight, she'd give them one. She looked around — so many... There had to be at least twenty of them. Thoughts of what they might do to her shook her focus, and fear swamped her again. She was going to be tortured and killed here in this strange land, and no one from her world would ever know what had happened to her. She breathed deeply and gritted her teeth. No. She would stand strong. She might die here, but she'd go out with fists and feet flying.

One of the red-cloaked Riders drew his horse up to within a few feet of her and dismounted. He pointed at Jaci, then at his horse. "You — get on." He spoke in a guttural accent, quite different from the horsemen's.

The other Riders remained on their mounts.

Jaci let out the breath she'd been holding. They wanted her alive. She wasn't sure if that was good or bad. Who knew what they planned to do with her when they got to wherever they were going? She might be trading a quick death for something worse.

The Rider pointed at his horse again. "Now."

Right. What was the saying — live to fight another day? Jaci stepped away from the tree and climbed onto the horse's back.

The Rider mounted behind her, his arms encircling her as he grasped the reins. Then he turned to the other Riders. "Kill them all."

No! Jaci cried silently. She caught the horse's mane and held on as the Rider kicked his mount into a gallop and headed away from the battle still seething behind them. Half a dozen of the Riders followed, while the others turned back to carry out their commander's orders.

* * * * *

No... gods take me, I cannot go through it again... Talan d'Lochlann sat on the hard ground, his back against a tree, his legs bent. Between his feet lay the diary he'd taken from Jacinda. He'd dropped it after reading the last few entries. He pounded his knee, then closed his eyes and rested his forehead on his fists. The pain was too much... the grief at the loss of his heart and soul, the rage at his helplessness — they cleaved through him like an axe, laying bare the memories he'd done his best to bury. Soneira... the name whispered through his mind, every syllable excruciating. Her smiling face teased him, her laughter beckoned him, drawing him in... He felt the soft brush of her dark curls against his cheek and groaned inwardly. *Why did you have to die? If only you had trusted me...*

"Talan?"

Solon's concerned voice roused Talan from his pit of misery. His friend's warm hand closed over his shoulder and squeezed. "What is it? Is your arm worse?" Solon fussed over the bandage on Talan's upper arm where the arrow had pierced the flesh.

"No. Leave it." Talan tried to clear his mind of the tormenting ghost. "What of the men?"

"Four dead, ten wounded — not counting you," Nickalonis said, coming up behind Solon. "Owen and Medres are tending the injured. Thirty of the Riders are dead. The Black Banders made short work of them. The rest are gone."

"Barayan?"

"No one has seen him or Jaci since the attack," Nickalonis said.

"Do you think they escaped?" Solon asked.

"We must hope." Talan closed his eyes for a moment. He couldn't get the image of Soneira out of his head.

Silence fell, then Solon spoke. "Do you think she really is Deirdre?"

"I don't know," Talan said.

"She had a *druidainoch* stone," Nickalonis said. "Where could she have gotten it? Did Deirdre have one?"

Talan rubbed his eyes wearily. "Not to my knowledge."

"Queen Selendria had one," said Solon. "Might she have given stones to Deirdre and —" He stopped, floundered for a moment, then continued awkwardly. "— I mean, in the way of mothers to daughters?"

"Neither was of age," Talan said quietly.

"Our late queen's stone is long gone. Galenock has it." Nickalonis spat out the name.

"If he's had it all this time, why hasn't he used it?" Solon asked.

"Only the Northern Enchantresses themselves can use *druidainoch* stones." Talan sat up as a new thought occurred to him. "Selendria's twin sister, Mirinesstra, had one, too."

"The lost queen?" Solon asked, startled. "She has been missing for over thirty years."

"Missing — yes, exactly," Talan said. "Disappeared without a word or sign."

"Just like Deirdre," Nickalonis said softly. "Are you saying they might have gone to the same place? And might still be alive? Where? How?"

Talan steeled himself against the horror of his memories and picked up the diary. "I don't know, but according to this, Deirdre has been alive, somewhere, for the past nineteen years. If Mirinesstra did, indeed, go to the same place and had a child..."

"Jaci?" Solon said doubtfully.

"It would explain the resemblance and the stone," Nickalonis said, thoughtfully.

"But that would make her a Tarshanian princess," Solon said in a stunned voice. "Do you realize what that means?"

"It means the royal family is no longer extinct," Nickalonis said. "Barring the sudden reappearance of Deirdre or Mirinesstra, Jaci would be the heir to the throne."

Solon shook his head. "This is too much to believe."

Talan found the page he'd been looking for. "There is more." He handed the diary to Solon. "Read this."

Solon read aloud in a hushed voice, his brother reading silently over his shoulder.

Free! I am finally free of that horrible place. Nineteen years of my life wasted, stolen by my aunt and uncle and those monsters who call themselves Doctors of Psychiatry. I must go back to Tarshane. I understand the drawings now. I know how to get through. And I have remembered another name — Galenock. When I return to Tarshane, I will find him. Perhaps he will help me to remember who I am and what this key unlocks. I'm sure the key is of vital importance. I must take it back.

"What does it mean?" Solon asked, bewildered.

"It means that Deirdre is alive, and she really does have amnesia," Nickalonis said. "She doesn't know who she is. And she obviously doesn't remember anything about Galenock, other than his name."

"*When I return to Tarshane...,*" Solon read again. "Return from where?"

Talan shrugged. "I have no answers."

"What about this key she mentions?" Nickalonis asked. He gasped. "It couldn't be... could it?" He lowered his voice. "The key to Ridaur's crypt?"

Solon's eyes widened. "Is that where it has been all this time — wherever Deirdre went? Galenock has moved heaven and mountain looking for that key."

"The more important question," Talan said, "is whether or not Jacinda has it. If she does —"

The distant cry of a hawk interrupted him.

Talan sat forward, listening. "Something is wrong. She wants us to come." He leaped to his feet.

"More Riders?" Solon asked tensely.

"No, something else."

The three raced to the camp, slowing only long enough for Talan to snap out orders. "Owen, come with us — and ten others. The rest get ready to move out."

The three dashed through the woods, following Sharrow's cries, with Owen and the other men close behind them. A half a mile into the forest, they burst into a trampled, bloody glade. Surrounded by six downed Riders, Barayan lay face down, arrows protruding from the back of his thigh and shoulder.

No, he can't be dead... Fear tightened Talan's throat. *Where is Jacinda?* He rushed forward and dropped to one knee beside Barayan. He searched for a pulse along the big man's neck. The weak pumping of lifeblood beneath his fingertips sent relief winging through him.

Owen knelt on the other side of Barayan and quickly evaluated his wounds.

"How bad is he?" Solon asked.

"He'll live," Owen said tersely, "if we can stop the bleeding." He pulled a sharp knife and bandages out of his healer's pack. "Tobias, help me."

Tobias dropped down beside Owen, and Owen handed him the bandages. "Clean the other wounds while I work on the arrows."

Owen soaked the knife blade with whiskey from his pack, then he probed the arrow wound in Barayan's shoulder. Tobias bandaged the oozing sword cuts he could reach, being careful not to interfere with Owen's work.

"The Riders are all dead," Nickalonis said, coming up beside his brother. "No sign of Jaci."

Nausea wrenched Talan's stomach. They'd taken her. He knew it as surely as if he'd seen it happen. *Oh, gods, not again... I can't...*

Barayan stirred, regaining consciousness. He groaned and tried to roll onto his side, signing agitatedly.

"Keep him still!" Owen barked.

Talan squeezed Barayan's arm. "Stay still, old friend. They are trying to keep you from bleeding to death."

Barayan grunted and ceased moving everything but his hand. He signed a message repeatedly, then blacked out again.

A crushing weight settled on Talan's shoulders.

"The Riders took Jaci," Nickalonis said softly.

Feeling as though he were about to vomit, Talan rose and led Solon and Nickalonis out of earshot of the other men. "Don't mention the key to anyone. The fewer that know about it, the better."

"But what if Jaci — Deirdre — whoever she is — does have the key to Ridaur's crypt?" Solon asked anxiously. "What if she gives it to Galenock?"

"Then we're done for," Nickalonis said grimly.

Talan shook his head. "Then all of Tarshane is done for."

CHAPTER 9

Jaci hunched her shoulders as the first few drops of cold rain
spattered over her and the red-cloaked Riders. They galloped across
a vast, grassy plain, their mounts' hoofbeats drumming like thunder. The late afternoon sun had disappeared behind ever-darkening
clouds. She grumbled under her breath as the cold soaked into her.
Not only was she even more saddlesore from riding all day, but now
it looked like she was in for a drenching, too.

Not far ahead of them, a high gray stone wall stretched for miles
across the plain, punctuated at intervals by enormous towers. Some
distance behind the wall, an immense castle loomed, with more
dark towers blending into the overcast. Jaci gazed at the castle, torn
between fascination and foreboding. She'd always imagined castles
as being romantic and fairy tale-esque, but this one was neither.
Even from a distance, it looked grim and intimidating, like it would
crush every enemy and grind them into the dust.

Light rain dogged them all the way to the wall, but the deluge
held off. Jaci unclenched her fingers from the horse's mane as the
Riders reined in their mounts at the massive gates of the walled
city. The gates stood open, but were blocked by two slow-moving

horse-drawn wagons, one loaded with casks going into the city, and one packed with full sacks and crates coming out.

Jaci flinched as her captor bellowed at the soldiers in red-trimmed black uniforms standing by the gates to get the wagons out of the way. The soldiers barked at the wagon drivers, who hastily whipped their horses into a faster speed.

Jaci stared at the gray wall in awe. Constructed of smooth granite, it had to be at least fifty feet high and thirty feet thick. It was even more impressive than the Great Wall of China, which she'd visited the previous summer while on vacation with her recently-ex-boyfriend. She craned her neck, looking up at the crenellations that edged the rampart, noting with apprehension the proliferation of soldiers patrolling its length. There was no way she'd ever be able to get out of the city undetected if she needed to escape.

The soldiers finally cleared the gates, and the Riders hastened through, galloping down cobblestone streets into a market still filled with people despite the rain. The crowds scrambled out of the way and Jaci closed her eyes, hoping no one would be trampled. When the shouts and clamor of the market faded, Jaci opened her eyes again and took in the city. They passed a multitude of colorfully painted houses, shops, and other businesses, arranged around grassy parks with carved stone fountains in the centers. Gables and decorative trusses adorned many of the buildings, and elaborate coats of arms graced the doors of the houses. *What a beautiful city,* she thought with surprise. She looked ahead to the castle, which still seemed miles away. Its dark bulk rose far above the surrounding buildings, like a diseased tree in a garden of flowers. Even at this distance, she could feel a sinister aura oozing from it.

The Riders rushed on toward the castle, their horses' hooves clattering over the damp cobblestones. Most of the city folk moved well out of the way before the Riders reached them, but a few older inhabitants stopped short where they stood, their mouths dropping open at the sight of Jaci. Younger family members pulled them to safety. Jaci wondered if these people, too, were possibly mistaking her for Deirdre.

She saw similar shocked expressions cross the faces of a gray-haired couple who were just coming out of a gabled red house. She caught a glimpse of the coat of arms on the door — hawks with talons extended as they dove toward their prey on either side of a large red square. She stiffened. *Red square.* The second symbol on the paper with the moon phases was a red-brown square. Could there be a connection? She tried to look back, but she had already passed too far beyond. The hawks reminded her of the horsemen. Tears burned her eyes. She hoped they had somehow survived the Riders' attack.

Rain pelted down harder as the Riders sped through the city. Finally they arrived at a tower, its lowered portcullis guarding a bridge over a wide moat filled with muddy water. The city's red-cloaked, black-uniformed soldiers raised the portcullis, and the Riders crossed the bridge to another high, thick curtain wall — this one surrounding the castle itself. Soldiers manning the open gates waved the Riders on through. Jaci shivered at the screeching clang of the gates closing behind her. A deeper fear iced through her blood. She was trapped. Alone. What would they do to her? How would she ever get home?

They trotted into a vast courtyard that opened into stables, smithies, and other buildings Jaci guessed to be storehouses and barracks. To her surprise, they rode past the castle's imposing main entrance, with its sweeping staircase and columned, high-arching façade, toward a side entrance near a garden overrun with late-blooming roses. Their fragrance sweetened the wet air.

The side door flew open. Two soldiers hurried out and stood at attention as the Riders reined in.

Jaci's captor pointed to the door. "Go in." He held the reins out of the way and sat back, allowing her to swing her leg over the horse's neck and jump down.

She bit back a cry as her sore legs crumpled beneath her, landing her on her knees.

The soldiers strode forward, lifted her to her feet, and ushered her inside as the Riders cantered off into the rain.

Jaci shrugged out of the soldiers' grip. "Thanks. I'm fine."

One of the soldiers closed and locked the door. The other strode off down a wide corridor lit by torches. The second soldier gestured for Jaci to follow the first, then fell in behind her.

Exhausted, hungry, and shivering, Jaci limped down what seemed like miles of deserted corridors and up three flights of stairs before stopping at the second of five wooden doors along a wider hall lit by decorative oil lanterns rather than torches. The leading soldier knocked on the door. After a moment, the door was opened by two girls, who beckoned Jaci to enter. The girls wore drab but clean floor-length dresses. Jaci estimated them to be in their mid-teens.

Uncertainly, she stepped inside. A fire glowed in the hearth, and the room was wonderfully warm. She breathed in the pleasant scents of woodsmoke and roses.

The soldiers took up posts in the hall on either side of the door. The taller of the two girls, who had long, sandy-colored hair done up in braids and pinned on top of her head, closed the door firmly, then turned and curtsied to Jaci.

"We are pleased to attend you, miss," she said with a smile and a lilt in her voice like Talan and the others. "I am Mandy, and this is Allina."

The smaller girl, her brown braids pinned up in a similar fashion, curtsied nervously and gave Jaci a shy smile.

"We have prepared a bath for you and brought you some clothes," Mandy said. "The kitchen girls will be bringing up some food. Come, let's get you out of those wet things." She eyed Jaci's sweater and jeans curiously. "I've never seen clothes like these before." She and Allina stepped forward and reached out as if to help her undress.

Jaci backed up a step and held up her hands in front of her. "No, wait. Please." This gentle reception was so completely not what she'd been expecting that it took her a minute to find words. "I— I'm not used to being undressed — by other people, that is." At the girls' worried looks, she hurried on. "I don't want to get you in trouble, and I would really *love* a bath. I'd just like to do it myself, if you don't mind." She closed her mouth to keep from babbling further.

The girls glanced nervously at each other.

Mandy said, "If we displease you —"

"No, no, not at all," Jaci interrupted. "You're perfect. I was just hoping for a little privacy. I haven't had much lately." She smiled reassuringly. "I promise I won't try to leave the room or anything. Please?"

Mandy nodded reluctantly. "All right, miss. We'll be in there, turning down and warming your bed." She pointed to an open door leading into an adjoining room. Then she and Allina disappeared into the bedroom.

Jaci took a deep breath and let it out slowly. She'd had visions of being dragged before some barbarian king and either being thrown in a filthy dungeon, tossed to the soldiers as a plaything, or being ravished by the king himself. Maybe things wouldn't be so bad here after all.

She glanced about the room, taking it all in: the mirrored oak dressing table on her left, with a hairbrush, cosmetics, and perfume bottles scattered across the top; the richly brocaded sea-green loveseat and chairs casually arranged around a low table in the center of the room; and the huge walk-in closet on her right, which was loaded with colorful dresses and paired with a full-length mirror attached to the wall.

On the far side of the room, she saw steam rising from behind a wooden tri-fold privacy screen. Her wet sneakers squinched as she crossed the slate-tiled floor and peeked around the screen. She discovered a white enameled tub filled with hot water and rose petals. *Yes! A bath, finally.* A thick, cream-colored robe and underclothes had been laid out on one of the brocaded chairs that had been pulled close to the tub.

She peeled off her wet clothes and shoes and dropped them on the floor. A tiny clink sounded. She looked down and suddenly remembered the key she'd found with the diary. Picking up her jeans, she saw the key lying on the tile. It must have fallen out of her pocket. She hid the key and her pendant on the chair, beneath the robe. Better to not let anyone see them until she knew whether she was among friends or enemies.

She climbed into the tub, and with a sigh, slid down into the comfortably hot water. She could have soaked for hours, but she wanted to be done and dressed before the two girls came back to check on her, so she used the flowery-scented soap she found on a small table beside the tub to lather herself and wash her hair.

Afterward, she wrapped her hair in one of the linen towels from a shelf beneath the table and dried off with another one. The robe fit her well, except that it was too long. The extra fabric pooled around her feet like a creamy puddle. The garment also had a revealing neckline, she observed with a frown. While the design was flattering, it wouldn't provide much concealment for her pendant. She considered a moment, then pulled the lace out of one of her sneakers, strung the key onto the pendant chain, and threaded the lace through the chain. Hiking up her robe, she knotted the damp lace around her thigh.

Just as she was finishing, she heard the soft steps of the girls approaching from the bedroom. She hastily dropped the hem of her robe and bent to pick up her wet clothes.

"You may leave them there, if you like," Mandy said, indicating the wet pile. "We will wash them out for you."

"Oh... thank you." Jaci straightened. She unwrapped her hair and began to towel it dry.

"May I help with your hair?" Mandy asked hopefully.

"Um... okay." Jaci handed Mandy the towel, then followed her to the dressing table and sat down.

Mandy gently dried Jaci's dark curls while Allina put more wood on the fire and cleaned up around the tub.

"You have beautiful hair, miss," Mandy said.

"Thank you. My name is Jacinda, but you can call me Jaci."

"Oh, no," Mandy said quickly. "Begging your pardon, but we are not allowed to address those above our station by name."

"What is your station?" Jaci asked.

Mandy set the towel on the corner of the table, picked up the brush, and began detangling Jaci's hair. "We are ladies of the chambers, miss. We tend to our master's guests."

"Who is your master?"

"Why, Lord Galenock, of course."

"Did you say *Galenock*?" Jaci blurted, then kicked herself mentally. *Don't broadcast your ignorance. Think before you speak!*

"Yes. Lord Galenock is master of this castle and the surrounding lands." Mandy hesitated. "Have you met him?"

Looking in the mirror, Jaci noted the shift in Mandy's expression to cautious curiosity.

"No, I haven't. I'm not from around here."

Mandy hesitated again. "I don't mean to be impertinent, but may I ask where you are from?"

It was Jaci's turn to hesitate. "Well... I'm from... a faraway land called White Plains. Please don't ask me how I got here — it's a very long and complicated story. But there is one thing I'd like to know — if Galenock is master of this castle, is he a king?"

A crash behind her startled Jaci. In the mirror's reflection, she saw that Allina had knocked over the small table holding the soap and towels. Allina shot Mandy a frightened glance and then hurried to clean up the mess.

Mandy turned back and continued brushing Jaci's hair. "Galenock is not a king," Mandy whispered, "because he is not related to the royal family."

Another frisson of fear prickled down Jaci's spine. Why was Mandy whispering? Who did she not want to hear her? Jaci didn't want to put the girl in danger, but she really needed information. "Where is the royal family? Do they live in another castle somewhere?" she asked quietly.

Mandy's brush froze in the middle of a downward sweep. Her eyes met Jaci's in the mirror. She seemed to be studying Jaci's face in a way she hadn't done before. "No. This is — was — their castle. They died."

A knock on the door made all three of them jump.

Allina's hand flew to her mouth, and she fled into the bedroom.

Mandy set down the hairbrush and turned toward the door, stopping momentarily to whisper in Jaci's ear. "Please do not speak of this anymore. It is dangerous." Composing herself, Mandy walked to the door and opened it.

Two girls in stained, patched dresses, their hair pulled back in ponytails, entered the room, each with a heavily laden silver tray of food and drink balanced on her shoulder. Bending under the weight, they slid the trays off their shoulders and set them on the low table in front of the loveseat. Painfully, they straightened, curtsied, and hurried from the room. Mandy closed the door behind them, but not before Jaci spotted the two soldiers still on guard duty in the hall. Obviously Lord Galenock didn't want her wandering around the castle on her own.

Mandy went to the bedroom door and called softly, "It's all right, Allina. It was just the kitchen girls." Then she came back to the table and filled a glass with an amber liquid. "Are you hungry?" she asked Jaci. "There is plenty."

Jaci eyed the food ravenously. "I'm starving." She left the dressing table and sat down on the loveseat.

Mandy handed her a plate filled with slices of cold meat, cheese, and fresh biscuits drizzled with honey.

"Absolutely delicious," Jaci declared after sampling a biscuit. She took a sip of the amber liquid. "And so is this. What is it?"

"It is a honey apple concoction that Bessa, the head cook, makes. I don't know exactly what is in it. She never reveals her recipes." Mandy filled two more plates and glasses, one set for Allina and one for herself. Allina left the bedroom long enough to collect her plate and drink, then hurried away out of sight again. Mandy stepped back from the table and curtsied. "We will leave you to your meal."

"Oh, please don't go yet." Jaci touched the loveseat beside her. "Come sit for a minute. There is something more I'd like to ask you."

Mandy reluctantly sat. "What is it?"

Jaci lowered her voice. "Will I be meeting Lord Galenock?"

Mandy nodded. "Yes, likely tomorrow. We — Allina and I — are to make you comfortable, with plenty of food and rest, so you will be fully recovered from your journey."

"What is he like?"

Fear flitted through Mandy's eyes, though she tried to hide it. "He is... very powerful." She opened her lips to say more, then closed them again, her face pale. Her voice dropped to the barest whisper. "Beware of him, miss. That's all I can say." She leaped up and ran into the bedroom.

CHAPTER 10

Jaci awoke to the sound of rain pattering on glass. She heard a swish and opened her eyes to find Mandy and Allina pulling back the sea-green draperies covering the windows. The gloomy grayness of the wet day leaked into the room.

"Good morning, miss," Mandy said with a smile. "Did you sleep well?"

Jaci stretched and smiled back. She *had* slept well and felt quite revived. A hot bath, a full belly, and a warm bed had been just what she needed. "Yes, thank you. I hope you did, too." Mandy and Allina shared a small chamber that opened off the bedroom.

"Yes, miss. Your breakfast will be here shortly. Then we'll help you dress... that is... if you will allow us..." Mandy trailed off uncertainly.

Jaci slipped to the edge of the bed. "Well, I don't have any other clothes than what I was wearing last night."

"Oh, we have plenty of clothes for you, miss," Mandy said, brightening. "Allina picked out a blue dress that is perfect for you. We will fix your bed and lay everything out while you're washing."

"All right, thanks." Jaci crossed to a door behind the tub and went into the tiny washroom, which contained a pitcher of water, a basin, and, she'd discovered to her relief, a toilet, of sorts — basically a seat with a hole that had piping below and a bucket of water beside it to wash down the waste. Mandy had shown it to her last night.

After washing up, Jaci emerged to find a satiny blue, medieval-style gown with fitted bodice and flowing skirt spread out on the coverlet along with a white shift and fresh underclothes. Mandy and Allina hovered nearby.

Jaci pointed to the undergarments. "I'll put these on, and then you can help me with the dress, all right?"

Mandy nodded. "Your breakfast is here, so we'll fill a bowl for you and come back."

Jaci smiled. "That's perfect."

By the time the girls returned, Jaci had finished her part, having donned the shift and underclothes. The girls assisted with the blue dress and matching flat-heeled shoes that laced up around her ankles. Like the robe, the dress was too long, and Jaci had to gather her skirt and lift the hem to walk without tripping.

After a breakfast of warm oatmeal and honey bread, Mandy tamed Jaci's unruly curls again, and Allina clasped her hands in delight at Jaci's appearance. Jaci smiled and hid her discomfiture at her décolletage. The neckline was quite a bit lower than she was accustomed to wearing, but she didn't want to hurt Allina's feelings by asking for another dress.

Someone rapped on the door. Allina started and Mandy tensed, fear shadowing their eyes. Allina ducked behind the privacy screen while Mandy squared her shoulders and went to the door. She admitted a bald man, thickset and of middling height, dressed all in black. A gray mustache and beard covered the lower half of his face, in sharp contrast to the bare skin of his head. He wore a jeweled dagger on his belt and a sword at his side, partly hidden by his long, black cloak. It was his eyes, though, that held Jaci's attention. They were cold and merciless, like a jackal evaluating its prey. She rose and stood beside the dressing table. *If this is Galenock...*

The man's gaze settled on Jaci. A hint of surprise cracked his cold mask, then vanished. "Is she ready?" he asked Mandy, without taking his eyes from Jaci's face.

Jaci noted his guttural accent, like that of the red-cloaked Riders.

Mandy swept into a deep curtsy, keeping her eyes downcast. "Yes, Castellan Felgarth."

"Good." He addressed Jaci. "Come with me." He strode from the room.

Jaci glanced at Mandy, who was chewing her lip and twisting her fingers nervously. Mandy quickly gestured for Jaci to follow him. Reluctantly, Jaci caught up the hem of her skirt and hurried after. The two guards outside the door fell into step behind her. Thank heavens, this man wasn't Galenock. But if Galenock employed frightening people like him...

Already halfway down the hall, the castellan neither turned nor spoke. She caught up with him just before he rounded a corner and followed him down a stairway and through several twisting corridors to a door in a curved wall that had to belong to one of the towers. He knocked twice, then opened the door and indicated with a jerk of his head that she was to enter.

She hastened past him into a spacious circular chamber that was half music room, half library.

Shelves filled with books covered the walls from floor to ceiling on the left side of the room, with comfortable-looking chairs and settees in front of them. The right side housed an assortment of musical instruments, including a harpsichord — she'd seen one in a museum once. There were two sets of skin-covered drums and several beautifully carved wooden harps inlaid with gold, some large and free-standing, others small enough to fit in the player's lap. Bugle-like horns, flutes, and other wind instruments, along with stringed instruments similar to guitars, had been carefully placed on shelves and stands. All were buried under a thick layer of dust.

Directly across from the door, splitting the room, stood a huge fireplace. The burning logs in the grate suffused the room with warmth and the faint smell of maple. Above the fireplace lay bare wall stained with a rectangular outline, as if from a painting that had been removed. Jaci wondered if it had belonged to the dead royal family.

"Ah, here you are," said a pleasant lilting voice. A man rose from one of the chairs half-turned away from the door. "Thank you, Felgarth," he said, with a nod to the castellan. "You may resume your duties."

Felgarth bowed without a word and left, closing the door behind him.

The other man stopped before Jaci with a welcoming smile. He was of average height and build, with a narrow face, brown eyes, and neatly trimmed reddish-blond hair and beard. He wore blue robes with a black mantle, and around his neck hung a long gold chain with an iridescent jewel pendant almost identical to hers. She tried her best to stifle her surprise and not stare at it.

He took both her hands in his. "Please let me welcome you to my castle. I am Lord Galenock."

So this was the man Deirdre had planned to seek out. His disarming smile seemed friendly enough. *But be wary,* Jaci's gut warned. *Don't antagonize him. He could still have you thrown in the dungeon.* Jaci inclined her head. "Thank you."

He held her gaze for a moment, then looked down at her hands and slid his thumbs over her knuckles, scrutinizing her fingers for a moment before letting go of them. Jaci had the odd impression he was looking for rings or signs that she'd worn them recently. As it happened, she wasn't wearing any. She hadn't put any on when she'd left White Plains. Her jewelry was in her suitcase in the trunk of her car. She wondered fleetingly what the people of Marston had done with her car and her belongings.

"And what is your name?" Galenock asked, shifting his scrutiny from her hands to her face again. He was studying her, much the way Mandy had last night.

"My name is Jacinda, or Jaci for short." She left off her last name, afraid she'd be required to demonstrate her lack of expertise on the harps in the room.

"Jacinda," he murmured. "A lovely name."

"Thank you."

He finally tore his eyes from her face and waved his hand toward the library furniture. "Come. Please sit and talk with me."

He touched her elbow and led her to one of the chairs near the bookshelves. She sat, noticing with relief that the library side of the room had been dusted.

Galenock sat across from her. "I hope you will forgive your manner of arrival. It was the only way to rescue you from that rabble."

"Rabble?" Jaci asked.

"Yes. Those men are a dangerous lot. Did they harm you in any way?"

"No. In fact, I owe them my life. They rescued me when I was attacked by a pack of wolves. They treated me well."

He forced a smile. "I'm very happy to hear it. I had hoped they wouldn't stoop so low as to mistreat a lady." He paused. "You say they rescued you from wolves — where did this happen?"

"I'm not sure exactly. They called the area 'Wolf Run.'"

His eyebrows shot up. "Wolf Run? That's leagues from any town or even a settlement. How did you get there? Were there others with you?"

"Well... that's a bit of a mystery," Jaci said, quickly deciding to fall back on her amnesia story. Galenock presented a friendly façade, but there had to be some unsavoriness somewhere or Mandy and Allina wouldn't be so terrified of him. "I don't know how I got there. I can't remember what happened. I think I might have fallen off a horse and hit my head or something. I found myself near a forest, and some wolves chased me up a tree. I have no memory of anything before that."

"I see." He considered. "Does your head hurt, now? I could have my physician —"

"No, thank you, that's not necessary. Other than the occasional headache, my head is fine."

"But you have amnesia. Are you certain about your name?"

"Yes, that is the one thing I do remember."

"I see," he said again. After a few moments, he continued, "I have never heard an accent such as yours. You don't remember where you are from?"

She shook her head. "I'm sorry." She'd been surprised by his accent, too. She'd expected him to sound like the Riders and the castellan. Instead, he spoke with the Gaelic-type lilt.

He studied her face once more, his eyes narrowed as if he were trying to decide what to do with her.

Jaci felt the hairs rising on the back of her neck. Galenock suddenly seemed menacing. His expression reminded her of something unpleasant, but she couldn't think what it was. She searched for something to say to break the uneasy silence. A sudden thought occurred to her. "May I ask you a question?"

"Of course." His face relaxed, and he spread his arms wide. "I will answer to the best of my knowledge."

"How did you know I was with — those men?" She hesitated to say their names to their enemy.

A too-quick smile crossed his face. "My Riders saw you and re-layed the message to me." He rose. "I would like to extend my hospitality to you and have you stay here in my castle as my guest until you have recovered your memory."

Jaci rose as well. "Thank you, that is kind of you. May I explore the castle?"

"For your safety, it would be best if you stayed in your room for now. There are dangerous elements about."

"In the castle?"

"Danger can lurk in the most surprising and innocent of plac-es." He walked with her to the door, where she discovered her guards waiting. They saluted, placing left fists over the right sides of their chests. "It was a distinct pleasure to meet you. We'll talk again soon." He inclined his head, then strode away down the cor-ridor.

The guards escorted her in the opposite direction, back toward her room.

Well, I've found Galenock — now what? Deirdre had planned to ask him about her identity and the key, but Jaci didn't feel comfortable broaching either subject. Something about him bothered her — something beyond the chamber girls' fear of him and the fact that he had a creepy chief of staff, though those were reasons enough not to trust him. His narrow-eyed, calculating expression had scared her, like someone had pulled a gun in the middle of a friendly, polite conversation, then put it away and carried on as if nothing had happened. And what had he meant by danger lurking in the castle? What kind of danger? Was he threatening her somehow?

What really frightened her, though, was that she was his prisoner, and if he decided he wanted her dead, there'd be nothing she could do about it. Rescue wasn't likely. There was no way Talan and his men could get her out of the castle, even if they felt so inclined. And why would they? They thought she was a spy — probably for Galenock. They'd be glad she was gone.

She remembered the diary entry about the two men battling with magical blue fire. Deirdre had described one as having gray-streaked dark hair, but the other one had short, reddish-blond hair and a beard — just like Galenock. If he had command of powerful magic, he'd be even more dangerous. Jaci would need to tread very carefully around him.

And then there was the pendant Galenock wore. She hadn't dared ask about it. How could two people from different worlds have the same type of pendant? She was glad she'd hidden hers. What if he had tried to take it from her?

As they neared her room, she found herself coming back to her original question — now what? It wouldn't do any good to try to escape on her own, since she wouldn't know where to go — unless she could find another grandfather clock like the one in the Brunswick house. Of course, finding one didn't necessarily mean it would work the same way... and who knew where she might end up if it did?

She decided the best thing to do, for now, was to talk to Mandy and Allina and convince them to tell her as much as they could about Galenock, the pendant, and the deceased royal family. Then maybe she could find out if there was a grandfather clock somewhere in the castle.

*****

Lord Galenock entered his war room and closed the door, eyes searching the dimly lit chamber for Castellan Felgarth.

The castellan stepped from the shadows. "So, my lord — is she, or is she not, Deirdre d'Gaire?"

Galenock picked up the single lantern and crossed the room to a map of Tarshane on the wall. "I don't know."

Felgarth paced the room. "She certainly looks like her, or an older version of the girl she was."

"Yes," Galenock agreed, studying the map, "and I'm sure I saw surprise and recognition in her eyes when she saw my *druidainoch* stone, though she tried to hide it. But she did not act nervous or afraid of me, which I might have expected. Perhaps she is just a very good actress. She has had plenty of time to perfect the art. On the other hand, her claim of amnesia could be true... it is difficult to say. I will have to talk to her more and try to force her into a mistake." He gestured toward the map. "I have traveled the length and breadth of Tarshane. I have never heard an accent like hers. There is also the question of how she got to Wolf Run."

"Well, if she isn't Deirdre, who is she? And why does she have such a strong resemblance to the royal family?"

"Who, indeed," Galenock mused. "Perhaps the late King Brannad sired a child on a commoner, though I find that highly unlikely. His greatest weakness was his devotion to his family."

"I could beat the truth out of her," Felgarth suggested with a sadistic smile.

Galenock's lip curled. "Beating women is so distasteful. They cry and beg, and it ruins their looks."

"Except for Soneira." Felgarth almost sounded admiring. "She took punishment like a man. Never did crack, no matter what we did to her."

"You failed me, there, Felgarth," Galenock snarled. "You killed her before we had the information." *And before I could take her to my bed one last time. Soneira...*

"She did that herself, my lord," Felgarth protested. "She used some sort of twisted magic to kill herself."

Galenock whirled on the castellan. "I should have used that 'twisted magic' on you."

Felgarth stepped back into a penitent bow. "Forgive me, my lord. If you wish to punish me again —"

Galenock reined in his anger. "Not now. There are more important matters at hand."

Felgarth straightened, but kept his distance. "We need an answer soon, my lord. The people are talking. Those who saw her when the Riders brought her in yesterday are saying Deirdre has returned, and that she will revive the royal line."

"I had Crawlin whipped for that. His orders were to bring her in under cover of darkness." Galenock turned back to the map. "As to how she got to Wolf Run... I wonder... Nineteen years ago, my spies told me Elshaer was trying to create magical portals that would allow the user to move from one place to another instantly. If he had perfected the magic... Soneira was his prize pupil, she might have known about it." He quashed a flash of jealous rage and faced the castellan. "The last time Deirdre was seen, she was with Soneira. What if Soneira sent her sister away somewhere, using a portal? And Deirdre has only just now found a way to return?"

"I leave magical possibilities to you, my lord. I have no knowledge in those matters."

"No, Felgarth. Unfortunately, you have very little imagination."

Felgarth's face remained expressionless. "What about the stone?"

"That would be a risk. If she is Deirdre, the *druidainoch* stone should react to her touch in some way. However, it would also awaken any magical abilities she might have, which could make controlling her difficult."

"You could just pronounce her to be Deirdre, proclaim her as heir to the throne, and marry her. Then the title of king would be yours without question."

"Yes, that is the most attractive prospect." He set the lantern back down on the table. "I must think on this a bit more. Make sure she stays in that chamber. I don't want anyone else seeing her."

"Yes, my lord." Felgarth left the room.

"Yes..." Galenock pictured Jaci in his own bedroom. "The most attractive by far."

*****

"What are we going to do?" Solon asked grimly.

Talan glanced around at his men, who were busy setting up camp on a clump of low tussocks in the hardwood swamp. None were within hearing range. "We have to get her out."

"Out of Castle d'Gaire?" Nickalonis asked incredulously. "How?"

"I don't know, yet," Talan said, "but we can't — I can't —" He looked away, unable to speak the words through the pain in his heart. *I can't let her die at Galenock's hands, not like...*

Solon clasped his shoulder. "We will get her out. We will find a way."

Talan took a long breath, in and out, and tried to bury the pain that clouded his thoughts. "Solon, you and Katar and half the Black Banders will ride with me to Cain's Hold. Cain might be able to get a few of us into the city in one of his market caravans. Nickalonis, the rest of the men will be under your command. Move them around the countryside, camp in a different location every night —"

"Why am I not going with you?" Nickalonis protested. "Katar is usually in charge of the men when we're away." His expression suddenly shifted to angry disbelief. "You don't trust me, do you? Because of what she said. You really think I'm a traitor."

"I think no such thing," Talan said sharply. "I trust you with my life, like I always have."

"Then why? I said I would leave her alone. How many times do I have to apologize?"

"It has nothing to do with that, either," Talan said, a tired hopelessness sinking into him. "There is a spell that can allow a wizard to see through the eyes of others. I read it once, in an ancient book of magic spells that Elshaer inherited from his great-grandfather Elsaesser. It is a very difficult spell to cast, requiring great strength and magical ability. It also requires the blood of the person through whose eyes the wizard wishes to see. You were wounded by one of the Riders. Your blood would have been on one of their swords. Galenock is strong enough to cast the spell, and since he defeated Elshaer, the book is now in his possession. So if Jacinda saw in you the brown eyes of someone who hated her — not once, but twice — it could have been Galenock using that spell. I think that's how he's been tracking us. If you go with us to rescue her, he'll know our every move."

Nickalonis sagged against a tree, the color draining from his face.

Solon, too, looked stricken. He stepped up beside his brother and put his hands on Nickalonis' shoulders. "Is there any way to know for certain if this is what is happening?" Solon asked.

"Have you felt any dizziness, like you were going to pass out, or like you were waking up from having passed out for a few seconds?" Talan asked Nickalonis.

Nickalonis grew paler. "Yes."

"What do we do? How can we stop it?" Solon asked.

"I—I'll put my eyes out," Nickalonis said shakily, "so he can't see."

"No!" Talan said sharply, then softened. "I know it will be hard, but we have to leave things as they are, for now. There is a counter-spell, but I don't know it. It is in the book. But right now, if this rescue mission is to succeed at all, I need him to think we are still out here in the wilderness." Talan squeezed Nickalonis' arm, wishing he had a way to comfort him, cursing his own lack of knowledge. *Soneira, why couldn't you have trusted me?* He gripped his emotions, shut them securely away. "I'll have one of the Black Banders watch you constantly to see if it happens again. If it does, you'll know to move camp before the Riders find you."

He let go of Nickalonis' arm and stepped back. "If we make it into the city, we'll seek help from Cranton and Zaiya —"

Sharrow's shriek of challenge startled them and drew their eyes upward. High above in the gray overcast, Sharrow circled closely around another, smaller hawk, blocking its descent. Then she ceased her challenge, and let the other hawk fly down toward them.

"That looks like one of Cranton's birds," Talan said, surprised. He raised his gloved arm, and the small brown-and-white hawk landed on his wrist. Talan removed the message capsule tied to its leg and handed it to Solon.

Solon drew forth a tiny, rolled scrap of parchment and read, "Must speak. Alquinon's playground. Urgent." He looked questioningly at Talan.

"He means the White Bluffs, where he sometimes trains his hawks," Talan said. Worry churned inside him. Was Cranton in trouble? Had something happened to him or his family? Living in the shadow of the castle as they did, Talan always harbored an undercurrent of fear that Galenock would discover he and Cranton were friends and would torture the family to torture him. He pulled a small stick of charcoal wrapped in wax paper out of his pocket and tossed it to Solon. "Write 'Yes' on the back of the note."

Solon did as instructed and slid the parchment back into the capsule. Talan pocketed the charcoal and reattached the capsule to the hawk's leg. Then he launched the bird into the air. The hawk flapped upward, caught an air current, and glided swiftly away.

CHAPTER 11

Jacinda stood by the window and stared out into the dismal gray noon. The rain had stopped, but the overcast still looked threatening. Below her in the courtyard, groups of soldiers hurried to and from the barracks and stables and other outbuildings, while non-uniformed people — castle workers, she guessed — hastened across on their errands, dodging the soldiers and mounted Riders as best they could.

So this is Castle d'Gaire, she thought, *and the city surrounding it is Catir Coronin, meaning City of Crowns, or Royal City.* Mandy had said it was the seat of power in Tarshane. The girl had listed six or seven provinces into which Tarshane was divided — Jaci couldn't remember them all. Most of them had sworn fealty to Lord Galenock, though the way Mandy said it made Jaci think that the governors of the provinces hadn't had any choice in the matter. The only free provinces left were Millianoch in the north, home of the Northern Enchantresses, and Hyanullis in the west, a desert land populated by nomads, who were experts at disappearing into the mazes of rocky canyons that shadowed the barren land.

Jaci had broached the subject after she'd returned from her audience with Galenock, saying she really didn't know much about

Tarshane and would like to learn more about the land and its people. Mandy had given her that look of guarded curiosity again but had talked of the various provinces and some of their customs. Castle d'Gaire and the City of Crowns lay in the largest province of Shiannora. Mandy and Allina were both from Shiannora, from the same outlying town. They had come to the castle three years ago seeking work to help support their families. Apparently, they each had several sisters and brothers. They'd worked their way up from the kitchen scullery to their current positions as ladies of the chambers.

Jaci had found the information quite interesting, but try as she would, she could not get Mandy to speak a word about Galenock or the royal family. Mandy had whispered that it was too dangerous to talk of Lord Galenock, and to speak of the royal family was forbidden. Jaci had looked to Allina once or twice, but whenever she did, Allina would blanch in fear, shake her head, and hurry away to another part of the room.

Jaci turned from the window, chewing her lip in frustration. There had to be a way to find out what she needed to know. Maybe she should try the one question, she hadn't asked yet.

"Mandy, is there a grandfather clock in the castle?"

"A grandfather clock?" Mandy repeated uncertainly.

"Yes. A timepiece like that one." Jaci pointed to a steeple clock on the mantel. "Only much bigger." She stretched her arm up as high as she could.

"I don't know, miss. I've never seen one, but there are many parts of the castle I've not been in."

"Is there any way you could find out? It would be really helpful for me to know."

Mandy looked at her doubtfully, and Jaci could see apprehension and what looked like indecision in the girl's eyes at Jaci's odd questions. *She probably thinks I'm nuts,* Jaci thought sourly. *Or maybe a spy for Galenock's enemies.* She grimaced to herself at the irony.

"I—I'm not sure," Mandy said. "I —"

A knock on the door silenced her, and she hastened to answer it, as if happy for the interruption. The same two kitchen girls who had brought the other meals entered, sagging under the weight of the heavy trays of food and drink on their shoulders. Mandy and Allina helped them set the trays on the low table.

Mandy threw Jaci an inscrutable look, then caught the kitchen girls' arms and whispered in their ears. The girls looked surprised and a little scared and quickly shook their heads. Mandy whispered something else to them, and the kitchen girls' eyes slid to Jaci. Reluctantly, the girls nodded. One of the girls put her hand on her back, bent over, and hobbled a few steps, as if she had hurt her lower back. She looked at Mandy, who shook her head. The girl exaggerated the performance, contorting her face into an agonized expression.

Mandy nodded and put her arm around the girl. Then she and the other kitchen girl "helped" her to the door. "I will return shortly," Mandy said. She stopped for a moment to speak to the guards, then she and the kitchen girls headed down the hall, the "injured" girl leaning heavily on the other two.

Allina shut the door behind them. Obviously frightened, she scurried to set out a lunch plate for Jaci.

Jaci sat and asked in a low voice, "What was that all about?"

"I don't know," Allina squeaked. She looked like she was going to cry. She flitted around the room, straightening and re-straightening everything, showing no interest in the food.

Jaci nibbled a honey biscuit. *I hope I haven't gotten Mandy in trouble.* Fear curled in her gut. What would she do if she had? She took a deep breath and let it out slowly. Well, she'd have to find a way to get her out of it. Her stomach churning, Jaci forced herself to eat.

Mandy returned just as Jaci was finishing her meal. Allina wiped her eyes and hugged her friend.

Jaci sprang to her feet. "Is everything all right?"

Mandy nodded. "Yes, miss."

Jaci's knees buckled in relief, and she sat back down. She'd been more scared than she'd realized. "I'm sorry to pester you with questions, but I don't know how else to find out —" She stopped. Just how much information was she herself willing to give up?

"Find out what, miss?" Mandy asked softly.

Jaci hesitated. She dropped her voice to a whisper. "I need to know about someone named Deirdre."

Mandy's eyes widened.

"And I need to know why some people look at me like... like..."

Someone knocked on the door, and Mandy opened it as if she were on autopilot, her eyes never leaving Jaci's face. The kitchen girls had returned to retrieve the lunch trays. Mandy ushered them in and shut the door. One of them, unfamiliar to Jaci, gasped, then gave her that open-mouthed stare.

"Like that," Jaci finished with a gesture toward the new girl — or rather, woman, Jaci realized. The replacement for the "injured" girl was middle-aged, about Jaci's size, with straight dark hair edged with silver around her temples. Most of her hair was covered by a dingy maid's cap.

"Your... Your Highness?" the woman whispered, her hand fluttering to her breast. She dropped into a deep curtsy.

Jaci stared, shocked. Her eyes met Mandy's. "Why is she doing that?"

Mandy took the woman's arm and drew her upright. "Nyelda, no — milady's name is Jacinda."

Nyelda shook her head vehemently. "No. She is Deirdre. She is the princess come back to us."

Jaci felt her own jaw dropping.

Mandy clamped her hand over the woman's mouth. "If the guards hear you, we'll all be punished!" she whispered heatedly.

The woman paled and nodded her understanding.

Mandy released her and stepped back, addressing the kitchen girl, too. "Take the trays before the guards get suspicious. Talk to Bessa — *no one else*. You know what will happen to us if the wrong people hear."

White-faced and tight-lipped, Nyelda and the kitchen girl lifted the trays with shaking hands. Mandy let them out of the chamber. The guards appeared bored and didn't even glance at them. Mandy closed the door and sagged against it.

Jaci gripped the back of a chair, too stunned to speak. Deirdre had been a princess?

Mandy roused and walked toward Jaci. "Are you feeling tired, miss?" she asked a bit too loudly. She continued before Jaci could answer. "Yes, miss, I think a nap would be just the thing for you." She waved Allina to the bedroom. When Mandy reached Jaci's side, she whispered, "Please come into the bedroom with me."

Jaci wasn't sure what Mandy was up to, but she turned and led the way into the sleeping chamber.

Mandy pointed to the window. "Allina, you close the curtains, while I turn down the bed."

Allina did as she was bidden. Mandy threw back the coverlet, then said, "Sleep well, miss." She looked at Jaci and made a gesture as if she wanted Jaci to speak.

"Um... thank you, I will," Jaci said, raising her voice to the same level as Mandy's.

Then Mandy held a finger to her lips and tiptoed to the door, beckoning for Jaci and Allina to follow. The three crept to the washroom and squeezed inside, closing the door silently behind them.

"I think if we are very quiet, we'll be safe talking in here," Mandy said.

"*Please* tell me about Deirdre," Jaci begged.

"I don't know all the details," Mandy said, "since everything happened before I was born, but my father told me some of the story, because he felt all Tarshanians should know the true history of what befell the royal family."

She lowered her voice. "Nineteen years ago, Tarshane was at peace, ruled by King Brannad and Queen Selendria. They had two daughters, Soneira and Deirdre. My father described them as being small of stature with dark curls, like their mother... and like you. Queen Selendria was one of the Northern Enchantresses. Soneira inherited her magical abilities, but it appeared that Deirdre did not.

"Soneira was being trained in magical studies by her mother and by Elshaer and Galenock of the Wizard's Guild. After a time, it became obvious that Galenock wanted Soneira, but she was in love with another — a young man named Talan."

Jaci started, her heartbeat quickening at the mention of her rescuer's name. Deirdre's sister was in love with him? In her diary entry, Deirdre had said Talan and her sister were fighting.

"Do you know anything about... about Talan?" Jaci asked, trying to sound casual.

"Not really," Mandy said. "I only know what my father told me — that he was an orphan who was also being trained by the Wizard's Guild, though no one knew where his magical talents had come from."

An orphan, Jaci thought, picturing the stern face of her rescuer in her mind. *Another person with a tragic childhood...*

"Then something happened during one of the training sessions," Mandy continued, lowering her voice even more.

Jaci felt so stiff with tension she thought she might crack. Allina listened wide-eyed.

"No one who is still alive — other than Galenock and perhaps Talan — knows what occurred. Galenock was banished to a magical prison on a deserted island in the Virulean Sea, to the far south. But Galenock had become much more powerful than anyone realized. He broke out of prison and came back to the city. Then he defeated the Wizard's Guild. He killed them all.

"At the same time, the army from the southern province of Ruusitar attacked Shiannora. The army wouldn't have made it inside Castle d'Gaire, except that Galenock had already weakened its magical defenses, and his spies among the castle folk betrayed their king to let the invading army in. Apparently, Galenock had been scheming for months to overthrow the royal family and had promised an alliance with the despicable governor of Ruusitar. That's why their army had been ready for war.

"The king and queen and Soneira were murdered and their bodies put on display..." Mandy faltered, then collected herself. "Not Deirdre, though. She had somehow disappeared. The Ruusitar army searched the entire kingdom of Tarshane, but she was never found. Galenock declared himself lord of Castle d'Gaire and all of Tarshane. He said he would destroy the other provinces if they did not bow to him. They all did, except for Millianoch and Hyanullis. The Enchantresses of Millianoch were able to magically protect themselves and their castle. Galenock could not defeat them, but neither could they defeat him. The nomads of Hyanullis had nothing Galenock considered valuable, so he has not bothered to pursue them."

"Is there no one who can challenge him?" Jaci asked.

Mandy shook her head. "His powers are too great. He has killed every member of the Wizard's Guild and every governor who opposed him. The Northern Enchantresses can do no more than hold him to a stalemate. They dare not leave their castle, for if he were to catch them individually, he would destroy them. There is no one else." Mandy hesitated, then looked at Jaci hopefully. "Except maybe for you, milady…?"

"What about Talan? What happened to him? You said he had magical talents." Jaci tried to keep her voice neutral and not betray the emotional turmoil thoughts of him produced. The pain and horror she'd sensed in him still haunted her. She wondered again what part he had played in this tragedy.

"No one knows, exactly," Mandy said. "Lord Galenock insists he is dead, but rumors say he is still alive and leading a small band of rebels made up of the remnants of King Brannad's army. I know such a group exists, as I have heard accounts of their deeds from market merchants. The band attacks Galenock's supply caravans and kills his minions. They've been a thorn in his side for many years, but he has yet to catch them. They always wear masks when they carry out their attacks, so no one knows for certain if it is Talan that leads them."

But I know, Jaci thought. *And now I understand.* Talan's pain must revolve around Soneira's death. Mandy said Soneira was in love with him, which means he was likely in love with her, too. Jaci found herself wondering what it would be like to be loved by someone like Talan…

Whoa! She straightened, appalled at herself. What was she thinking? Her only goal was to get home in one piece. Mandy appeared willing to help her, and Jaci's instincts told her she could trust the girl. She glanced at Allina, who hadn't spoken a word since they'd entered the washroom. Could she trust her? The smaller girl was so timid. *But I have to take the chance...*

"Mandy, Talan *is* their leader. I've seen him and spoken with him. He and his men saved my life when I was treed by wolves. Galenock's Riders attacked Talan's men and captured me and brought me here. I don't know if Talan or his men survived the attack." She swallowed the lump in her throat as she remembered Barayan's sacrifice. "I'm lost, and I need to get out of this castle, so I can try to find my way back home."

Mandy leaned forward. "What if your home is here? What if you really are Deirdre and you just don't remember, because of magic, or — or some other reason..."

"I'm sorry," Jaci said softly, "but I know for certain that I am not her."

Mandy's shoulders sagged, and a hopeless expression settled on her face. Jaci could see she was trying not to cry.

"I'm really sorry," Jaci said again. "Though I'm glad you shared all this with me. May I ask what made you change your mind about telling me?"

Mandy wiped her eyes with the corner of her sleeve. "Because I'm tired of being frightened all the time. Galenock is a monster, and I thought that you... that your coming might be a sign that his reign might be ending. You asked so many questions about the royal family, and you look so much like them, that I began to think that maybe you were trying to find out what happened to them without revealing who you really were..." She took a deep breath and drew herself up. "I know you wish to leave and go back to White Plains, wherever that is, but before you try to escape this castle, there is something you need to see — something I found by accident when I was a linen maid. It will be dangerous, but I believe it is of vital importance that you see it. Please don't ask me any questions about it now. I will explain tonight, after I've had time to arrange things." Desperation tinged her voice. "Please, miss — please say you'll do this one thing for me. Afterwards, if you still feel the same, I promise that we will do our best to help you get away from here."

Jaci looked at Mandy's pleading eyes and knew she couldn't refuse. She nodded. "All right."

Hope blossomed in Mandy's face again.

Jaci followed the girls back to the bedroom. *What am I getting myself into now?*

*****

The shriek of a hawk, higher pitched than Sharrow's cries, tore through the leaden sky, its fierce and lonely sound echoing on the brisk autumn wind as Talan wended his way through the last of the evergreens. He reined in just inside the edge of the forest, signaling a halt to the men behind him.

Rolling fields stretched away from the line of trees. Close on his left, white cliffs rose toward the lowering clouds. Two men stood near the base of the cliffs, their green cloaks billowing in the breeze. One was older with gray hair and beard, the other, tall and brown-haired. The younger man launched another hawk into the gray sky, and its piercing shriek echoed after the first.

Solon drew his horse up beside Talan's. "Good. They're here."

He and Talan dismounted and handed their reins to Katar and one of the other Black Banders.

"Wait here," Talan said. Then he and Solon slipped through the trees to the base of the white bluffs.

Sharrow flew out of the evergreens and soared above the fields, catching thermals and spiraling upward with the other two hawks. The falconers caught sight of her and looked toward the woods. Talan waved. The older man spoke to the younger one, then strode across to where Talan and Solon waited.

"Talan, Solon, thank you for coming." He greeted them warmly with a hug and a handclasp. "It is good to see you."

"And you, Cranton," Talan said. "How is your family? No trouble, I hope." He couldn't hide the worry that had plagued him since he'd received Cranton's urgent note. If Galenock had hurt any of them...

"No, no trouble. They are well, thank you." Cranton laid a reassuring hand on Talan's shoulder. "No, my message was about something else entirely." He hesitated, as if choosing his words. "A group of Riders returned to the city yesterday. They passed our house on their way to the castle, and I saw — Zaiya and I both saw — that they had someone with them — a woman."

Cranton eyed Talan keenly, and Talan fought to control the sick feeling that twisted his insides as he waited for the older man to tell him what he already knew.

"As impossible as it sounds, Zaiya and I... we swear it was Deirdre," Cranton said softly.

Talan swallowed. Solon said nothing, waiting for him to speak.

"We know," Talan said finally.

Cranton's eyebrows lifted. "You do?"

"We found her in Wolf Run. She was alone, with no horse, no pack — nothing. She wore a style of clothes like we've never seen and spoke with an accent we've never heard. She said her name was Jacinda..." He stopped, her face clear in his mind, her eyes flashing fire as she threatened to unman Nickalonis. A stab of fear stole his breath. *What if they were torturing her right now? What if she was already dead?*

"She claimed to have amnesia," Solon said.

Talan caught Solon's glance of concern, but he couldn't frame any more words.

"She said she couldn't remember anything except her name," Solon continued. "The Riders attacked us yesterday morning and took her. We had just decided to ride to Cain's Hold to see if Cain could get us into the city in one of his caravans, when we got your message."

Cranton's eyebrows rose higher. "You're going to try to rescue her? From Castle d'Gaire?"

"Yes," Talan said, finding his voice. His chest felt so tight, it was hard to breathe.

"She had a *druidainoch* stone," Solon added.

"Deirdre didn't have one, did she?" Cranton asked.

"No," Talan answered. "She wasn't of age."

Cranton pursed his lips in thought. "Could she be one of the Northern Enchantresses? Though I didn't think they dared leave their castle."

"We don't know," Solon said.

"Getting into the city was difficult enough," Cranton said. "But now Galenock has increased the Guard tenfold, as if he expects a rescue attempt. They search everyone who passes through the gates. And gaining entrance to Castle d'Gaire..." He shook his head.

"We have to try," Talan said quietly.

Silence fell for a long moment. The hawks soared overhead, the two smaller ones alternately diving to land on the young falconer's forearm and taking off again into the wide expanse.

"Quinton has grown tall," Talan observed.

"Yes," Cranton agreed. "Both my grandsons have outgrown me. They make me proud." He inhaled deeply, then exhaled a long breath. "Well, this task you've set for yourself — I can help you on one part. I will send one of my hawks with a message to Cain to expect you. I'll also send one to my cousin, Willem, who owns the gristmill in Sagetown. He owes me a favor. Have Cain include the mill on his route."

"Why the mill?" Solon asked, perplexed.

"My cousin took up smuggling a couple of years ago, because of Galenock's increased taxes. There is a passage — a long and dangerous one — through the river and caves beneath the mill that connects to the sewer system underneath the city. He asked me if he could continue the passage up into my wine cellar and use the space as a storeroom for his contraband. I told him that as long as he kept my cellar well-stocked with fine wines, he could put whatever he wanted down there."

"Cranton, you old fox," Solon said with a grin.

The older man grinned back.

"Are you sure that's wise?" Talan asked. "If you are discovered—"

Cranton waved him off. "I am too old to fight, now. You must allow me my own form of rebellion. Besides, it gives us an escape route if Galenock ever comes for us. The old tunnels down there are endless."

"So we are to follow that route to your house?" Solon asked.

Cranton nodded. "Yes. Once you arrive, we can work on the problem of getting you into the castle. Can you swim?"

"Swim?" Solon looked perplexed again.

"The beginning of the smuggler's route involves diving into the river beneath the mill and swimming through a short underwater tunnel," the older man explained. "Willem discovered it when we swam there as boys. He got sucked down through it before we knew it was there. I thought he'd drowned for sure, and ran to get my uncle, but by the time we got back, there he was swimming toward us. Scared me half to death. I thought he was a ghost.

"After that, we swam back and forth through the tunnel and explored the caves on the other side." Cranton smiled in reminiscence. "Lots of fun for a pair of young boys." He sobered. "It's a bit tricky, though, if you've never done it before. Willem can explain what to do."

"It would do him no good to explain it to me. I cannot swim," Solon said.

"I can," said Talan.

"You cannot rescue her by yourself," Cranton pointed out.

"We have Black Banders with us," Talan said. "Some of them may be able to swim."

"I hope so." Cranton looked west to where the late afternoon sun would have shone if it hadn't been obscured by the overcast. "When do you expect to reach Cain's Hold?"

"Late tonight," Talan answered.

Cranton nodded. "Then I will look for you to be in my wine cellar, two nights hence."

"Thank you," Talan said, hope stirring in his chest. The feeling surprised him, yet he didn't quite dare examine it too closely, for fear it might wither and die under scrutiny. It had been so long since he'd had any hope at all.

"You're welcome, my friends." Cranton embraced them both again. "Good luck, and may the gods speed you on your journey."

"And may they keep you and your family safe," Talan replied.

With final farewells and waves goodbye, Talan and Solon headed back to the Black Banders.

"I don't like it," Solon said.

"You heard what he said about the increased Guard," Talan said. "It is the only way into the city."

"I don't like it, because I can't go with you."

"It's best this way. If I do not return, the men will need you to lead them. You have the maturity and common sense that Nickalonis has not yet shown."

"And likely never will," Solon said with a forced laugh. He fell silent, his footsteps slowing, then stopping altogether.

Talan halted beside him. "What is it?"

Solon held his gaze. "Tell me truthfully. The spell that is on him — will we ever be able to remove it?"

Talan read the anxiety in his friend's eyes and put his hand on Solon's shoulder. "The counterspell is in Elshaer's spellbook. If we can get the book, we can remove the spell. Or we can do it by killing the wizard who cast it."

"A task I would gladly do," Solon growled.

Talan smiled grimly. "As would many. We just have to find a way to defeat him. And Jacinda may be our best opportunity."

"How so?" Solon asked.

"If we can get her out of the castle and let the people see her, it won't matter if she is Deirdre or not. If enough of them think she is, they might rally behind us and the 'royal family' and fight back."

Solon considered the idea. "It might work."

Talan started walking again. "It might at least give them hope — something we've been without for a very long time."

*****

Jaci paced the room as she waited for the kitchen girls to bring her evening meal. Anxiety and excitement gnawed at her, along with not a little curiosity. Mandy had explained the plan: After the meal, Jaci would exchange clothes with Nyelda and take the empty trays back to the kitchen with the other girl, while Nyelda stayed in the room and went to bed early, pretending to be Jaci, indisposed. Once in the kitchen, Bessa, the head cook, would hide Jaci in Bessa's own room, just off the kitchen, until all the castle slept. Then one of the linen maids, an older woman named Ione, would fetch Jaci and take her somewhere to see whatever it was Mandy wanted her to see. Afterward, Ione would return Jaci to Bessa's room, where she would stay until it was time to deliver Jaci's breakfast trays. Jaci and the kitchen girl would go to Jaci's chamber, and Jaci and Nyelda would change places again.

Jaci shivered and paced some more, trying not to think about all the things that could go wrong.

The awaited knock startled her. She hurried forward as Mandy let in the kitchen girls with their heavily laden trays. Nyelda looked scared but determined. The other girl just looked scared. Nyelda curtsied to Jaci again before leaving.

Jaci picked at her food, too nervous to eat much. Mandy and Allina did the same, seeming even more nervous than she was. When the time neared for the kitchen girls to return, Mandy helped Jaci remove her outer clothing.

The knock sounded. Allina let the girls in. With Mandy's and Allina's help, Jaci and Nyelda hastily exchanged clothes. Jaci put Nyelda's maid's cap on her head and shoved her curls up into it. Nyelda showed her how to carry the dish-laden tray and use it to shield her face from the guards.

"Luck be with you," Mandy whispered.

"Thanks," Jaci said. "And with you."

Jaci took a deep, steadying breath. Keeping the other kitchen girl between her and the guards, she stepped out into the hall.

CHAPTER 12

They reached the kitchen without mishap. The guards had barely glanced at them as they'd carried the trays away, and no one they'd passed in the halls had given them the slightest attention.

Jaci followed the other girl through the kitchen and, keeping her face averted, set the tray down on the table next to the huge vat of hot, soapy water in which the scullions were washing dishes.

A rotund woman with gray hair pulled back in a bun met them at the table. She eyed Jaci sharply, then handed her a large metal pitcher, half full of water, in a basin. "Take these to my room and be quick about it," she ordered, her words twisted by a thicker lilt than any of the others Jaci had heard. The woman pointed to a closed wooden door on her right.

Jaci nodded wordlessly. The kitchen girl touched her arm and dropped into a curtsy. Hastily, Jaci curtsied, then hurried across the kitchen, trying not to spill the water. Balancing the pitcher and basin on her hip, she opened the door, stepped inside, and closed the door behind her. She leaned back against it and let out a long breath. Whew! She'd made it this far. She hadn't thought to ask what Bessa looked like, but she had to assume that was her.

Two candles ensconced on the walls lit the room. The small, windowless chamber contained a bed, a wooden stand, a trunk, and a tiny fireplace with a wood bin. All were spotless. A threadbare rug, greenish-blue and rectangular, lay on the floor near the hearth.

Jaci set the pitcher and basin on the stand. Mandy had said she was to stay in Bessa's room until Ione came to fetch her. She thought about sitting on the bed, but wasn't sure if Bessa would approve, so she sat on the rug, near the fireplace. Only a few glowing embers still burned, and the room was quite chilly. Jaci took a chunk of wood from the small metal bin near the hearth and set it in the embers. After a few moments, flames bit into it, curling up around the wood. She held her hands out toward the fire, grateful for the warmth.

Sometime later, the door opened and the gray-haired woman strode in, closing and locking the door behind her.

Jaci started at the woman's arrival, and realized she'd dozed off. She rose. "Are you Bessa?"

"Yes." Bessa eyed her up and down. "Well, take that silly cap off and let me see you."

Jaci pulled off the maid's cap and shook out her curls.

Bessa gasped. "Bless my pots," she whispered.

"I'm not Deirdre," Jaci said quietly.

"Who are you, then?"

"My name is Jacinda."

"Where did you come from?"

"A place called White Plains."

Bessa frowned. "Never heard of it."

"It's very far away."

"In what province?"

"I—I'm not sure, exactly." Jaci quickly changed the subject. "Do you know what it is that Mandy wants me to see?"

Bessa regarded her appraisingly. "Yes, but I'll not tell you. You'll see for yourself soon enough. Ione will be here in a bit. Now I need you to turn around so I can dress for bed. I need my sleep."

Jaci turned to the wall while Bessa pulled things out of her trunk and washed up. She considered asking Bessa for more information about the royal family, but the head cook's brusque manner made her decide against it.

"All right, you can turn around again," Bessa said finally. She now wore a dark, floor-length night dress, and her gray hair hung loose to her hips. She handed Jaci two brown woolen blankets. "You'll have to sleep by the fire. I'm sorry I don't have a proper bed for you, but if I don't get my sleep, I'll never be able to keep up with all my kitchen girls. I swear the girls that come here looking for work get younger every year." She blew out one of the candles and muttered, "If his *lordship* would stop taxing their families to death —" She closed her mouth and shot Jaci a wary glance.

"Thank you for helping me," Jaci said. "I know you're risking a lot."

"We are risking, at best, our livelihoods and, at worst, our lives. This had better be worth it."

Jaci didn't know what to say.

Bessa drew back the covers and sat on the bed. "Ione will knock twice, then twice again. When you hear that, you can open the door. Any other knock, wake me." With an effort, she slid her large body into bed and turned on her side, away from Jaci.

Jaci sat on the rug again and wrapped herself in the blankets. They were scratchy, but warm. She gazed into the crackling fire, thinking about Bessa's — and so many others' — reaction to her face. Even Tom, the mechanic in Marston, had commented on her resemblance to Deirdre. Could she really look that much like another person? Jaci had seen Deirdre on the night of the accident, but her hair and half her face had been covered in blood, and she'd lain in the shadow of her wrecked car. Even though the memory was still clear as a blue-sky day, there was no way to tell what Deirdre really looked like. Jaci shuddered and wished again there'd been some way to save her. She deserved so much more than the terrible life she'd had.

A short time later, a chime sounded somewhere out in the kitchen — a clock marking the half hour, Jaci guessed. She hadn't heard the chimes earlier, probably because of all the noise from the kitchen workers cleaning up after the evening meal.

Then a soft knock interrupted her thoughts — two taps on the door, followed by two more. Throwing off the blankets, Jaci rushed to the door. She undid the lock and eased the door open.

"I am Ione," a tall, thin woman whispered in a lilting voice. She carried a shuttered lantern.

Jaci let the woman in, then quickly closed the door and locked it again. She faced Ione. Wisps of gray-brown hair frizzed out beneath the woman's maid's cap. Ione's eyes widened in the familiar stare, her hand flying to her mouth with a sharp intake of breath.

Jaci stifled the impulse to roll her eyes and nodded to her. "I'm Jacinda." She retrieved Nyelda's maid's cap and pulled it over her curls. "Shall we go?"

Ione recovered her composure, though she couldn't seem to erase the shock and uncertainty from her eyes. "Follow me, miss. Listen sharp for the night patrols."

They tiptoed through the silent kitchen, staying well away from the scullions bedded down by the fireplace. Ione led Jaci down many dank, unlit corridors, up several flights of stairs, and through more corridors. Only their rapid breathing and the soft scuff of their steps whispered through the darkness. Jaci shivered as the glow from the half-shuttered lantern chased creepy shadows across the floor. The death-like silence weighed on her as she listened for any other sound. The thought that, at any moment, a night patrol might walk around a corner and see them frayed her nerves. *This is worse than walking through a mausoleum at midnight.*

Finally, Ione stopped before an arched wooden door. She handed the lantern to Jaci. "Hold this, if you please, miss, while I get the key," she whispered. She drew a large ring with at least two dozen keys out of her pocket.

"Where are we?" Jaci asked softly.

"This is the north wing of the castle. The royal family lived in those rooms down the hall, behind you." Ione tried one key after another, but none would fit. Her hands began to tremble. "No one is allowed in this wing, except for Lord Galenock, Castellan Felgarth, and House Mistress Grundelle. She cleans these rooms. She is from Ruusitar, and neither knows nor cares anything about the royal family. If we are caught here, we'll be killed."

Jaci heard a catch in Ione's voice and realized the woman was truly frightened. Ione twisted the ring around to try another key and nearly dropped them.

Jaci closed her fingers over Ione's shaking hands and took the keys from her. "Please, let me try."

"I'm sorry, miss. I'm so scared." Ione took the lantern back and held it so Jaci could see the keyhole.

"It's all right," Jaci said. "I'm scared, too." She tried six more keys to no avail. The seventh key turned and clicked in the lock. The door opened.

"You did it, miss!" Ione wiped away a tear.

They hurried inside and locked the door. Ione opened the shutters on the lantern and led the way toward the back of the room, past piles of wooden crates and clusters of old furniture that had been crammed together and covered with sheets.

"What room is this?" Jaci asked.

"A storeroom," Ione said. "Mandy and me, we hid it back here after we found it."

"Found what?" Jaci could barely contain her curiosity.

"This." Ione reached into a narrow space between an armoire and the back wall and drew forth a large, sheet-covered, rectangular object. "It is the only portrait left of the royal family. His lordship had all the others destroyed, but he missed this one." Reverently, she pulled off the sheet and let it slip to the floor. She held the lantern close.

Jaci gasped and knew the wide-eyed stare on her face easily matched the looks everyone else had been giving her. She knelt in a daze, unable to comprehend what she was seeing. The portrait showed the king and queen and their two daughters in regal attire, golden crowns encrusted with jewels on their heads. The older girl, Soneira — then in her late teens, Jaci guessed — looked so much like her it was beyond uncanny. The same shape of face and complexion, the same nose, the same dark curls, though Soneira's were longer. The only differences were eye color — Soneira's blue to Jaci's brown — and fineness of features. Soneira's were more delicate and refined, with higher cheekbones and perfectly arched eyebrows. Jaci had always considered herself attractive, but Soneira was breathtakingly beautiful. *No wonder Talan was in love with her,* she thought with a pang.

The younger girl had to be Deirdre, around age nine or ten. Jaci's breath stopped. Deirdre looked even more like her than Soneira did. The same eyes, though blue, and slightly coarser features — she looked just like Jaci had at that age. Jaci felt like she was seeing an old school photo of herself.

"How is this possible?" she murmured. Her gaze slid upward to the dark-haired queen, and she nearly fell backward in shock. "Mother!" she breathed.

"That is Queen Selendria," Ione said, surprised and uncertain.

"No, it's my mother!" Jaci moved closer, studying the face that was identical in every way to her late, beloved mother — "No, wait..." *Something's missing.* "It can't be her, there's no scar on her face."

Ione gripped Jaci's arm. "Scar? Where?"

"Just above her right eyebrow — there." Jaci pointed to Queen Selendria's temple. "My mother had a two-inch scar right there. She said she'd gotten it when she fell off a horse when she was young."

Ione's hand fluttered to her mouth. "The lost queen!"

"Lost queen? I thought you said *she* was queen." Jaci gestured at the portrait.

"What was your mother's name?" Ione asked in a shaky voice.

"Miri."

Ione took a step backward and sank down on the arm of a sheet-draped sofa. "Mirinesstra's child," she whispered. Then she knelt beside Jaci and bowed her head. "Your Highness."

Taken aback, Jaci touched her arm. "Oh, please don't call me that. I'm not royalty."

"But you are," Ione insisted. "You are the lost queen Mirinesstra's daughter."

"Who is Mirinesstra?"

"Selendria and Mirinesstra — Miri — were sisters — identical twins."

"Sisters?" Jaci repeated, dumbfounded.

Ione nodded. "They were Northern Enchantresses — daughters of the High Enchantress of Millianoch."

"But... but that's impossible." Jaci looked at the portrait, her eyes tracing Selendria's features, seeing her mother inside them. "H—how was she lost?"

"Well, Your Hi — miss, it's a bit of a long story." Ione glanced back at the locked door of the storeroom before continuing. "Not quite forty years ago, King Brannad was looking for a wife. He wanted an alliance between Shiannora and Millianoch, so he asked the High Enchantress for the hand of one of her daughters in marriage. She agreed. Miri was firstborn, so it was decided that she would marry the king." Ione nodded toward the portrait. "Selendria was terribly jealous, though. *She* wanted to be queen of the realm.

"Miri, however, had no wish to be queen. She refused the king's hand outright. She was nineteen at the time and very headstrong. Both twins were wild and willful. They hated each other, though no one knew why. They competed over everything, always trying to outdo each other. The scar on Miri's forehead came from one of their riding escapades. Miri told me what happened. I was her lady's maid after she came to live at Castle d'Gaire, and she would often complain to me about her sister. They'd been riding breakneck through a forest to prove who was the better rider when Miri's horse threw her, and she hit her head on a rock. Miri blamed Selendria. She said her sister had struck her horse with a riding whip. Selendria denied it. The High Enchantress would have healed the scar, but Miri wanted to keep it. She said she liked being able to look in the mirror and not see her sister's face."

Jaci listened as if in a dream. Could this wild teenager really have been her mother?

"The High Enchantress forced Mirinesstra to marry King Brannad," Ione continued, "so Miri became queen of Shiannora and all of Tarshane. But she was furious at having no choice in the matter. She refused all queenly duties and wouldn't let King Brannad into her bedroom. The king was an honorable man, and he had no wish to force himself upon her, so he left her alone and waited, hoping she would eventually accept her position and, perhaps, begin to care for him."

A look of sorrow creased Ione's face. "Sadly, this never happened. Miri wanted nothing to do with the king and spent most of her time with Elshaer and the Wizard's Guild. She and Selendria had both inherited strong magical abilities from their mother, and Miri wanted to learn from the wizards so she could become more powerful than her sister."

Jaci reeled inside as she tried to reconcile her memories of her kind and loving mother with the portrait Ione's words were painting. She felt like not only the rug but the entire floor had been yanked out from under her.

"A year passed," Ione said, "and King Brannad finally ran out of patience and forbade Miri from training with the wizards until she agreed to assume her role as queen. She again refused. That night, she disappeared. She just vanished from a room that was locked from the inside. I was sleeping in an adjoining alcove, and I never heard a sound. King Brannad was terribly upset and had the entire kingdom searched. Both the Enchantresses and the Wizard's Guild tried to scry her, but neither could find her.

"Rumors flew that the king had secretly disposed of her, but he vehemently denied them. The Enchantresses threatened to go to war against Shiannora to punish the king for what he supposedly had done. To prove his innocence, King Brannad submitted to a truth test they devised. He passed without question. Then he accused the Enchantresses of using magic to spirit his wife away, because she was unhappy. The Enchantresses denied the charge.

"While both sides were debating what to do, Selendria offered to take her sister's place. She would marry King Brannad and become queen of Tarshane, in every sense of the word, just like she'd wanted.

"Some months later, this came to pass, since neither side could prove the other was to blame for Miri's disappearance. Selendria and King Brannad were quite happy together." Ione looked at Selendria's smiling face in the portrait, then her expression grew pensive. "Miri was never found, and to this day, no one knows what happened to her. Everyone eventually assumed she was dead."

Jaci's thoughts flew in a rapid whirl. Miri — her mother — an Enchantress — able to work magic — traveling through a portal like the clock that had transported Jaci to this world. She had disappeared from within her own room, so the portal had to be somewhere in that room — if Jaci could find it, she could go home...

Ione touched Jaci on the shoulder. "Miss?"

Jaci blinked and met Ione's gaze. "She wasn't dead — at least, not then. This is going to sound crazy, but she magically transported herself to another world — my world. She was alive and well up until about two years ago when she got sick and — and died." Grief clogged her throat. She still missed her mother so much. "A few days ago, I stumbled across some kind of magical portal by accident and ended up here. I want to go home, back to my world, but I'm not sure how."

Ione stared at her blankly, uncomprehending.

Jaci abandoned her attempt at explanation and went right to the point. "I need to get inside Miri's room. You said the royal family's rooms were just down the hall. Will you show me?"

Ione nodded. "Yes, of course." She reached for the sheet to cover up the portrait.

Jaci took one more look at the painting and noticed a detail she'd missed the first time. Queen Selendria wore a jewel pendant exactly like hers. "Wait. The pendant the queen is wearing — do you know what it is?"

Ione squinted at the portrait. "It is her *druidainoch* stone. All the Northern Enchantresses have them. They receive them in a coming-of-age ceremony when they turn eighteen. The stones have magical properties that enhance and help focus the Enchantresses' powers. Lord Galenock has it now... the swine," she muttered under her breath. She draped the sheet over the portrait and slid it behind the armoire. A thoughtful look crossed her face. "I wonder what happened to Miri's stone?"

Jaci pretended not to hear her. "We should get going. How far down the hall is — is Miri's room?" She couldn't get her head around the idea that her mother had been a queen of this realm. She felt like she was talking about a stranger, not someone who had raised her and doted on her for twenty-seven years.

"It is four doors down on the right," Ione said. "It was also Soneira's room. She moved into it during her early teen years. The king and queen didn't want her in there, after what happened with Miri, but what Soneira wanted, she always got, and she finally wore them down. They relented and let her have the room."

"I wonder why she wanted it so badly?" Jaci asked. Could she have known about the portal? Mandy had said Soneira was training with Elshaer, the same wizard who had trained Miri.

"I don't know," Ione said. "She tended to be secretive about things."

They made their way to the front of the room, and Ione listened at the door. "I don't hear anything," she whispered. "I think it is safe to go out."

They left the room and crept down the empty hall to the fourth door. Ione fitted a dozen keys in the lock before she finally found the correct one. They slipped into Miri's old chamber, and Ione re-locked the door.

"May I see that key?" Jaci asked quickly, before Ione let it drop and mingle with the others.

Ione handed her the key, with the key ring dangling from it.

"Thanks." Jaci examined the ring and found a way to remove the key.

"What are you doing?" Ione asked anxiously.

"I need this key." Jaci successfully detached it from the ring. "I might need to get into this room again."

Ione looked horrified. "But if House Mistress Grundelle finds out we took it..."

"I thought these were your keys," Jaci said, surprised.

Ione shook her head. "I took them from the House Mistress. She has a weakness for brandy, and when she's in her cups, she sleeps like the dead. I left a bottle where she would find it, so I would be able to get the keys tonight. I have to sneak them back to her before she wakes."

Jaci clasped the key tightly. "I'm sorry, but I have to have this key." She gave the key ring back to Ione. "You shouldn't have to worry. Even if she discovers it's missing, she will have no way of knowing who took it. You should be safe."

A loud bong vibrated through the chamber. Jaci nearly jumped out of her skin.

"Gods save us," Ione cried, and for a moment, Jaci thought the woman was going to faint.

Another bong sounded, very familiar.

Jaci pulled herself together. She took Ione's arm and squeezed it gently. "It's just a clock."

Ione nodded and took several deep breaths.

Jaci turned around and, across the room, beheld a massive grandfather clock, one that was identical to the clock in the Brunswick house. She stared at it, scared and excited at the same time, hardly believing she'd actually found it. Feeling as if she was moving in slow motion, she walked toward it.

The clock continued to bong, ceasing at eleven. Jaci touched the burnished ebony wood, her fingers tracing the gold inlay. Everything about the clock was exactly the same as the Brunswick clock, except for one detail: the pane of glass protecting the pendulum was blank. No etching decorated its surface. Her excitement turned to dismay. Did that mean this clock wasn't a portal?

She stepped around behind the huge timepiece, while Ione watched her with a 'what on earth are you doing?' expression. The clock had been set away from the wall, just like the Brunswick clock. With that one, Jaci had accidentally fallen against it, and the door in the back had popped open. She moved her hand over the back, inch by inch, pressing and prodding, trying to recreate what she'd done without falling.

Partway down the left edge, she felt a strange warmth in her fingers and heard a tiny snick. A door sprang open. *Yes!* She gestured for Ione to bring the lantern. The light shone into an empty space.

"How did you know that was there?" Ione breathed.

"There's a clock just like this where I come from. It's how I got here." She closed the narrow door, then popped it open again twice to make certain she knew where the release mechanism was. Leaving the door closed, she stepped back around to the front of the clock. This had to be a portal. Why was there no etching?

Maybe it was because the time wasn't right. She calculated in her head. This was her fifth night in Tarshane. If the moon phases in this world shifted in a similar manner to how they did on Earth, it would be two more nights before the next phase listed on the parchment hidden in the diary — the word *"ris,"* opposite a red-brown square, whatever that meant.

Jaci put the clock between herself and Ione and whispered the word she'd seen on the calendar — *saelarin*. Nothing happened. Well, she hadn't really expected it to. Not really.

Another thought occurred to her, and she turned to Ione. "On the night that Miri disappeared — do you remember if there was a full moon?" On the parchment, the full moon corresponded with a clock face — hopefully the Brunswick clock face, and not another one hidden somewhere else.

Ione looked surprised at the question. "Oh, my, that was so many years ago... let me think." After a few moments, she said, "Yes... yes, I think it was. It had to have been — it was the night of the Harvest Festival, and that is always on the first full moon of autumn."

"What about Deirdre? Was it a full moon then?"

Ione's face crumpled. "Oh, I don't know, miss. Please don't ask me about that horrible time. I don't want to remember it."

"Never mind." Jaci touched Ione's arm in sympathy. "I'm sorry."

"Thank you, miss." Ione looked toward the door. "Can we go now?"

Jaci glanced wistfully around the darkened room. She would love to look around and see if she could learn anything more about Soneira, since she was the last to use this room, but Ione was anxious to leave.

"All right," Jaci agreed, and they headed for the door.

"Was — was she happy, miss?" Ione asked.

Jaci reached for the door lock. "Who?"

"Miri. Was she happy, wherever you say she went?"

Jaci smiled. "Yes, she was. Very happy."

Ione gave her a tense smile. "I'm glad."

Out in the hall, the scrape of booted feet and the murmur of low voices filtered through the door. Jaci froze, her hand on the lock.

Ione went rigid with fright. "The night patrol," she whispered.

Jaci backed away from the door. "Douse the light."

Ione shuttered the lantern. Jaci grasped her hand, and they stood silently in the pitch dark, holding their breath.

Footsteps strode near, and Jaci heard rattling sounds as the night patrol checked all the doors in the hallway. The footsteps halted before their door. Jaci squeezed Ione's hand. The door latch rattled, then the footsteps moved on down the hall, testing doors as they went.

Jaci exhaled. That was way too close. They'd almost walked right into the patrol. "How long before they're gone?"

"They should be out of this wing in another few minutes," Ione answered, a shaky edge to her voice. She opened the lantern enough to emit a pale stream of light.

"How about if we wait until the clock strikes the half hour, then leave? Do you think that will be enough time?"

Ione nodded nervously. "I think so."

"Okay." Jaci held out her hand. "May I have the lantern? I'd like to look around. Don't worry, I'll leave everything as I found it."

Ione reluctantly gave her the lantern.

From the look on her face, the woman obviously didn't think snooping was a good idea, but Jaci couldn't contain her curiosity. She examined first a desk, then a chest of drawers, then a vanity, opening all the drawers and searching for places where things — she didn't know what — could be hidden. The drawers were all empty, and she couldn't find any odd spaces that might be secret caches. Then she checked the bed, looking underneath the mattress and the bed itself. Nothing — not even dust bunnies. House Mistress Grundelle did her job well.

She did a quick search of the bare bookshelves, the empty closet, and the washroom. Still nothing. She glanced about the room, disappointed. She'd really wanted to find something of Soneira's, though she wasn't sure why. The clock face read five minutes until the half hour. The only thing left in the room was the fireplace.

Crossing to the hearth, Jaci set the lantern on the floor and ran her hands over the stones to see if any were loose. The outside of the fireplace was rock solid. She got down on her knees and, bending low, stuck her head into the fireplace and felt the inner wall of stones.

Her breath caught. Her fingers had slid across another warm spot like the one on the back of the clock, and one of the smaller stones had shifted.

The clock bonged, reverberating through the room. So intent was she at working the stone free, she barely noticed the sound. Out of the corner of her eye, she saw the lower half of Ione's dress appear.

Ione bent down. "Miss? What are you doing?"

"Hold on, I've almost got it." Straining, Jaci wiggled the stone out of the wall. "There!" She looked at the hole. She was going to feel really silly if there was nothing in it. Hoping no creepy-crawlies lived in the wall, she reached into the hole. Her fingers touched something smooth, definitely not stone. Excitement rushed through her as she pulled out a small book bound in soft blue leather.

Ione crouched beside her. "Oh, miss! What did you find?"

Jaci brushed the rock dust off the cover and opened it. Unfamiliar words and phrases, written in a delicate script, filled the first page, and the second, and third. Jaci thumbed through more pages. Half the book was filled with similar writings.

Ione backed away. "Those be words of magic, miss. Don't speak them!"

Jaci shoved the stone back into place, then stood, the book gripped in her hand. "Why not?" Not that she actually would try to say any of the words. Now that she knew her speaking the word *saelarin* had likely opened the magic portal, she was definitely thinking twice before saying any more unfamiliar words.

"Magic is dangerous."

"Whose book is this — Soneira's or Miri's? I don't see any name on it."

"I don't know, miss. I've never seen it before. I don't know how you found it. His lordship searched this room dozens of times after — after..." She stopped, her voice catching in a sob. She cleared her throat. "He never found what he wanted. He was always so angry."

"I felt a warmth in my fingers when I touched where it was hidden," Jaci said. "I felt it on the back of the clock, too."

"A magical ward of hiding," Ione said. "I heard Miri speak of it once."

"But isn't Galenock a wizard? Why wouldn't he have felt it?"

"Perhaps it was done in such a way that only another Enchantress could find it."

Jaci stared at Ione. "Are you saying *I'm* an Enchantress?"

"You are Mirinesstra's daughter."

Whoa. Jaci's legs wobbled. She gripped the mantel for support. She was not ready for that kind of speculation.

"Are you all right, miss?" Ione asked anxiously.

Jaci breathed deeply to calm herself. She wanted badly to clasp her pendant, now hanging by her thigh, and let it soothe her anxieties — wait, was that a form of magic, too? She swallowed hard.

"Yes, I'm okay. Don't tell anyone about any of this, all right? The fewer people that know, the less likely it will reach Galenock's ears."

Ione nodded quickly. "Can we go now, miss? *Please?*"

"Yes." Clutching the book and the room key in one hand, Jaci picked up the lantern and gave it to Ione. "Let's go."

CHAPTER 13

Jaci sat by the fire again, listening to Bessa's soft snoring. Ione had led her safely back to the head cook's room. Thankfully, they hadn't run into any more patrols. Jaci had memorized every twist, turn, and stair, making certain she could find her way back to the grandfather clock. She gripped Miri's room key in her hand. If she was lucky, in just over a week, that clock would send her home. She hoped Ione would be able to return the other keys to the House Mistress without difficulty. Jaci couldn't bear the thought of anyone else getting hurt because of her.

Lifting up the hem of her dress, Jaci untied the shoe lace from around her leg and threaded Miri's room key onto her pendant chain alongside the key she'd found in Deirdre's clock. She wasn't sure what the extra weight would do to it. She was having enough trouble keeping the knotted shoe lace from slipping down her leg as it was. Her fingers closed around her pendant and she shut her eyes, relaxing in a glow of serene warmth... warmth like what she'd felt on the back of the clock and on the stone in the fireplace wall. Her eyes flew open. Enchantress magic, traceable only by other Enchantresses — *her*? Could that be possible? When Ione had identified Jaci's mother as an Enchantress, Jaci had been shocked. She'd managed to get a tenuous grip on the idea, but she'd never thought to take it further — to think that she, herself, might be one, might have inherited magical abilities. She shook her head. It still seemed impossible.

And yet she'd worked the magic of the clock portal, and she'd found the "wards of hiding," as Ione called them, that even Galenock hadn't been able to find. Didn't that prove she had some kind of magical talent? *I am an Enchantress.* The thought thrilled and frightened her at the same time.

She thought of her mother again, remembering through her grief their times together. Miri had been a free spirit, very competitive as Ione had said, and headstrong, quick to anger and just as quick to forgive and forget, but she was mostly warm and loving. Jaci could not recall her mother ever doing or saying anything that might have been even remotely magical. Nor her father, either, who she was certain had been from her world. He'd been killed in a plane crash when she was nine. What she remembered most about him was his kindness, his friendly smile, and his infectious laugh. He and her mother had been so happy together. Miri had grieved for a long time afterward, but she and Jaci had helped each other through the pain and become closer because of it. *Why didn't she ever tell me?*

Jaci tied the shoe lace around her leg as tightly as she could without cutting off her circulation and then drew the woolen blankets more closely about her. She knew she should try to sleep, but there were too many thoughts whirling around in her brain. She picked up the little blue book she'd taken from the fireplace in Miri's room and slowly thumbed through it again. Had this belonged to her mother, or to Soneira? The words might have been written in some African dialect for all the sense they made to her. What could they mean? She wondered if her mother had regretted giving up the use of her magical abilities in her new world. Or maybe she hadn't. Maybe she'd only used them in secret. Jaci would never know.

She turned a page, and a folded piece of parchment fell out of the book into her lap. She set the book down, picked up the parchment, and unfolded it.

Dearest Talan —

With a sharp intake of breath, she dropped the parchment back into her lap. She swallowed hard. Well, that answered the question of whose book it was.

She stared at the parchment, torn between what she *should* do and what she wanted to do. Her mother had raised her with better manners than to read other people's letters, but... She chewed her lip. Who would know if she did? Soneira was gone, and Jaci wouldn't likely be seeing Talan again. She frowned, not liking how that realization hurt. She really didn't want to see him again, she told herself. If he was still alive — what if he'd been killed in the Riders' attack? That thought hurt even more. *Don't go there... just don't.* She looked back at the letter. The fire crackled and spit while she argued with herself. Curiosity won out again. She picked up the parchment.

Dearest Talan —

I am sorry for what I said. You were right about Galenock. I know it is dangerous to work with him, but I've discovered he is so much stronger than the other wizards — even Elshaer. He is teaching me spells that none of the others know. I want to become as powerful as he is. Then I will surpass him and be the most powerful Enchantress Tarshane has ever seen.

There is something that worries me, though. I read some notes of his that I wasn't supposed to see — notes about Ridaur's crypt and a map of where to find it, along with some magical phrases I'd never heard. With the notes was a strange-looking key. It was short and copper-colored with a wire of black metal twisted around it.

Jaci gasped. The key from Deirdre's clock. She whipped up the edge of her dress and looked at the key, hanging from her pendant chain. It matched the description exactly. Was that what Galenock had been searching for in Soneira's room? Cold fear washed through her. She had something Galenock wanted very badly, and she had the feeling it would be very bad for her and everyone else if he got it. Her heart thumped in her chest as she rearranged her dress and continued reading the note.

The phrases were so evil they made my skin crawl when I read them. I copied everything into my spellbook. I will show it to my mother when she returns from Millianoch tomorrow.

Talan, I miss you. Please come back and tell me you forgive me. I want us to be together again.

Love always,

Soneira

Jaci released the breath she'd been holding and slowly read the lines again. They must have been written after the fight Deirdre had witnessed between Talan and her sister.

Then I will surpass him and be the most powerful Enchantress Tarshane has ever seen.

Jaci remembered what Ione had said about Miri, and Soneira's mother, Selendria, always competing, always trying to outdo each other. Apparently, Soneira had inherited her mother's competitiveness, as well as her magical abilities. Ione had also said something about Soneira being secretive and always getting what she wanted. Recalling Soneira's face in the portrait, Jaci could see imperiousness in the girl's eyes and in the lift of her chin. *I bet she was as wild and spoiled as her mother.*

Jaci chided herself. *Don't think ill of the dead.* And why was she being so critical, anyway? She looked back at the letter. Who was Ridaur? Obviously he was dead if he was in a crypt. She wondered if the evil magical phrases had anything to do with the "something" that had happened and gotten Galenock banished. Mandy had said only Galenock and maybe Talan knew the whole story...

Scenes of the past played before her eyes, brought to life by her vivid imagination. She saw everything as if she had been there: Soneira showing her mother the notes with the evil magical phrases she had copied from Galenock; the king banishing Galenock for whatever it was the wizard had been planning; Galenock storming back with a vengeance; the Ruusitar army attacking; Soneira taking the key and sending it with Deirdre as far away as she could to a place she hoped Galenock wouldn't know about, right before she was dragged off to be murdered with the king and queen...

Jaci sat, shaking, her hands over her eyes as tears poured down her face. How horrible! And now she'd been dropped right into the middle of everything and had brought the key back. She wiped her tears on her sleeve. What should she do? She couldn't let Galenock have it. She thumbed through the rest of the pages in the book. The last ten pages, separated from the others by a blank page, contained notes about Ridaur's crypt, more foreign-looking words, and a hastily sketched map. She studied the map for a few moments, reading the unfamiliar place names, and wondered where the crypt was in relation to Catir Coronin. She closed the book. The information Soneira had copied was still there. If Galenock's notes had been destroyed when he'd been banished — she would have destroyed them if she'd been the king — then the wizard would be after this book, too.

She looked at the fire. She could burn the book and destroy the information for good. Unless there was another copy of it somewhere else. Galenock seemed too shrewd to have kept only one copy of something that important to him. And burning the book wouldn't get rid of the key. Well, she'd just have to take the key back with her through the portal.

She lifted the book to toss it into the fire, then hesitated. Destroying the book suddenly felt wrong to her. Something — conscience? instinct? — was telling her not to do it. She lowered her hand uncertainly. Then another thought struck her. What if Talan and his men could somehow use the information against Galenock? Maybe it could help them find a way to defeat him. But how could she possibly get the book to them? She couldn't get out of the castle, and she hoped to be home in nine days. She chewed her lip again. Well, technically, she could get out of the castle, if the clock really was a portal. In two nights, it could send her to whatever place the red-brown square was, though the odds of that being anywhere near Talan were astronomical. Then she'd be stranded who knows where and miss her chance to get home. Besides, if she found Talan, she'd have to give him the letter. He'd know she'd read it. Her cheeks flamed. She looked back at the fire. Or she could burn it. Guilt pricked her sharply. She tried to squash the feeling, but didn't succeed.

She rubbed her eyes, exhausted. This was all too confusing. She needed to sleep on it and hope things would be clearer in the morning. Which meant she needed a place to hide the book. Sighing deeply, she glanced at the still-snoring Bessa, then silently crawled to the trunk and opened it. She searched through the clothing until she found a pair of brown knitted stockings. Making certain everything in the trunk was exactly as she'd found it, she went back to the fire and pulled on the stockings. They rose up over her knees.

She stuck the letter back into the book, then stuffed the book down inside the stocking, thinking all the while that she had to be out of her mind.

* * * * *

A rough shake of her shoulder woke Jaci. She sat up, blinking, disoriented. Where was she? What time was it?

Bessa loomed above her, bristling, a severe frown on her face. She'd already dressed for the day, her long hair twisted up in a tight bun.

Oh, right. Bessa's room off the kitchen. Jaci hadn't even heard the woman get up.

"There is a washroom around the corner." Bessa pointed to the right. "You'd best hurry. It will be time to take the breakfast trays up soon. I'll come get you." She stomped toward the door.

My goodness, what had put her in such a foul mood? Jaci started to rise and saw the stockings she'd borrowed on her feet. "Bessa, wait," she said quickly.

The woman turned, still scowling.

Jaci improvised. "My feet were freezing last night, so I borrowed a pair of stockings. I would have asked, but I didn't want to wake you. I'd like to wear them up to my room, and then I'll wash them out and have the kitchen girls bring them back down to you. Would that be all right?"

Bessa's face relaxed, her animosity fading. "Yes. Just make sure they get back to me. Give them to Nyelda."

"I will, thank you."

Bessa unlocked the door and went out.

Whew. One disaster averted. Jaci repositioned Nyelda's maid's cap and, shielding her face with her hand, hurried around the corner to the washroom. The kitchen was such a hive of activity, she was pretty sure no one noticed her.

A short time later, Bessa helped Jaci balance a loaded tray on her shoulder and sent her and the other kitchen girl on their way. After lugging the tray up a second flight of stairs, Jaci could see how the girls could very easily injure their backs.

"Tell Bessa not to send up so much food," she whispered to the other girl. "This is way too much to carry."

The kitchen girl gave her a tiny, scared smile.

When they approached her guest room, Jaci kept her head down and tried to keep her arms from shaking from both fear and exhaustion. The tray she carried screened one side of her face from view, while the kitchen girl's tray blocked the other. Jaci held her breath as they stepped between the bored guards. The kitchen girl knocked on the door, which was opened instantly by Mandy, who waved them into the room and shut the door.

Once they had deposited the trays on the table, Jaci and Mandy rushed to the bedroom, where Nyelda and Allina waited. Mandy helped Jaci remove Nyelda's clothes and don a robe, while Allina helped Nyelda into her dress. Then Nyelda and the other kitchen girl left the room. Jaci and Mandy listened at the door, but heard no challenge from the guards. They both let out long breaths and leaned against the door, smiling at each other.

Mandy gestured toward the table, where Allina was filling a bowl with honey-sweetened oatmeal. Jaci nodded and went and sat on the loveseat, suddenly ravenous. She could feel Mandy's undercurrent of excitement and knew the girl must be bursting with questions, but was holding them in until they could talk safely. *How much am I going to tell her?* Jaci thought, with a touch of apprehension.

"When you're done, we'll get you into a proper dress," Mandy whispered. She and Allina spooned themselves out some oatmeal and sat on the chairs to eat.

"The dress I wore yesterday was beautiful," Jaci said, "but do you have any with higher necklines? I'm a little more comfortable with that style." *And I need to be able to wear my pendant around my neck*, she thought silently. She'd felt the shoe lace inching down her leg while on her way up with the tray. "Oh, and some thick stockings would be nice, too. I borrowed a pair from —"

A sharp look from Mandy stopped her from saying the head cook's name.

"— From the closet last night to keep my feet warm," Jaci finished, horrified at her almost-slip. What if someone really was listening? *Sorry*, she mouthed silently to the girl.

Mandy took a breath. "Oh, yes, miss. We'll see what we can find." She and Allina quickly finished eating and headed off to the closet.

After Jaci had eaten breakfast and washed up, the girls dressed her in a yellow silk dress with a round collar that, Jaci noted with relief, was high enough to hide her pendant and the keys. They also produced stockings equal to Bessa's and pins they'd had sent up from the seamstress to tack up her dress so she wouldn't have to hold it up whenever she walked.

"Is that better?" Mandy asked.

"Yes, much better, thank you." Jaci pointed to the washroom and raised her eyebrows.

Mandy nodded eagerly.

The three squeezed into the small room and shut the door.

"Did you see it?" Mandy whispered.

Jaci nodded. "It was amazing."

"You look just like them, miss. You say you're not Deirdre, but you have to be related, somehow. I just know it."

Jaci took a deep breath, feeling like she was about to jump into an abyss from which she'd no idea if she could escape. "My mother's name was Miri. Ione said she was Mirinesstra, Queen Selendria's twin sister."

"The lost queen!" Mandy's eyes shone. "You are the lost queen's daughter — that makes you a princess of the realm. I knew it!" She covered her mouth to stifle an excited laugh. "Is Queen Mirinesstra in White Plains? Will she be coming back?"

Jaci smiled sadly. "I'm afraid not. She died two years ago, from an illness."

Mandy sobered. "Oh, miss, I am so sorry."

Allina touched Jaci's arm in sympathy.

"Thank you," Jaci said. "I do miss her very much."

"Her disappearance was a great mystery — hers and Deirdre's," Mandy said. "We always hoped they would return some day and help us defeat Galenock."

"About Deirdre..." Jaci hesitated. Should she tell them? She couldn't decide which would be crueler — letting them know Deirdre was dead and dashing all their hopes, or letting them go on hoping for something that would never happen.

"Yes? Do you know something about her?"

Jaci closed her eyes for a moment, made her decision. "I'm sorry to have to tell you this, but Deirdre is dead, too."

Mandy gasped. "No!"

Allina covered her mouth with her hand, eyes round with shock.

Before Jaci knew what she was doing, she spilled the whole story of Deirdre's accident, finding the clock in the old house, being transported to Tarshane, her rescue from the wolves by Talan and his men, and her capture by the red-cloaked Riders, leaving out only the details about the key, her *druidainoch* stone, and Soneira's spellbook and letter.

"There is another clock in Soneira's old room," Jaci finished. "I saw it last night after seeing the portrait. I think I can use it to get home."

"But you are our princess," Mandy said in dismay. "No, you are more than that — you are heir to the throne — our queen!"

Whoa. *Queen?* "Now — now wait a minute," Jaci stammered. "I am *not* a queen. I'm just an ordinary person. I don't belong here — I want to go home."

Tears filled Mandy's eyes. "You can't leave us. We need you! Tarshane is dying under Galenock's rule. If Queen Mirinesstra and Deirdre are both dead, we have no one left. You have to help us defeat him."

"*Me?* What could I possibly do against him? You told me yourself he is very powerful."

"But you are the daughter of an Enchantress. You must have magical abilities, too."

"Well, if I do, I don't know what they are or how to use them," Jaci countered. "I'd certainly be no match for Galenock."

"The Enchantresses — that's it!" Mandy said. "If we can get you to the Enchantresses, they can teach you what you need to know. You'd be safe there. And with your added power, the Enchantresses will be able to overcome him!"

"But —" Jaci began.

Mandy went on as if she hadn't heard. "Now, how can we get you there?"

"Where do they live?" Jaci asked, curious in spite of herself.

"The Northern Mountains."

"Did you say *mountains?*" Jaci asked. The fourth symbol on the scrap of parchment with the moon phases was mountains.

Mandy nodded. "Their castle is built around the highest peak."

Jaci's mind spun. It would be two weeks and two days before the portal could open into the mountains. But who knew what mountains they would be? If it were the Northern Mountains, she could meet her mother's relatives, and maybe learn about magic... How mind-boggling would that be? But if the portal opened elsewhere, she could die of exposure on top of an isolated icy peak somewhere... Of course, it would make sense for an Enchantress to make a portal connection to her home castle. But no, the risk was too great. Then again... what if she could actually control magic?

A mental image of Deirdre's words describing the two wizards fighting with blue fire all around them filled Jaci's mind.

"Miss?"

Jaci shook her head. "I — I have to think." She fled the washroom, feeling Mandy's and Allina's anxious gazes following her as she ran into the bedroom and closed the door.

CHAPTER 14

Jaci dragged herself out of bed and stumbled to the washroom as Mandy and Allina pulled back the curtains on a brilliant sunny morning. She'd slept badly, her mind a constant turmoil of *should she* or *should she not*. All the rest of the previous day, the chamber girls had tread carefully around her, tense and anxious, waiting for her to decide — would she help them or abandon them?

Jaci hid in the washroom and splashed cold water on her face. All she could see in her mind's eye were their hopeful, pleading faces. She wanted to go home, but how could she live with herself if she went back to the comforts of her world and left them to the tragedy of theirs?

She inhaled deeply, then let it out slowly. Tonight would be her seventh night in Tarshane — the night of the rising half-moon and the red-brown square. She needed to know if the clock was a portal before she could make any kind of decision. The only way to find out was to go back to Miri's room tonight. If an etching appeared in the clock's glass door, and if the magic word triggered the same electrical charge in the air she'd felt in the Brunswick house, she'd know the clock was a working portal. If not...

She splashed more cold water on her face. No. She would wait until then to think beyond. She wondered if Nyelda and Bessa would be willing to do the switch again, after dinner. She wouldn't need Ione this time. She knew the way, and she already had the key to the room. Nyelda would be up soon with the breakfast trays. Jaci had washed out Bessa's stockings and given them to Nyelda yesterday evening to take back, so there wouldn't be any trouble over that detail.

Jaci finished up in the washroom and went back to the bedroom to dress and tell the girls what she had in mind.

*****

It was late morning when Talan descended the iron ladder, following Cranton's burly cousin, Willem, down into the bowels of the rock beneath the gristmill. He stepped off onto the damp stone floor, his eyes sweeping the underground cavern. Solon, Katar, and seven other Black Banders climbed down the ladder behind him.

Lanterns hanging from hooks driven into the rock lit the vast space. An arm of the river that flowed past the gristmill crooked down through a high crack in the stone wall on the right and cascaded into a ten-foot-wide channel, worn deep by the endlessly pounding water. The channel sliced through the stone floor for a dozen feet, then widened out into a rippling pool, some twenty feet across, before narrowing again into another short channel that cut down through the floor at the base of the far wall, rushing on out of sight. Several lumpy, tarp-covered piles lay in the shadows of the back wall — goods destined for Willem's smuggling trade, Talan guessed.

"Watch your step," Willem warned, as he picked his way across the swath of slippery, uneven rock along the left side of the channel. He stopped about two-thirds of the way around the pool.

Talan and the others gathered around him.

Willem pointed across the pool. "Over there, on the far side near the bottom, about ten feet down, there's a hole big enough to fit three men swimming through together, one on top of the other two. You won't really have to do much swimming. It's a short tunnel, mostly downhill, and the current will suck you through right quick. You have to take care, though, because the tunnel quirks to the left partway through. If you don't have your arms out in front of you to guide yourself through the tunnel, you'll ram your head into solid rock." He rubbed the side of his head. "I can tell you right now, you'll be sorry." He chuckled. "Coming back through is trickier. It's very difficult to swim back up through the tunnel. The current is too strong. There's a tarred rope anchored to the right of the hole that you can use to pull yourself hand-over-hand back up through. Once you're out of the current, you can let go and surface. The hard part is holding your breath long enough to do it. You also have to do it blind. It's pitch black in the tunnel."

"Talan —" Solon began in a worried voice.

"We have no choice," Talan cut in. "How long does it take to get to Cranton's wine cellar, Willem?"

"It will take you most of the day," Willem said. "If you don't get lost, you should arrive right around dinner time." He pulled from his pocket a flat parcel, wrapped in waterproofed tarp. "Here is a map. The path is clearly marked. Leave it in Cranton's wine cellar when you go off to do whatever it is you're going to do. *Don't get caught with it.* Are all of you going?"

Talan shook his head. "Five of us." Katar and three of the Black Banders could swim well. Solon and the other four would be staying behind to guard their exit.

Willem turned and addressed the whole group. "Those of you that are staying, I would ask that you stay down here in the cavern and keep quiet. Every so often, Galenock's men will come by, unannounced, and start poking around to see if they can find a reason to raise my taxes. I don't want them stumbling across you by accident. I will provide food and blankets."

Solon nodded. "Thank you. We will do as you ask."

"Yes, thank you," Talan said. He shook Willem's hand. "I appreciate your help."

"You're welcome, my friend. I'm always willing to help anyone who can put a stitch in Galenock's plans. Good luck."

Talan tucked the parcel with the map into his belt pouch. He and the others going with him had strapped their weapons securely to their backs, so they wouldn't be a hindrance while swimming.

Talan removed his cloak and handed it to Solon. "If we're not back in three days, you know what to do."

Solon accepted the cloak reluctantly. "Yes."

Talan held Solon's gaze a moment, reading his friend's unspoken apprehension, knowing there was nothing he could say to alleviate it. He squeezed Solon's arm, then turned away. Katar and the other three Black Banders stood at the edge of the pool, awaiting his word. He nodded to them, took a deep breath, and dove into the pool.

*****

Jaci washed down another mouthful of roast chicken with honey-apple cider, forcing herself to eat her usual amount of the dinner Bessa had sent up, so as not to arouse attention. She wished her stomach wouldn't tie up in knots when she was nervous.

Nyelda and Bessa had agreed to do the switch one more time, though neither was pleased with the idea. Nyelda and the other kitchen girl would be back up soon to collect the trays. Jaci drained her glass, mentally reviewing the path to her mother's old room for the hundredth time. Nyelda had told her that Ione would leave a lit, shuttered lantern just inside the door of the pantry for her to use in navigating the dark corridors.

Jaci pushed her plate away, unable to eat any more. Mandy and Allina had finished their meals and were hovering in the back of the room, waiting to help her out of her dress. Taking a deep breath to calm her butterflies, Jaci rose.

Three sharp raps on the door froze her in place. That was definitely not the kitchen girl's knock. Before Mandy could get to the door, it flew open, and Castellan Felgarth marched in. Mandy and Allina immediately dropped into curtsies.

Jaci caught the flash of terror in their eyes before they bowed their heads, and Mandy's words about being frightened all the time slid through her mind. Anger rose within her. How dare these monsters terrorize people this way?

"Castellan Felgarth," Jaci said coolly, her anger smoothing the nervousness out of her voice. "What brings you here at this hour?"

"Forgive the intrusion," the castellan said, oozing false penitence, "but Lord Galenock wishes to speak with you."

Jaci nearly lost her composure. "Now?" Did they know? How could they have found out?

A cruel little smile played over the castellan's lips. "Yes. *Now.*"

Jaci searched for a way to refuse, but couldn't think of any excuse that wouldn't have unpleasant consequences. Hiding her fear behind an icy smile, she said, "Of course, if that's what he wishes." She swept her arm toward the door. "After you."

He inclined his head, then turned on his heel and left the room. Jaci gave the girls a quick smile on her way out, hoping it might reassure them that she would be okay, though she was more worried about them than she was about herself. If Galenock had discovered their plan, the girls, Nyelda, and Bessa would suffer the most.

Jaci followed the castellan down the hall, accompanied by the two guards. She wondered where they were going this time. They were headed in the opposite direction from the way that had led to the library and music room. What could Galenock want? He'd said they'd speak again, so maybe this was nothing other than very bad timing... but then again, if he *had* somehow found out what they were planning... No, she wouldn't go there. To keep from scaring herself with speculation, she concentrated on memorizing the path they walked and the turns they made.

They passed no one in the halls, and a short time later, they arrived at another door. Castellan Felgarth knocked twice and let her into a spacious chamber, very similar to the sitting room of her guest chamber, but quite a bit larger and much more opulently furnished, with a color scheme of blue and gold. The castellan gave her a mock bow, then closed the door and left. She heard his footsteps fading down the hall. She had the wild urge to bolt for the door and make a run for it, but dismissed the idea immediately, knowing the two guards would still be out there.

She glanced around, looking for Galenock, but the room was empty. Where was he? Shivering with a sudden chill, Jaci crossed to the large fireplace that occupied half the left side of the room. She stood with her back to it and let the heat from the roaring fire sink into her bones.

A door opened on the far side of the room, and Galenock emerged from an adjoining chamber. Jaci caught sight of what looked like the corner of a bed, and another wave of coldness chilled her. Galenock had dressed in green this time, his velvet robes threaded with gold. The *druidainoch* stone he'd taken from Queen Selendria seemed to sparkle iridescently in the firelight. He approached Jaci with a wolfish smile.

Anger crept up inside Jaci again, her cheeks growing hot with outrage. His wearing that stone was an insult to her family. He'd murdered her aunt and uncle and cousin, then stolen their throne. The indecision she'd felt earlier vanished. She'd see him pay for his crimes, no matter what she had to do.

"Ah, Jacinda. Please forgive the lateness of the hour. I've been wanting to resume our conversation, but have only now found the time." He took her hand and raised it to his lips.

Jacinda stifled the impulse to wipe her hand off on her dress. "I'm sure you're quite busy."

"Yes. Let us go sit on the divan, shall we?"

Warning flags sprang up in Jaci's mind. Was he going to try to seduce her?

She smiled sweetly. "If you don't mind, I'd like to stay here by the fire a while longer. I'm a bit chilly."

"Of course," he said, a hint of displeasure in his eyes. "Have you remembered anything more since we last talked?"

"No, I haven't." Jaci began to breathe easier. This appeared to be another round of twenty questions, rather than an interrogation concerning her 'roaming-the-castle-at-night' activities. The women who had helped her should be safe.

"That is unfortunate," Galenock said. He regarded her a moment with that calculating look that made the hair on the back of her neck stand on end. "The men who found you in Wolf Run — where were they taking you?"

"I don't know," Jaci said truthfully. "They didn't say."

"Did they mention my name?"

"No. In fact, they talked very little. They communicated mostly with hand gestures that I didn't understand."

"I see." He paused again, eyes searching her face. "Your resemblance to Deirdre is truly remarkable, but you also bear a striking resemblance to Soneira."

He was watching her closely, no doubt looking for a reaction. Jaci assumed a blank look. "Who?"

"Soneira — a young woman who once lived in this castle. She and Deirdre were sisters."

"You speak of them in the past tense."

"Sadly, Soneira died years ago. The man who you say rescued you was responsible for her death."

"Was he?" Jaci struggled to keep a look of only mild interest. "What did he do to her?"

"Nasty lover's quarrel. When he found out that Soneira, the woman he loved, loved someone else, he snapped. Very tragic. Those men are all murderous outlaws. You are fortunate that my men found you and were able to rescue you."

"Yes. Thank you. I had no idea." *Liar!* she fumed silently. "What happened to Deirdre?"

"She vanished nineteen years ago. Her disappearance is a mystery we've not yet solved — an enigma, like you." Galenock walked around her, from one side to the other. "The questions you arouse are many. If you are Deirdre, do you really have amnesia, or are you playing games? If you are not, then who are you, and how is it you look so much like her?" He stopped in front of her and stroked his beard. "And where did you come from? Absolutely no one in Tarshane speaks like you, which leads me to believe you come from somewhere else — where, I don't know. That only brings me to another question. How did you get to Wolf Run — a wild place out in the middle of nowhere?"

"I'm sorry, I can't answer your questions."

"Can't or won't?"

"Are you saying you don't believe me?"

He started pacing again. "Do you want to know what I think? I think you *are* Deirdre. I'm sure you recognized my *druidainoch* stone, which once belonged to your mother. I think you were sent somewhere by Soneira, your sister, using a portal Elshaer helped her create — magic they selfishly kept to themselves. And I think you've only just now found a way to return, but then, you never did have any magical talent to speak of." He stopped again before her. "Am I correct?"

Jaci held his gaze steadily, her anger simmering at the scorn in his voice. "My name is Jacinda. As to your other questions, I couldn't say. I have amnesia."

Galenock smiled in amusement. "You still insist on playing games? Age has given you spunk" — he eyed her up and down — "along with some other desirable attributes."

An angry blush rose in her cheeks again, and she had to bite her tongue to keep from telling him what she thought of him. She couldn't risk any slip that might condemn those that had been helping her.

He cupped her cheek, then lifted her chin to examine her profile. "The truth is that it doesn't matter what you call yourself. If I say you are Deirdre, then you will be Deirdre, to me and to everyone else in Tarshane." He let go of her chin. "The princess returning from afar. The people will have their *beloved*" — he sneered the word — "royal family again. You and I will marry, and I will be king!"

"You can't force me to marry you," Jaci snapped.

"Oh, yes, I can." He gripped her upper arm. "You seem to have forgotten that I rule here, and you are at my mercy." He pulled her closer. "And I would like a taste of our future marital bliss, right now."

"Well, I wouldn't." Jaci stomped on his foot and twisted in his grasp.

He snarled in pain and snatched at her with his other hand, jerking her toward him at the same moment she yanked away. Her dress tore off her shoulder, not quite exposing her breast, but revealing her *druidainoch* stone. Surprise and perplexity flitted across his face, then he shouted in triumph. He'd seen the copper key.

Jaci's self-defense training took over. She lunged toward him and speared him in the throat with rigid fingers. He choked and stumbled to the side, clutching his throat. She kicked him hard in the groin, ripped Selendria's stone off over his head, then smashed her elbow into his jaw. He spun around and fell into the fireplace.

He screamed as the fire blinded him, the flames searing his skin and igniting his robes.

Jaci leaped back, horrified. She hadn't meant for that to happen. Galenock scrambled on his knees out of the fire, his robes aflame, his hair melting to ash, the skin of his hands and face red and blistering.

Don't just stand there — move! her brain prodded her. Sickened, she dashed to the door. Just as she reached it, the guards burst into the room.

"Galenock is hurt! He needs you!" she cried, pointing to where he was rolling on the floor, his robes still burning.

They rushed to his aid.

Gripping Selendria's *druidainoch* stone in her hand, Jaci ran out the door.

She raced through the empty corridors, following the way back to her guest room. She didn't dare stop there, though. She had to get to Miri's room. Now.

She flew past the guest room and on toward the kitchen. She heard shouting behind her, and the distant thump of running feet in pursuit. She stumbled down the last set of stairs and almost fell into the kitchen, catching herself on a table, her chest heaving as she tried to catch her breath. Bessa and the kitchen workers ceased what they were doing and stared.

Bessa took a step toward her, eyeing her torn dress. "Are you hurt, child?"

"No. Hide — all of you!" Jaci gasped out into the silence. "Before the guards come through... and question you... about where I went."

The clamor of approaching soldiers floated into the kitchen. The workers' eyes widened in terror, and they scattered for the exits.

"Will you be all right?" Bessa asked anxiously.

"Yes. Now go, and thank you," Jaci said, touched by the woman's concern.

"Gods be with you," Bessa whispered, then hastened after the scullions.

Jaci gathered herself and dashed to the pantry, relief wobbling her knees when she found the lantern. *Thank you, Ione!* Opening one of the shutters, she raced through the darkened corridors toward her mother's old room. "Up the stairs, around to the left, at the end of the hall turn right..."

She whispered the directions as she ran, sending fervent thanks to the chamber girls for pinning up her dress. When she finally reached the door to Miri's room, she shifted Selendria's stone to her lantern hand, whipped the pendant chain from around her neck, and found the key. She was shaking so badly, she could hardly make it fit in the lock.

The stomp of many running feet reached her ears, coming from her left, then a guttural voice from the right shouted, "This way!"

Castellan Felgarth! How had he known where she was going? Had Galenock recognized Miri's room key on her chain?

Panicking, Jaci stabbed the key at the lock, got it into the hole on the third try, and unlocked the door. She pulled the key out, darted inside, and locked the door again. Draping the pendant chain back around her neck, she ran across the room to the grandfather clock. *Please, please let this work!*

She held the lantern up close to the glass front. The glass seemed dark, shadowed, with faint long lines tracing upward at an angle from the bottom to most of the way up to the top of the left side of the glass, as if some long, thin things leaned against a wall. Something bulky and darker filled the right side of the glass. *Yes!* There was an etching. But what in the world was it?

Thud! A shoulder crashed into the door.

Jaci whirled, just managing to swallow her shriek.

"Break it down!" the castellan ordered.

Another thud. The hinges groaned, but held.

Jaci turned back to the clock and whispered, *"Saelarin."*

The familiar electrical charge zinged the air around the clock. With a sob of relief, Jaci pressed the release mechanism, and the back of the clock opened. Shuttering the lantern and clutching it to her, she crammed herself into the tiny space and pulled the back shut.

Thud! She felt the room shudder, heard the chamber door crack. Then silence.

CHAPTER 15

Talan paced the floor of Cranton's study, racking his brain for a workable plan to get himself and the Black Banders into the castle. They'd arrived in Cranton's wine cellar two hours ago, having followed Willem's map without difficulty. They'd eaten the hearty dinner Zaiya had cooked and discussed various ways to breach the castle gate, but with the heightened security, none were likely to be successful. He knew his men would follow him anywhere, but he would not risk their lives unless there was at least a slim chance of achieving their goal. After dinner, the Black Banders had retired to the cellar, and he and Cranton had gone to Cranton's study to continue working on a solution.

Cranton poured himself a glass of red wine and sat in a high-backed chair near the fire. "Wearing a path in my carpet is not going to solve the problem, Talan. Sit down, relax, have some wine. Your mind will work better."

"I can't sit down, and I'm sorry, but the wine will cloud my thoughts, not sharpen them." Talan raked a hand through his hair. "There has to be a way in that won't leave most of us dead."

Cranton took a deep swallow. "I cannot believe how much she looked like Deirdre."

Talan said nothing. The last thing he wanted was to reminisce.

"You know the girls used to come here often — Soneira and Deirdre — to visit my daughters when they were all growing up. In fact, they were here not a month before —"

"Cranton, please." Talan tried to keep the rough edge out of his voice, but couldn't.

"Talan, you need to talk about them. It's been nineteen years. You need to grieve and let go, to ease the pain in your heart before it kills you."

Talan turned away, shaken by the raw anguish the mere mention of their names always brought. He clenched his fists. "Sometime, perhaps, but not now. I have to concentrate on finding a way to get Jacinda out. Every moment she is in there, the danger to her grows. I can't let Galenock do to her what he did to... It may already be too late."

"What happened to Soneira was not your fault. You have to stop blaming yourself. I know this sounds harsh, and it pains me to say it, but she knowingly chose the wrong path, and she paid the price."

Even as he rose to defend her, Talan knew in his soul it was true. "She didn't — she wasn't —" He stopped. He didn't even know what he was trying to say, his thoughts fragmenting beneath a mountain's weight of guilt. "If I had been there —"

"You would be dead, too."

Talan turned away again, Cranton's words of quiet sorrow echoing in his ears. "It would have been better that way," he whispered.

The opening of the front door out in the foyer ended their conversation. They heard voices talking, then Quinton burst into the study, followed by Zaiya.

"Grandfather, something is happening up at the castle," Quinton said breathlessly. "Everything is in an uproar. The streets are full of Riders. They are emptying the taverns and telling everyone to go home, saying there is a curfew, starting immediately. They chased my friends and me out of the Whiskey Barrel just now."

"You'd best be getting home, then — quickly," Cranton said, his voice tense.

Quinton nodded. "I'm on my way, but I had to stop and tell you."

"Thank you," Cranton said.

Cranton and Zaiya accompanied him to the front door. Talan followed as far as the hall leading into the foyer.

"Take care!" the older couple called after their grandson as he rushed out the door and blended into the streams of people hurrying to their homes.

Cranton closed and bolted the door, then stood with his back to it, his face pale. "You'd best hide in the cellar," he said to Talan, "and be ready to go back into the tunnels, in case the soldiers start going door to door to see that their curfew is being observed."

Talan shook his head. "I need to know what's happened."

"You can't go out there. I won't let you."

Talan stepped toward his friend. "I have to know."

Zaiya joined her husband at the door. "Talan, no, you can't!"

Cranton gestured toward the door. "You heard what Quinton said. The streets are full of Riders. How do you know they're not looking for *you*? They may have somehow discovered you're in the city. If you go out there now, you will join your Jacinda as a prisoner in the castle. How will you rescue her then?"

"At least I'd be inside the castle."

"You'd be in his dungeon, strapped to a rack, or whatever hideous device he has down there," Cranton said. "Listen to reason!"

Talan raked his hand through his hair again. "But what if this has something to do with —"

A muffled thump silenced him.

"What was that?" Zaiya asked in a small voice.

"I don't know," Cranton said. "Was it outside?"

The three of them glanced about, searching for the source of the noise.

"I don't think so." Talan looked down the hall behind him, his hand on the hilt of the knife at his belt. "It sounded like it came from back there."

Cranton moved up beside him. "One of your men coming up from the cellar?"

"Perhaps..." Why did he feel a strange aura swirling through the air, as if someone had cast a magic spell? A sudden fear froze his blood. *Galenock? No, he can't be here. How will I protect Cranton and Zaiya?* He concentrated, trying to keep his wits about him through his rising panic. *No, it's not Galenock — that's not his aura. But whose is it, then?* As far as he knew, the only others who could cast spells were the Enchantresses.

Another faint bump sounded.

"Stay back," Talan warned. Making certain his friends were well behind him, he trod silently down the hall.

*****

Jaci shoved what felt like a piece of clothing hanging on a wall out of her face and tried to assess her situation. She couldn't see a thing. It seemed she'd traded one tiny, cramped, dark space for another. A jumble of hard objects littered the floor beneath her feet. Every time she moved, she stepped on something unstable and stumbled against a wall. The confined space was so small, she couldn't even stretch her arms out full length, and she'd already bumped her head on a board that stuck out from one of the walls.

She pulled her torn sleeve back up over her shoulder for the tenth time and forced herself to relax. She tried to open the shutter on the lantern, but it had stuck fast, and she couldn't see to tell what was wrong with it. Grumbling under her breath, she groped around with her other hand and found something tall and skinny, like what she'd seen in the etching in the glass door of the clock. She ran her hand up and down it — hard like wood, smooth, round — it felt like a broomstick. Was she... in a *closet*?

She shifted her feet. Whatever she was standing on slipped sideways, and she fell back against the wall. Then the wall was yanked away, and she fell backward with a cry into a pair of strong arms. A familiar masculine scent filled her senses; warm tingles like an electrical current shivered through her body. She knew who held her even before she heard his exclamation of stunned disbelief.

"Jacinda!"

Talan. Her heart leaped — *He's alive! I can't believe I found him!* — then sank — *Oh, no, the letter!*

He lifted her onto her feet, and keeping one hand on her arm, took the lantern from her and set it on the floor. He seemed reluctant to let go of her, as if he feared she might disappear if he did. "Are you all right?" he asked.

Before she could answer, the torn sleeve of her dress slid off her shoulder again, and Talan's eyes burned with the same frightening fury she'd seen at the river.

His hold on her arm tightened. *"Did he hurt you?"*

"No!" Jaci said quickly, knowing what he was asking. She shook her head. "No one hurt me. I'm fine."

His grip eased. He took a breath, and she could feel him gathering himself, getting his anger under control.

She hitched her sleeve back up and held it in place, keeping her pendant chain covered, glad her sleeve hadn't slid far enough down to reveal what hung from it. She'd also managed to keep Selendria's *druidainoch* stone hidden in her clenched fist when Talan had taken the lantern from her. She wasn't ready, yet, to talk about the copper key or the stone, or where she'd gotten them.

A gray-haired couple came up beside Talan. They both stared at her in astonishment. They looked vaguely familiar — a memory snapped into her mind: the older couple, coming out of the house with the hawks and the red square on the door, the day the red-cloaked Riders had brought her into the city. They'd given her that same look they were giving her now. The red square — she'd been right! It was the same square that was on the parchment.

"How in Brackan's name did you get in our closet?" the man asked.

"Through a magic portal," Jaci said. "It's a very long story, but I don't have time to explain. Galenock's men are after me. I have to get out of here!" She stifled a squeal as Katar, knife in hand, and three other muscular men appeared at the other end of the hall, drawn by the commotion. Black Banders, she realized with relief.

"Check the tunnels, make sure they are clear," Talan ordered. "We'll be leaving shortly."

Katar and the Black Banders disappeared back the way they'd come.

Talan turned back to Jaci. "How did you make the portal work?"

"I said the magic word."

"You worked magic?" he asked in amazement. "I felt the aura of a spell being cast, but I had no idea —"

"Wait!" Jaci interrupted. "I felt an aura, too, around the clock when I said the word. How long does the aura last? Will Galenock be able to feel it and find the portal? And end up here?"

Zaiya gasped. "No!"

Talan looked grim. "The aura usually dissipates quickly. I can no longer feel it here, so it should be gone from wherever you were. Was he near you at the time?"

"No, but his men were." She shuddered. All she could see was Galenock thrashing on the floor, burning.

He bent closer. "Are you sure you're all right?"

She nodded, warmth stealing through her at the concern in his voice. "I'm fine." Outside, rapid hoofbeats clattered past the house. Jaci tensed and looked toward the front door. "How are we going to get out of the city?"

"We're going underneath it." Talan picked up the lantern and led her down the hall and through a kitchen toward another door.

The older couple followed.

"Cranton, I will leave Katar and the Black Banders with you as a precaution," Talan said. "I don't think you need to worry. If Galenock could find the portal, I think he would have already, but to be safe, I'll have them put a lock on the closet door to prevent your being caught by surprise. If nothing happens in the next few days, you can send them back to me. They will know where to find me."

"But Talan, there is only one map," Cranton said. "How will they get back?"

"I will leave the map. I don't need it. I remember the way." Talan turned to Jaci. "Can you swim?"

"Swim?" Jaci repeated, surprised. "Yes. Why? Are we crossing a river or something? I thought you said we were going underground."

"There is a water-filled tunnel we will have to swim through."

"We have to swim underwater? Okay, I can do that." She looked down at herself. "But not in this dress."

He halted before the door and eyed her dress, momentarily at a loss.

The gray-haired woman took Jaci by the hand. "Come with me." She led Jaci toward another hall off the kitchen. "We will only be a few minutes. Cranton, dear, pack them some food to take with them."

The older woman brought Jaci to a cozy bedroom lit by a single candle.

"Let's get that dress off you, now," she said and helped Jaci remove the garment. "My name is Zaiya, by the way."

"I'm Jacinda — Jaci for short. Thank you, Zaiya, for your help."

"You're quite welcome, dear."

Jaci slid out of her shift while the older woman pulled some pieces of clothing from a chest of drawers and tossed them onto the bed beside Jaci — a soft, warm undershirt; a dark green, lace-up overshirt; dark brown pants; and a brown leather belt.

"These are my husband's, but I think they will work if you roll up the sleeves and wear a belt," Zaiya said, as Jaci hastily donned the clothes. Jaci covertly pulled Soneira's spellbook out of her stocking and slid the book and Selendria's stone into the pants' pockets.

"Now, let's see about those trouser legs." Zaiya took a pair of scissors from a drawer in the vanity next to the chest and trimmed several inches from the pant legs. "There, how is that?"

"That's great," Jaci said. She cinched the belt as tight as she could. "What will you do with the dress? I wouldn't want anyone to find it here."

"We'll burn it as soon as you and Talan leave." Zaiya stood before Jaci and looked in her eyes. "When I first saw you a few days ago, I could have sworn you were Deirdre, but looking at you now, I can see the differences."

"What do you see?"

"Your eyes are brighter, bolder. More like Soneira's, but without the guile."

"Are you ready?" Cranton called from the kitchen.

"Yes," she called back. "We will be right out." She clasped Jaci's hand. "I wish we could talk more, dear. I would love to hear all about you. Go gently with Talan. He is a fine young man, but his heart holds so much pain. I think you will be good for him." She patted Jaci's hand, then headed back to the kitchen.

Jaci followed, puzzled. *What does she mean 'I'll be good for him'?*

Talan, now carrying a light pack on his back, stood waiting for her at the door. After Zaiya had given Jaci a pair of sturdy boots to slip on, Talan hugged the old woman and Cranton. "Thank you for all you've done. Send word to me if there is trouble, or if you need anything."

"We will," Cranton said.

Zaiya kissed him on the cheek. "You're welcome, dear. Take care of yourself." She glanced at Jaci. "And our young lady."

"I will," Talan promised. He picked up the lantern and handed it to Jaci. "Watch your step." Then he opened the door and descended into the cellar.

With a quick thank you to Cranton and Zaiya, Jaci trod carefully down the stone stairs, her way lit by the lantern light from below. Part way down, Talan took her arm and guided her over the last few uneven steps.

The wine cellar stretched some twenty feet to her left and even farther to her right. Massive casks and racks filled with dusty bottles lined the walls. Smaller kegs and freestanding racks of bottles trailed through the interior space, creating haphazard passages throughout the cellar. Katar and the Black Banders waited silently about halfway down one of the right side passages.

Talan led Jaci a few steps to the right, then halted.

"Wait here for a minute. I must speak with Katar."

Jaci watched him as he and Katar conversed in low voices. She still couldn't believe he'd been here at the exact moment she'd needed him. Why was he even in the city? From what Mandy had said, it would be suicidal for him to come here. Her breath caught. Was he here for her? Had he come to try to rescue her? Warmth rose through her body again, blushing her cheeks. That he would risk so much for her...

But what if that wasn't why he was here? What if he had come for something else entirely? She frowned, wondering why she suddenly felt forlorn. What was the matter with her, anyway? It didn't matter why he was here, as long as he helped her escape the city. Maybe she could get him and his men to take her to the Enchantresses, since that was where Mandy seemed to think she should go. They must know how to find the castle in the mountains where Mandy had said they lived, and she would feel much safer traveling with them. She wouldn't even mind being around Nickalonis. He might be a womanizer, but compared to Galenock —

She stopped in mid-thought, the warmth in her body turning to ice as her brain finally registered the absence of Nickalonis and Solon. She'd had the impression they always traveled with Talan. Had they been hurt or killed in the Riders' attack? She clenched the handle of the lantern in worry.

Talan finished his conversation, and he and his men strode swiftly toward her. Katar and the Black Banders passed by and mounted the steps to the kitchen.

Talan stopped beside her. "Come. This way."

He led her through the maze of kegs and bottle racks and around a corner to the right. The cellar extended much farther than she'd realized, spanning another thirty feet before hooking to the left. This end of the cellar lay swathed in darkness, past the range of the burning lanterns pegged along the walls.

He stopped again and reached for the lantern she carried. "May I?"

She let him take it. "The shutter is stuck." She'd probably squeezed it too hard when she'd jammed herself into the clock.

He examined the shutters, straightened a bent piece, and opened it. Light glowed around them, illuminating several tarp-covered piles strewn between the kegs and racks. After checking the oil level and the burning wick, he adjusted the shutters until only small streams of light showed through the cracks.

"We'll be moving through the sewer system beneath the city," he said. "The sewer tunnels connect with another series of tunnels out beyond. Once we are away from the city, we can talk, but until then we have to be as silent as possible — light steps and no words." He made his way around the piles, heading toward the back corner of the cellar.

Jaci hurried after him. "Okay, but before we go, there's something I have to know."

"What is it?" he asked over his shoulder.

"Solon and Nickalonis — they're not here. Are they all right? Or were they hurt when those Riders attacked?"

"They were not hurt. They are in other places." Talan slipped between two of the huge casks lining the walls.

Jaci eased through behind him. "What about Barayan? He tried to lead the Riders away from me, and he took an arrow in his leg, and... please tell me he's not dead."

"No, he lives. He was badly hurt, but he is recovering."

"Thank God," Jaci breathed. "I was worried..." She trailed off. "What are you doing?"

Talan had lifted the lantern high and was running his fingers along the wall above his head. "Somewhere up here, there is a —"

Jaci heard a click. With a faint grinding noise, a four-foot-wide by six-foot-tall section of the stone wall swung outward into what, judging by the smell, must be the sewer.

"One last question?" Jaci said quickly.

He peered out into the sewer tunnel, moving the lantern so he could see better. "Yes?"

"How did you happen to be here?"

He started to look back toward her, hesitated, then fiddled with the lantern instead. Jaci had the impression he was deliberately avoiding looking at her.

"We were trying to figure out a way to get you out of the castle."

"You really were trying to rescue me," Jaci said softly, a warm, sort of bubbly, irrationally happy feeling effervescing through her.

"Fortunately for us, you rescued yourself." He sounded impressed.

She touched his arm. "Thank you." She caught his eyes for a brief moment, felt the anguish rise within him.

He looked away. "You're welcome." Then he stepped out into the sewer.

CHAPTER 16

They crept through the sewer tunnels for hours. Night had long since fallen. Exhausted from the previous night's sleeplessness and the stress of her confrontation with Galenock, Jaci did her best to move stealthily and not slosh through the grungy, knee-deep water or slip on the flat, slimy edge stones. They halted frequently, listening, then easing past innumerable storm drains, shuttering their lantern to hide its faint glow until they were well beyond the openings. The smells curdled Jaci's stomach. She refused to think about what might be swirling around in the water she was slogging through.

An almost nonstop parade of cantering horses and running or marching feet pounded the streets overhead. It seemed Galenock had sent out his entire army to hunt her down. Shouts and the occasional frightened cry or scream of pain filtered down to them through the storm drains, some near, some distant, all terrifying.

Please let those who helped me be all right, Jaci thought. She moved closer to Talan, grateful for his presence.

Talan rounded a corner and halted, and she nearly ran into him. He put a finger to his lips for silence, closed the lantern, and pointed to a storm drain just ahead of them, a dim, oblong shape against the dark of the sewer. Stumbling footsteps had stopped beside it, up in the street. More footsteps strode near, approaching from both sides.

Jaci and Talan ducked back behind the corner and peered around it at the storm drain.

In the street above the drain, a guttural voice growled, "What are you doing out here after curfew?"

A slurred voice responded. "I wazsh on my way home... but lozsht... I got lozsht."

A woman giggled, sounding mildly intoxicated. "I told him it was the other way, but he wouldn't listen." She and the drunk man spoke with the lilt of Shiannora.

"Do we bring her?" another guttural voice asked.

"Lord Galenock said bring all women, small built, with dark hair," the first soldier said. "Take her."

Jaci heard the scrape and thrash of a struggle, then the woman screamed.

"Shut your mouth or I shut it for you," the second soldier barked.

Several people strode away, the sound of their heavy footsteps dwindling.

"Let go... her of... !" the drunk man yelled. "Bring... her back!"

The first soldier laughed nastily. "You will not need her, you Shiannoran dung heap. Do you not know the penalty for being out after curfew?"

Metal rasped.

"No... I... wait!" the drunk man cried, then he groaned.

Something heavy hit the ground with a sickening thud. A dark liquid trickled through the storm drain and dripped into the sewer water below.

Jaci clapped her hand over her mouth to keep from crying out. Talan's arms went around her, and he drew her away from the corner, holding her against him as if he would shield her from the brutality. The familiar tingling enveloped her, strangely soothing this time instead of galvanizing, swathing her in layers of warmth and protection. She laid her head on his chest and closed her eyes, letting the sweetness enfold her.

She heard the tread of the other soldiers walking away, then silence descended.

"They took her because they thought she might be me," Jaci whispered, tears brimming. "What will they do to her?"

"I don't know. When they see she is not you, hopefully they will let her go."

Jaci tried to hold back her tears, but she couldn't stop a few from sliding down her cheeks. "They're monsters — all of them!"

"Yes." He stroked her hair. "Don't worry. I'll not let them take you again."

Jaci wiped her eyes. "Thank you. I'd be lost without you."

He let go and stepped back, eyes averted, all at once seeming miles away from her. "If you are all right, we should keep going."

"I—I'm okay," she said, disconcerted by his sudden shift in manner.

He led the way back around the corner, past the storm drain still leaking blood, and on through the tunnels.

She followed, confused as much by her own feelings as by his abrupt withdrawal. For a few moments, he'd seemed to truly care for her, and she had to admit, as intimidating as he was sometimes, she could have stayed within the tender circle of his arms until the sun stopped rising. The realization both scared and tantalized her.

But why had he let go so suddenly? Her heart thudded to the floor. *In his mind, he was probably holding Soneira and not me.* That hurt much more than it should have, and in her exhaustion, she had to fight back another round of tears. *It doesn't matter,* she rebuked herself sharply. *You're not staying in this world. Once Galenock is defeated, you're going home.*

*****

An hour deeper into the tunnels, Jaci splashed out of the stinking water and up onto the fouled rocks, too tired to move quietly anymore. Her foot slipped on the slick stones, and she would have fallen if Talan hadn't caught her arm and steadied her.

"I can't go any further," she said between breaths. "Can we rest for a few minutes... please?"

"The door to the outer tunnels is just down here," he said, leading her a few steps further along the sewer wall. "Once we're through, we can stop."

They continued on another dozen feet, then Talan reached up above his head and pressed a slight depression in the rock wall. A door grated outward into darkness. They stepped through into another set of tunnels, this one clean and dry and fresher smelling. Talan pushed the door shut, the lock clicking into place.

He gave a long exhale. "Now we can rest." He drew her around a bend to a cleft in the wall. It was narrow at the top, then about three feet from the ground it widened from a thin crack into a two-foot triangular opening at its base. "We should be safe in here. I'm sorry we have to enter this way, but follow me." He got down on the floor and, holding the lantern in front of him, wormed his way through the opening.

"You've got to be kidding me," Jaci muttered under her breath. The tunnel darkened around her as the lantern light dimmed, blocked by Talan's body. Seeing the creeping darkness close in, she suddenly felt very alone. She dropped to all fours and crawled through the hole.

She found herself in a cavern the size of a small bedroom. A brown tarp and two wooden crates lay against the side wall. Talan gave her a hand up, then shook out the tarp and glanced through the crates. Jaci wasn't sure if he was checking out the supplies or looking for vermin. She hoped it was the former. Apparently satisfied, he shoved a square block of stone in front of the opening to seal the entrance. The crack above it was filled with mortar, so no lantern light would be visible out in the tunnels to give away their presence.

Talan spread out the tarp so they could sit, holding part of it up along the wall until Jaci sat down and put her back against it. Wet and cold and exhausted, she draped one edge around her shoulder like a blanket.

Talan shrugged off the pack of food from Cranton and Zaiya and sat beside her. "Are you hungry?"

"I'm too tired to eat." *And too filthy*, she thought to herself. She tipped her head back against the wall and closed her eyes.

Completely spent, she drifted, half-in, half-out of sleep, kept awake by her own shivering. She felt herself being lifted; strong arms drew her close. Hardly aware of what she was doing, she leaned into his warmth, her ear against his chest, her mind lulled by his steady heartbeat.

"*Mirochnae...* sleep," he whispered.

Feeling warm and safe, she slipped into oblivion.

* * * * *

A gentle touch on her hair woke her. She blinked for a moment, confused, then her memory sharpened, and she realized her position. She was sitting sideways in Talan's lap. He'd wrapped the tarp around them both to conserve warmth. Blood rose in her cheeks as she sat up.

"Forgive me for moving you," he said, avoiding her eyes as he helped her shift onto the tarp beside him, "but I feared you would take ill from the cold."

"It's okay," she said quickly. She took a deep breath, trying to calm her unruly emotions. "Thanks. I'm much warmer... and I slept a lot more than I would have... otherwise." She was still tired, but she definitely felt better. "Do you know what time it is?"

"I'd guess a little past sunrise, though I don't know for certain." He handed her the pack from Cranton and Zaiya. "We'll eat, then head out."

"Where are we going?" She pulled out two small water flasks and poured a bit of water on her hands from one of them to wash off some of the grime. Then, trying not to think about her still dirty hands, she broke off chunks of bread and cheese and gave the pack back to him.

"These tunnels lead to a cave beneath a gristmill, owned by a cousin of Cranton's — the man whose house you were in last night. Solon and four of the Black Banders are there waiting for us." Talan took out a portion and began to eat.

"Who are the Black Banders, exactly?" Jaci asked between bites.

"They were members of King Brannad's Elite Corps — experts in weaponry and combat. They fight for me now, in hopes of one day overthrowing Galenock." Talan sighed. "Our rebel band was once several hundred strong, with what was left of the king's regular army and the Black Banders. We had some successes in the beginning, but over the years our numbers dwindled, and truth be told, we're not much more than an annoyance to Galenock now. We could never get much help from the townspeople. They were too terrified of Galenock to risk defiance, and they had families to protect." Talan's voice had grown quiet.

Jaci put her hand on his arm. "I'm sorry for what you've had to bear. Mandy — one of the chamber girls — told me what happened to the royal family, though she didn't know all the details."

He finally met her eyes. "Who are you? Please — I must know."

Jaci took another deep breath, shaken again by the depth of his anguish. "I'll be honest with you. My name is Jacinda — that much was true. I don't have amnesia. I only said that because I didn't think you would believe me if I told the truth. I came here accidentally from another world, through a magic portal. My mother's name was Miri. Ione, one of the other castle workers, told me my mother's real name was Mirinesstra, and that she came from this land."

"The lost queen. I guessed as much when I saw your *druidainoch* stone, though I dared not believe it."

"My mother never told me. I never knew there was another world out there that she'd been a part of. She gave me the stone two years ago... right before she died."

"Mirinesstra is dead?" His countenance fell, and Jaci knew he must have been thinking about the possibility of the lost queen returning to Tarshane. He roused himself. "I'm sorry for your loss. How did it happen?"

Jaci looked down and twisted a remnant of bread between her fingers. "My father died in an accident when I was nine. I don't think my mother ever fully recovered from her grief. She lived many years afterward, but when she came down with pneumonia, she kept talking about going to be with him in the afterlife. She had no wish to live anymore. She let the illness take her..." Jaci closed her eyes, fighting back the tears that burned her eyelids.

"It must have been very hard for you."

She nodded, getting her emotions back under control.

He took a drink from one of the flasks. "If you didn't know this world existed, how did you find it?"

Jaci shot him a glance, dreading having to tell him. "That is a very long story — one that I fear will be more painful for you than for me."

His brows furrowed slightly, and he seemed both puzzled and apprehensive. "Please tell me."

Reluctantly, she told him about Deirdre.

His face became a mask of stone. "So Deirdre is dead, too." He tipped his head back against the wall and closed his eyes. "Oh, gods, no," he whispered, his mask breaking as he fought back tears of his own.

Jaci gasped as his agony pierced her own heart, and she felt him drowning in a well of grief and guilt.

She threw her arms around him and held him tight. "I'm so sorry."

He clasped her close, his body racked by silent sobs. After a few minutes, he quieted. He drew back and wiped his face on his sleeve. "I had so hoped she was still alive somewhere, and after reading the diary you gave me..." He trailed off, his emotions raw. He wiped his face again and pulled himself together. "The diary — have you read it?"

"Yes."

"Toward the end, it mentions a key. Do you know anything about it — what it looks like, where it is?"

Jaci pulled her pendant chain out of her shirt and held up the key she'd found with the diary.

He caught his breath. "The key to Ridaur's crypt. You do have it." He cupped his fingers around her hand and the key. "I can feel the evil in it." He gripped her shoulders. "Does Galenock know you have it?"

She nodded, fear crawling over her. "He saw it, right before I escaped."

Talan's face grew grim. "We need to get you as far away from here as possible."

He snatched up a spare lantern from one of the crates, made sure the oil font was full, and lit it. Then he put out the other lantern, filled it from a container of oil he found in the second crate, and relit it. Shouldering his pack, he shoved the rock away from the opening. He picked up the lanterns, handing one to Jaci. "As soon as we're into the tunnels, you can tell me everything."

CHAPTER 17

"You knocked him into the *fire?*" Talan stopped short in the middle of the tunnel.

Jaci turned back. His look of utter amazement was priceless. "I didn't mean to. That's just where he happened to fall after I hit him."

"You *hit* him — *Galenock?*"

"Yes. Twice, as a matter of fact. And I kicked him, too. Right where it hurts. His intentions toward me were not in the least gentlemanly, and I was furious with him anyway after hearing what he'd done to the royal family, which — which is *my* family." She was still having a hard time getting her head around that notion. "And the way he was talking to me was so scornful and condescending… but then his robes caught fire, and his hair, and his hands and face were all red and blistering, and he was screaming…" She shivered. "It was horrible."

Talan started walking again. "Then what did you do?"

"The guards burst into the room, so I told them Galenock needed help, which was obvious, so when they went to help him, I ran — all the way to the clock. From there, I ended up in Cranton and Zaiya's closet." She'd told him the entire story as they'd hurried through the tunnels, from her getting lost and ending up in Marston only to witness Deirdre's accident and be transported through the clock in the Brunswick house, to seeing the portrait of the royal family and finding the clock in Miri's old room, so that she could make her escape. She'd described her meetings with Galenock and related everything that had happened during her stay in Castle d'Gaire. Well, everything except two small details. Was she ready to share them?

"There is one other thing," she said after a few moments' thought. "This." She drew the stone she'd taken from Galenock out of her pocket. The stone's iridescence caught the lantern light in muted tones.

Talan stopped again, a look of wonder on his face. "Is that...?"

Jaci smiled. "Queen Selendria's stone. I snatched it from him right before I hit him the second time."

Talan shook his head. "Do you realize — you did more damage to Galenock in the space of five minutes than my men and I have done in nineteen years?"

She blushed at the admiration in his voice and gave a little shrug. She didn't know what to say.

Talan shook his head again, and they continued down the tunnel.

The passage they followed wound through gray-brown stone streaked with veins of darker gray and white. The place was like a rabbit warren, with tunnels branching off in all directions. Jaci would have been lost long since, but Talan appeared to know exactly where he was going.

"Will Galenock be able to heal himself — being a wizard and all?" Jaci asked.

Talan considered. "I don't know. A true healing talent is rare. I've only known two with such a talent: the High Enchantress of

Millianoch — who would be your grandmother — and one of the wizards from the Guild who was murdered by Galenock." Talan's voice took on a bitter edge. "Galenock was always good at the art of killing."

"Do all wizards have a particular thing they're good at?"

"Wizards can have many talents, but, yes, they generally have one in which they excel."

"What is your talent?"

"Mine?"

"Yes. Mandy said you had magical abilities and that you trained with the Wizard's Guild."

Talan was silent for several steps. Finally, he spoke. "I do not know what my talent is, or if I even have one. My abilities are limited, or so I was told, and so my training was limited as well. I was an orphan, and not given priority — I was trained only when the wizards had time to spare. Most thought me a waste of time."

"Oh, but you're not! You do have magic — I've felt it. Every time you touch me, it makes me feel... *alive*."

Surprise washed the bitterness from his expression.

"The first time it happened," Jaci said, trying to explain, "was when I rode with you, after you rescued me from the wolves. You held me like this." She stopped him and pressed back against him, drawing his arm around her waist like she was riding with him again. The familiar tingling current sizzled through her. She took a deep breath, drawing it in. "When I'm close to you like this, everything is so much sharper and clearer. The dark of the tunnels has lightened to gray, and I can see further down them. I smell fresher air that way" — she pointed to a tunnel on her left — "and I can feel rain sweeping in from over there." She gestured to the right. "There's a family of mice in that right-hand tunnel behind us, and there are some lizards up ahead. They're talking to each other, but I can't quite understand them. It's like" — she searched for words — "like I can hear and feel the music of the world. It's so beautiful..." She trailed off, suddenly feeling embarrassed. She let go of his arm and stepped away. "Anyway," she finished quickly, "there's no question you have magic."

She took a few steps down the tunnel, then turned around. Talan hadn't moved.

"Is everything all right?" she asked tentatively.

"Yes." Avoiding her gaze, he started walking again.

They pressed on silently through the tunnels. Jaci glanced at Talan every so often, but he seemed to have withdrawn into himself, as if thinking deeply. She wanted to ask more questions, but she couldn't discern his state of mind and was hesitant to disturb him. She also needed to tell him about Soneira's spellbook, but she hadn't quite been able to make herself do it, particularly after his reaction to the news of Deirdre's death. She didn't want to hurt him any further.

When he finally did speak, she jumped, startled. He didn't appear to notice. He seemed to be talking half to himself, like he was thinking out loud.

"You must have inherited the Enchantresses' magic, since you were able to work the portal. Have you worked any other magic?"

"No."

"I knew Elshaer was trying to perfect some kind of spell, but he kept it secret from everyone except... She would never tell me. An actual working portal — I wonder how many there are..."

"There are at least three that I know of, besides the clocks," Jaci said.

"There are? Where? And how do you know?"

"Cranton and Zaiya's closet, the meadow near the forest where you found me in Wolf Run, and somewhere in the mountains that

I'm guessing might be the Enchantresses' castle. They were listed on the parchment in the diary."

He frowned. "I saw no parchment."

"It was hidden in the back cover. Do you have it? I'll show you."

Talan stopped and pulled out the diary, which was wrapped in waterproofed tarp inside his belt pouch. He unwrapped it and gave it to her. She opened the back cover, slid the tiny folded parchment out of the hidden pocket, and opened it, revealing the faded red-brown words and drawings.

"I discovered that the words correspond to the phases of the moon." She indicated the sketches. "There's the clock. The trees and grass drawing refers to Wolf Run, the square is the closet, and I don't know where the mountain portal is, but the Enchantresses' castle seemed an obvious guess. The word that works the magic is there at the bottom."

Talan took the parchment from her with shaking fingers. "It's written in blood," he said in a hoarse whisper. "She must have written it at the last minute, then given it to Deirdre and sent her through the portal right before she was taken."

He looked stricken, his face white, his hard exterior on the verge of cracking under the weight of his grief. Sharing his agony, Jaci slipped her arms around him and gave what comfort she could, not caring who he thought her this time, only wishing to bring him peace. Slowly, his arms came round her, returning the embrace, and they stood that way for a long time.

Jaci finally roused herself. "Why don't we rest for a little bit? I heard a stream just up ahead. We can sit and eat."

He said nothing as she took his hand and led him around a bend to where a small, burbling stream flowed out of the rocks into a small pool. They sat by the wall near the stream.

He handed her the food pack. "Go ahead and eat. I don't want anything right now."

She toyed with it for a moment, her conscience prodding her about the spellbook. *Better to give it to him now than to traumatize him again later.*

"There's one last thing I have to show you."

He started to look toward her, then stopped, his eyes focusing on the pool of water instead. "What is it?"

She bit her lip, hurt despite her resolution to remain neutral. Hoping she was doing the right thing, she reached into her pocket, drew out Soneira's blue spellbook, and laid it in his hands.

"Where did you get this?" His ragged voice matched his expression.

"I found it hidden behind a stone in the fireplace in her room. It was guarded by what Ione called a 'ward of hiding.' I hesitated to give it to you, because I know how much it hurts you to think about her. But there's something in there you need to see. And maybe some of the information might be useful in the fight against Galenock." She squeezed his arm in sympathy. "I'm sorry."

She rose and took the pack over to the pool, where she scrubbed her hands and face and then sat, angled away from him, and nibbled on a biscuit. She heard him unfold the letter, and her face grew hot again. Soneira's words played through her mind, and she realized she'd memorized them. *Dearest Talan — I am sorry for what I said...* She forced herself to think about something else — anything else. But it was so hard when her mind wanted only to dwell on the feel of his arms around her, the touch of his hand on her hair. The way his nearness electrified her.

Sighing deeply, she finished the biscuit and drank, then brushed the crumbs from her lap and washed her hands again. She'd heard him refold the letter, but he'd made no other sound.

She decided to focus on figuring out how long they'd been traveling since they'd left Cranton and Zaiya's house. It had to have been after midnight when they'd stopped to rest in the cave, and Talan had thought it was just after sunrise when he woke her. She hoped he'd slept during that time, too. She guessed it to be somewhere near midmorning.

She heard Talan stir, and out of the corner of her eye, she saw him rise and walk toward her. He held out his hand and helped her up, then picked up the pack and slid it onto his shoulders.

"Thank you for the book," he said quietly, his eyes still not meeting hers.

She wished again for some way to ease his pain. "You're welcome."

"It isn't much farther to the mill. We should be there within the hour."

They trod the rest of the way in silence. Talan was lost in thought or memory, Jaci didn't know which.

Half an hour later, they reached the branch of the underground river that flowed out from beneath the gristmill. They followed the rushing water upstream to where the tunnel dead-ended in a deep pool, eight or ten feet across. Set back from the pool, along the wall, lay a pile of tarps and more crates. Right at the edge of the dark water, on the back wall, hung a coiled rope with knots at about one-foot intervals. It was fastened to a metal peg driven into the stone, one end trailing down into the pool.

"Is this where we go swimming?" Jaci eyed the pool apprehensively. She was no stranger to water, but she could tell the current was strong, probably a lot stronger than she was.

"Yes. There's an underwater tunnel about halfway down the back wall where the river comes down through from underneath the mill." He gestured toward the coiled rope. "We have to use that rope to pull ourselves up through it into the upper pool. Once we are out of the current, we can let go of the rope and surface. It's a short tunnel, but a very fast current. Do you think you can do it?"

"Honestly, I don't know, but I'm willing to give it a try. What do we do with the lanterns?"

"Willem said to leave them here. His men will take care of them later." Talan searched through the crates until he found another length of rope. "I will tie us together, so we don't get separated, and help you as much as I can." He looped the rope around her waist and knotted it snugly, then tied it around himself, leaving room between them so they could swim freely if necessary. "If you need to, hang on to me, and I will pull us both up through."

"Can you do that?"

He smiled faintly, his gaze rising from the rope to her chin before shifting away to the pool. "You are not heavy."

She bit her lip again and sighed, dispirited by his continued avoidance of her face.

He looked back. "Are you all right?" His eyes touched hers for a brief, searching moment, then slid away again.

"I'm fine," she said. "Maybe a little scared."

His eyebrows rose. "You? Scared? After how you manhandled Galenock, this shouldn't bother you at all." He smiled at her.

She gave him a half smile in return, distracted by the way his smile changed his face, made him look younger, less careworn...

His smile faded behind the ache of his grief, and he looked away.

She touched his arm. "I wish it didn't hurt you to look at me."

He closed his eyes for an instant, then looked down. "I'm sorry."

A sudden idea struck her — something Zaiya had said. "Would you try something for me?"

"If I can."

"I'd like you to look at me, but instead of seeing how similar my face is to Deirdre's and Soneira's, I want you to look for differences. In what ways do I *not* look like them — other than the obvious, like having brown eyes and not being anywhere near as beautiful."

He shot her a quizzical glance. "Why do you say that?"

"I've seen the portrait. So... what do you see that's different?"

She could almost feel him steeling himself as he lifted his eyes to her face. After a few moments, his expression relaxed a little, and she could tell he was seriously considering what she'd asked.

"Your eyes are different," he said. "There is honesty in them and openness, strength and kindness... no conceit or deception."

"Except when I'm lying about having amnesia," she said with a rueful smile.

He smiled back. "Your smile is different, too. It quirks up on one side, and mischief dances in your eyes when you laugh."

He brushed his thumb over the corner of her lip and cheek, and she suddenly found it very hard to breathe. He tore himself away, his gaze once more on the pool. He cleared his throat. "Are you ready to swim?"

She nodded, unable to speak.

They crossed to the edge of the pool near the back wall. Talan unfastened the coiled, knotted rope and shook it out. He held it out to her.

"Grip the knots and pull yourself along with them. Take hold right above where my hands are."

She grabbed the rope where he indicated, her fingers sticking to the tar.

"We will go on the count of three. All right?"

She nodded again, scared, but determined.

He paused and looked into her eyes, and she couldn't breathe again. "You should not consider yourself less beautiful than your cousins," he said softly. "You are every bit their equal." He turned back to the pool. "One… two… three!"

CHAPTER 18

The water was freezing. The shock of it nearly cost Jaci what little air she'd managed to gulp before jumping into the pool. Talan's words and the way he'd looked at her had stolen her breath, left her trembling and weak-kneed.

She concentrated on gripping the knots in the rope and pulling herself along through the water, despite being half-blinded by the current pounding into her face. They had jumped in right at the back wall. The underwater tunnel appeared as a darker space of black about halfway down the wall, as Talan had said.

They faced each other as they climbed the rope up into the tunnel. Talan's hands kept pace with hers, holding the rope two knots below her. She tried to catch the knots with her feet to help her climb, but her boots kept slipping off them. The tunnel walls were slippery, too, worn smooth by the endlessly flowing water, and she could find no purchase there, either.

The faint light darkened to black. Dragging herself upward in pitch darkness, she kept her body as elongated as possible. She'd already scraped her back and elbows against the rock walls more than once. The tunnel bent to the right, and she struggled to pull herself around the corner. She was so cold that she could hardly get her numb hands to move, and she was rapidly running out of air.

Fighting the torrent and her rising fear, she reached for the next knot, but couldn't quite grasp it. Her hand slipped off the rope. In a panic, she grabbed for it. Talan caught her wrist. Holding the rope with one hand, he wrapped her arm around his neck. Then he slid his arm about her waist and held her tight to him. She let go of the rope with her other hand, slipped her arm over his shoulder, and locked her hands behind his neck, her head beneath his chin.

Hand over hand, he pulled them the rest of the way through the tunnel. Jaci's lungs burned; she had no more breath. She started to panic again, when suddenly they were out of the torrent and into the upper pool. Talan pushed off the bottom, swimming upward with strong strokes. They burst through the surface. Jaci gasped and coughed, trying to take in air and cough out water at the same time. Talan kept her head above the surface. She heard a shout, then something splashed into the water next to them — a small buoy attached to a rope. Keeping one arm around her, Talan flung his other arm around the buoy, and they were pulled to shore. Many hands lifted them out of the water.

Jaci heard Solon's voice as she coughed and retched, but she couldn't catch his words.

"Jacinda?" Talan slipped his arm around her shoulders. "Are you all right?"

She nodded weakly. When she finally stopped coughing, she wiped her mouth and sat back.

Someone pressed a couple of blankets around her. She wrapped herself in them gratefully and just breathed. It didn't feel like she would ever get enough air back into her lungs.

"Katar and the others?" Solon asked Talan as he draped a blanket over his friend's shoulders.

Jaci could see by Solon's expression he feared the worst.

Talan rose. "They are fine. I left them with Cranton and Zaiya as a precaution."

Solon exhaled in relief. "Your arm is bleeding again."

Jaci turned sharply, suddenly remembering the arrow wound in Talan's arm. She could see red stains on the elbow of his shirt, where blood had dripped down from beneath the blanket.

"It is nothing," Talan said. "Find Willem and ask if it would be safe for us to leave now."

Solon nodded, hurried up the ladder, and disappeared through the trapdoor.

Talan turned to one of the Black Banders, a rugged man with gray hair and grizzled beard. "Has anything happened since we left?"

The Black Bander shook his head. "All has been quiet, though we have not seen Willem yet this morning for news."

Solon reappeared at the trapdoor and climbed back down into the cavern. "Willem says the roads are crawling with soldiers, and it won't be safe to leave until after dark."

Talan cursed under his breath.

"He also said there was a crate of spare clothes and some bandage material under one of the tarps," Solon continued. He and the Black Banders crossed to the back of the cavern and started poking through the piles of supplies and contraband.

Talan sat beside Jaci and untied the rope from around their waists. "I'd hoped we could leave now and get you out of here." He lowered his voice. "The others will want to know what happened. You should tell them your story — all of it — except for the key. Don't mention the key to anyone."

"I won't," she whispered. "How bad is your arm?" she asked in a normal voice.

"Not bad. Are you sure you're all right?"

"Yes. Thank you for pulling me out of there. I owe you my life again."

He smiled, his eyes meeting hers this time. "You're welcome. It was a difficult swim. You were brave to try it."

Her breath caught, and she couldn't speak, her cheeks turning rosy at the compliment.

"We found some clothes," Solon said, striding over to them. He handed Jaci a pile of garments. "If you go back there around the corner, you'll have some privacy." He pointed toward the back wall. The Black Banders had all moved forward, near to where she and Talan were sitting. Solon knelt beside Talan. "Now, if you will take off your shirt, I'll rebandage your arm — and don't argue. We have plenty of time to do it."

As Jaci rose to go change, Talan peeled off his wet shirt and dropped it onto the rock floor, revealing a blood-stained bandage on his upper arm and a well-muscled torso that quickened her pulse. Whoa! No wonder he could carry her so easily. She caught herself staring, blushed even more, and hurried to the back of the cavern.

She hastily removed her wet clothing, dried herself with one of the blankets, then threw on the tan shirt, olive green tunic, and black trousers Solon had given her, transferring Selendria's stone to her new pocket. The garments were big, but with Cranton's belt, they would do. As she rolled up her pant legs, she took several deep breaths to cool her heated emotions. It wasn't like she'd had that many boyfriends before, but she'd never had this kind of a reaction with any of them. Of course, none of them had had that kind of muscle... Heat rose within her again, sent a tremble through her limbs. She took a couple more deep breaths and put her cold hands on her face to try to stop herself from blushing.

Hoping she had herself under control, she stepped back around to where the others were sitting. Solon was tying off a new bandage around Talan's arm. Jaci set her wet clothes on top of Talan's drenched shirt and found a dry spot on which to sit. She tried not to stare, half of her wanting him to put on another shirt to ease her temptation, the other half wanting him to stay as he was. She started drying her hair with another blanket to distract herself.

"There, that should feel better," Solon said. He rose.

Talan took Solon's offered hand and stood up beside him. "Thanks." He patted Solon on the shoulder, picked up the dry clothes one of the Black Banders had been holding for him, and headed to the back corner to change.

He emerged a few minutes later, and they all gathered and sat in a small circle toward the back of the cavern. Talan and Solon sat on either side of Jaci.

"Now, which of you is going to tell us what happened?" Solon asked, his eyes shifting from Talan to Jaci and back.

Talan nodded to Jaci. "Jacinda can tell it best, since I had very little part in it."

Jaci glanced at him in protest. "I wouldn't say that. If not for you, I wouldn't be here." She took a deep breath and brushed back her damp hair. "Before I start, there are some things you need to know..."

She told her story again, from the beginning. When she spoke of Deirdre's death, Solon clenched his fists and looked away, eyes wet with tears. Talan kept his head down, eyes closed, and the Black Banders bowed their heads in silent grief.

They listened without comment as she shared the details of her stay at Castle d'Gaire. The look of shock on Solon's face when she described her altercation with Galenock almost made her laugh. Even the Black Banders appeared impressed.

When she finished, no one spoke for several heartbeats.

"I can't believe you actually hit him," Solon said finally.

"Well, what was I supposed to do? Let him have his way with me?" Jaci asked.

"Well — well, no," Solon stammered. "It's just that most women don't usually... well..."

"Fight back?" Jaci said.

Solon struggled for words. "It's not that they don't try to fight back, it's that most don't know how."

Jaci sat up straighter. "I am not 'most women.'"

"For which we are profoundly grateful," Talan said with a look of admiration.

She smiled, warmth flooding her cheeks again.

"May we see Queen Selendria's stone?" asked the Black Bander Talan had spoken with earlier. He seemed to be the oldest member of the group — mid-fifties, Jaci guessed.

She slipped the stone from her pocket and held it out.

He made no move to take it. The four Black Banders bowed their heads again in a moment of silence.

"You have honored our queen," the man said, lifting his head. "Thank you."

"You're welcome," she said softly. "Will you tell me your names?"

"I am Carrick." He indicated the two men on his right, the first with shoulder-length sandy gray hair and light scruff on his face, and the other taller and darker, with flecks of gray in his beard and a long dark braid. "They are Jarand and Arnos." He turned to the stocky, grizzled, long-haired blond sitting on his left, who reminded Jaci of a Viking. "This is Liundur."

Jaci nodded to them. "I'm pleased to meet you."

The four of them gave her deferential nods.

"The honor is ours, Your Highness," Carrick said.

She shifted uncomfortably. "Please, you shouldn't call me that. I'm not from this world —"

"It does not matter where you are from," Talan said quietly. "You are the last surviving member of the royal family. That makes you heir to the throne of Tarshane."

"But..." She chewed her lip. How could she say she didn't plan to stay in this world?

"We would not make you stay, if you do not wish to." Talan's gaze met hers briefly, and she sensed a new pain in him, as if his heart had begun bleeding again, but for a different reason.

She laid her hand on his arm in concern. His eyes remained downcast. If they had been alone, she would have asked what was wrong, but she didn't feel comfortable broaching something so personal in front of the others.

"So, where do we go from here?" Solon asked.

"That depends on Jacinda," Talan said. He raised his head, his face expressionless. "Where do you wish to go?"

Jaci studied his eyes, but whatever he was feeling, he hid it well. She sighed inwardly. "My goal is to get home, but now that I've learned what Galenock did to my family, I would like to see him defeated first. Mandy suggested I go to the Northern Enchantresses. She thought they could teach me how to use whatever magic I have, and she said I'd be safe there, because they're equal in power to Galenock. Maybe my being there might tip the balance in their favor. Would you be willing to take me there?"

Talan stiffened. Silence filled the cavern, a sudden tension thickening the air. Jaci saw Solon's eyes slide to Talan, an "oh, crap" look on his face. Talan looked down at his hands in his lap and said nothing.

Solon cleared his throat. "We are not welcome there."

"*I* am not welcome there," Talan corrected. He rubbed his hands over his face wearily.

"I see." Jaci did her best to hide her disappointment. *It must have something to do with Soneira,* she thought, but she couldn't bring herself to ask. "Well, the portal will open in the mountains when the moon is waning. Maybe you could take me back to where you found me in the meadow, and I could use that portal to get there."

Talan shook his head. "You don't know for certain that's where it goes. You could be sent to some other mountain range and be left stranded and alone, and we would have no way to find you."

"How far away is their castle?"

"About two weeks travel by horse."

Jaci considered. "Where had you planned to take me, when we left here?"

"To one of our bases, a few days from here. I had not thought beyond that."

"We could take her close to the castle, couldn't we?" Solon ventured. "It makes sense — what she said about learning from them. And what if she *could* tip the balance? They might be able to overpower Galenock and end this madness." He nodded toward the Black Banders. "Some of us could see her the rest of the way." He fell silent.

Talan let out a long exhale and turned to Jaci. "Yes, I agree it makes sense. We will take you there, if that is where you wish to go."

"I would like to go there," Jaci said slowly, "but I don't want to put you at any more risk."

"The risk is of no importance," Talan said. "We are yours to command."

The four Black Banders rose as one, drew their weapons, and knelt before Jaci, their heads bowed, their swords upright in front of them, sharp points touching the floor.

"We will serve you and guard you with our lives," Carrick said. "We swear it."

"We swear it," repeated the other three, in unison.

"As will I," said Talan, kneeling with his blade, as they had.

"And I," said Solon, following suit.

Jaci stared, speechless. That these strong, courageous men would willingly give their lives for her completely overwhelmed her. Who was she to receive such homage? She'd never done anything important in her life, and she didn't even plan to stay here. "I — I thank you," she finally stammered, "but I'm not worthy of such an honor."

Talan raised his head. The look in his eyes left her tongue-tied. "To us, you are."

At the front of the cavern, the trapdoor flew open. The Black Banders moved between Jaci and the opening almost before she registered what was happening. A man descended the ladder awkwardly, then dropped to the rock floor, landing in a crouch, cradling his bandaged arm that had been tied in a sling. Someone up above, out of sight, closed the trapdoor. The man rose and staggered against the wall. His shirt was soaked with sweat, and he was breathing as if he'd just run a great distance. He looked familiar to Jaci — she was pretty sure he was one of Talan's men.

"Tobias!" Talan said as he and Solon rushed forward and steadied him.

"Talan... Solon... thank the gods I found you," Tobias said between breaths. "It's Nickalonis... he's taken ill."

"What's wrong with him?" Solon asked tensely.

"We don't... exactly know."

"What do you mean you don't know?"

"Solon." Talan laid his hand on his friend's arm. "Let him speak." He turned to the Black Banders, who had sheathed their weapons. "Carrick, some water."

Carrick picked up a water flask and gave it to Tobias, who took a long drink.

"Thank you. It started last evening. Nickalonis was fine, and then suddenly his face and his hands started turning red and blistering like he'd been badly burned, and his hair turned gray like ash, and his eye — it... it..." Tobias shuddered. "He was in horrible pain. We couldn't understand what happened, because he'd not been anywhere near a fire. Then more burned spots appeared on other parts of his body. Owen did what he could to ease the pain, but Nickalonis passed out. He was unconscious when I left. I came as fast as I could to find you."

Her stomach clenching in dismay, Jaci pushed forward, between the Black Banders. "It's my fault, isn't it? Galenock's burn wounds —"

"It is not your fault," Talan said sharply. "You are not responsible for Galenock's actions."

"Do you mean Galenock found a way to transfer his burn wounds to Nick?" Solon asked, horrified.

"It appears that way," Talan said grimly.

Solon leaned his hand against the wall for support. "We have to go to him. He may be dying... or — or dead..."

"He was alive when I left, but —" Tobias' words cut off, and for a fraction of a second, he looked blank. An instant later, his hazel eyes shifted to brown and settled on Jaci with venomous hatred.

She gasped and backed into Liundur, who swung her behind him. Talan snatched up a blanket and flung it over Tobias' head as the Black Banders closed ranks.

Tobias cried out. "What's going on? What did I do?"

Talan gripped his shoulders. "Stand still. Close your eyes." He turned to Solon. "Find me something to use as a blindfold."

Solon ran to the back of the cavern and returned with more bandage material.

"Are your eyes closed?" Talan asked Tobias.

"Yes," Tobias said shakily.

"Don't move and don't open your eyes." Talan lifted a corner of the blanket until he could see Tobias' face. Satisfied, he removed the blanket and tossed it to the floor. Solon quickly blindfolded Tobias.

"I'm sorry to have to do this to you," Talan said more gently, "but Galenock is using you, seeing through your eyes. I don't have time to explain everything right now. You're just going to have to trust me. Sit down right where you are, and no matter what happens, *don't take that blindfold off.*"

Tobias squatted, felt the floor beneath him, and sat silently.

Talan pounded the wall with the edge of his fist. "I should have told them to watch everyone who'd been wounded, not just Nickalonis. Solon, find Willem again and get him down here."

Solon headed for the ladder, then stopped and turned, sudden fear shadowing his face. "What about your arm?"

"They don't have the arrow that hit me," Talan said.

"Are you certain of that? What if they go back and find it?"

Talan said nothing for a moment, his gaze locked with Solon's. He slammed the wall again, and Jaci jumped. "Damn him to the Abyss!"

Solon hurried up the ladder in search of Willem.

Talan turned to the Black Banders and gestured toward Tobias. "Carrick, watch him. Liundur, stay with Jacinda. Arnos, Jarand, help me pack up our gear. As soon as Solon returns with Willem, we're leaving."

CHAPTER 19

A few minutes later, Solon slid down the ladder, followed by Willem.

"What's happened?" Willem asked. "Solon said it was urgent you leave now —" He stopped as he caught sight of Jaci. His eyes widened. "Well, I'll be jiggered," he said softly.

Talan strode forward. "Willem, this is Jacinda, daughter of Mirinesstra, the lost queen. Jacinda, this is Willem d'Archer, Cranton's cousin, who owns this gristmill. He allowed us to hide here while we went in search of you."

"Thank you, Willem, for your help," Jaci said. "I know it was done at great risk."

Willem swept into a bow. "Your Highness, you honor me." He glanced at Talan. "I can see now why you risked going into the city."

"Yes." Talan gripped Willem's arm. "You are in danger. Galenock has been using the blood of my men who were wounded in battle to cast the spell that allows him to see through their eyes. He just did so with Tobias, here. Galenock saw us, but he was so focused on Jacinda that I don't think he saw anything that would reveal our location. I can't be certain, though. He may come for you."

"Let him come," Willem said with a grim smile. "My men and I will set up a few surprises for him. We don't cause as much mayhem as you do, but we're always happy to poke a few thorns in Galenock's side when we have the chance."

Talan clapped him on the shoulder. "We are glad of the help." He sobered. "One of my men is in trouble. We have to leave now. Can we get to the woods without being seen?"

Willem shook his head. "There are Riders and soldiers everywhere. They nearly caught your man, there." He nodded toward Tobias. "It was pure luck they didn't see him." Willem thought for a moment. "There are two wagons from Twain's Crossing due in. They should be here any time now. The wagonmaster is a good man. He might be willing to smuggle you out. I'll let you know as soon as he arrives." He nodded to Jaci. "We'll need to find some kind of disguise for you, Your Highness."

"We'll take care of it, if we can borrow some more of your clothes." Talan gestured toward the crates.

"Take whatever you need." Willem bowed to Jaci again. "Your Highness." He hastened up the ladder, back to the main floor of the mill.

Jaci and the others dug through the crates, pulling out a couple of bulky tunics and a knitted hat. Jaci put on the tunics over the clothes she already wore, to hide her slenderness. Then she shoved her dark curls up into the hat.

Talan swept a cloak about her shoulders and fastened the clasp. "If you keep the hood up, no one should be able to see your face."

She smiled. "Thanks."

He flashed her a smile, his eyes lingering on hers for a moment before he turned away to help put the unused clothing back into the crates. She smiled to herself, the irrational, bubbly, happy feeling spilling through her again.

A short time later, Willem returned.

"He'll do it," Willem said, "but you'll have to go with him as far as Garsondale. Will that work?"

Talan nodded. "We should be able to make our way back to the woods from there. We left our horses hidden with one of my men."

"Good," Willem said. "They're loading the sacks of flour and meal now. They said they could leave spaces within the piles of sacks to hide four of you. The other four will have to ride guard. He'll leave his men here, and your men will take their places. He said he could pick up replacements in Garsondale, enough to get him home safely. I'll arrange to get his men back to him."

Talan regarded Willem keenly. "The wagonmaster and his men — do you trust them?"

"Yes. They're good men."

Talan turned to Jaci. "I think we should let them see you to give them proof that the royal family has returned. It will give them hope for the future."

"Okay." Jaci lowered her cloak hood and pulled off her hat.

The trapdoor opened. "They're ready," one of the millworkers called down.

"All right. Let's go," Talan said.

They ascended the ladder to the main floor of the mill and hastened to where the loaded wagons stood. The millworkers and the men from Twain's Crossing had clustered around the backs of the wagons. The mouths of the wagonmaster and three of his men dropped open as Jaci and the others approached.

"Y—Your Highness?" the wagonmaster said in a shocked whisper.

Willem introduced them. "Kent, this is Jacinda, daughter of Mirinesstra, the lost queen. Your Highness... Kent d'Raflinger of Twain's Crossing." He put his hand on the wagonmaster's shoulder.

"If you can get her and Talan and his men out of here safely, all of Tarshane will be greatly in your debt."

Kent dropped to one knee. "It is my honor to serve the royal family, Your Highness." His men knelt where they stood. "We will get you through."

"Thank you," Jaci said, awe stealing through her again at the sight of these people kneeling to her, freely transferring their love and respect for the royal family to her.

Kent rose, as did the others. "We can hide you and three of the men in the wagons." He indicated tunnel-like spaces in the backs of the wagons, surrounded by two rows of sacks, the topmost layers supported by planks not visible from outside the wagons.

"We will ride guard," Carrick said, with a nod toward the other three Black Banders. "We are the least recognizable."

Jaci noticed that they had slid their black arm bands up beneath their tunic sleeves.

Talan looked for a moment like he might argue, but Solon spoke first. "He's right," he said firmly. He waved his arm toward one of the wagons. "Why don't you and Jaci take that one? Tobias and I will take this one."

Talan acquiesced. He shook hands with Willem and Kent, while the Black Banders tossed their gear into the front of the hideaways. Then Talan helped Jaci climb into the small space. Solon assisted the still-blindfolded Tobias into the other wagon. Jaci sat sideways and hitched her way to the front with her knees tucked to her chin, grumbling to herself about tiny, cramped spaces as she gave Talan room to squeeze in next to her. The wagonmaster's men piled more sacks onto the back of the wagon, leaving chinks here and there for air and light.

"Do you think this will work?" Jaci whispered, inching back toward him until their shoulders and knees touched. A warm tingling buzzed through her, and she pressed closer without thinking.

He didn't pull away. "It has to. Kent is risking his life for us. I don't want him or any of his men to get hurt."

"Everything is loaded," she heard Willem say to the wagonmaster. "I'll get your men back to you tonight. Good luck and may Brackan see you through."

"Thank you, Willem," said Kent. The wagon creaked as he climbed up and settled in the seat.

"And spread the word," Willem added. "The royal family has returned!"

"I will." Kent cracked the whip, and the wagon jerked forward.

Guilt pricked Jaci like a cold knife. "The royal family" had only temporarily returned. She bit her lip. So many people were risking so much for her. How were they going to feel when she left? How was she going to feel? *Like a heel,* she thought dismally.

They hadn't gotten two hundred feet from the mill when Jaci heard the sound of cantering hoofbeats ahead of them.

"We are about to have company," Kent said grimly. "Stay quiet."

The wagon slowed to a halt as the hoofbeats surrounded them. Jaci saw flashes of red through the chinks in the sides — red-cloaked Riders. She stiffened nervously and held her breath, hoping they wouldn't recognize the Black Banders. Talan's hand closed over hers. He squeezed her fingers reassuringly.

"What is your business?" asked a guttural voice.

"We just picked up a load of flour and meal from the mill back there and are on our way home," Kent said in a conversational tone.

"Where is your home?"

"Twain's Crossing."

"Have you seen anyone on the road?"

"No."

"We search for a woman — small, with dark hair — and for Talan d'Lochlann and his men. If you see them, you must report it immediately. There is a generous reward for their capture."

"I will keep my eyes open," Kent said.

No one else spoke.

"See that you do." The Rider barked a command, and the troop rode off down the road in the direction of the mill.

The wagons started forward again. Jaci let out the breath she'd been holding. Talan relaxed and squeezed her hand once more, then let go. He flexed his arm a couple of times, as much as he could in the cramped space.

Jaci suddenly realized she was leaning against his injured arm, and she drew away. "I'm sorry. I shouldn't have been leaning on you like that. Does it hurt badly?"

"No. You are not hurting me. It stiffens up sometimes, if I don't move it."

Jaci hesitated, then asked the question that had been gnawing at the back of her mind. "Do you think they really would go back and find the arrow?"

"I don't know," he said after a moment, and a surge of frustration, anger, and doubt washed through Jaci, leaving behind the bone-deep tiredness of a battle against despair he seemed to be losing. "If you see his eyes in mine..." He trailed off, as if the thought were too abhorrent to speak.

She clasped his hand in both of hers, wishing there was something she could say to ease his burden.

"We've got more trouble coming," Kent said. "A group of soldiers on foot. I've run across them before. The leader is particularly nasty."

Moments later, another guttural voice rang out. "Halt your wagons!"

Jaci sucked in her breath. She recognized the voice — it was the soldier who had murdered the drunk man back in the city. In a panic, her eyes sought Talan's. All she could see in her mind was the same fate befalling Kent... and then the rest of them.

Talan squeezed her hand again and raised his finger to his lips for silence.

The wagons rolled to a stop. The heavy tramp of footsteps surrounded them.

"You! You four get off your horses."

Jaci heard the creak of saddle leather as the Black Banders dismounted, and she wondered how badly they were outnumbered.

The soldier's voice moved around the other side of the wagon. "Get down on the ground — face down in the dirt where you Shiannoran dung heaps belong."

Talan tensed again, and Jaci could feel his anger rising.

The Black Banders must have complied, for no skirmishes erupted.

"What have you got in your wagons?" The soldier now stood to Jaci's left, near Kent.

"Like I told the Riders a few minutes ago, flour and meal from the mill," Kent said in a flat voice.

"You been talking to Riders?"

"They questioned us."

"Then you know who we look for."

"Yes."

"Have you seen them?"

"No."

"Flour and meal. Is that all you carry?"

"Yes."

The soldier walked toward the back of the wagon, halting about halfway, where Jaci and Talan sat with their backs to him. "Then you won't mind if I do this."

Jaci heard a slitting sound, then his sword cut through the sacks, the point slicing through right between their heads. Jaci shrank back and just managed to keep from screaming. Only about two inches of the blade protruded, but it would have drawn blood if it had hit them. The blade hissed out of the sacks. Corn meal spilled into their hiding place.

The soldier strode around to the back of the wagon, thrusting his sword in again, inches from Talan's leg. Jaci clamped her lips tight to make certain no sound escaped. The soldier continued on to the other side. Jaci and Talan scrunched their knees back as far as they could beneath their chins. The soldier's sword thrust brushed Jaci's pant leg.

The soldier's footsteps receded toward the second wagon. Jaci listened anxiously for the sound of either Solon or Tobias crying out, but heard only the hissing of the blade through the sacks and the faint swish of spilling meal.

The soldier stalked back to the lead wagon. "I want that reward money. If I find out you knew something and kept it to yourself, or told someone else, I will come for you. You and your wife and children will wish you had never lived."

Kent said nothing.

"Bring the horses." The soldier stepped away from the wagon. "Remember what I said."

"You're stealing my horses?" Kent said, his voice deepening with anger.

The soldier spit on the ground. "Be glad that is all you are losing."

Jaci heard creaking saddles again as the soldier and some of his men mounted the horses and rode away toward the mill, the other soldiers jogging after them.

"I am going to kill that man," Kent swore, as his men plugged the holes in the meal sacks with strips of cloth. Then he urged the wagon team forward again. "Are you all right back there?"

"Yes," Talan said. "Thank you for not revealing us. I'm sorry about your horses. We will get them back for you as soon as we can."

"Don't worry about them," Kent said. "They are replaceable."

Carrick walked up near the wagon. "Should we have acted?"

"No," Talan said. "As infuriating as it was, you did the right thing. Are Solon and Tobias all right?"

"Yes. They guessed what was happening and were not touched by the blade."

"Glad to hear it."

Carrick moved away from the wagon to take up his guard position.

"Willem wasn't kidding about Galenock's men being everywhere," Jaci whispered, so only Talan could hear. "Those soldiers were headed toward the mill. Do you think they'll harass him?"

"I'm sure they will," Talan said grimly.

Jaci sensed his worry, felt the helpless anger seething through him. Kent wasn't the only one who wanted to kill that soldier. "Willem sounded like he'd be ready for them, though, didn't he?"

"We can only hope." Talan turned toward her. "You were incredibly brave back there. When that sword came through, you never made a sound. Most people would have cried out and given us away."

Jaci's face grew warm with pleasure. "I don't know how I didn't cry out. I was so scared."

"It is one thing to be scared, but it is quite another to be scared and still keep your wits about you. You have done so the whole time."

"The whole time?"

"You were transported here to a place you'd never heard of, where you knew no one, and had no idea how to get back to your own world. You've been chased around, kidnapped, imprisoned in an impregnable castle, from which you escaped — by yourself. You are one of the most courageous people I have ever met."

The warm glow burned all the way to her toes. "Thank you," she finally managed to say. "It's been both a frightening and exciting experience." She put her hand on his arm. "I can't tell you how glad I am that you were the one who found me."

Their eyes held for several heartbeats, then he shifted and looked straight ahead. "I am glad, too."

Jaci closed her eyes for a moment and tried to still the rampant trembling that quivered through her whole body. When he looked at her like that, all she could think about was how badly she wanted to be in his arms again. *Whoa! This has got to stop.* She turned and looked out through the chinks at the passing greenery to calm herself and suddenly became aware of the buzz of voices and the clatter of other wagons coming toward them.

She twisted to get a better view. "Where are we? Is that a town?"

"We are coming into Sagetown."

Jaci saw snatches of weather-beaten houses, shops, and a village green with a fountain surrounded by market stalls, where merchants were hawking their wares to the many passers-by.

"When we came through earlier," Kent said, "there were Riders at the other end of town, searching wagons. It is likely they are still there."

"Thanks for the warning," Talan said.

They rolled through town behind another wagon heading in the same direction. They were stopped and questioned without incident by two more troops of Riders — one at the edge of town, the other a few miles outside of town, who, after a brief interrogation, galloped away cross-country. The wagon in front of them turned off onto a side path, and Kent's two wagons continued on toward Garsondale, alone.

After they'd traveled a few more miles unmolested, Jaci began to relax. Maybe they'd make it safely through after all.

Talan shifted again, rubbing cramped leg muscles. "If anyone should ask me, I would definitely not recommend traveling this way."

Jaci laughed quietly. "Yes, I have to say I'm getting a bit tired of being stuck in tiny spaces — first the clocks, then the closet, now this. It's a good thing I'm not claustrophobic."

"What is it like — your world?" he asked softly.

"Well…" She thought for a moment, not knowing where to start. "It's hugely different from this world, much more technologically advanced." She talked about cars and airplanes and skyscrapers and cell phones — she'd described Deirdre's death as a carriage accident, earlier, because she hadn't wanted to confuse the issue by trying to explain what a car was — but she felt like she was making a jumbled mess of everything. There were so many things she wanted to convey, but he had no point of reference with which to even begin to imagine what they would look like or how they would work. She trailed off, at a loss.

He fiddled with the edge of his belt pouch, his eyes downcast. "You must have family — husband — friends — who are greatly worried about you."

"I don't have a husband, or any family that I know of. My father and his parents died many years ago. If they had other relatives, they never told me. My mother was the only family I had, and now she's gone. I do have some close friends, and yes, they're probably worrying and wondering where I am." She thought about Courtney, the friend she was supposed to be visiting right now. Courtney had likely called every police department in the state, multiple times.

"I give you my word that I will do all I can to get you back to them safely."

"Thank you." She hesitated. "Maybe you could come through with me, and I could show you my world."

He gave her a brief smile touched with sadness. "Your world sounds wondrous, but I think it would be beyond my understanding." A deep heartache welled up inside him, squeezing her own heart.

She clasped his hand. "You're hurting again. Why?"

"It is nothing." He tipped his head back wearily and closed his eyes, his fingers still curled around hers. He did not let go this time.

CHAPTER 20

Jaci shot Talan a sidelong glance and wished she knew what he was thinking. This new pain that bled in him like an open wound worried her. She'd thought he'd moved past her resemblance to Soneira and that his heart had begun to heal. While they were in the tunnels, he'd let out some of the grief he'd buried for so long, and he'd been able to look at her without the agony she'd felt ripping through him when they'd first met. But now...

She glanced at him again, but he didn't open his eyes. His breathing deepened, and his fingers around hers relaxed. The rolling of the wagon had lulled him to sleep. She sighed. Well, so much for getting any answers. She was glad he was sleeping, though. She'd felt his weariness. Gently, she brushed an errant strand of dark hair away from his face. He looked so peaceful when he slept, his haggard lines smoothed away, his shoulders relaxed... those broad shoulders, which carried such a heavy load — not only the weight of his grief and the guilt he felt over Soneira's and Deirdre's deaths, but the burden of leading an endless, seemingly futile rebellion. He was responsible for the lives of his men and so many others. The hopes of all the people of Tarshane rested on him.

What would he be like in my world? She tried to picture him in a suit and tie, working in a high-rise; or in casual khakis and a polo shirt, going out to dinner or to the movies; or even in jeans and a T-shirt, doing construction work; but she couldn't do it. The images were all wrong. He didn't belong in a world hemmed in by skyscrapers any more than a lion of the Serengeti belonged in a cage.

She sighed deeply. She was going to miss him — a lot more than she wanted to admit. Thoughts of his touch and his strength and his dark eyes looking into hers filled her with a sudden sharp longing. She closed her eyes. *No, you can't fall in love with him!* But no matter how hard she tried to stop it, the sweetness of the memories kept enfolding her like the warmth and strength of his embrace, eroding her will to resist where her heart was going...

"We're being followed," Carrick said.

Jaci snapped out of her reverie and turned sharply toward the front of the wagon, where the Black Bander's voice had come from. She hadn't heard him approach.

"Can you tell who it is?" Kent asked.

"They're too far back, but my guess would be the soldiers who took the horses," Carrick said.

"What do you want to do?" Kent asked.

Jaci listened for Carrick's response, but none came, and she realized the question had been directed at Talan.

"He's asleep," she said. "Do you want me to wake him?"

There was a brief pause, then Carrick said, "No, not yet. I don't think they will approach us until we reach our destination. They'll wait and watch and see what we do. When he does wake, please tell him."

"I will," Jaci promised.

She sat back, fear shivering through her. Did the soldiers know she and Talan were hidden here? In her mind's eye, she could see them beating the information out of Willem and the millworkers, maybe even torturing them. The memory of the murdered drunk man thudding to the ground, his blood dripping into the sewer water, flashed through her mind. She shuddered.

Talan stirred in his sleep, disturbed by her tension. She took a long, deep breath and forced herself to calm down. If the soldiers knew she was here, they would be here right now, tearing the sacks out of the wagons. No, they were just suspicious, and greedy for the reward. She looked out through the chinks at harvested fields stretching between stands of evergreens, stone walls separating them from chewed-down pastures that rose into rocky hills. Clouds obscured the sun, and she couldn't tell what time of day it was, but she thought it must be getting on toward late afternoon. She thought of Willem and the millworkers again, worry for them plaguing her. Anger began to needle her, rising into the burning outrage she'd felt when she'd seen the fright in Mandy's and Allina's eyes as Castellan Felgarth had walked into her room. These Ruusitarans had terrorized the people of Shiannora long enough. She would see them driven back to Ruusitar if it was the last thing she did.

*****

Shouts and the clang of metal on metal shocked Jaci awake. Completely disoriented, it took her a moment to figure out where she was. Apparently, the motion of the wagon had lulled her to sleep, too.

Talan was twisting around, trying to see what was going on through the chinks.

Jaci gasped as her brain clicked into focus. "The soldiers!"

"What soldiers?" Talan asked sharply.

"Carrick said we were being followed. He thought it was the soldiers who stole the horses."

Talan peered through another chink. "No, it's not them. Why didn't anyone tell me?"

"I asked Carrick if I should wake you, but he said not yet, which I was glad of because you really needed the sleep." She squinted through one of the chinks. "Who's out there?"

The clash of weapons ceased, and silence settled around them.

"Drag their bodies into the bushes." Kent's voice reached them from somewhere off to the side.

They heard footsteps approaching, then Kent climbed back up onto the wagon.

"What happened?" Talan demanded.

"A band of brigands, trying to steal the load. It would fetch a good price on the black market."

"Was anyone hurt?" Talan asked.

"None of us, anyway. Your men are impressive. They took down three times their number without hardly breaking a sweat."

"They are all out of sight now," Carrick said.

Jaci could see the dark of his cloak as he drew near.

"Good. Thank you." Kent cracked the reins, and the wagons moved forward again.

"What's this about our being followed?" Talan asked.

"The foot soldiers that took the horses are trailing us," Carrick said. "Arnos went back and scouted them. There are twenty of them, but they're keeping their distance."

"How far to Garsondale?" Talan asked.

"About two miles," Kent answered. "There's a livery stable toward the other end of town. The owner is a friend of mine. We can drive both wagons inside and get you out without anyone else seeing. We'll have to be quick, though, so you can escape before the soldiers reach town."

"All right," Talan said.

Three wagons passed them in the opposite direction as they neared their destination. Kent greeted them in a neighborly manner, receiving similar calls in return. A few minutes later, they reached the outskirts of Garsondale.

Garsondale was a bustling town, much bigger than Sagetown, but nowhere near the size of Catir Coronin. Jaci watched through the chinks as they passed by houses, mercantile buildings, inns and taverns, woodworking shops, smithies, and what looked like a jail. Crowds of people walked along the sides of the street, and the street itself was clogged with wagons traveling in both directions, slowing their progress.

Come on, hurry up, Jaci urged, her nervousness growing by the second. She wanted to be out of this tiny hole and away, so as not to put Kent in any further danger. She wasn't too keen on meeting those soldiers, either.

Finally, they reached the livery stable. Kent spoke to a stable boy, who dragged open a huge set of double doors and waved them in. As soon as both wagons were inside, the boy shoved the doors closed. Talan had directed the Black Banders to stay outside and watch for the soldiers. Jaci peered through another chink as Kent jumped down from the wagon and tied the reins to a hitching post. He called to the boy, and when the boy came near, he said something quietly to him, gave him a coin, and sent him running off through a side door. Then he went around to the back of the wagon and began pulling the end sacks off and dropping them to the floor.

"Kent, it's good to see you!" piped a jovial voice from the back of the stable. "What are you doing?"

Jaci put on her hat and drew her hood up around her face. She couldn't see who spoke, but she could hear his curiosity.

"I'm sorry to do this to you, Donnel." Kent yanked off the last of the bags. "Those Ruus soldiers are after us — the nasty ones." He stepped back so Talan could climb out of the hole.

"You mean Vorstun and that vile gang of his?" Donnel asked, sobering.

"Yes."

Talan jumped down, then reached his hand in for Jaci. She grabbed the gear and, with Talan's help, slid out of the wagon. Her cramped muscles complained as she straightened beside him, keeping her face averted.

"Talan, you need to get out of here," Kent said as he reached for one of the bags he'd just pulled off the wagon. "Those soldiers will be here any minute."

"Not until we cover up these hidey-holes. If the soldiers see them, they'll kill you." Talan gripped the end of the heavy sack and helped Kent lift it back onto the wagon.

"You are Talan d'Lochlann," Donnel said, a touch of awe in his voice. "How can I help?"

Kent gestured toward the second wagon. "You can help get the others out." He and Talan swung another sack into place.

Donnel headed to the other wagon.

As Talan and Kent hastily repacked the wagon, Jaci glanced around. The wagon teams were champing their bits and pawing the ground restlessly, the jingling of their harnesses floating up into the rafters. The livery stable was huge — an airy barn, well-lit by at least a dozen paned windows spread high along the length of each side. An open area, wide enough for two wagons abreast, spanned the middle from one large set of closed doors to another. Rows of horse stalls, some filled, took up the far side of the barn, while a tack room and several wagons and lighter buckboards lined her side. Broken and spare wagon parts lay strewn against the wall, close by.

Jaci hurried over to the wall and poked through the wagon parts, looking for something she could use as a weapon. What she wouldn't give for her can of pepper spray. She found a round metal bar, about a foot long and an inch in diameter, sticking out from beneath a broken wheel. She jerked it free and slipped it up her sleeve, letting it drop into her hand a couple of times to make sure it slid easily.

"This'll work," she said to herself. She could do some serious damage with it. Holding the bar tightly up her sleeve, she hastened back to the wagon just as the stable boy returned with four rough-looking men who bristled with weapons.

Kent thanked the boy and sent him back out. Then he turned to the four men. "I need your help getting this load home. I'll pay you well."

The men nodded and lent a hand with the sacks.

"Talan, you should get going," Kent said. "We'll finish —"

A frightened scream from somewhere outside startled them. Before anyone could move, one of the far doors burst open and a dozen soldiers with weapons bared streamed in, followed by the four Black Banders and the rest of the soldier troop. The Black Banders had been disarmed. Vorstun entered last, dragging a young girl of about ten or twelve years, his knife at her throat. Blood seeped from a knife cut on her cheek.

Vorstun kicked the door shut behind him. "Stand where you are," he bellowed, "or I will cut this girl up into little pieces."

The girl whimpered, her eyes round with terror, her tears mixing with the blood dripping down her face.

"Oh, no," Jaci whispered, horror clenching her chest.

Jaci felt Talan go rigid beside her, his fury so sharp she could almost taste it.

The soldiers shoved the Black Banders up against the side of the first wagon, then spread out and surrounded everyone.

Vorstun handed the girl off to one of his men, who wrapped his arm around her chest with a grin and waved his knife in her face. She cringed. Vorstun laughed. He pointed at Solon, Kent, and the others. "Take their weapons. If they resist, cut the girl... or kill them... or both." He laughed again, his men chortling along with him.

The soldiers disarmed Solon, the still-blindfolded Tobias, and the wagonmaster and his men.

Vorstun swaggered up to Talan and took the sword and knives from Talan's belt and stuck them in his own swordbelt. "Talan d'Lochlann, we finally meet. You are going to bring me a lot of money." He turned to Jaci. "And you must be the one Lord Galenock has had us chasing uphill and down after. You are going to bring me even more money. Come, let us have a look at you." He grasped her arm.

She snatched it away. "Don't touch me, you filth."

He raised his hand to strike her. Talan sprang between them. The young girl shrieked as the soldier's blade cut into her face. Talan froze, his fists clenched.

"You want to hit me? Go ahead," Vorstun goaded. "That girl will have more wounds than a battlefield full of dead men."

Talan didn't move, his fury barely controlled.

Horrified and angry at what her kneejerk refusal had caused, Jaci stepped around Talan and Vorstun toward the middle of the stable. "Fine. You want a look?" She pushed her hood back and ripped off her hat, tossing it onto the wagon. "Here I am."

Vorstun couldn't contain his surprise, and she heard some gasps from a few of the other soldiers. He started circling her. "Well, well, the lost royal daughter has returned."

"My name is Jacinda, daughter of Mirinesstra," she said flatly. "I am *not* Deirdre."

Vorstun stopped in front of her. "I don't care what your name is, as long as I get my gold." He walked around her again. "I knew there was something suspicious about these wagons. The men at the mill didn't have much to say when we questioned them. They have even less to say now, since we burned the place to the ground... with them in it."

Jaci stiffened. *Oh, no... Willem and the millworkers dead... no!* She fought back her tears. She wouldn't give him the satisfaction of seeing her cry.

Vorstun sauntered past the Black Banders, as if daring them to attack him. "My suspicions were confirmed when you fought those brigands. Only Black Banders could have dealt with so many, so quickly and efficiently." He stopped before Carrick and ripped the sleeve of Carrick's tunic, revealing the black arm bandanna underneath. He spit on the bandanna, grinned at the hateful glare Carrick shot him, and walked away. He trailed past Kent and his team. "You are all going to die for helping a wanted criminal." He speared a finger toward Talan. Then he spread his arms, encompassing everyone but the soldiers and Jaci. "In fact, you are all going to die right now." He glanced up at the wooden beams that crossed the width of the stable. "Get some rope," he ordered his men. "We'll string them up right here and leave them to rot. Then all of Shiannora can see what happens to those who oppose Lord Galenock."

No! Jaci looked at Talan. His face was expressionless, save for the helpless rage burning in his eyes. She saw the Black Banders glance at each other, then at Talan. Would they sacrifice themselves, or the girl?

A few of the soldiers searched the stable and produced several lengths of rope. They began tying nooses in the ends of them.

Jaci racked her brain. She had to *do* something. Her eyes fell on the soldier holding the girl. He was quite a bit taller than Jaci, but he didn't look too intelligent — a typical flunky — and there wasn't another soldier within ten feet of him.

The girl whimpered, and Jaci realized the soldier was fondling her. Something inside Jaci snapped.

"You there." She strode toward the soldier.

He stopped what he was doing and eyed her guardedly, his knife hovering beside the girl's face.

"Yes, you," Jaci continued, walking toward him in a calm manner. She felt Talan's fear for her tightening his throat, constricting his whole being.

None of the other soldiers moved. They watched her advance with amused grins.

"What are you doing, woman?" Vorstun demanded. "Get back where you were!"

Jaci ignored him. She walked up to the soldier, keeping away from his knife arm. *If she could just get him to move the blade away from the girl's head...* She forced aside her anger and smiled at him. "You look like a smart man."

He leered at her, his knife arm lowering a bit.

Some of the other soldiers snickered, their grins widening.

"I said get back here!" Vorstun strode toward her.

The soldier glanced at Vorstun, then looked back at Jaci.

Jaci moved right up next to him and looked him in the eye. "You should be in charge here. You're much smarter than *he* is." She stabbed her finger toward the approaching Vorstun.

The moment the soldier looked toward Vorstun, she seized his arm, which held the girl, and wrenched it around backward. The soldier howled. The girl twisted free and ran. Jaci ducked behind the soldier before he could swing his blade at her and drove her heel into the back of his leg, dropping him to one knee. The metal bar slipped down into her hand, and, wielding it like a baseball bat, she cracked him upside the head. With a grunt, he toppled over.

Vorstun lunged at her, but ran into Talan, who was suddenly between them. Jaci darted to the side and stayed back out of the way. From then on, everything was a blur. Shouts and groans and the whinnying of frightened horses filled the air as Donnel and the second wagon driver tried to control the panicked teams. The Black Banders were everywhere, sweeping through the soldier ranks, while Solon hung back, protecting Tobias. Talan was beating the tar out of Vorstun, punching him repeatedly in the face and gut. Vorstun reeled and fell flat on his back. Talan snatched his knives from Vorstun's belt, then reclaimed his sword. Vorstun struggled onto his hands and knees. Talan went after him, but was waylaid by another soldier, who delayed Talan just long enough for Vorstun to stumble to his feet and escape the stable. The remaining soldiers tried to flee, but the Black Banders cut them down, and soon every last soldier lay face down in the dirt, dead. Carrick spit on the nearest one as he dropped his borrowed weapons and retrieved his own.

Jaci turned away, sickened by the sight of so much blood and death. A movement caught her eye, and she saw the girl cowering beneath one of the buckboards. The girl had long brown hair and a pixyish face that reminded Jaci of a slightly younger version of Allina.

Jaci wended her way to the buckboard and knelt. "You can come out now. It's safe." She reached in, took the girl's hand, and drew her out. Then she ripped a piece of cloth from the bottom of one of the oversized tunics she wore and gently pressed it against the girl's face to stem the bleeding.

The girl shrank back as Talan and Liundur came up beside them.

Jaci slipped her arm around the girl's shoulders. "It's okay. They're friends. I'm fine," she said to Talan, before he could ask.

He cupped her cheek, the look in his eyes stealing her breath again. "Stay here."

Liundur planted himself nearby.

"Where is Vorstun?" Kent demanded, having searched through the dead soldiers.

"He escaped through that door," Talan said, indicating the open side door as he strode to Kent's side.

One of the mercenaries rushed in through the door. "Vorstun took one of the horses and bolted."

Kent's face blanched. "My family!" He called to the other wagon driver. "Stay with the load. The rest of you come with me." The four mercenaries followed him out the door.

"Jarand, go with them," Talan said. "See his family to safety. You know where to take them."

Jarand nodded and left on the run.

Jaci heard the sound of galloping horses fading into the distance and hoped they would be in time to save Kent's family, assuming that was where Vorstun had gone. For all anyone knew, he could still be nearby, waiting to ambush them. She shuddered at the thought.

"Are you all right, miss?" the girl asked, her eyes flicking back and forth between Jaci and Liundur. The girl was uneasy around the Black Bander, but Jaci was glad of his presence, especially with Vorstun still on the loose.

"Yes, I'm fine, thanks." Jaci tore off another piece of cloth and wiped away some more of the blood from the girl's face. "I'm so sorry for what they did to you. One of these cuts is my fault."

"It's all right, miss. You saved me. Thank you." The girl gave her a shy smile, then winced at the pain in her cheek.

"Talan!" Carrick pointed to one of the side doors further down the stable.

The door was opening slowly. Head and shoulders poked through — one of the townsmen, a big man built like a football player. He entered, carrying a scythe, a look of shock on his face as he surveyed the dead soldiers. More people pushed in behind him, a few of them carrying weapons, and Jaci heard startled exclamations and murmuring.

The other doors opened, including the big doors. People streamed in, filling the stable. It was as if the entire town had massed outside the building, listening to the carnage, but had been too afraid to enter even when the soldiers hadn't come out. Jaci could almost see their fear, so strong it clung to them like a garment.

Liundur stepped in front of Jaci and the girl, his hand resting on the hilt of his sword. Talan, Carrick, and Arnos gathered around them, followed by Solon, who was leading Tobias.

"Lani?" a woman called out, her voice edged with hysteria. "Where are you?"

"Lani!" a man shouted hoarsely.

The girl turned to Jaci. "They're looking for me." She glanced nervously at Talan and the Black Banders, not quite daring to walk past them.

Jaci smiled at her. "It's all right. They won't hurt you. Go ahead."

"Thank you, miss." The girl eased away from Jaci and slipped between Talan and Carrick, who moved aside to let her pass. She rushed toward the growing crowd. "Mother! Father!"

A middle-aged man and woman burst out of the crowd into the open, about twenty feet from where Talan and the Black Banders stood with Jaci safely encircled.

"Lani!" they both cried and swept the girl into their arms.

The big man with the scythe shoved through the crowd and came up beside Lani and her family. He eyed the girl's bloodied face with grim anger. Then his gaze shifted to Talan and those with him. "Who are you? What happened here?"

"I am Talan d'Lochlann, and these are my men. We killed the soldiers before they could kill us. We mean no harm to any of you."

Jaci heard Talan's name whispered through the crowd that now completely surrounded them.

"Talan d'Lochlann is dead, according to Lord Galenock," said a man richly dressed like a merchant, in a suspicious tone.

"Galenock lies," Talan said simply.

"How do we know you're not part of that band of brigands that's been thieving and killing around here for the last two months?" the merchant asked.

The big man with the scythe swept his arm out, indicating the dead soldiers. "No brigands could have done this."

"There is only one group of men who could have," said a graying man with thick biceps and a blacksmith's hammer. He gestured with the hammer toward Carrick's arm. "Black Banders."

Jaci heard the respect in his voice and in others' voices as his words carried through the crowd. Yet there were still murmurs of unease rippling through the people. She could feel a rising tension, an undercurrent of dread. She could see it in their faces. They were like a herd of spooked cattle on the verge of stampeding.

"You should be thanking them," said the liveryman, Donnel, who'd been off on the other side of the stables, calming the horses in the stalls. He strode into the space between Talan and the crowd. "They just rid us of the most vile Ruusitaran whoresons Shiannora has ever seen."

"That's all well and good," the merchant said, "but what are we going to do when Lord Galenock discovers what these Black Banders have done here? He will send his Riders and they will kill every last one of us."

"Yes, they are going to kill us all!" cried a female voice.

"We're done for!" cried another voice.

The rampant murmurings grew louder, and Jaci saw many heads nodding, fear edging toward panic. The herd was about to stampede. Talan and Solon and the Black Banders stood tensely, hands on their weapons. None of the doors would be easy to reach with so many people in the way.

"Stay between us," Talan whispered to her over his shoulder.

Anger sparked within her. Talan and his men had given up nineteen years of their lives fighting Galenock and the Ruusitarans, trying to win back freedom for these people and the rest of Tarshane. They had just killed a bunch of murderous soldiers, and instead of showing any sign of appreciation, the townspeople were condemning them. Yes, the people were frightened, and with good reason. Galenock and the Ruusitarans had beaten them down until they'd lost their will to fight. But somewhere, a line had to be drawn. What these people needed was a sharp kick in the pants to rouse them from their cowed position and get them fighting again.

"There is a price on their heads," the merchant continued. "Maybe if we hand them over to the Riders, they will give us the reward and forget about what happened here."

Arguments broke out between the blacksmith, and the merchant, and many others, tempers flaring, hysteria rising.

Jaci had heard enough. She slid between Talan and Liundur and jogged into the open space.

"Jacinda!" Talan called.

She heard the anxiety in his voice, but she didn't turn back. She stopped beside Donnel and shouted, "What is the matter with you people?"

The blacksmith and the merchant and those nearest to them went silent, looking at her in surprise.

"What is wrong with you?" she shouted again.

Slowly, the silence spread throughout the crowd.

"Are you men and women or spineless cowards?" Jaci demanded. "Where is your backbone, your courage? You want to know what to do when the Riders come? Fight back! You have weapons. Use them! They can only terrorize you if you let them!"

"Who are you?" the merchant asked rudely.

Jaci felt Talan's spike of anger at the merchant's disrespect. Talan and the others had followed her and now stood close behind her.

The circle of people closed in around them, and the muttering began again. But before she could say anything further, the blacksmith's face spread into the familiar look of shock. "Hold your tongues — all of you!" His voice boomed into the rafters, quieting the entire crowd. "By Brackan's shroud... are you... Deirdre?"

Many eyes widened and mouths dropped as the townspeople took a good look at her. She heard the name repeated over and over again, amid gasps and exclamations of disbelief and joy.

"No," Jaci said, projecting her voice as far as she could. "I am not Deirdre. My name is Jacinda. I am the daughter of Mirinesstra."

"The lost queen," said the blacksmith, his voice hushed now, his words echoing through the crowd.

"Queen Mirinesstra has been gone for over thirty years," said another gray-haired man. "Where have you — and she — been? Where is she now?"

"We were a very long, long way from here," Jaci said. "Sadly, Mirinesstra died of an illness, two years ago. I am sorry we were not here to help you in the fight against Galenock, but I am here now, and I will do all I can to defeat Galenock and send the Ruusitarans back where they belong."

"What can *you* do?" the merchant asked skeptically. He gestured toward Talan and those with him. "They have supposedly been fighting against Galenock for years, and I cannot see where they've made any progress. We are still under Ruusitaran rule."

"And how much help have they had?" Jaci snapped. "Have *you* gone out there and risked your life to help them fight?" She raised her voice. "Have any of you? The people of Shiannora need to band together and fight! You can't just cower beneath your beds with your tails between your legs. You are the men and women of what was once the most powerful province in Tarshane. Act like it. Fight!"

"But Galenock has magic," countered a man on Jaci's right.

"So do I," Jaci shot back. "And I will use it."

"How will you defeat him?" asked another.

"I don't know yet," Jaci answered, "but I will find a way. And that is a promise."

No one spoke.

Lani stepped forward hesitantly. "I believe her. She saved me from the soldier who was hurting me." Lani touched her cut cheek. "She confused him, she twisted his arm so I could escape, then she hit him with something, and he fell."

Jaci let the bar slip down into her hand. She held it up for all to see. "I hit him with this. A wagon part I found over there." She pointed to the wall where the pile of parts lay. She swept her hand toward Talan and the others, who stood by silently. "They did the rest." She took a step forward. "You don't need to have the skill of a Black Bander to defend yourselves. You just need the will... and a little creativity."

The blacksmith knelt. "Your Highness, my hammer is yours. I am honored to serve the royal family."

Others knelt, some resolutely, some uncertainly. Jaci watched in awe, goosebumps shivering over her skin as, in a wave, the townspeople lowered themselves to one knee and bowed to her. Even the merchant followed suit, though Jaci could tell by his shrewd expression that he was more interested in keeping on the good side of his customers than in serving the royal family.

"What would you have us do?" asked the blacksmith.

Jaci took a deep, calming breath. "First and foremost, organize yourselves and plan a defense of your town. Spread the word throughout the other towns to do the same. The more that help, the greater our successes will be. Secondly, you can help us get rid of these... soldiers." She indicated with distaste the corpses lying on the stable floor. "The stable needs to be cleaned up before any more soldiers or Riders come."

"We will dig a pit outside of town to bury them in," the blacksmith said.

"Thank you." Jaci turned in a full circle, addressing everyone. "Thank you all for whatever help you can give. Trust in yourselves, stand together, have faith. We will do our part to see this through."

"Where will you go?" asked Lani's father.

Jaci thought fast, knowing it wouldn't be prudent to reveal their real plans. "To where we are needed most," she said, after only a moment's hesitation. "We have a lot of work to do."

The townspeople looked at her expectantly, and she finally realized what they were waiting for.

"Oh — please rise, and thank you again. You honor *me*."

The townspeople rose and milled about, their conversations hushed and urgent. Many came forward to say a word to Jaci personally. She was a bit overwhelmed by all the attention, but the Black Banders kept an open space around her, eyes scrutinizing everyone. None of the townspeople dared get too close to them. The blacksmith and several other men spoke with Talan about the town's defenses, then went in search of shovels to start digging a pit. A wagon was driven inside, and another group of men loaded the soldiers' corpses into it.

After one last thank you from Lani's parents, Jaci and the others made their way to a side door, the crowd parting to let them through.

CHAPTER 21

Moonlight filtered through the narrow windows as Galenock stalked down the corridor behind Castellan Felgarth, furious at being awakened before his full recovery time for casting the sight spell. He'd been irritated enough before he'd gone to sleep, partly because he was still weakened from transferring his burn wounds, and partly because his sight spell had been stymied again. He'd finally chosen a blood sample that had allowed him to see something useful, instead of the endless forests and swamps he'd been seeing through the eyes of those wretched rebels. He'd finally found Deirdre — or Jacinda or whatever it was the wench called herself — but before he could determine where she was, that cur Talan had blocked his vision.

It irked Galenock even more that the woman had somehow managed to rejoin Talan and his men. Galenock still didn't know how she'd escaped the castle. She had to have used a magic portal, but he could find no trace of one anywhere. Felgarth had felt his wrath that night, as he would again this night if this soldier Felgarth was bringing him to meet didn't have earth-shaking news. Galenock's ranks would be minus a soldier — and perhaps a castellan, as well.

"In here, my lord." Felgarth opened the door to a small ante-room.

Galenock swept past him into the torchlit room. Felgarth followed, closing the door behind him.

A dirty, disheveled Ruusitaran soldier who was braced against a table straightened painfully. His left arm, which had been cradling his abdomen, slid upward, his fist moving to his right shoulder in salute. "My lord."

Galenock noted the soldier's black eyes, bloody nose, and split lip. Someone had given him a thorough beating. He wondered who. "What is your report?"

"I found the woman you wanted. She was in a livery stable in Garsondale. She and Talan d'Lochlann had been hidden in wagons traveling from a mill just outside of Sagetown."

Galenock lunged forward and grasped the man's collar. "Where is she? Why isn't she in this room right now?"

The soldier didn't flinch. "They had Black Banders with them. They killed my men."

"But not you."

"I escaped to bring you this information."

Galenock backhanded the soldier across the face. "You should have brought the woman!"

The soldier took the blow stoically. "I failed, my lord. It won't happen again."

Galenock eyed him, considering whether or not to have him flayed for his failure. The cold-blooded malice in the man's eyes, along with the way his voice had dripped hatred when he'd spoken of the Black Banders, persuaded him to give the soldier a second chance. Vengeance would drive him, and that could prove very useful.

"What else do you have to report?" Galenock asked, pacing away from the soldier.

"They were aided by the mill owner, Willem d'Archer, and by a man from Twain's Crossing. I burned the mill with d'Archer and his workers in it. If you will allow me more soldiers, I will kill the other man and his family and burn his home to the ground. Then I will find that woman again and bring her to you, and I will kill Talan d'Lochlann and every one of those Black Banders. I swear it."

Galenock looked at him skeptically. "If you could do that, I would make you general of my entire army."

"There is one other thing, my lord."

"Which is?"

"She said her name was Jacinda and that she was the daughter of Mirinesstra."

"Mirinesstra," Galenock repeated, pacing again, puzzle pieces fitting together in his mind. That would explain the *druidainoch* stone around her neck... and her more spirited personality. It didn't explain, however, how she'd gotten the key to Ridaur's crypt. Soneira had stolen the key, so she must have given it to Deirdre before sending her off... somewhere. Perhaps Mirinesstra and Deirdre had gone to the same place. But if that were the case, then where were they now? Why had only Jacinda returned? He clenched his fist. He needed that key to set his final plans in motion — plans that had been on hold for nineteen years. He had been so close, and then that wench had attacked him with surprising ferocity and knocked him into the fire. He stifled a shudder at the horror of it. He would not underestimate her again.

He faced the soldier. "Very well. You will have your soldiers. I will hold you to your vow to bring the woman to me and kill all those with her. But mark my words well, if she is harmed in any way, I'll have you flayed and tortured until your screams are heard across the entire province. Do you understand me?"

"Yes, my lord. I will not fail."

"Go, choose your men. I don't want to see you back here until you've accomplished your mission."

The soldier saluted and limped from the room.

"I know his reputation," Castellan Felgarth said, after he'd closed the door again. "He is completely unscrupulous and will use whatever means necessary."

Galenock paced slowly, the earlier use of his magic weighing on him. "A mill outside Sagetown. How in Brackan's name did she get there?" He spoke more to himself than the castellan. "And where is she now?" *With Talan d'Lochlann... just like Soneira...* The thought infuriated him. He whirled on the castellan. "Send word to all the Riders to converge on the area around Sagetown and Garsondale. They are to take orders from that soldier that just left. What is his name?"

"Vorstun, my lord."

"I want the woman found, and everyone with her, dead." If only he could scry her, it would be so much easier, but he needed something that belonged to her to work the spell... Wait! When she'd come to his rooms, she'd been wearing a yellow dress. But when he'd first spied her through Talan's man's eyes, she'd been wearing some strange outfit, the likes of which he'd never seen. Her old clothing might still be here.

"Stop!" he ordered Felgarth, just as the castellan was walking out the door.

"Yes, my lord?"

"After you send the messages, go to Jacinda's room and find the clothes she was wearing when she was first brought here. Bring them to my chambers."

"Yes, my lord."

"Oh, and Felgarth — don't wake me again."

Felgarth paled at the menace in Galenock's voice. "As you wish, my lord." He hastened from the room.

*****

Jaci jogged through moonlit darkness, her breath frosty as she tried to concentrate on the hard, uneven ground. Talan ran a few feet ahead of her. Liundur kept pace a few steps behind. Carrick had taken the point, scouting out the path ahead. Somewhere behind her, Solon led Tobias, their arms linked to keep Tobias from stumbling. Arnos kept rear guard. They'd headed south out of Garsondale to throw anyone watching them off their trail. Then they'd circled around to the northeast, making their way cross-country to where Talan and the others had hidden their horses. Their progress had been slowed considerably by the fact that Talan wouldn't let Tobias remove his blindfold. He couldn't take the risk of Galenock seeing their location.

Rapidly approaching hoofbeats rang in the chill air, and Carrick waved them to cover. They ducked behind a stone wall as red-cloaked Riders galloped across a nearby field. Several times, they'd had to hide from troops of Riders headed toward Garsondale. As soon as the Riders passed from sight, Carrick signaled them onward. They'd run for what seemed like hours, and even though their pace hadn't been swift, Jaci's legs were starting to feel like lead. Guilt and worry weighed her down even more, like a heavy yoke around her neck. So many Riders going to Garsondale. The merchant's words haunted her.

That's all well and good, but what are we going to do when Lord Galenock discovers what these Black Banders have done here? He will send his Riders, and they will kill every last one of us.

Would the Riders kill the townspeople, even though they weren't involved in the massacre of the soldiers? Had her angry outburst condemned the entire town? Or what if they did try to fight and were killed for their efforts? Either way, the result was the same: the population of an entire town annihilated because of her. Just like Willem and the millworkers, who were dead simply because they'd helped her. It was too much to bear. She surreptitiously wiped away the tears that wouldn't stop trickling down her face, glad of the dark and the shadows that hid them.

Talan halted in front of her and turned around, and she just managed to stop herself from running into him. He caught her shoulder, his thumb brushing across her wet cheek.

"What's wrong?" he asked softly.

"All those Riders," she said in a quavering voice. "All the townspeople... they're going to die, and it's my fault... and — and Willem... and all the millworkers..." Her voice failed her, and tears poured down her face in earnest.

He drew her close. She buried her face against his chest and sobbed. He stroked her hair and let her cry.

When she'd quieted, he brushed her tears away again. "Jacinda, listen to me. Nothing that has happened is your fault. Galenock is the evil here, not you. You have to understand that — yes?"

She nodded wordlessly. She understood, but it didn't make her feel any less guilty.

He sighed heavily. "The Riders are headed to Garsondale, and yes, some of the townspeople may die, but many lives will be saved because of what you said to them." His tone grew more hopeful. "Your words and your passion inspired them to move beyond their fear and take up arms. When the Riders arrive, they will be prepared. The women and children will have been moved to safety, and if we are lucky, a full scale rebellion will have begun."

He shook his head. "For years I've tried, with very little success, to rouse the people of Shiannora and get them to fight." He smiled. "You have a gift for making people rise above themselves."

She smiled faintly, heartened by his words. "Thank you."

He squeezed her shoulders. "I know how much it hurts to lose those who've befriended you." His voice grew rough with the pain of loss. "But you must not dwell on it. What's happened has happened and cannot be undone. We have to move on and look forward — always forward — to our goal. Such is the way of war."

She nodded. "That's a lot easier said than done, but I'll try." She saw that the others had gathered around them, and tried not to feel embarrassed by the fact that they'd seen her cry.

"We also must thank you," Talan continued, "for your brilliant maneuver in freeing the girl. You saved her life and spared us from having to make what would have been the most terrible decision we've ever had to make."

All of them bowed their heads respectfully.

Warmth rose in her face. She didn't know what to say. "I... sometimes my temper gets the best of me. I'm glad what I did worked."

"Your bravery is as much an inspiration as your words." He gave her shoulders one last squeeze, then let go. "We'll rest for another few minutes and eat, then move on."

They crossed to a nearby pine grove and sat beneath the trees, mostly hidden from the light of the moon.

Jaci accepted her portion of bread and jerky from Solon, Talan's words of praise still ringing in her ears. She glanced at those around her. To have won the respect of battle-hardened men such as these... It boggled her mind. And to think, she had actually saved a life. She, whose life had been one of ease and indulgence. Not that she'd been spoiled. Her parents had taught her the importance of hard work and of treating others as she would want to be treated.

But life on her parents' horse farm and at the private school and college from which she'd graduated had been peacefully uneventful. Her father's death so many years ago and then her mother's recent passing were the only real upheavals in her humdrum existence. She'd never done anything truly important in her entire life.

Now, she was in the middle of a rebellion, where everything she did was of utmost importance. The kingdom of Tarshane depended, not just on Talan anymore, but on her, too. She was a marked woman, a fugitive, and if Galenock caught her... The reality of the situation terrified her, and yet it exhilarated her at the same time. She'd never felt so alive, so vital, so... *needed*.

All through her self-defense classes, she'd wondered what she would do if she was ever threatened for real. Would she be strong and fight, or would she freeze up in fear and become another victim? Now, she knew. She was discovering a whole new side of herself she'd never known existed. And she would do her best to use that newfound strength to save this land.

More Riders charged by, not far away, chilling her. Doubts began to creep around the edges of her resolve, fueled by thoughts of Willem's death and the dire threat the Riders posed to the people of Garsondale. She closed her eyes and prayed that her best would be enough.

*****

It was nearly dawn when they finally reached the cave where the horses had been hidden. The cave delved deep into a rocky hillside and was protected from view by an overgrown blackberry thicket. Talan signaled the Black Bander inside with the same bird call Solon had used at the ruins. The Black Bander pulled back a part of the briar thicket along the stone face of the hill and let them in. Solon and the other Black Banders readied the horses, while Talan spoke with the horse guard, named Iain. Solon could hardly contain his impatience to get going, concern for his brother plain on his face. Jaci wondered, with another stab of guilt, if Nickalonis was still alive.

They led the horses outside and mounted up. Jaci rode in front of Talan. Tobias remained with Iain, who stayed behind to take care of the horses belonging to Katar and the other Black Banders who were still with Cranton and Zaiya. Jaci hoped Katar and his men would be able to escape from the tunnels beneath the mill safely now that the mill had been destroyed.

They turned their horses' heads to the northeast and rode out at a gallop. Tobias had told them where the encampment was the night before, saying that the men should still be there, because Owen, the medic, had declared Nickalonis too near death to be moved.

The orange sun had lowered toward the western horizon by the time they rode into the forest camp. A series of bird calls had alerted the sentries to their coming, and they were met by Medres, the other medic.

Solon leaped from his horse almost before it had stopped and collared Medres. "Is he alive? Where is he? Take me to him."

Medres' hands sprang up, and he pressed them against Solon's chest. "Solon, calm down! Yes, he lives. Follow me." He turned and led the way into the encampment. Jaci jumped down from Talan's horse with Talan right behind her and, despite her weariness, hurried after them. Medres led them toward a shelter made from thickly woven evergreen branches.

Before they reached the shelter, Owen blocked their path. He grasped Solon's arms.

"Owen, let go!" Solon fought the restraining hands. "I have to see —"

Owen tightened his grip. "Solon, stop! You have to listen to me first. His wounds are grievous. He needs rest and quiet, so you can't go barreling in there. *Rest and quiet.* Do you understand?"

Jaci watched, her heart in her throat, as Talan gently laid his hands on Solon's shoulders from behind. Solon ceased struggling. He looked from one to the other, then his face crumpled, and she saw tears running down his cheeks. He took several deep shuddering breaths. When he faced Owen again, he had himself in hand. "Can you save him?"

The look in Owen's eyes said no.

Jaci's hand flew to her mouth, a sick feeling clutching her stomach.

"I don't know," Owen said after a moment. "I won't lie to you. He is fading."

"Please let me see him," Solon whispered.

Owen let go. Talan kept his arm around Solon's shoulders and walked forward with him into the shelter. Jaci followed, dreading what she would see.

Nickalonis lay on a pallet padded with blankets, naked except for another blanket covering his loins and the swaths of bandages covering his head, neck, and chest, his lower arms and hands, and two or three places on his legs, as well as the older sword wound on his side.

Solon knelt slowly beside his brother. Talan stood behind him, his hand on his friend's shoulder. Jaci edged up beside Talan and curled her fingers around his other hand, his sorrow heavy in her heart. He clasped her hand tightly.

Owen came in and sat opposite Solon.

"Is there nothing more you can do for him?" Solon asked in a hoarse whisper.

Owen shook his head. "I've done all I can. Only magic could heal him now."

"Magic?" Solon turned desperate eyes on Talan.

Talan squeezed Solon's shoulder. "I cannot heal others. You know that. I've tried. The Guild wizards tested us —"

"Us?" Solon asked.

"Yes — we —" Talan stumbled over his words. "She — she and I tested at the same time... without success."

"Oh." Solon turned away, hope crumbling.

Jaci's heart ached, both for Solon in his grief and for Talan in his struggles with his past. It disheartened her to know he still couldn't think of Soneira without pain.

Then Solon whipped around again, this time eyeing Jaci. "You have magic. Can you heal?"

Jaci was taken aback. "*Me?* I — I don't know."

"But you worked the portal magic. Can't you try?" Solon begged.

"All I did was read a word on a page," Jaci said, at a loss. "I didn't actually *do* anything. If you know any healing words, I'll gladly say them."

Talan looked at Jaci. "Your grandmother is a true healer. It's possible you could have inherited her talent."

Jaci swallowed hard. She felt like she was floundering in water over her head. "Do you know what she does — what she says when she heals?"

"No," Talan said, "but I do know that to use magic, you must draw on the celestial energies around you and focus them on what it is you want done. You also have your *druidainoch* stone to help you."

Jaci looked at Nickalonis and wet her dry lips. She was afraid to touch him. She had no idea how she had worked magic. What if whatever she did made him worse? *He's nearly dead,* her conscience chided. *How much worse could you make him?*

She shifted her gaze from Nickalonis' still form to Solon's pleading face to Talan's expression of cautious hope. She took a deep breath. "When you tested with the Guild, do you have any idea what words you used?"

Talan looked blank. "No, I — it was so long ago —" His eyes lit as if with a sudden thought, and he tore through his belt pouch. He pulled out and unwrapped Soneira's spell book, then leafed through it, scanning the pages. About a quarter of the way through the book, he stopped. "Yes, this is it. *Syelonin henaltroth sepalinata.*"

"What does it mean?" Jaci asked.

"It means 'simple healing spell' in the archaic language of ancient wizards. We had to study the language, because most magic spells are derived from it." He showed her the phrase, then pointed to a phrase on the next line. "These are the words you must say."

Jaci read them silently. "And what do they mean?"

"Literally, 'heal the flesh,'" Talan said.

Jaci looked back at Nickalonis. She was tired and scared and full of doubt, but she couldn't just step away. He was dying because of something she'd done. Despite what Talan had said, she still felt responsible. "All right, I'll try." Jaci knelt beside Solon.

Owen removed one of the smaller bandages on Nickalonis' leg, revealing a five-inch by three-inch oval burn, the damaged area bright red with darker patches, clear fluid seeping from around the edges. "You can try on this one. I don't want to disturb the bad wounds unnecessarily."

Jaci grimaced. This wound looked bad enough, matching the images of second degree burns she'd seen in a first aid book. She didn't want to imagine what the "bad" ones looked like. "Do I touch the wound?"

"The Guild wizards had us put our hands just above the wounds, not quite touching them," Talan answered. "Then you say the words and repeat them over and over for as long as you can."

For as long as I can, she thought nervously. *Why wouldn't I be able to keep saying them?*

Owen doused Jaci's hand with whiskey for disinfection, in case she accidently touched the wound. She shook off the excess drops, then held her right hand about an inch above the wound, her left hand gripping the *druidainoch* stone she'd drawn out of her shirt. *Here goes nothing...*

She spoke the words: *henalto falaishia.* The familiar electrical charge crackled in the air. Her stone glowed faintly with soft iridescence. She heard Talan's sharp intake of breath. He must have felt it, too. She repeated the words, concentrating on healing the wound, picturing in her mind an undamaged leg. After only about ten minutes, an intense weariness dragged at her, and she had to stop to catch her breath. She looked at the wound in disappointment. It didn't appear to have changed any.

"Why does it exhaust me so much?" she asked when her breathing had slowed.

"You have never used this kind of magic before," Talan said. "Wielding magic can be draining for even experienced wizards, unless they are using their particular talent. Apparently, healing is not yours." He said the last softly, without censure. "Thank you for trying."

"But working the portal didn't tire me," Jaci argued.

"The portals appear to have been created with Enchantress magic, which is subtly different from the ancient magic. I think that is why Galenock hasn't been able to find them. Enchantress magic would be easier for you to use, since you are descended from them."

Frustrated, Jaci looked back at the wound, then looked again, more closely, a sliver of hope rising in her chest. "Owen, is it just wishful thinking on my part, or do the darker spots appear a bit lighter to you?"

Owen studied the wound. "I think you're right. There is a change — a very slight one. At this rate, though…" He left the thought unfinished.

"…it won't really help much," Jaci finished for him, deflating again.

Solon looked desperately from one to the other. "Can't she — you — keep trying? Perhaps with more practice…?"

Owen looked doubtful.

Jaci thought hard. What she needed was more strength, more power. She caught her breath. "I have an idea. Remember when we were in the tunnels," she asked Talan, "and I told you about how your magic affects me when I'm close to you?"

"Yes." She saw speculation in his eyes and knew he had caught on to her idea, but he didn't seem very excited about it. She wondered why.

"I'd like to try the healing spell again with you sitting close to me and see what happens."

She sensed reluctance in him, but he nodded.

"What are you talking about?" Solon asked.

"I'll explain later." Jaci rose and had Talan sit cross-legged next to Nickalonis. Then, hoping no one would notice her blushing, she lowered herself into Talan's lap. He eased her into a sitting position, then hesitated, so she slid his arms around her waist, her back firmly against his chest. Warm tingles zinged through her as if someone had flicked on a light switch, brightening and sharpening the world around her. Heat of another kind sizzled through her as well — a sudden desire to turn around and kiss him completely distracted her. She took several deep breaths, under the guise of preparing herself for the healing, to curb her rebellious hormones and slow her speeding heart. When she had herself under control, she noticed with surprise that his heartbeat had quickened to almost the same rate hers had been. Could he be nervous about working the magic?

She settled back against him and tried to exude confidence. "Are you ready?" she asked over her shoulder.

"Yes," he said, breathing deeply.

"Here we go." She placed her hand above Nickalonis' wound, grasped her *druidainoch* stone, and recited the healing spell. Light burst from the stone, brighter this time, and a powerful influx of energy, drawn from the earth and the trees and the very air itself, swept through her like a raging river. The force of it knocked her for a loop. She closed her eyes and struggled to contain the vast power. Talan somehow helped her corral it, so she could focus the energy on the burn wound.

Jaci repeated the words as many times as she could, lasting twice as long as the last time, before slumping forward, her head in her hands, more exhausted than she'd ever been in her life.

"Jacinda!" Talan turned her sideways and touched her cheek.

"...all right," she mumbled. She was having a hard time forming coherent thoughts. "Just need sleep. Did it work?"

"Yes, to some degree," Owen said. "Better than the first attempt."

Solon helped Jaci up. She swayed, the darkness of sleep overtaking her. Talan rose and then lifted her in his arms. She laid her head on his shoulder and drifted away.

CHAPTER 22

Jaci woke to warm sunshine and sparrows chirping in the trees over her head. She rubbed her eyes, trying to remember where she was. Waking up in a different place every morning kept throwing her off balance.

She heard footsteps walk by, and Owen saying, "She's waking. Get Talan."

The shrill cry of a hawk cleared the rest of her cobwebs. *Sharrow.* She sat up and looked around. She'd been lying on a blanket on a bed of pine needles, just outside the evergreen bower that sheltered Nickalonis. A few paces away, Liundur rose from where he'd been sitting ripping a beige tunic into strips. He gave her a nod, then headed off into the forest. Owen was already ducking into the shelter, his hands full of clean bandages. Jaci threw back the covering blanket and followed after Owen.

She halted at the edge of the shelter. Owen sat down next to Medres, near Nickalonis' shoulder. Solon was sitting across from them, looking like he hadn't moved since Jaci's healing attempt the night before. He had such a look of grief on his face that Jaci's heart stopped.

"He's not... is he...?" She couldn't get the words out.

Owen glanced at her. "Dead? No." He and Medres carefully unwrapped the bandages from around Nickalonis' head and neck.

Jaci choked. Most of the skin on one side of his face had burned off down to the muscle. His eye looked badly damaged. The other side had red patches centered with black, one extending down his neck and beneath the chest bandages. Charred frizz covered parts of his scalp, his long, blond hair burnt away. Her stomach heaved. She stumbled away from the shelter, caught herself on a tree and vomited.

"Jacinda?" Talan cupped her shoulders from behind. "Are you all right?"

She spat and wiped her mouth on her sleeve. "It's — it's — horrible... I can't even —" *Oh, God, what have I done?* Her stomach heaved again, but she fought it down.

"Come with me." Talan led her away from the shelter to a log, where he had her sit. He brought her some water.

She rinsed her mouth, spat again, and drank a few swallows. "Thanks."

He sat beside her. "How do you feel?"

"Sick." Jaci closed her eyes, but all she could see were those terrible wounds. She looked down at the ground and poked at a rock with her foot. "I've never seen burn wounds that bad."

"I've not seen them, but Owen described them to me. He said your second effort at healing did some good. He thought that if you — we — kept trying, we might have a slim chance of saving him." Talan hesitated, gazing off across the forest. "He said it would take many days, though, and not to get our hopes too high."

Jaci shook her head. "Those wounds looked catastrophic. How could we heal something like that? The skin is gone. There's nothing to replace it with. Can the healing spell create new skin?"

"I don't know, but I would like to keep trying."

Jaci looked away. The thought of having to see the wounds again made the bile rise in her throat. "I'm not sure I could handle it." *But you can't not try*, her conscience told her grimly.

"When you woke, did you feel any ill effects from using the healing spell?"

Jaci thought back to when she'd first awakened. "No, I felt fine. The twelve hours of sleep helped a lot. What about you? Did channeling your magic through me exhaust you, like using the healing spell exhausted me?"

"No."

"Maybe that's your natural talent, then — gathering the magical energies around you and boosting the magic of others. Tell me, the heightened sensitivity I felt, do you see and hear and feel that all the time?"

"Yes, when I choose to."

"Did you ever tell anyone? The Guild wizards, I mean?"

"I tried to explain it once to Elshaer, but he was so caught up in... other things... that I don't think he ever really listened."

The sharp spike of pain in Talan's heart, and hers, startled Jaci. She'd only felt that kind of pain in him when he was thinking of Soneira. Mandy had said Soneira had trained with Elshaer. Jaci wondered exactly what they'd been doing.

"What was Elshaer's talent?"

"He was an inventor. He could manipulate magic and create new ways to use it. I think it was Elshaer who conceived the idea of the portals. He made time for me when he could, but his talent wouldn't let him rest. He was driven to create, always full of ideas. I believe he was a good man at heart, and I do not blame him for —" He stopped abruptly, his knuckles white on the log, his eyes sliding away to look at nothing.

Jaci struggled to find something to say to ease his pain, but all she could come up with was, "I'm sorry." She covered his hand with hers and squeezed it.

He shot her a fleeting smile, then looked away again. "You need not be sorry. As I said before, what's happened has happened and cannot be undone. We must look forward."

Jaci had the distinct impression it was himself he was trying to convince, not her. "You know," she began, trying to get his mind off Soneira, "I'd be willing to bet that the power you can wield with your talent is stronger than the magic of all those Guild wizards put together. It sure threw me for a loop, last night."

"I'm sorry. I've never used it in that way before. I didn't know that I could. The wizards always had me try to cast spells, which never worked very well, and I thought that was how magic was supposed to be used."

"Did anyone else besides me ever mention being affected by your magic, when they were close to you?" She immediately regretted the question.

His gaze dipped downward, and he stared at the ground unseeingly. "No."

Jaci upbraided herself mentally. Not only had she made him think of Soneira again, she'd conjured up images in her own mind of Talan and Soneira together that stung her with needles of jealousy. At least it didn't sound like Soneira had shared his magic, Jaci thought with a kind of sour satisfaction. She was probably too busy fooling around with Elshaer...

"Did Elshaer have dark hair with gray streaks in it?" Jaci asked, struck with a sudden thought.

"Yes." Talan looked at her questioningly. "How did you know?"

"I was just remembering one of Deirdre's diary entries. She described two wizards battling, one with dark, gray-streaked hair and the other with reddish-blond hair, who I assume must have been Galenock."

"Ah, yes, I remember reading that as well. She must have witnessed part of the final battle after Galenock had murdered all the other Guild wizards. Elshaer was incredibly powerful, but that wasn't enough. In the end, Galenock killed him too."

"Did you see any of what happened?"

"No," he said in a hoarse whisper. "After she... she and I... we fought... I left the castle." He studied the ground, his body so tense Jaci feared he might snap. "I wasn't there."

She wanted desperately to ask more questions — what had they fought about, what had Soneira done to anger him so much — but his anguish wrenched her heart until she could hardly bear it, and she cursed herself for having brought up the subject in the first place. She twined her arm around his, clasped his hand, and leaned against him sympathetically.

He closed his eyes and neither spoke for several moments.

Some distance away, Liundur rose and carried the new bandages he'd made into the shelter. She wondered where Carrick and Arnos were. She hadn't seen them since she'd awakened. Then she realized with a start that they weren't the only ones she hadn't seen. She straightened and glanced around at the empty forest. The encampment was gone.

Talan roused at her movements.

"Where did everyone go?" she asked, before he could speak.

"They have been moving to a new location every day, so that if Galenock uses the sight spell, he won't discover where we are."

"I see. I'd forgotten it wasn't just us." She nodded toward Liundur, who was coming out of the shelter with empty hands. "Did Carrick and Arnos go with them?"

"No. They are serving as lookouts, to warn us if Galenock's men come near."

In case he looks through your eyes? Jaci thought apprehensively. She shuddered inwardly. *It can't happen to him... it just can't...* "What is Galenock's talent?" she asked, trying to hide her anxiety.

She caught the grim despair that flickered in his eyes before he looked away. He'd guessed what she'd been thinking.

"Galenock is also an inventor of sorts," Talan said. "However, he twists the magic, perverts it in ways that should not be. He creates spells to destroy things and to hurt and control others."

"What a lovely guy," Jaci murmured.

She looked down at their hands where they rested on the log, their fingers still twined together. She leaned in close against him once more, letting his magic fill her with the essence of the world. A gentle breeze whispered through the forest. She listened to its voice, older than the ages, yet still young and playful as it ruffled her hair. Birds sang of warmer lands and long journeys, and she sensed a herd of deer passing through the trees to the south. What would it be like to see and hear like this all the time?

Then another thought chilled her, as if the breeze had suddenly turned icy. What if Galenock found out what Talan could do? What if Galenock captured and imprisoned Talan, then tortured those he cared about to force him to boost Galenock's power? She could hardly imagine such horror. Talan's life would become one of unspeakable pain and torment, with far-reaching consequences: the Northern Enchantresses would fall, and the world of Tarshane would be doomed.

Talan turned toward her, his face lined with concern. "What has frightened you?"

"We can never let Galenock find out what your talent is," she said in a low voice. "He would try to use you in horrible ways." She shivered. "Thank God, Elshaer didn't listen to you. If they'd known what you could do, back then…"

Talan slipped an arm around her, his other hand cupping her cheek. "Jacinda, don't worry so. He's tried for many years but he hasn't caught me yet."

"But he's making a much more concentrated effort now — because of me. I couldn't bear it if something happened to you because of my being here. Maybe I should —"

"Don't say it," he said firmly. "You'll not go anywhere alone."

The fierce protectiveness in his eyes silenced the argument she'd been about to make. Her breath caught. She sat motionless, lost in the depths of those dark eyes. His fingertips lingered on her cheek, traced the line of her jaw. Her lips parted. Slowly they leaned toward each other as if drawn together by an invisible cord. Jaci closed her eyes, trembling, yearning for his lips to touch hers.

"Are you two ready to try again?" Owen called from across the way.

Talan shot to his feet as if the log on which they were sitting had suddenly become electrified. Jaci gasped, startled, her breath coming fast. She cursed Owen silently.

Talan raked his hand through his hair. "Yes… I think so." He half turned toward her, his gaze on anything but her, which was just as well, she thought. If he'd looked her in the eye again, she would have thrown her arms around his neck and kissed him, regardless of who was watching.

"Are you ready?" he asked.

She rose. "Almost. I just need to… wash up." She jerked her thumb toward a stream running close by. She'd heard its silvery song when she'd shared Talan's magic. "I'll be right back."

She took a few steps toward the stream, then stopped in her tracks, gasping as heat seared through her body and white light burst from her *druidainoch* stone. The light flared outward, enclosing her in a shimmering, iridescent bubble. She yanked the stone out from beneath her shirt, but the bright light blinded her, and she dropped the stone back down out of sight. "What's happening?" she cried.

Talan, Liundur, and Owen ran forward and surrounded the bubble.

"Don't touch it," Talan said sharply to the others. "Is it hurting you?" he asked Jaci.

Jaci squinted at him through the milky translucence. "No. I just feel really hot, like I've spent all day in a desert."

"Have you ever seen anything like it?" Owen asked Talan.

"No." Talan studied the smooth iridescence.

"Why is it doing this?" Jaci reached toward the shimmering wall with the flat of her hand, not quite touching it, feeling a continuous throb of energy like a heartbeat.

Talan did the same from the outside. "Enchantress magic," he said slowly. "The bubble is shielding you from something." He recoiled, a look of revulsion on his face. "Galenock! I feel the aura of his magic."

"*What?*" Jaci jumped back from the bubble's edge. "What's he doing?"

Talan blanched in alarm. "He didn't get any blood from you, did he, while you were at the castle?"

Jaci clamped down on her rising panic and forced herself to think, to remember her days with Mandy and Allina. "No, he didn't."

"You are certain?"

"Positive."

Talan exhaled a long breath, his relief so overpowering that Jaci felt almost blown away by the force of it. He took a moment to collect himself, then frowned, thinking. "He could be trying to scry you, but he would need something of yours to do it. Did you leave anything in the castle —" He stopped. "Your clothes!"

"My clothes!" Jaci said at the same time.

Talan turned to Liundur. "Find Carrick and Arnos and tell them to increase their vigilance and set some traps. This bubble may block the scrying spell, but if it doesn't, we'll need the extra warning."

Liundur nodded and dashed off into the woods.

"What is that?" Solon asked, as he came up beside them. His haggard, tear-stained face wrung Jaci's heart.

"I'm not sure, but I think it is shielding her from Galenock's scrying spell," Talan said.

"He's scrying her?" Horror etched Solon's face. "The Riders — Nick is too weak to move."

"I don't think the spell is getting through." Talan held his hand close to the wall of the bubble again.

"Can you be certain?" Solon asked anxiously.

"The aura of his magic is fading, and the wall is still strong."

"But can you be certain?" Solon repeated.

"No," Talan said quietly.

Moments later, the light from the *druidainoch* stone winked out and the shimmering bubble vanished. Jaci glanced about, but no remnants of the bubble remained. She took a deep breath, her body cooling quickly. *Well, that was weird.*

Talan caught her arms and looked her up and down as if to reassure himself that she was unharmed.

"I'm fine," she said, "and it didn't tire me."

Owen touched her forehead with the backs of his fingers. "You have no fever."

"No, the heat went away when the light from the stone went out."

"Has that ever happened to you before, either here or in your own world?" Talan asked.

Jaci shook her head. "Never."

"What do we do?" Solon asked.

"If you are going to try the healing, it needs to be done now," Owen said. "I want to finish wrapping the wounds."

Jaci cringed inwardly at the thought of having to face those horrible wounds again. But what choice did she have? "All right." She straightened resolutely. "We'll try this again." She pointed in the direction of the stream. "I'll be right back."

She found some bushes in which to relieve herself, then washed her hands and face in the stream, all the while mulling over what had just happened. She wondered if Talan was right about the bubble acting as a shield against hostile magic. The magic of the *druidainoch* stone — Enchantress magic — had acted on its own. She'd had no inkling she was in danger, but she must have been, since Talan had sensed the aura of Galenock's magic around her. She filled her cupped hands with water, lifted them to take a drink, then stopped in mid-motion. Could that be *her* natural talent — to be able to shield herself against magical attacks? The sudden image of herself battling Galenock in Elshaer's place, with Galenock's blue lightning bouncing off the iridescent bubble around her, slid into her head. She almost laughed. Here she'd been frightened of him, when in reality, his magic couldn't harm her. Of course, that was assuming her magic was as strong as his. What if it wasn't? If Galenock's magic was powerful enough to defeat the entire Wizard's Guild, what were the chances her magic could stand up to it? Likely slim to none. She drank the water in her hands, then scooped up some more. She honestly hoped she'd never have to find out.

Footsteps approached, and she hurriedly finished her drink and headed back toward the shelter, meeting Talan as he came to check on her.

"Are you sure you're up to this?" he asked.

She nodded, not sure at all, and they made their way to the shelter.

Inside, Solon had resumed his place near his brother's shoulder. Medres and Owen sat opposite him. Jaci and Talan knelt beside Solon. Jaci swallowed, trying to settle her still queasy stomach.

Owen lifted the bandage covering the leg wound she'd healed the night before. "As you can see, there is some improvement."

The wound now looked more like a first degree burn rather than a second, still red and seeping in places, but definitely better. Jaci frowned. Not as much improvement as she'd hoped for, though. She thought again of the terrible burns on Nickalonis' face and neck. At the rate she was going, he'd be dead before she could do any real good.

Owen covered up the leg wound and removed a section of bandage that lay over Nickalonis' chest. Jaci steeled herself. It was all she could do not to turn away.

"I'd like you to work on this one," Owen said.

The burned area, larger than the leg wound, wasn't quite as bad as the wounds on Nickalonis' face, but it was still deep and angry-looking, with charred edges and oozing red flesh. Jaci swallowed hard, fighting her nausea as Owen disinfected her hand.

Talan sat and drew her into his lap. "Close your eyes," he whispered in her ear. "Let me guide you."

She did as he asked, and he took her hand and held it above the wound. His magic swelled and flowed into her, much more gently this time, like a deep, slow-moving river instead of the raging torrent from before. She let the energy fill her to overflowing, then channeled it outward into the wound. Over and over she repeated the healing words until exhaustion claimed her once again, and she faded into sleep.

CHAPTER 23

When she woke again, it was late afternoon. The sun slanted through the trees, patching the ground with light and shadow, the fragrance of evergreens strong in the cool air. She lay on her bed of blankets and pine needles, blinking. *Right. The encampment. The healing.* She must have slept a good eight hours. She wondered how long she'd lasted with the healing this time, and how much progress had been made. She'd kept her eyes closed to lessen her nausea and had focused so hard on healing the wound that she'd lost track of time.

Her stomach growled as she sat up. She wasn't nauseated anymore. She was famished. She pushed her hair back out of her face, wishing fervently for a brush to tame the tangled mess her curls had become. She wrinkled her nose. Another bath would be nice, too.

The Black Banders were nowhere to be seen. Liundur must have been assigned lookout duty as well, she surmised. At least no Riders had appeared. If the scrying spell had worked, if that was truly what it was, it seemed likely they would have found the camp by now.

She spotted Talan sitting cross-legged in front of a small fire a short distance away. Two steaming metal pots hung from a makeshift spit over the flames. Jaci was surprised he'd risked a fire. She watched a thin curl of smoke rise into the leafy canopy and hoped no one would see it.

Talan was sitting half turned away from her and hadn't noticed yet that she was awake. She started to rise, then stopped when she realized what he was doing. He was thumbing slowly through Soneira's spellbook, stopping to read here and there before moving on. He turned a page, and Soneira's letter fell out into his lap. He set the book down and opened the letter, reread it. Then he refolded the parchment and stared into the fire, holding the letter in his hands.

Throw it in, Jaci urged silently. *Burn it up. Get rid of it.*

His gaze shifted to the letter, and he looked at it for several long moments. He glanced at the fire once more, then picked up the book and carefully placed the letter back between the pages.

Jaci sank down again from her knees onto the blanket, crestfallen. He just couldn't forget the past, forget... *her*. Even after being dead for nineteen years, Soneira still had him bewitched. Jaci narrowed her eyes, her temper flaring. Someone needed to drag him out of the pit of memories he continued to wallow in, and it looked like that someone would have to be her. She rose determinedly and walked to the fire.

He caught sight of her and smiled, looking both relieved and genuinely happy to see her. "You're awake. Did you rest well?"

"Yes," she answered, her heartbeat quickening at his smile. She bent over and kissed him on the cheek, then sat down beside him.

His eyes darkened, smoldering with a fire of another kind. "What was that for?" he asked softly.

"To thank you... for everything. You've done so much for me, and I don't think I ever really thanked you for it."

Their eyes held again and the world stopped, everything slowing until it seemed nothing moved except her racing heart.

"Aren't they ready yet?"

Owen's demanding voice startled her. She whirled. Eye contact lost, the world began turning again. Owen strode up next to her and glared into one of the bubbling pots. She had to restrain herself from kicking him in the shin. Both shins.

Talan cleared his throat. "Yes, I think they're ready now."

"Took long enough," Owen muttered. Using a folded cloth, he lifted one of the pots off its hook and carried it back to the shelter.

Frustrated, Jaci regrouped, her moment lost. "Find anything useful in there?" She nodded toward the little blue book Talan still held. Then she caught a mouth-watering aroma wafting from the other pot. "Oh, that smells wonderful. What is it?"

"Stew. Are you hungry?"

"Very."

He stuffed the spellbook into his belt pouch, then spooned out a bowlful for her.

She hesitated. "As much as I'm looking forward to hot food, I'm a little worried someone might see the smoke."

"That was my worry as well," he said as he handed her the bowl, "but Owen is concerned that one of the wounds on Nickalonis' neck might be starting to fester. He insisted we needed to boil the bandages to try to stem any further infection." Talan sighed heavily. "I couldn't deny him. If infection sets in, Nickalonis is lost. So, if we have to have a fire, we might as well have hot food."

Jaci dug into the stew. "What happened with the wound we healed?"

"Some improvement."

"Only some?" Jaci couldn't hide her disappointment.

"It does look like the spell is rebuilding the flesh that was burned away, but it is a slow process."

Jaci ate a few bites in silence. How were they going to save Nickalonis if "some improvement" was the best they could do?

"To answer your other question, I'm not sure."

"Not sure about..." It took her a moment to remember what she'd asked him.

"About whether there is anything useful in the spellbook. I read the writings and translated the spell related to Ridaur's crypt. It's an ancient spell of regeneration that Galenock has twisted into a spell of binding. From what I can decipher, Galenock wants one of Ridaur's bones. He plans to use it in some sort of ritual to revive Ridaur's spirit and bind that spirit to him, giving him access to Ridaur's vast magical powers."

"Who was Ridaur?"

"He was the most powerful wizard Tarshane has ever known. He lived about a hundred and fifty years ago. He and Elsaesser, Elshaer's great-grandfather, were childhood friends. According to the story, Ridaur was born with a crippled leg. As he grew older, he became obsessed with finding a way to make it whole. Apparently, there were no true healers at that time, and no one else was able to repair it. He began spending most of his time in old libraries, searching for books dealing with the curing of maladies. Elsaesser helped him when he could, but nothing they tried did any good.

"Then one day, Ridaur and Elsaesser discovered an ancient spellbook of unknown origin, containing both benevolent spells and ones with evil intent. Ridaur wished to keep the book secret. Elsaesser agreed, on the condition they only experiment with the benevolent spells."

A chill goose-pimpled Jaci's skin. "Somehow I have the feeling Ridaur didn't stick to the agreement."

"No, he didn't." Talan took her empty bowl, refilled it, and handed it back. "Using one of the malevolent spells, he found a way to heal his leg."

"By transferring the damage to someone else, like Galenock did with his burn wounds?"

"That would be my guess. The stories say Ridaur continued to experiment with the evil spells and that his use of them changed him. His power grew to frightening levels, and so did his craving for even more power. Elsaesser realized what was happening and tried to get the book away from him. Ridaur almost killed him. Elsaesser managed to escape and took his family into hiding. While Elsaesser was recovering from his injuries, Ridaur declared his supremacy over all the other wizards and rulers of the kingdoms. No one could stand up to him."

"Sounds like a past incarnation of Galenock." Jaci finished her stew and set the bowl down.

"Perhaps he is an ancestor. I don't know. Eventually, Elsaesser returned. He tried again to defeat Ridaur, but failed, barely escaping with his life. Since he couldn't defeat Ridaur in a face-to-face battle, he and his son, Saegan, set a trap, using illusions and Elsaesser himself as the bait to draw Ridaur out. They trapped Ridaur in a crypt on the Isle of Lorn with a binding spell so powerful it required the blood of a willing sacrifice to make it work. Elsaesser used his own blood to work the spell and permanently seal both Ridaur and himself in the crypt. Grieving for his father, Saegan took the key to the crypt and hid it in a place where it was never to be found."

"But Galenock found it," Jaci said.

Talan nodded. "I don't know how, but he did. Saegan also took the ancient spellbook, which he kept and passed down to his children. Elshaer inherited it. Galenock took possession of the book after killing him."

"So Galenock wants to revive Ridaur's spirit and use his power to enhance his own."

"That is what I suspect."

Jaci shook her head. "And I conveniently brought the key back to allow him to do it."

"Do not blame yourself. You didn't know about any of it."

"What if we destroy the key?"

"It cannot be destroyed. It is bound to the magic that imprisoned Ridaur in the crypt."

"Then it makes even more sense to take it to Millianoch, where it will be within the Northern Enchantresses' sphere of protection."

Talan was silent for a few moments. "Perhaps." He stared into the fire, brooding.

"You don't trust them?"

"No." He exhaled loudly and ran his hand through his hair. "I'm sorry. I know they are your relatives, and I do not mean to —"

Jaci put her hand on his arm. "Don't apologize. I know nothing of them, so you're not insulting me. Why don't you trust them?"

"It is... complicated. You can judge for yourself when you meet them."

"If we meet them," Jaci said, half to herself. "I don't know what to do about Nickalonis. We don't seem to be making much progress, no matter how hard we try — wait a minute. You said the High Enchantress was a true healer. How long would it take us to get to Wolf Run?"

He eyed her warily. "That depends. Without Nickalonis, about two days hard ride. With him, a week or more. Why?"

"We have about a week and a half before the portal opens into the mountains. I'm certain the portal opens either in or around the

Enchantresses' castle. I'm sure of it," she said earnestly. "If we can get Nickalonis stabilized enough so that he can be moved and then get him to Wolf Run by the waning moon, we can take him to the High Enchantress and she can heal him. What is her name, anyway?"

"Keiresta." Talan raked his hand through his hair again. "I know I said we'd take you there and we will, but I don't think this is the way to do it."

"Why not?"

He hesitated, and Jaci could feel tension and frustration building in him. "Because she won't likely do it, particularly if I am there, and I cannot let you use an untried portal without me unless I know for certain where it goes."

His protectiveness warmed her through again, and she tried to keep her thoughts coherent as she savored the feeling. "Why wouldn't she heal him? How could she refuse to help someone who could die without her skills?"

"You do not know her."

Jaci shrugged helplessly. "I don't know any other way to save him. I don't want to keep on trying to heal him for days and days and not be successful and end up watching him die."

Talan looked back at the fire and let out a long breath. "I know."

Sharrow's shriek startled them. The bird glided overhead, followed by another, smaller shadow that arrowed out of the sky toward them. Talan leaped to his feet. He donned a glove that had hung over his belt and lifted his arm. A small gray and white falcon swooped in and landed on his upraised hand.

Jaci rose and kept her distance from the bird's sharp beak.

"He won't hurt you. He belongs to Cranton." Talan detached the message capsule and tossed it to Jaci. "There should be a message inside." The bird flapped its wings, then rebalanced on Talan's hand.

Jaci drew out a tiny parchment and read, "'All fine. They are leaving.'" She looked back at Talan. "What does it mean?"

He relaxed visibly. "It means that he and Zaiya are all right, that Galenock's soldiers haven't come to the house in search of you, and that Katar and the others have left and are on their way back through the tunnels."

"Will they be able to get out of the tunnels with the mill... burned?" A fresh wave of guilt and grief rushed over her as she thought of Willem and his men who'd been lost in the fire, murdered by Vorstun and his thugs. She blinked back her tears.

"If they can't get out through the mill, I am sure there are other exits from the tunnels," Talan said gently, his grief close to the surface as well. "They have the map to guide them." He drew out the wax-paper-wrapped charcoal and gave it to Jaci. "Write 'MR' on the note and slip it back into the capsule."

Jaci did as he asked and handed the capsule back to him. "MR?"

"Message received." Talan reattached the capsule and sent the falcon on its way.

She held out the wrapped charcoal to him. "Shall we try another healing session?"

"If you are ready." He put the charcoal back into his pocket.

She nodded.

He kicked out the fire and followed her to the shelter.

They spent the next hour working on the neck wound Owen was most concerned about, healing raw edges that had grown red and hot.

Afterward, Jaci slept again, waking this time near midnight. A smattering of stars were visible through the canopy overhead, dimmed by the waxing moon, and the wind carried the smells of wild forest and damp marsh. She shifted in the darkness and saw the still form of Talan sleeping close by. He lay on his back with one arm crooked behind his head, his cloak half-draped over his torso. She could just see the faint rise and fall of his breath.

She bit her lip, wanting so much to slide over and curl up beside him, lay her head on his chest, feel his arms slip around her, draw her close. She'd kiss him on the lips this time — give him something else to think about besides Soneira...

And then what? She lay back, trembling, her face flushed, the heat of her own need rushing through her. What would she do? Make love to him? Make him fall for her, so he'd forget Soneira? To what end?

She recalled the look he'd given her after she'd kissed him on the cheek. That had definitely not been a look of platonic friendship. Cold horror froze the fire in her blood. What was she doing? *You don't plan to stay in this world, remember?* To make him fall in love with her and then leave him would be crueler than letting him stay as he was, lost in the agony of his memories of Soneira. How could she do that to him — and to herself? *How long will you deny your own feelings?* her conscience prodded.

Oh, God, what should I do? she cried inwardly. How could she stay in this world with no electricity, no modern conveniences, no flush toilets? He'd probably never be able to truly love her anyway. He'd been obsessed with Soneira for so long that she was likely all he would ever see — in Jaci or in anyone else. She had no desire to spend the rest of her life trying to live up to Soneira's perfection.

Confused and distressed, she sat up slowly so as not to wake Talan and caught a movement out of the corner of her eye. She turned sharply. A dark shape leaned against a tree, over near where the cook fire had been. She recognized the stocky form of Liundur, on watch. The faint rasp of a whetstone reached her ears as he sharpened one of his blades. Relieved, she let out the breath she'd been holding. She felt his eyes on her, but he didn't speak. She rose silently and headed to the shelter, too upset to sleep anymore.

Inside the shelter, Solon sat in his usual place near Nickalonis' shoulder. Owen sat opposite, grinding herbs and a dab of water into a paste with a mortar and pestle. He glanced at her as she entered, then went back to his work. Solon gave her a weak smile. Dark circles rimmed his eyes and he seemed thinner, his cheeks hollowed by anxiety.

Jaci sat next to him, eyeing him with concern. "Don't you ever sleep? You're going to make yourself sick."

"I don't want to sleep," he said softly, his gaze shifting back to his brother. "I fear he will pass on while I'm not here. I want to be with him, every minute he has left. He is the only true family I have."

Jaci looked down and fiddled with the hem of her tunic as the pain of her own losses — of family she'd cherished in her world and family she'd never known in this one — gouged her heart. "I'm sorry," she said after a few moments. "What happened to your family?"

"Our father was a member of the Royal Guard. He died trying to protect the king and queen from the Ruusitaran soldiers. Our mother and our siblings were killed in the aftermath. Nick and I survived because we weren't in the castle when the Ruusitarans invaded. We'd gone in search of Talan. We were worried about him, after his fight with Soneira."

Soneira again. So much seemed to revolve around her. "Tell me about Soneira," Jaci said impulsively. "What was she like?"

Solon's eyes grew distant. "She was enchantingly beautiful, and mysterious and clever —"

"And proud and ambitious and manipulative and deceitful," Owen said under his breath, but loud enough that Jaci could hear him. She looked at him in surprise.

"— and I don't think there was a man alive who'd seen her who wasn't, at least a little bit, in love with her," Solon finished.

"Speak for yourself, man," the medic growled.

Solon glared at him. "I heard what you said. How can you say such things?"

"Tell me one thing I said that wasn't true," Owen retorted in a low voice. "You forget, I was court physician during King Brannad's reign. Yes, Soneira was beautiful and all that, but her parents spoiled her rotten, and whatever she wanted, she got, no matter who might be hurt in the process. She used her royal pedestal to bask in the glow of her countless admirers, doling out just enough of her favors to keep them all at her feet. Poor little Deirdre was forever in her shadow."

"You are painting a horrible picture of her," Solon protested. "You're leaving out all the good works she did as princess of the realm."

Owen snorted. "All I know is that she was just like her mother — driven by her ambition to be better than everyone else at everything, and her actions cost not only the royal family but the entire kingdom everything."

Solon's eyes narrowed. "What do you mean?"

"I mean," Owen said, his voice taut with anger, "if she hadn't been sleeping in the wrong bed, the whole thing never would have happened."

Solon's expression darkened. "If she hadn't been sleeping in the wrong bed, we never would have known it was coming. She warned us —"

"Too little, too late," Owen snapped, and went back to grinding herbs as if he would crush every atom of life out of them.

Solon lapsed into silence, sullen and brooding and lost in his thoughts.

Jaci stared at them, speechless, stunned by their reactions.

* * * * *

Talan lay rigid and silent, eyes closed, awakened by the conversation in the shelter. So many emotions stormed through him all at once he could hardly bear it. Indignation, fury, denial, love, anguish, guilt and grief — all spinning together like whirlwinds in his mind and heart. Owen's words cut him as only harsh words could, yet Talan, try as he might, could not deny that everything Owen had said was true. Talan was sure Soneira had loved him, but her ambitions had always come first. She'd had to be the best at everything, and she'd done whatever she thought necessary to achieve her goals. Talan had suspected she'd shared much more of herself with others than she'd admitted, to further her ambitions, but he'd deliberately blinded himself to the truth. He hadn't wanted to know. Even when he'd found irrefutable proof that she'd lied to him, more than once, he'd still let her talk him down to her feet once more. One look in those mysteriously bewitching blue eyes and he'd been lost... until he'd found out about Galenock... about how they'd —

He couldn't think anymore, the agony of his shattered heart tearing at him like shards of glass. They'd fought then, and he'd raged at her, said terrible things, and even though the words were true, he hated that those were the last words she'd heard from him. He'd left the castle, not knowing where he was going, only knowing he had to get away from her. When the unthinkable happened, he was so far away he couldn't get back in time to save her.

He wiped damp eyes, wondering again what would have happened if he had saved her. She might have been so grateful she would have claimed him for her own, forsaking all the others. The two of them together as he'd always dreamed — until the next time her ambitions took her to someone else's bed and shattered his heart all over again. No... his dream was fatally flawed. He would never have been able to trust her to remain faithful to him, and he couldn't live otherwise. He needed to let go, to say goodbye to Soneira and his dream. As Cranton had been telling him for years, nothing that had happened had been his fault. He'd always known that deep down, but the knowledge had been buried too far beneath the horror and the guilt to ever see the light of day. Now that truth was finally cracking the surface, brought to the forefront in the light of the moon instead, but just as freeing. All that was left was to forgive himself and say, *Goodbye...*

Soneira's face coalesced in his mind, her beauty, her dark curls, her lovely lips quirked up in a half smile, her mischievous brown eyes full of warmth and honesty...

He almost cried out in shock. Saying goodbye was unnecessary, he realized. Without even knowing it, he already had.

CHAPTER 24

Jaci looked from Solon to Owen and back and searched for something to say. "I—I'm sorry. I didn't mean to —"

She nearly cried out as a rush of fierce emotions — rage, passion, helpless anguish — floored her, left her breathless. *Talan.* Was he dreaming, or had he overheard them? The violent feelings, as confused as hers, tore through her heart like a saw blade, leaving ragged edges of pain and grief. She wanted to go to him, to comfort him, but she didn't dare. Her own feelings were so muddled and uncertain, she didn't trust herself.

Then shock jolted her, followed by a lessening of the pain as the heartache slowly faded into a fragile, troubled peace. *What could it mean?*

Solon touched her arm. "Jaci? Are you all right?"

She blinked and nodded, trying to collect her scattered wits.

"It is we who should be sorry," Solon said. "We should not have subjected you to such rantings."

Owen grunted something unintelligible and demolished more herbs.

Jaci sat silently, her thoughts still whirling around Talan. She wanted desperately to go talk to him, to see if he was all right and find out what had just happened, but she needed time to sort through her own feelings before she became hopelessly ensnared in his.

Nickalonis moaned faintly and shifted his bandaged head, the first time Jaci had seen him move since she'd arrived at the camp. She hoped it was a good sign.

"His sleeping draught is wearing off again," Owen said. He reached down into a pack and drew forth a dark-colored bottle. Holding it near the lantern light, he tipped it at an angle. "There isn't much left."

Jaci tried to put Talan out of her mind, at least temporarily. "You mean he wakes up? I thought he was unconscious from his wounds."

"He's unconscious because of this." Owen set the bottle back into the pack. "As soon as he fully wakes, we'll give him water and medicine and some herbal broth, and then put him back to sleep. The pain would be too much for him otherwise."

"I see." Jaci shuddered. She couldn't imagine the agony of those burns. "Owen, I'd like your opinion on something. Do you think we could heal him to the point where he could be safely moved?"

Owen eyed her keenly, his anger of a few moments ago gone. "To where, and why?"

She explained her plan.

"Would it be possible?" Solon asked the medic, hope shining through the anxiety in his eyes like a new morning pushing back the darkness of an interminably long night.

Owen considered. "Well…" He glanced at Nickalonis. "His pulse is a bit stronger, and I think you've stopped the infection. We have a few days yet before we'd have to make a decision. What does Talan think — or have you asked him?"

"He doesn't think it's a good idea," she admitted.

Owen grunted. "That's not surprising."

"I'm not trying to circumvent his authority," Jaci said hastily. "I just wanted to know if you thought it was possible."

Owen shrugged. "I won't say it's impossible. Why don't you go wake him and bring him in. The more healing you do, the better our chances."

"You don't need to wake me." Talan stepped into the shelter, his expression inscrutable.

Jaci glanced at him nervously, her emotions on edge. How much of their conversations had he heard?

Nickalonis stirred, another low moan escaping him. Solon gently took his brother's bandaged hand in both of his.

"Can we heal him when he's waking?" Jaci asked Owen.

"You should be able to. It takes some time for him to fully come to."

Without a word, Talan sat beside Jaci and lifted her into his lap. She pressed back against him, unable to stop herself. Her body hungered for his touch — any touch at all. She felt him take a deep breath and relax. She tried to do the same, but it was going to take a lot more than deep breaths to calm her inner trembling. He slipped his arms around her waist, holding her firmly, and she felt his cheek against her hair. She closed her eyes with a wistful sigh, wishing they were alone and concentrating on each other, rather than preparing for the task at hand.

"You can start now," Owen said with dry amusement.

Jaci snapped her eyes open, her face flaming. She looked down at the wound Owen had uncovered, and her stomach roiled.

"Close your eyes," Talan whispered, "and we'll work as we did the last time."

"All right," she said, grateful for his help.

He took her hand and held it over the wound as she absorbed his influx of power and recited the healing words.

*****

For three days and nights, Jaci did nothing but sleep, eat, and heal Nickalonis. Though they weren't making anywhere near as much progress as Jaci would have liked, she noticed that Owen seemed more relaxed, and Solon had lost some of the pinched worry lines around his eyes and mouth. Solon had even slept a few hours, after Owen had finally convinced him that his brother's death was no longer imminent.

When Jaci awoke around midmorning on the fourth day, she found Talan and Solon building a sturdy litter with which to carry Nickalonis. By the time she'd washed up and eaten, they'd transferred Nickalonis onto the litter and were dismantling the shelter.

Jaci knelt beside Owen, who was wrapping another blanket around his patient. "How is he doing?"

"He's stable, improving little by little."

"Where are we going?" she whispered.

"Toward Wolf Run," Owen said quietly. "We discussed your plan earlier, and Talan agreed to it, but he's not happy about it, so I would avoid the subject if I were you."

"I will, thanks." She rose, a mixture of relief and trepidation sifting through her. She was glad they were finally moving. It had begun to seem like they were in a holding pattern, everything they did revolving around the immediacy of Nickalonis' wounds, while their plans for joining the Enchantresses were indefinitely postponed. But what if Nickalonis worsened, his burned body overtaxed by the traveling? She closed her eyes. *Please let him be okay.*

They traveled east for two hours through woodland and valleys, moving slowly and carefully, with frequent breaks to allow Owen to monitor Nickalonis' condition. Jaci rode Nickalonis' horse. Talan and Owen carried the litter for the first hour, then switched off with Solon and Medres, while the Black Banders rode guard. Sharrow soared on the wind currents high above them.

Just past midday, they stopped to rest and eat in a small forest clearing. Owen examined Nickalonis again and pronounced him unharmed by the venture. Jaci and the others shared smiles of relief. Even Talan smiled faintly, though Jaci could tell by his tenseness that he still thought this endeavor a bad idea.

After they'd finished eating, Talan and Owen debated the merits of continuing on a while longer before setting up camp, since their progress would slow considerably once they reached the eastern mountains.

A screech from Sharrow silenced them, drawing their eyes to the circle of sky ringed by the spiky tops of the surrounding evergreens. The hawk screeched again, then sped westward, back in the direction from which they'd come.

Talan leaped up. "Riders! Solon, Liundur — take the others and hide them. Carrick, Arnos — with me. We'll try to draw them off."

Talan and the two Black Banders swung aboard their mounts and galloped back into the forest.

Jaci watched them go, fear for them clutching her throat. Only three against how many? She snatched up her horse's reins and mounted. How had the Riders found them? Had Galenock used his sight spell on Talan? *Oh, please — not that. Let the Riders have found us by accident...*

Solon and Liundur were already astride their horses, leading the two belonging to the medics. Owen and Medres lifted the litter bearing Nickalonis and hurried after Solon, who kicked his mount forward through the trees. Jaci followed, Liundur behind her.

Jaci looked back as the distant clang of metal on metal jarred through her bones. She heard shouts, more sword clashes, and a chaotic rush of hoofbeats.

"They're coming!" Liundur called to Solon.

Solon pulled up and turned around.

Liundur drew his sword and pointed to a thick grove of spruce just ahead on the right. "Put him in there where he won't get trampled."

Owen and Medres veered toward the grove. As soon as they'd set the litter down among the trees, they mounted their horses and drew their own weapons.

Solon caught the reins of Jaci's horse. "Hide with Nick. Stay out of sight."

Jaci jumped down and ran to the grove. Crouching beside Nickalonis, she watched as Solon tied her horse to a tree, then moved to the forefront with Liundur, far enough away so as not to draw attention to the grove, but close enough to defend it.

Jaci heard the hiss and thunk of arrows flying and striking trees and dirt. Solon and the others dodged among the trees. Splotches of red on horseback cantered through the forest — Jaci counted at least ten of the red-cloaked Riders spreading out around them. Solon and Liundur spurred forward and attacked two of the Riders. Owen and Medres intercepted two more. Jaci caught a glimpse of Carrick standing with his back to a wide bole, fighting off three Riders swinging at him from horseback.

More arrows flew. She shifted her position, but with everyone battling in and out between the trees, she couldn't see if any of the arrows had hit their marks, and she couldn't tell if the cries and groans she'd heard were from Talan's men or the Riders.

Jaci sucked in a breath as Talan galloped into sight, caught one of the Riders, and knocked him off his horse. Then an arrow thunked into the neck of Talan's horse and it reared, whinnying in fright. Another arrow grazed its head. The horse shied violently, stumbled over some tree roots, and went down.

"No!" Jaci cried. She scrambled to the other side of Nickalonis, trying to see what had happened to Talan. Finally she saw him weaving among the trees, battling two Riders on foot with two more on horseback coming up behind him. Just as she was about to scream out to him in warning, she saw a flash of metal flick through the air, then another. She stared open-mouthed as the two Riders tumbled off their mounts, knife hilts protruding from their throats.

A man in forest colors, a black bandanna on his left arm, galloped up beside Talan, and they quickly dispatched the two Riders Talan had been fighting. Jaci got one clear look at the man's face before he rode off to help the others. She sagged back in surprise and overwhelming relief. Of course, the knives — she should have known. *Katar.*

A few minutes later the clash of battle ceased. Talan and his men gathered by the grove.

"Jacinda?" Talan called anxiously, peering in through the branches.

"Here." She rushed out and embraced him.

He held her tight for a moment, then they let go and stepped back.

Jaci did a quick headcount and found no one missing. "Are any of you hurt?"

"No, Your Highness," Carrick said.

"At least, not seriously," Owen amended, after giving them all an appraising glance. "Medres?"

Medres' voice floated out to them from the grove where he was checking on Nickalonis. "I'm fine. And Nickalonis' condition is unchanged."

Jaci couldn't see anything other than a few scrapes on Talan. Solon and the Black Banders, including the three who had come with Katar from Cranton's house, also appeared to have fared well, with only a few minor lacerations between them.

Katar, who'd been prowling the woods on foot, strode up beside Talan. "I count seventeen Riders — all dead. There are no tracks leading away from here, so none could have escaped."

Talan clasped Katar's forearm and clapped him on the shoulder. "That's another one I owe you, my friend."

Katar grinned. "No, I think we're even, now."

"Either way," Talan said, "your timing couldn't have been better."

Katar gestured with his chin toward one of the dead Riders. "We've been tracking this lot since early morning. After we left the tunnels, we picked up our horses. Iain is taking Tobias back to the other camp. He told us where they'd left Nickalonis, so we headed there, but then we ran across this troop and decided to see where they were going."

"How did they find us?" Solon asked Talan uneasily.

Jaci slid her eyes back to Talan. His uncertainty, his indecision over blindfolding himself, and his revulsion for the need were tying her stomach in knots.

"I don't know," Talan said grimly. "I haven't felt any of the symptoms of the sight spell." He turned to Katar. "Were they traveling with a purpose, or did they seem to be scouting and just ran across us by happenstance?"

Katar considered. "Could be either. They were definitely heading in the same direction we were. Then they spread out and searched and eventually found the campsite you'd abandoned earlier. From there, they followed your trail."

Talan cursed under his breath. "All right, we'll clean up here, then move on. There's a small stream over there." He pointed to his left. "Make certain every weapon is cleaned. Leave no trace of our blood anywhere."

The Black Banders scattered, following Talan's orders. Solon helped Medres carry Nickalonis out of the grove. Owen produced his healer's pack and moved from one to the next, giving everyone involved in the battle a thorough going over and bandaging their cuts and scrapes. Jaci removed the tack from all but two of the Riders' mounts that hadn't run away and let them go free. Carrick's horse had been shot out from under him, and Talan's had broken a foreleg when it had fallen over the tree roots. Both had to be put down. Jaci shared Talan's sadness at the loss.

They stacked the Riders' bodies in the grove, and when the area had been cleansed to Talan's satisfaction, they gathered again.

"I should have you go and attack Galenock's supply lines and stir up more villages against him," Talan said to Katar. "With so many of his men out looking for us, the wagons won't be as well guarded and we could use both the supplies and the distraction."

Katar shook his head. "You'll need us if you run into any more Riders. And Willem said he is already planning to do just that —"

"Willem?" Talan said sharply.

"He's alive?" Jaci blurted, not quite daring to believe it. "But they burned the mill."

"Yes," Katar said, "but Willem and his men escaped through the river tunnel. He showed us another way out and said those soldiers would regret destroying his mill."

Solon and the others grinned at the wonderful news. Jaci was so happy she could have jumped up and down. If she hadn't been so afraid of Katar, she would have hugged him.

"Well then, let's mount up." Talan took a strip of bandage from Owen's pack, folded it double, and held it out to Solon. "If you would, please?" His tone had grown bitter.

Solon reluctantly took the cloth strip. "Are you sure it's necessary?"

"No, but I would rather do it and find out it's not, than not do it and lead Galenock's men right to us."

Solon tied the blindfold. He put his hand on Talan's elbow. "What next?"

"I will ride with Jacinda, since she is the lightest. Carrick, take the point. Katar, take rear guard."

As soon as they'd all mounted, they headed east again, riding silently, their wary eyes scanning the surrounding forest. Owen and Medres took the first shift carrying the litter. Solon and Arnos rode beside them, with Jaci, Talan, and Liundur behind. Carrick and one of Katar's three men rode up front. Katar and the other two brought up the rear. Sharrow still glided overhead, a shadow of dark wings against the blue sky.

Jaci took a deep breath, her insides quivering at Talan's nearness. He sat stiffly, his hold about her waist as loose and impersonal as when she'd first ridden with him. She knew he was brooding over the possibility that his sight had been violated by Galenock. His anger and his hatred of the wizard churned around him like a thunderstorm.

Jaci shivered, rattled by his fury.

She sensed his anger lessening, shifting to apprehension. He drew closer, his arms tightening, his lips by her ear. "What's wrong?" he asked softly.

She covered his hand with hers. "Please don't despair," she whispered over her shoulder. "We'll find a way to beat him. I know we will."

With an effort, he stilled himself. She felt the storm of his thoughts and emotions dissipating. "I'm sorry. I don't know how or why you feel what I'm feeling. You must be extremely empathic, though I've never heard of anyone in your family having such a talent. Or at least, your family in this world."

Jaci guided her horse around a fallen tree, following Arnos. "My father was always good at sensing how other people felt about things. He was a natural peacemaker. But if it was some talent I inherited from him or some other ancestor, you'd think I'd feel everyone's emotions. I don't. It only happens with you."

"I can't explain it. I'll try to keep a better hold on my feelings —"

"Oh, no, please — don't hold everything inside because of me," Jaci said. "You'll go crazy. Besides, I want to know when you're hurting, so I can help you —" She broke off, her face flaming again.

He leaned forward, his chest solidly against her back. He slipped his other hand out and pressed it over hers. "Thank you. You have already helped me, in more ways than I can ever say."

His gratitude filled her, the warmth of a thousand smiles enfolding her, edged with another emotion so strong he barely contained it before she could determine what it was. The irrational bubbly happy feeling swept every other thought from her mind.

*****

At sunset, they made camp in a narrow, secluded valley sheltered by a stand of maples. The sky darkened, the air cooling as they ate; a chorus of crickets surrounded them. Jaci caught a glimpse of Sharrow dipping down through the dusk and alighting in one of the trees. The Black Banders, already done with their evening meal, chose their guard shifts and either dispersed to the perimeter or slept. Solon and Medres bedded down. Talan, still blindfolded, and Owen remained awake, in anticipation of another healing session.

Jaci looked up into the twilight at the moon, a circle of gold already well above the horizon, and realized with a start that it was full. This was the fourteenth night since she'd come to Tarshane — the night the portals opened in the clocks. She stiffened. If she were still at the castle, she could have gone home. *Home.* A flurry of sharply conflicting emotions buffeted her: the bitterness and frustration of missed opportunity, the fear and exhilaration of her ongoing fight against Galenock, her desire to see her old friends again and go back to her old life yet be with Talan in her new one. She closed her eyes and tried to make sense of her confusion.

What would she be doing right now if she'd gone back through the clock? She'd be in the Brunswick house, probably stranded. The Marston sheriff would surely have impounded her car with her belongings by now. The Brunswick phones would have been disconnected, so she'd have to walk back to that hotel to call Courtney and the state police and somehow get everything straightened out. She didn't trust the authorities in Marston.

Then what? Go to Courtney's, fawn over her new baby, and pick up life where she'd left off like nothing had happened? But so many things *had* happened. Unbelievable things. She'd been swept up by a band of rebels who considered her a princess of the realm. Her — a princess! She'd fought with and bested an evil wizard. She'd discovered relatives she'd never known existed — she was a granddaughter of a High Enchantress! She'd even used magic...

She had to admit that being able to work magic beat anything she'd done in her own world. And the traveling by horseback she was doing now was much more visceral than the guided tours of other countries she'd been on. Of course, if she were alone here, it would be a different story. It wasn't like she could order pizza or drive to a grocery store to find food. She didn't know how to hunt or fish, and she had no knowledge of edible woodland plants. This world seemed a lot more rough — less civilized than hers — where a woman traveling alone would be in great danger. Then she thought about the streets of New York City, so close to White Plains. She'd gotten lost there once and driven through some streets where no one would be safe traveling alone.

The main attractions of her world were her friends and the modern conveniences — how she missed toilets and hot showers! But how much did she really miss the rest? She had to admit, she hadn't thought about any of her friends other than Courtney, her only really close friend, the entire time she'd been here. She'd found new friends she liked equally well. And would she really mind not being able to watch television or go to a movie or surf the Internet? Or even drive anywhere? Horseback riding might be a lot slower than car travel, but it was much more enjoyable. And this world held just as much wild beauty, but there were fewer people... less crowding — at least, that appeared to be the case.

Of course, no one in her world was trying to kidnap her and bend her to his will, or maybe even kill her. What she'd gone through these past two weeks made her old life seem pretty boring, but that had its merits. Her old life was familiar, comfortable. She knew her way around and could take care of herself... and she could do laundry without a washboard... and cook on something other than a wood fire...

She sighed. All that thinking, and she'd resolved nothing. She still didn't know what she wanted... well actually, truth be told, she did know, but... Her eyes settled on Talan, being led by Owen to where Nickalonis lay. She wished she knew what *he* wanted. Her? Or a clone of Soneira? Or had she completely misinterpreted what she'd seen in his eyes and heard in his voice? Maybe it *was* only gratitude that he felt. She sighed again, frustrated.

Owen gestured to her, ready to start the healing session.

Forcing her mind away from her inner turmoil, she brushed the crumbs from her hands and rose. It was time to use her magic. The thought brought a smile to her lips.

CHAPTER 25

It took them seven more days to reach Wolf Run. Storm clouds brooded, darkening the late afternoon into premature twilight as they rode into the meadow bordering the forest where Jaci had entered Tarshane. She pushed back her wind-tossed hair and scanned the meadow, trying to remember exactly where she'd come through the portal.

"I'm not sure how far across the meadow I was," Jaci said over her shoulder to Talan. "Do you remember where you rescued me from the wolves?"

Talan hesitated, then lifted his blindfold long enough to get his bearings. Jaci bit her lip and watched his eyes, her senses rubbed raw by his intense frustration over his forced blindness.

Talan pointed to a spot halfway down the meadow. "Over there, in behind that twisted pine. Do you see it?"

Jaci looked quickly. "Yes."

He lowered the blindfold. "You'll need to show Carrick."

She released her breath. "I will. Hold on. I'm going to speed up."

He tightened his arms around her waist as she urged their horse into a canter. She pulled up alongside Carrick and passed on Talan's message, pointing out the twisted pine tree.

"We can camp there under the trees and build a temporary shelter," Talan said. "We need to hurry. It's about to rain."

Carrick waved everyone forward and they hastened to the edge of the woods. The first drops of rain caught them just as they passed beneath the verge of the forest canopy.

They moved far enough back under the trees to be out of the range of the windblown rain, then constructed another shelter of pine boughs for Nickalonis. He'd survived the trip none the worse for wear, bolstered by the few healing sessions Jaci and Talan had been able to fit in around the traveling. She was glad they hadn't run into any more red-cloaked Riders. She only hoped it wasn't because Talan was blindfolded.

As the men worked on the shelter and set up camp, Jaci helped untack the horses and rub them down. The steady motion soothed away some of the nervousness that had been building inside her since they'd neared Wolf Run. She couldn't stop thinking about the Enchantresses. *The High Enchantress — Keiresta — is my grandmother.* What would she be like? Imperious and manipulative like Soneira and her mother, Selendria, or fiercely independent, but still caring and compassionate, like Jaci's mother, Miri? The fact that Talan didn't trust the High Enchantress worried Jaci. She wondered what dealings they'd had with each other that had caused the rift. Did Keiresta blame Talan for Soneira's death? Or had she objected to Talan's relationship with her granddaughter, thinking him — an orphan of unknown birth — too far beneath her?

She chided herself. Worrying about it wasn't going to help the situation. She'd just have to play it by ear. They'd already decided on a simple plan of action. She, Talan, Solon, and Owen, guarded by Carrick, Arnos, and Liundur, would take Nickalonis through the portal. Katar and the others would stay behind, check on the main camp, then return to the meadow in seven days. On the seventh night, the portal would open in Wolf Run, and they would meet whoever came back through.

Of course, that was providing Jaci could actually find the portal in the meadow and work the magic. And then there was the possibility the portal might open into some other mountain range, and they might all freeze to death, or be attacked by predators, or who knows what, before they could return. Now that the time was near, she wasn't half so confident of the portal's destination. Her hand paused in its rhythmic rubbing of the horse's back. What if the portal opened into another tiny, closet-like space? How would they all fit?

Stop it! she told herself severely. *Just don't think about it.* They'd find out when the time came and deal with whatever happened as best they could. She let out a long breath and resumed rubbing down the horse. If only so many things didn't depend on *her*. What if she couldn't convince the High Enchantress to heal Nickalonis, or what if the High Enchantress refused to have anything to do with her because of her friendship with Talan? Jaci needed someone to train her in the use of magic. She scowled to herself. The High Enchantress would have to be incredibly mulish, or incredibly bitter — or both — to let old grudges keep her from seeing Jaci's arrival as anything other than a legitimate chance to finally defeat Galenock. Jaci couldn't believe the Enchantresses liked being trapped perpetually in their own castle.

"This has to work," she whispered under her breath. "It has to."

*****

The rainstorm had blown past with the deepening of twilight into night, its only remnant a stiff breeze that whistled through the pines. The waning half-moon shone silver. Its soft light glistened on the wet, windswept meadow and the dripping leaves edging the forest.

Taking a deep breath, Jaci stepped out of the trees into the tall grass. She shivered, the sharp wind colder than she'd expected. Catching Talan's hand, she clasped it tightly and led the way across the meadow to where she thought the portal should be. Talan followed reluctantly, every muscle and sinew taut as a bowstring that had been stretched to its limit. He'd also clamped down on his emotions. She couldn't sense them, and that troubled her. Solon and Owen carried the litter with Nickalonis, the three Black Banders behind them. The others watched from the treeline.

"I think it's somewhere around here," she said, keeping her back to the wind. She looked toward the grassy moonlit hills bordering the meadow, remembering how, when she'd first arrived in Tarshane, the three horsemen — Talan, Solon, and Nickalonis — had galloped out of the hills straight past the place where she'd hidden here in the grass. A troop of red-cloaked Riders had pursued them down the meadow. The hills looked to be about the same distance away as they had then.

Talan shoved his blindfold up over his forehead, but kept his eyes closed. Solon cast him a worried glance. The Black Banders watched him, awaiting orders, Jaci guessed. She wondered what they thought about the possibility of his vision being compromised. They hadn't said anything when Talan had originally asked Solon to blindfold him. They'd carried on with business as usual. If they'd had any doubts about his ability to still be in command, they hadn't shown it.

"Everyone move in close, link arms and hold hands, as we planned," Talan said.

Liundur, his long gray-blond hair whipping in the wind, moved over beside Jaci. He, Jaci, and Talan stood in a row facing the litter bearing Nickalonis. Carrick and Arnos lined up on the opposite side of the litter and they all gripped hands and arms, creating, with Solon and Owen, a human chain around and including Nickalonis.

"Everyone ready?" Talan asked.

"Yes," they chorused.

Solon swallowed hard.

Talan half-turned toward Jaci, his eyes still closed. "All right, Jacinda. Go ahead."

Jaci took another deep breath, painfully aware of everyone watching her. They tensed as she spoke the word. *"Saelarin."*

The air around them crackled with energy, and for a moment, it seemed the whole world held its breath.

Talan squeezed her hand. "I feel it," he whispered.

Then in the blink of an eye, the wind stopped, and the air shifted from the evening chill of the meadow to a humid warmth, pungent with the smells of horses and dung and hay.

Jaci looked around. They were in a stable, in a shadowed back corner with a pile of grain sacks on one side of them and a mound of hay on the other. She heard the stamp of horses' hooves and the swish of their tails, though she couldn't see the animals. She did a quick headcount and released her breath, thankful they'd all made it through the portal. But this was definitely not where she'd expected to be.

"Where are we?" Talan asked tensely. "It smells like a stable. Can you see the horses? What do they look like?"

Jaci shot him a confused glance. *Why would he ask that?*

"It is a stable, but I can't see the horses from here," Carrick said. "I don't know where we are."

A man rounded the end of a box stall in front of them, yelled in surprise, and brandished a pitchfork. "Who are you? Where did you come from?" His voice had a musical, sort of Scandinavian tone.

Carrick and Liundur slid in front of Jaci, their swords half drawn before she could stop them.

She caught their arms. "No, wait! This is supposed to be peaceful, remember?"

"Tell *him* that," Owen said with a nod toward the man with the pitchfork, who was edging backward and shouting to coworkers for help.

Carrick and Liundur let their blades slide back into their scabbards as Arnos joined them in front of the litter.

Jaci gritted her teeth against Talan's emotional battle to keep his eyes closed.

"Someone tell me what's going on," he demanded.

Jaci heard whispering behind her as she stepped forward and held her hands out in a gesture of peace. "Please, we mean you no harm. We just want to talk to you." She looked more closely at the man they'd startled and realized he was actually a tall youth in his teens.

He stopped retreating and watched her warily as two stable hands ran up beside him. They appeared to be a few years older. One carried another pitchfork and the other gripped what looked like an awl.

Then an older man with gray hair and mustache approached in a shambling jog. "What are you... hollering about?" he demanded between breaths. He cuffed one of the young men aside before anyone could answer him. His eyes widened as he took in Jaci and the Black Banders. "By the Enchantress' robe!" His hand dropped to the knife at his belt.

Jaci gestured again for peace. "We're not here to hurt anyone. We only want to talk."

The stable master took the pitchfork from the youth and shoved the boy behind him. "Get Aegis Nordrel."

The boy raced away.

Jaci felt Talan stiffen in recognition at the name, confirming that they were at least somewhere near where they needed to be.

"You, get a lantern," the stable master ordered one of the other young men. The youth with the awl rushed around the corner of the box stall, out of sight. "Who are you?" the stable master asked Jaci, holding the pitchfork in a defensive manner, his gaze flicking back and forth between her and the Black Banders. Out of the corner of her eye she saw that Talan had pulled his blindfold down, perhaps hoping he wouldn't be recognized.

"My name is Jacinda. I am Mirinesstra's daughter, and I need to speak with the High Enchantress."

The young man returned with a lantern and held it up high.

The stable master stared at Jaci, his face paling. He opened his mouth, but no words came. When he finally spoke, his voice had grown hoarse. "Miri? That's impossible." He continued to stare as if he couldn't take his eyes from her. "How... how did you get in here?"

"We came through a magic portal we think was created by Soneira. We need the Enchantresses' help. Can we talk to them?"

The stable master's face went paler still at the mention of Soneira's name. His voice shook. "That will be for Aegis Nordrel to decide."

The thud of swiftly marching feet filled the stable. The horses snorted and paced in their stalls, unsettled by the commotion.

Here we go, Jaci thought nervously. She turned quickly at Liundur's touch on her arm and moved back between him and Carrick.

Moments later, an imposing figure of a man in chainmail and a gray and blue uniform stood before them. A sword and two daggers hung from his belt. His short-clipped hair was stone gray, but traces of red showed through in his neatly trimmed beard and mustache. More uniformed and armed soldiers packed the open space behind him. The youth who had fetched him hovered around the fringes, stretching to see over their shoulders.

"Aegis Nordrel," the stable master said with an arthritic bow. He gestured with the pitchfork toward Jaci and the others. "These people just appeared here." He stared at Jaci again.

"They really are Black Banders," Nordrel said in surprise. "The boy said they had black arm bands, but I didn't believe —" His words stopped as his gaze fell on Jaci. "By the gods of the sky," he whispered. *"Deirdre?"*

Jaci stepped forward again. Carrick, Arnos, and Liundur moved with her, their eyes trained on Aegis Nordrel and the soldiers behind him in silent warning.

Nordrel's eyes narrowed.

"I'm not Deirdre," Jaci said hurriedly. The last thing they needed was to have a fight break out. "My name is Jacinda. I am Mirinesstra's daughter. I need to speak to the High Enchantress... my grandmother. We need her help. Will you take us to her?"

"Mirinesstra is long dead," Nordrel said sharply. Jaci could see him sizing up the others with her. "I will only ask you this once more. Who are you? How did you get here, and why did you come?"

Jaci bit down on her temper. "I am who I say. Mirinesstra died two years ago in a land far from here. She gave me her *druidainoch* stone right before she passed away." Keeping the keys hidden, Jaci lifted the stone above her neckline. "I have it here, as you can see."

Nordrel uttered an exclamation, a look of shock on his face.

The soldiers behind him murmured among themselves.

"Silence!" Nordrel bellowed, startling the horses again.

The soldiers fell stiffly quiet.

Jaci let the stone drop back down beneath her shirt. "We came here through a magic portal we think was created by Soneira. Our friend is badly hurt." She swept her hand back toward Nickalonis.

"We'd hoped my grandmother could heal him. I also need training in magic, which I hoped she could help me with, so that just maybe we could tip the balance of power and defeat Galenock. That is why we are here. Now are you going to take us to her or not?"

Aegis Nordrel regarded her silently. She hoped the possibility of defeating Galenock would sway him to her favor.

"Let me see your wounded man," he said.

Jaci and the others stepped back so he could see the bandaged form of Nickalonis.

"What about him?" Nordrel gestured toward Talan. "Why is he blindfolded?"

"He is injured as well," Jaci said, which was actually true. The arrow wound on his arm hadn't completely healed yet.

"Very well," Nordrel said slowly. "I will take you to the High Enchantress, but first you will hand over your weapons."

Talan unbuckled his sword belt. The Black Banders reluctantly followed his lead.

After they all had given their weapons to the soldiers, Aegis Nordrel led the way through the stable toward the door, half his soldiers in front of them, half behind. Jaci glanced into a box stall as she walked by, curious to see what kind of horses the Enchantresses kept and why Talan had asked what they looked like. She saw the fine head and arched neck of a tall, dark brown stallion — She stopped short, dumbfounded. "He — he has wings!"

Carrick's guiding hand kept Talan from running into her. "Yes," Talan said with a wistful note in his voice, as if he'd ridden a winged horse once and longed to do so again. "That is how they travel between their mountain cities and towns."

Jaci stared at the dark glossy feathers folded tightly against the horse's body. "That's incredible."

The soldiers urged them onward, out of the stable.

CHAPTER 26

They emerged from the stable into a snow-dusted courtyard of dirt and stone, its wide expanse lit by luminous spheres atop stone pedestals. Jaci shivered in the frosty night air. Large buildings like barracks and other smaller outbuildings hemmed them in on the right.

The sound of running water from off to her left caught Jaci's ear. She turned and gasped. A massive stone palace, lavender-hued in the moonlight, projected outward from the face of a snow-capped mountain peak like something out of a fantastical dream. She craned her neck, staring. The palace rose ten stories into the night sky, all gables and dormers, arched windows and balconies. Intricate scrollwork laced the edges. Towers and turrets soared even higher, their pinnacles lost in the stars.

A grand staircase flanked by statues of winged horses bridged a half-frozen waterway as it ascended to a porticoed veranda looking out over more mountains that dropped away several thousand feet. A steaming waterfall flowed out from under the ice beneath the stairs and cascaded off the edge of the world. The rising mist froze into frothy patterns along the base of the veranda.

Jaci realized she was gaping, but she couldn't help it. This palace surpassed any fairy tale edifice she'd ever seen or imagined. Even King Ludwig II's famous Neuschwanstein Castle, which she and her mother had visited a few years ago, paled in comparison. She'd always wondered why her mother hadn't been particularly impressed by the beauty of Neuschwanstein. Now she understood.

"This palace — what's it called?" she whispered to Talan as they crossed the courtyard, their footsteps crunching in the snow as they headed toward the staircase.

"Catir Enseidrinocha — City of Enchantresses."

"City? It looks like a palace, not a city."

"Part of the city lies beyond those outbuildings and part lies within the mountain. It is much larger than it appears."

Jaci noticed a faint milky translucence in the sky similar to the Milky Way, except that it formed a huge dome over and down around the mountain, enclosing the palace and a good distance further, past the outbuildings. It reminded her of the iridescent bubble that had protected her from Galenock's spell.

"Is there some kind of shield around this place or does the sky have that sort of filmy appearance naturally?"

"I would guess it is the magical shield the Enchantresses have been using to prevent Galenock from attacking them."

The soldiers herded them up the staircase, the rush of the waterfall rising above the tread of their feet as they passed through an ornate iron door into an immense foyer that was softly lit with more of the luminous spheres on slim pedestals. Jaci drank in the scent of roses as her gaze traveled upward, taking in the balconied floors rising to a vaulted ceiling hidden in deep shadow. Beneath her feet, a mosaic depicting a rising sun spread outward to the walls, which echoed the mauve and gold of the ornamental sky. Niches along the walls contained delicate porcelain vases filled with the sweetly fragrant roses. Jaci wondered how in the world they grew in the frigid mountains.

"You will wait here," Aegis Nordrel said. He strode to the far end of the foyer and out through a set of double doors.

The soldiers surrounded them but kept their distance. Many stared curiously at Jaci.

Solon and Owen set Nickalonis' litter down as the Black Banders moved to keep everyone within their protective triangle. Talan stood tensely, his fists clenched. Jaci could feel tendrils of dread snaking around him. She reached for his hand, hoping to ease his mind and lessen her own nervousness.

He clasped her fingers warmly.

A few minutes later, Aegis Nordrel returned. "Come, this way."

The soldiers escorted them through the double doors into another expansive room — a throne room, Jaci realized. They walked between two rows of lavender columns, their gilded tops several stories high, rising from a mauve and cream tiled floor. The glowing spheres were brighter here, illuminating the cathedral ceiling inlaid with mosaics of flowery swirls and colors. Tapestries of mountain vistas, blooming gardens, and winged horses in various settings graced the walls. Behind the dais with its high-backed, intricately carved gold chair, hung a silky banner of a white winged horse flying across a starry sky.

The soldiers fanned out on either side and behind them. Nordrel signaled for a halt near the empty throne.

Jaci bit her lip, wondering where the High Enchantress — her grandmother — was. How late was it? Had the woman already turned in for the night? She'd have to be at least in her seventies by now. Or maybe the Enchantresses aged differently because of their magic.

A door to their left opened and a petite woman with silvery white hair strode into the room, her lavender robe with cream accents sweeping the floor behind her. A golden circlet crowned her head, and she moved with the poise and authority of an assured ruler. A retinue of six women in blue robes followed closely, all similarly petite with graying dark hair, their manner that of guardians.

Jaci couldn't help but stare as the High Enchantress swept up beside Aegis Nordrel. The resemblance to her mother was astonishing.

"Lady Keiresta." Nordrel bowed. He waved his arm toward Jaci and the others. "These are the people I spoke to you about."

The High Enchantress turned imperious eyes on the group. When her gaze touched Jaci, her eyes widened, and she looked momentarily taken aback. She pointed at Jaci. "You, come forward. Who are you?"

The Black Banders tensed, and Jaci felt Talan's anxiety ratcheting upward.

She wet her dry lips and stepped up beside Liundur. "I am Jacinda, daughter of Mirinesstra. Your granddaughter."

Keiresta's eyes narrowed. "You are *not* my granddaughter. I will not recognize you. Mirinesstra ceased to be my daughter when she refused her royal duties and brought shame to my kingdom and to me. I have only one daughter — Selendria. She fulfilled her royal destiny in every sense of the word. She was perfect." Grief etched the High Enchantress' features, chased by bitter anger. "You will leave my kingdom. I don't ever want to see you or your mother again." She nodded to Aegis Nordrel. "Take them to the border and leave them." Then she turned on her heel and swept back toward the door through which she'd entered, her retinue accompanying her.

Jaci swallowed her shock. "Wait! Don't you even want to hear what I have to say?"

The High Enchantress lifted her hand in a gesture of dismissal as she walked away. "I have no interest in anything you might say. Go back to wherever it is you've both been *hiding* all these years."

Jaci bristled at the slight toward her mother, and her temper flared. "Even if it might mean Galenock's defeat?"

Keiresta spun around. "Do not speak to me of Galenock. If Mirinesstra had been here, we would have been strong enough to overpower him, but she stubbornly refused her duty — selfishly ran away, abandoned her own family. She was such a disgrace."

"I can't help what happened in the past," Jaci said fiercely, "nor am I responsible for my mother's actions. Miri is dead now. She died of an illness two years ago. She gave me her *druidainoch* stone right before she died." Jaci revealed the stone amid gasps from Keiresta's retinue. "I also inherited her magical ability, but I don't know how strong it is. If you will train me to use that magic, I will help you overthrow Galenock."

Keiresta eyed Jaci silently, the burning anger in her gaze shifting to an icy shrewdness Jaci found unnerving. The women in the retinue glanced at each other, then at the High Enchantress.

Keiresta walked slowly back toward Jaci, her sharp gaze examining Jaci's companions more closely. "Just what sort of magic do you think you have —" Her breath caught; her face twisted in fury. She brushed roughly past Jaci and shoved Solon aside, halting before Talan. She ripped the blindfold from his face. "You! How dare you set foot here again!" She slapped him hard.

He recoiled into Arnos.

"Because of you, Selendria and Soneira are dead!" The High Enchantress stalked away from him, shaking with rage.

Talan straightened, closed his eyes, and bowed his head. Jaci winced at the swell of anguish that threatened to drown his spirit. "He is here because I asked him to bring me," she said sharply.

"Then he can blame you for his death!" The High Enchantress turned suddenly and swept her arm forward at Talan, chanting words of magic. Her *druidainoch* stone glowed white as blue light swirled around her hand.

"No!" Jaci leaped between them. She backed against Talan and gripped his forearms.

Blue lightning streaked toward them, and Jaci heard an unfamiliar mental scream of anguish as Talan cried, "Jacinda, no!" and tried to swing her to the side. Before he could do so, white light blazed from Jaci's *druidainoch* stone, and an iridescent bubble materialized around them. Jaci gasped from the intense heat like liquid fire in her veins. The lightning hit the surface of the bubble, fizzled, and dissipated harmlessly.

Shocked silence filled the room.

The bubble vanished, the heat it had sparked draining away, leaving Jaci cold. Shaking, she pried her fingers from Talan's arms. Their eyes met for a brief moment, reassuring themselves the other was unharmed. He looked as shaken as she.

Jaci faced Keiresta and tried to marshal her thoughts. Not welcome here, Talan had said. Heavens above, could that have been any more of an understatement? Why hadn't he told her the High Enchantress would try to kill him? And where on earth had that emotional outcry come from? It was just like the strong emotions she felt from Talan, but it hadn't been him... highly unlikely it would have come from any of the soldiers, and it definitely wasn't from the High Enchantress... one of the retinue?

She focused on them for a moment. They were staring at her in open amazement, and so was Aegis Nordrel.

"Well, well, so it seems you do have some magic in you." Keiresta stepped close, examining her with that cold scrutiny, like an aristocrat considering how best to use a new beast of burden. "You must be tested." She turned to her retinue, addressing one with dark eyes and a gray-brown braid curling over her shoulder. "Cristella, prepare her." She gestured toward Aegis Nordrel. "Escort the rest of them off the mountain and see that they don't return."

Aegis Nordrel bowed as she passed. "Yes, my lady."

"No," Solon whispered in dismay.

Jaci lurched forward desperately. "Now — now wait a minute. Please," she added quickly. "I'd hoped that you might heal my friend."

The High Enchantress laughed derisively as she strode toward the door. "Why, by the mountain heights, would I do that?"

"Because he's wounded and you're a healer," Jaci snapped, losing her grip on her temper. "How can you just walk away from a dying man?"

Keiresta turned, rigid with fury. "How dare you judge me! You know nothing of a healer's curse. There are always people who need healing. If I were to heal every man, woman, and child in this world whenever they were injured, I'd be doing it every hour of every day for the rest of my years. That is more than I am willing to give."

Jaci held her ground. "I'm not asking you to heal the world, just one man."

"No." Keiresta lifted her chin. "It is galling enough that I must have you in my house. I'll do you no favors."

"I see," Jaci said coldly. *If that's the way you want to play...* "I was going to give you something as a token of our goodwill — something I thought you might want, since it belonged to your daughter... your so-called *only* daughter." Jaci drew Selendria's *druidainoch* stone from her pocket and let it dangle from its chain.

Keiresta drew in a sharp breath, her hand flying to her own *druidainoch* stone. Aegis Nordrel muttered something, and Jaci heard murmuring among the retinue and the soldiers.

"But since you are unwilling to help me," Jaci continued, "I don't feel the need to be generous, so I'll just keep it." She slipped the stone back into her pocket.

Talan, Solon, and Owen tensed behind her, the Black Banders like tight coils prepared to spring.

"Where did you get that?" the High Enchantress asked in a hoarse whisper.

"I took it from Galenock. He was planning to declare to everyone that I was Deirdre and force me to marry him so he would become part of the royal family. We fought and I escaped, with the help of Talan and his men."

Keiresta stepped back toward Jaci as if drawn against her will. "That stone belongs with me."

"I will freely give it to you." Jaci pointed at Nickalonis. "If you will heal him."

The High Enchantress stood eye-to-eye with Jaci. "I could have my guardians or my soldiers take it from you."

Her retinue had moved in behind her, hands held in front of them as if poised to cast spells.

Jaci kept her hand over her pocket. "Many would die. I don't want that to happen."

The High Enchantress glanced at Liundur, who stood glaring down at her, only a few inches from Jaci's side.

"I had hoped this would be a friendly meeting," Jaci said. "A family reunion of sorts, for the benefit of all of Tarshane. Can't we forget the past and start over?"

Keiresta regarded her with the look of a cat that had just been bitten by the mouse it had been batting around. Without a word, she strode past Jaci. She looked down at Nickalonis. "What is wrong with him?"

"He's been badly burned," Owen said. "I gave him a sleeping draught to keep him unconscious."

"Remove the bandages and lift him up," she ordered.

Owen carefully unwrapped Nickalonis' wounds, then he and Solon hoisted the litter.

Keiresta studied the wounds impassively.

Jaci turned away, her stomach churning. On the edge of her vision, she saw the High Enchantress place her hand just above Nickalonis' face. Wordlessly, the High Enchantress began moving her hand over the burned areas, her *druidainoch* stone glowing softly. At Solon's sharp intake of breath, Jaci looked back. Her jaw dropped. Wherever Keiresta's hand hovered, flesh and skin grew quickly, spreading over bare muscle and bone until, within minutes, all of Nickalonis' wounds had been healed. His face looked exactly as it had before he'd been burned, with no scars, no pockmarks... nothing. Even his hair had grown out to shoulder length.

"That's amazing," Jaci whispered.

The High Enchantress finished the healing, then stepped back.

"Thank you," Solon said roughly, tears misting his eyes.

Keiresta looked at him coldly and said nothing. She turned her hard eyes on Jaci, held out her hand expectantly.

Jaci set Selendria's stone on Keiresta's open palm. "Thank you for saving his life."

Keiresta's fingers closed tightly over the stone. She gave Jaci an inscrutable look, then walked past her toward the door.

"I have one more request," Jaci called after her. "I'd like one of my friends to stay here with me."

Keiresta turned sharply.

"No offense," Jaci said, "but I don't feel comfortable being here alone."

To her surprise, the High Enchantress didn't immediately refuse.

"Very well," Keiresta said, an annoyed frown darkening her brow. She pointed at Talan. "But not *him*." She swept out of the room.

Jaci sagged, exhausted. That didn't go at all how she'd hoped.

Aegis Nordrel strode forward, his soldiers slowly closing in.

"Wait, can't we have a minute to talk?" Jaci pleaded.

Nordrel slowed to a stop, his soldiers halting as well. "A brief one."

"Thank you." Jaci huddled with the others. "Where will you go?" she whispered anxiously to Talan. "If they make you leave the city, how will you get back to the portal?"

He turned toward her, his eyes closed. "Don't worry. We will not be far. Liundur will stay with you." Then his eyes opened and locked with hers, as if he couldn't leave without one last look at her face. "Jacinda..."

"I'll be fine," she said, with as much assurance as she could muster.

Talan suddenly cried out and dropped to one knee, head bent, his hands over his eyes. "No!" He moaned low in his throat.

"Talan!" Jaci knelt and threw her arms around him, frightened by the fierce struggle she felt twisting inside him. A mental cry of anxiety cut into her mind, startling her again, just as the light from her *druidainoch* stone burst forth. Heat blazed through her as the iridescent bubble enveloped the two of them. Their companions, the soldiers — everything around them blurred behind the milky wall of the bubble.

"Talan, what's wrong?" Keeping one arm firmly around his shoulders, Jaci brushed his hair back from his face. "Please tell me."

"Galenock used... his spell on me."

"The sight spell? Oh, no." Jaci held him tight. "I'm so sorry."

Talan's harsh breathing slowed. His body unclenched, freed from the spell by the bubble. He pounded the floor. "Damn everything to the Abyss. I should never have opened my eyes."

"It's not your fault." Jaci helped him to his feet.

The bubble faded away, and Jaci shivered with cold.

Solon grasped Talan's arm and steadied him. "Are you all right?"

"What happened?" Aegis Nordrel demanded. He'd gotten as close to the bubble as he could without touching it.

A blue-robed woman with a gray-brown braid stood beside him. Jaci recognized her as the one Keiresta had spoken to earlier.

"Galenock was trying to use a spell on Talan," Jaci said. "I blocked it, or rather, the bubble did."

"You blocked one of *Galenock's* spells?" Nordrel asked incredulously. He and the woman exchanged glances.

Solon looked horrified. "Not — not the..."

Jaci nodded.

"Did he see anything?"

Nordrel frowned. "Did who see what?"

"I don't know," Talan rasped, his eyes tightly closed. He leaned on Solon as if he'd used all his energy fighting the effects of the spell.

"I'll explain everything and answer any question you ask," Jaci said to Aegis Nordrel. She touched Talan's arm. "But first, he needs rest and time to recover. I know she doesn't want him in the castle, but it's freezing and dark out now. Couldn't you let them stay somewhere inside where it's warm, for the night at least? As I said before, we're here to help, not cause trouble. Please?" She looked at Nordrel beseechingly.

"Blindfold," Talan whispered. "Where is it?"

One of the soldiers picked up the knotted cloth and tossed it to Arnos. Arnos passed it to Owen, who slipped it into place over Talan's head.

Nordrel wavered. He looked at the woman beside him.

Jaci turned to the woman. *"Please?"*

The woman met her gaze, and Jaci caught her breath in shock. The woman had Talan's eyes.

A flicker of fear crossed the woman's face, and Jaci felt the resonance in her own heart.

The woman looked away. "Lock them, under guard, in one of the barracks for the night," she said to Aegis Nordrel, her lyrical voice tight. "I will take responsibility."

"As you wish, milady." Nordrel wiped the apprehension from his expression, and he and his soldiers escorted Talan and the others from the throne room.

CHAPTER 27

Jaci watched with trepidation as the others left the throne room. Her heart ached for Talan's plight.

Liundur shifted beside her, and she turned back to the woman with the gray-brown braid and Talan's eyes. Jaci could feel the woman's anxiety beating inside her own heart like a caged bird desperate to escape.

"I am Cristella." The woman inclined her head nervously. "If you would come with me?" She walked quickly toward a side door.

Jaci followed, Liundur a step behind her.

They traversed several corridors and climbed five flights of stairs. Jaci tried to pay attention to their direction, but her thoughts strayed, whirling around Cristella and Talan and their similarities. She wished Talan had gotten a good look at Cristella and seen her eyes. They had to be related somehow. And Cristella's fear and anxiety were affecting Jaci the same way Talan's did, which meant the two emotional outcries she'd felt earlier must have come from her. And yet, Talan was supposed to be an orphan. He'd lived at Castle d'Gaire and trained with the Wizard's Guild, but no one had known where his magical talent had come from.

Jaci studied Cristella's slender form as she hurried on ahead. The woman's thick brunette braid was generously sprinkled with gray, though her face, Jaci recalled, had only the barest touch of crow's feet around the eyes. Could she be old enough? But then why —

Cristella had followed a dimly lit hall to the end. She opened a door to a darkened chamber. "This will be your room."

Jaci stopped in front of her and blurted, "You're his mother, aren't you?"

Cristella went white, and a spike of fear pierced Jaci's heart. The Enchantress ushered Jaci and Liundur into the chamber. She whispered a few words, and light bloomed in spheres ensconced on the walls. A roaring fire burst to life in the fireplace. She closed the door behind her.

"Please, you must not speak of this," she said in a low voice.

Jaci moved closer, matching her low tone. "Why not? Are you his mother?"

The Enchantress hesitated, glanced at Liundur.

"He won't repeat anything," Jaci assured her.

Cristella wrung her fingers. "No one must know. You must promise me you won't tell anyone."

"I won't tell anyone but Talan," Jaci said.

"No, you can't tell him!"

"He has a right to know."

"Keiresta would banish me if she found out. She might even kill me. She hated Elshaer —" Cristella's hand flew to her mouth.

"What's Elshaer have to do with —" Jaci gasped. "Elshaer is Talan's father? The wizard?"

"I must go," Cristella said, gripping her *druidainoch* stone in agitation. "Please, *please*, don't tell *anyone*." She rushed toward the door.

Jaci beat her to it. She stood with her back to the door and her arms outstretched, barring the exit. "I'm sorry, but you're not leaving this room until you tell me everything."

Cristella took a step back and glanced wildly around the room as if looking for another exit. Liundur had slipped behind her to cut off any escape. She wrung her hands again. "I can't! You don't know how spiteful and unforgiving Keiresta can be."

Jaci stepped toward her slowly, her hand held out in front of her in a calming gesture. "I'm not going to do or say anything that will get you in trouble. You have to believe that." She sensed Cristella's overwhelming fear and switched tack. "Talan has lost nineteen years of his life fighting Galenock. I want him and all of Tarshane to be free. The only way that will happen is if we can defeat Galenock. I'm willing to help, but I need all the information you can give me."

Cristella wavered, glanced at Liundur again.

"I will stand guard." Liundur headed for the door.

"Thank you," Jaci said. "Oh, but please don't leave the room. I'll feel much better if I can see you. I don't trust the Enchantresses not to try to cast a spell on you if you're out in the hall alone."

"As you wish, Your Highness." Liundur stood beside the door.

Jaci turned back to Cristella. "I'm sorry, I hope I didn't offend you with what I said."

"I am not offended." Cristella gave her a nervous smile, then sobered. "You are wise to be wary."

Jaci took the woman's hands in both of hers and led her to the bed. They sat down, facing each other.

"Please tell me about Talan," Jaci said softly. *"Please?"*

Cristella closed her eyes for a moment as if gathering her thoughts. "When I was a young girl growing up, your mother Miri and I were good friends."

"You knew her?"

Cristella nodded. "We were the same age, and we liked to do many of the same things."

"What was she like then?"

"She was strong and impetuous, stubborn, determined to forge her own path. She wanted more than anything to study magic — ancient magic as well as Enchantress magic — and be inducted into the Wizard's Guild. By the time we came of age and received our *druidainoch* stones, she had already mastered every spell in the *drinoch arcantus* that Keiresta would allow her to try. She was a better spellcaster than Selendria. In fact, she was better than her sister at most things. Selendria hated her because of it, but she hid her feelings so well that very few people knew."

"Was that Miri's natural talent — her affinity for spellcasting?"

"That was what everyone originally thought. She also had a talent for working with animals, particularly horses. But one day when she and Selendria and I were training with Keiresta, Selendria cast a mutated spell at her sister that would have seriously hurt or perhaps killed her. A protective bubble formed around Miri and blocked the spell, just like the one that protected you from Keiresta's spell. Selendria claimed that she'd cast the spell accidentally, that she'd misspoken the words. Keiresta believed her, but Miri and I both knew her twisting of the spell had been intentional."

Selendria could twist spells, just like Galenock, Jaci thought. *I wonder if Soneira could, too?*

"Miri badly wanted to get away from her sister and begged her mother to let her go and study with the Wizard's Guild," Cristella continued. "Keiresta had been reluctant to give her consent. She would never say why, but she finally agreed. Selendria wanted to go, too, but her mother refused to allow both her daughters — her heirs — to leave the kingdom, and no amount of pleading would change Keiresta's mind.

"As Miri was preparing to go, a royal delegation from King Brannad of Shiannora arrived. He proposed an alliance between the two kingdoms, to be sealed by marriage to one of Keiresta's daughters. Keiresta agreed, and since Miri was firstborn and was already going to Castle d'Gaire to study with the wizards, Keiresta chose her to marry King Brannad. Miri was furious. She had no wish to be married to a stranger and had no desire to be queen. She and Keiresta had a terrible row, but in the end, Miri was forced to marry the king." Cristella smoothed the coverlet, her expression pensive.

"When I was at Castle d'Gaire," Jaci said, "one of the women I met told me about how Miri came to the castle, but refused to be queen."

Cristella nodded. "Miri could be incredibly stubborn. Keiresta was so angry with her. King Brannad was patient with Miri, but Keiresta was not. She sent me to Castle d'Gaire with a message for Miri — either Miri would perform her duties as queen, or Keiresta would disown her and give whatever inheritance she might have had by birthright to Selendria. I guess she thought that, as her friend, Miri might listen to me. I knew it would be a wasted endeavor, but I went anyway." Cristella smiled. "I was glad to see a new place. I'd never been to Catir Coronin.

"Miri was very happy to see me. She'd been lonely and a bit homesick, though she loved studying with the wizards. She ignored her mother's message, as I'd known she would, and instead she told me all about the new magic she'd been learning. She even let me come with her to study with the Guild."

Cristella looked down at her hands. "That was when I met El-shaer. I was nineteen, and he was twice my age, but he had this way about him... this intensity. When he looked at you, it was like you were the only person that mattered to him." Her cheeks blushed pink. "His magic filled him with ideas. He was constantly driven to create new ways to use the celestial energies. His talent wouldn't let him rest, and he sought release in... other ways." She flushed a deeper shade of rose. "I know I was not the only one in whom he sought solace... there were many... and I shouldn't have..." She stumbled over her words. "But he was a good man, and kind. He would not take what was not freely given."

Jaci put her hand on Cristella's arm to show she understood, and Cristella gathered herself. "I think Miri was the only woman in the castle he didn't touch. She said that even though she refused to be queen, she wouldn't dishonor King Brannad by sleeping with another man, and Elshaer respected that. She didn't love either of them. She'd always said she wanted to wait until she found a man she could love."

Jaci thought about her mother and father and how they'd looked at each other, and blinked back tears. Miri had found her true love.

"When I realized I was with child," Cristella said, "I panicked. I was terrified of what Keiresta would do. She had taken me in after my parents died and let me live in the castle because Miri and I were such good friends. If she found out that a man she hated had fathered my child, I feared she would either banish me or kill me, so I told no one. I tried to work up the courage to at least tell Miri, but then she disappeared, and everything was in an uproar.

"I returned to Millianoch, and Keiresta locked me in my room and questioned me relentlessly about Miri's actions and whereabouts. She didn't believe I didn't know where Miri had gone. But I was as in the dark as everyone else, and when her truth spells finally convinced her of this, she let me go. I fled the castle and went to live with a childless couple who had been friends of my parents. They took me in and treated me like I was their own daughter." Tears filled Cristella's eyes. "But when my baby was born, I feared for his safety. Keiresta and King Brannad were still threatening each other with war, and Keiresta had summoned me back to the castle. She thought she might have need of my talent."

"What is your talent?" Jaci asked.

"I can't say. Keiresta told me never to reveal my true talent."

"Is it, by any chance, the ability to boost others' magical powers?"

Cristella looked at Jaci in shock. "How did you — ?" Then a smile curved her lips, and her expression mirrored one Jaci had seen on her own mother's face when she'd done something well — parental pride. "Is that his talent?"

"Yes."

"Thank you for telling me." Cristella exhaled a deep sigh, her face awash in sadness again. "I knew he would have magical abilities of some kind, which is why I didn't want to leave him with the couple who was caring for me. I wanted him to have the proper training he deserved. And I didn't dare bring him to Catir Enseidrinocha, so I delayed my return as long as I could by saying I was unwell and secretly took him to Castle d'Gaire. It broke my heart to leave him, but I could see no other way." She covered her face with her hands and wept.

Jaci slid over beside her and hugged her. "I'm so sorry."

After a few minutes, Cristella pulled a cloth from her pocket and wiped her eyes. "I did have news of him from time to time. After Selendria took Miri's place and married King Brannad, our kingdoms were on friendly terms again. And then he came here a few times with Soneira. I used to watch him from a distance. He was tall and dark and strong, yet kind and considerate — a mother's dream for a son. I was so proud of the way he'd grown up. His presence always raised Keiresta's ire, though. I think she saw Elshaer in him. I always wondered why she hated Elshaer so much. I think she might have trained with the Wizard's Guild when she was much younger. She and Elshaer would have been within two or three years of each other. Perhaps they had a relationship that ended badly. I don't know."

Cristella wiped her eyes again. "Talan seemed like he was doing well, but I couldn't help worrying about him, because he obviously loved Soneira, and she was —" Cristella bit off what she'd been about to say. "It doesn't matter now. After Galenock's betrayal and the murder of the royal family, Keiresta and I both lived in agony, our children dead. But then I learned Talan still lived, and I was overjoyed. I wished I could bring him here to give his heart time to heal in safety, but I knew it would be impossible. Keiresta's actions today proved that." She took Jaci's hands and squeezed them. "Thank you for saving him."

"Of course, and thank *you* for telling me all this." Jaci hesitated. "Keiresta said it was Talan's fault that Selendria and Soneira died. Do you know why she blames him?"

Cristella shook her head. "No, I don't. And I must ask you again to please not tell anyone what I've said. The consequences could be dire for both him and me."

"I can't promise I won't tell him, but I certainly won't tell anyone else. You have my word on that."

Cristella squeezed Jaci's hands again, then let go. "You are so much like your mother. You said earlier that Miri died of an illness. As strong as she was, I would never have thought that she would succumb to any kind of ailment. I hope she didn't suffer long."

"No, she didn't." Jaci wiped a tear from the corner of her eye. "I think her spirit died years before, when my father passed away from an accident. After that, she just went through the motions.

She never even tried to fight the illness. She was ready to go and be with him in the afterlife." Jaci swept more tears away with her sleeve. "They were so happy together in life, and I know they are happy to be together again in spirit."

Cristella hugged her. "I'm sorry. It had to be terribly difficult for you. I'm glad to know that Miri did find happiness in life and love." Cristella rose. "I must go now. And you must get some rest before the testing tomorrow."

Jaci stood more slowly, exhaustion from the day's events dragging on her. "Testing — what exactly does that mean?"

"Keiresta will have you cast spells and will challenge your defenses, to see how strong your magic is."

Jaci walked Cristella to the door. "That sounds scary."

"Just remember to be on your guard at all times. You already know she can't hurt you physically. Your magic will protect you. But she likes to play mind games and she can be cruel, so no matter what she says or how she acts, remember she is not your friend." Cristella gave Jaci another hug. "I'm glad we met. And next time, I want to hear all about you and Miri and where you've lived all this time."

Jaci nodded. "It's a deal."

Liundur opened the door.

Cristella squeezed Jaci's hand one last time and left the room.

*****

Talan paced the back of the barracks room, his hand trailing along the rough wooden wall to keep himself oriented. Aegis Nordrel had locked them in and set guards at the door, as ordered. Solon had described their temporary quarters — a sparsely furnished room with a long table and twelve chairs in the middle. Three sets of double bunks and some chests filled with clothing and linen lined two of the walls. A large fireplace split the back wall, opposite the door. Nordrel had allowed Solon and Owen to carry in wood and light a fire. Then he'd grilled Talan about the sight spell and about Jaci. That had been hours ago.

Talan skirted the hearth, his arm outstretched, his fingers skimming the stone mantel. The fire snapped and hissed, its heat blazing outward. The smell of burning pine curled around him. He heard the shifting of his companions in the beds as they tried to sleep. He knew Carrick guarded the door, though he couldn't see him.

He cursed Galenock for the thousandth time. The violation of his mind sickened him. And Galenock would undoubtedly attack him again. Galenock had to know it was Talan he'd cast the spell on. No one else could have fought the spell like Talan had. His magic had resisted its mind-controlling effect. He'd known what was happening, and he'd been able to close his eyes and keep them closed. Then Jacinda had banished the spell with her magic. She'd saved him twice — from the High Enchantress' attack, and then from Galenock's. Talan knew Keiresta hated him, and that coming here might well get him thrown in the dungeon to rot, but the savage spell she'd cast had caught him by surprise. And then Jacinda had leaped in front of him, directly in the path of the blue lightning. The terror he'd felt stopped his breath again. He struggled for calm. She was safe. Her magic and her *druidainoch* stone had protected them both.

He breathed deeply, in, out. He couldn't bear to live if anything happened to her. She was so courageous and strong and beautiful. He saw her in his mind — her guileless brown eyes, that mischievous half smile, her dark curls so soft... His heart fluttered and raced and grew cold again with fear. What was happening to her right now? Being stuck out here in the barracks was torture. Not that he would be of much use as a protector, blindfolded as he was.

His fists clenched at his helplessness, and he cursed Galenock again. At least she had Liundur with her. Of all the Black Banders, Liundur and Katar were the most highly skilled. But what if..."

Someone stirred in one of the beds.

Solon said, "Nick... Nick, can you hear me?"

Talan ceased pacing and listened.

A low groan, and then Nickalonis' voice. "Oh, my head."

"That's from the sleeping draught," Owen said. Talan heard him cross the floor. "It will wear off in an hour or so. How do you feel, other than your head?"

"Fine. What happened? Where are we?"

"We're in one of the barracks in Catir Enseidrinocha," Solon answered.

"What in Brackan's name are we doing there?"

"He'll need a blindfold," Talan said. "Close your eyes, Nickalonis. Owen, do you have any bandage cloth left?" Talan heard rustling as Owen dug into his healer's pack. His profound relief at Nickalonis' recovery was marred by the fact that Nickalonis was still vulnerable to the sight spell.

"Yes, I have some," Owen answered.

"Talan?" Nickalonis said. "You're blindfolded. Why? And why do I need one?"

"You don't remember?" Solon said.

"Remember what?" Nickalonis' voice rose in confusion. "If I knew what you were talking about, I wouldn't be asking. Ow, not so tight."

"What's the last thing you remember?" Owen asked.

Silence, as Nickalonis considered. Talan moved along the wall toward where the others had gathered until Arnos took his arm and directed him to a seat on a bunk.

"I remember leading the men through every cursed forest and swamp between the White Bluffs and the Velstand Mountains, while you all went off to rescue Jaci. Where is she? Is she still in Castle d'Gaire?"

"No," Talan said. He couldn't keep his anxiety for her out of his voice. "She is with the High Enchantress."

"Oh, gods, that witch. But *how* did you manage to get her out of the castle?"

"We didn't. She got herself out." *And now she's in an equally dangerous place...* Talan clamped down on his emotions. "It's a very long story, and we will tell you, but first I need to know if you remember why you didn't come with us to rescue her?"

"I don't —" Nickalonis gasped. "The sight spell. That's why you wanted me blindfolded." A pause, then he said, appalled, "He used the spell on you, too?"

"Yes," Talan said roughly. "But it's worse than that. Do you remember anything more?"

"No. What could be worse?"

"Galenock and Jaci fought, and she knocked him into a roaring fireplace," Talan said. "He was very badly burned. He used another spell and transferred his burn wounds to you."

"You would have died," Solon said, "but Jaci convinced Keiresta to heal you."

"I — I don't remember that," Nickalonis said in a shaky voice.

"We gave you the sleeping draught so you wouldn't feel the pain," Owen said.

Talan heard more shifting and rustling.

"What are you doing?" Solon asked.

Nickalonis said, "I don't see any wounds or scars."

"You don't have any," Solon said. "You're fully healed."

"But he could do it again, couldn't he? Any wound he had he could give to me, or to you, Talan, or to anyone else whose blood he collected. How do we stop him?"

Talan heard the desperate note in Nickalonis' voice, and the same feeling clenched his own gut. "I don't know. Jacinda is with the Enchantresses now. She is to be tested. We can only hope that her magic, combined with the other Enchantresses' magic, will be enough to defeat him."

"But unless he's killed instantly, he'd have time to cast the spell and transfer his death wound to one of us, wouldn't he?" Nickalonis asked. "How long does it take to say the words? A few seconds?"

Cold despair settled over Talan as he acknowledged the truth of Nickalonis' words. "In all likelihood, yes."

No one spoke as the horror of the possibility sank in.

Solon's strained voice broke the silence. "We'll find a way to do it. We have to."

Talan struggled to find similar words of encouragement, but none came. He heard the creak of someone sitting on one of the bunks.

"I just hope Jaci is all right," said Solon.

Talan's heart echoed the sentiment a thousandfold.

"Wait... did Talan say that Jaci has magic?" Nickalonis asked.

"She is Queen Mirinesstra's daughter," Solon said.

"Ah... so Talan, you were right about where she got her *druidainoch* stone!" Nickalonis paused again. "I can't believe Keiresta agreed to heal me. She accepted Jaci?"

"Not willingly." Talan rose and paced the wall again while Solon recounted what had happened since they'd gone to rescue Jaci from Castle d'Gaire.

"That is one spirited little minx," Nickalonis said when Solon had finished. "So what do we do now? Do you think they'll throw us out of the city in the morning, or leave us locked in here?"

"I don't know," Talan said. "If they do escort us out, we'll find a place to camp. We have to stay nearby in case she needs help." All he could see was Keiresta turning on Jaci, attacking her in some way.

"A lot of help we'll be, blindfolded," Nickalonis said in disgust.

Talan pounded the wall with the edge of his fist. "Don't you think I know that?" He took a deep breath. "I'm sorry. I'm just worried about her."

"You're a lot more than just worried." Talan heard Solon walking toward him, dawning comprehension in his voice. "You're in love with her, aren't you?"

Talan didn't answer. He paced to the corner and turned. Yes, he was in love with her — wildly and deeply. He'd loved her since... he didn't even know when he'd started to fall.

"Have you told her?"

"No," he said sharply, "and neither will you."

"But... she should know. You have to tell her —"

"No."

"Why not?" Solon demanded.

"Because she doesn't want to stay in this world. She wants to go back to her own world, and I don't want her to feel like she has to stay out of pity or some sense of obligation to me."

"But if she knew you loved her, she might want to stay. She obviously cares for you —"

"No. I want your word you won't tell her."

"Talan —"

"Your word!"

"All right," Solon said reluctantly, "I won't tell her, but I really think —"

"Someone's coming," Carrick said from his post by the door.

"Is it morning already?" Nickalonis asked.

"Yes," Owen said. "The sun is just coming up over the mountain."

"I never realized how much I would miss being able to look out a window," Nickalonis said.

Talan stepped away from the wall. "Arnos." Arnos took his elbow and guided him toward the door.

"Let's see what they have in store for us," Talan said grimly.

CHAPTER 28

"Genelistonia finisoldun onandri ispenak." The words of ancient magic whispered in the air, floating around the ring Galenock twisted in his fingers — the silver ring with the purple faceted stone he'd taken from a chain around Elshaer's neck after he'd crushed the life out of him. The ring had once belonged to Keiresta, the High Enchantress of Millianoch. Galenock had seen her give it to Elshaer, one of the many times he'd spied on them.

He whispered the words again, and the ring began to glow with a faint aura as the magic melded to it. *Yes! The spell is working.* He'd finally gotten the mutation right. He set the ring down atop the open book of ancient magic lying on the table before him and rubbed his eyes. Working the old magic tired him immensely, though twisting the spells did not.

A knock on the door roused him. He recognized Castellan Felgarth's sharp rap.

"Enter." Galenock picked up the ring again, watching as the glow faded, the ring now completely imbued with the magic.

Felgarth strode into the dim, windowless chamber. "Please forgive the intrusion, my lord, and my delay in delivering this message. I couldn't find you, and when one of the guards told me you had gone to your old rooms in the Wizard's Guildhall, I nearly throttled him for insubordination."

Galenock looked up, his patience thinning quickly. "The message, Felgarth?"

"Yes. Reports are coming in from Garsondale and the surrounding towns. The people are fighting back against the Riders and the Ruusitaran foot soldiers. There are pockets of organized resistance, spreading the seeds of rebellion." Felgarth's eyes fastened on the ring. "A lovely trinket, my lord."

"This little 'trinket,' as you call it, will bring about the downfall of the Enchantresses."

Felgarth's eyebrows lifted. "How? You can't get past their shield."

"Ah, but I can." A smug smile curved Galenock's lips at the success of his twisted spell. "It seems that as long as the spells I cast don't directly affect the Enchantresses or those under their protection, I can get through." He'd proven that when he'd used the sight spell on Talan. The spell had worked, even though Talan had been in Catir Enseidrinocha. In the brief moment before Talan had closed his eyes, Galenock had recognized the distinctive colors of the palace throne room. The gamut of emotions he'd experienced at that moment swept over him again: elation at discovering he had a blood sample from his hated rival, frustration and fury that Talan and Jacinda had reached the Enchantresses' castle — *curse you, Soneira, for not sharing with me your portal magic* — and surprise and uneasiness, first that Talan had enough power and control to block Galenock's vision, and second that someone had completely stopped his spell. Had it been a combined effort by the Enchantresses? He found that hard to believe, knowing how Keiresta felt about Talan. But what other explanation could there be? Jacinda? Could she really be that powerful? His scrying spell had been stopped cold the same way when he had tried to find her. If her magic was as strong as her mother's and grandmother's, and if she joined forces with the Enchantresses, it would jeopardize everything. He needed to tap into Ridaur's power before they could organize an attack on him. He had to get that key to Ridaur's crypt *now*.

Felgarth cleared his throat. "With all due respect, my lord, what good will it do, if you can't affect the Enchantresses directly?"

Galenock smiled again. "I won't have to. Keiresta's greed and ambition will get me what I want." His fingers closed around the ring. "I need a few hours of rest. Then the endgame will begin. As for the rebellious towns, send as many troops as necessary. Kill everyone who resists and burn every last building to the ground."

*****

Jaci took a deep, steadying breath and focused once more on the ancient script in the *drinoch arcantus*. The massive tome lay open on the pedestal before her in the center of the small tower room to which she'd been brought early that morning. Keiresta sat in a gilded chair across the room and glowered at her, drumming her fingers on the chair arm while she waited for Jaci to speak the words of the spell again. Her retinue, including Cristella, stood tensely on either side of her, while Liundur stood equally tensely by the door.

Jaci's stomach growled. They'd dragged her out of bed at the crack of dawn and hadn't allowed her so much as a bite to eat. She could see out the window that the sun was now high in the sky. It seemed Keiresta's goal was to make this as unpleasant an experience as possible. Worry over Talan and the others slipped into Jaci's mind, and she wondered where they were and if they were all right. Marshaling her thoughts, she forced herself to concentrate and repeated the spell, stumbling over the pronunciation, the words sounding awkward and strange as they hovered in the air and then dissipated into nothing.

She cringed inwardly as Keiresta sprang from the chair and stalked toward her. "No, no, no. You're not speaking the words correctly. It should sound like this." Keiresta spoke the magic phrase with precise inflection, her voice rising and falling in unexpected places. Bright light filled the unlit globes on the wall.

Jaci's temper rose. "Well, if you would tell me how to pronounce them beforehand, I might be able to say them properly."

"I shouldn't have to tell you. Your mother didn't need any such help."

"I'm not my mother."

"Obviously."

Jaci gritted her teeth at the scorn in Keiresta's voice.

Keiresta halted a few feet away, pointed at Jaci, and shouted a spell. Blue lightning erupted from her fingertip.

Jaci bit off her startled cry as the iridescent bubble from her *druidainoch* stone swallowed her and blocked the attack. She shivered, cold replacing intense heat as the bubble faded. She glared at Keiresta. "Why do you keep doing that? You know it won't hurt me."

Keiresta closed the distance between them. "To remind myself that you might be of some use to me, despite the fact that you can't even cast simple spells."

"You don't know if I can cast them or not. You're not giving me a chance. What I need is *training*, not this farce you call 'testing.'" Jaci got a grip on her temper. "I'm sorry if my mother hurt you, but you don't need to take it out on me. That won't solve anything. I'm here because I want to help you defeat Galenock. Once that's done, I'll leave, and you'll never have to see me again."

Keiresta eyed her coldly. "So you're going to run away, just like your mother."

"I'm not running away. I'm leaving because I don't belong here."

"That's for certain."

Jaci's fists clenched. "How about I try that blue lightning spell? I've heard that enough times to say it correctly."

Out of the corner of her eye, Jaci could see Liundur's lips twitching as if he were trying not to smile.

Keiresta gave her a withering look. "You have your mother's impudence, but none of her talent."

"Stop comparing me to my mother! I am not her! And I'm not Soneira or Deirdre! They are all dead. Do you hear me? Dead. Gone. Never coming back. This whole world needs to stop living in the past and start thinking about the future. A future without Galenock. I am Jacinda. I can help you defeat him. But you have to let me." She put her hands on her hips. "So are you going to let me help you or not? Because if you're not, I'll just leave now, and you can all stay stuck in this palace for the rest of your lives."

Gasps from the retinue hushed into a brittle silence as Jaci and Keiresta glared at each other. The retinue remained frozen, faces pale, a few with hands over their mouths or hearts.

A tentative knock sounded at the door. Liundur's hand slid to the hilt of his sword. Keiresta ignored the knock and continued to glare at Jaci. Jaci refused to back down.

Another knock sounded, louder this time, along with a muffled female voice. "My lady? I must speak with you."

With a dismissive toss of her head, Keiresta turned away from Jaci and moved toward the door. "Enter!"

The door opened, and a brown-haired woman in a flowing blue dress hurried up to Keiresta and whispered in her ear.

Keiresta stiffened, then addressed her retinue. "There will be no more testing today. Cristella, take *her*" — she crooked her thumb over her shoulder at Jaci — "back to her room. Then come to the West Tower."

"Yes, my lady," Cristella said, as the High Enchantress swiftly exited the room, along with the rest of her retinue and the woman in the blue dress.

"What was that about?" Jaci asked.

Cristella rushed toward the door. "I don't know. Please, come with me."

Jaci hastened after her with Liundur following, Cristella's shared anxiety filling her with a sense of dread.

When they reached Jaci's room, Cristella ushered them inside and whispered the light spell. The orbs along the walls glowed with a soft luminescence.

Jaci looked at the orbs. "How do you do that so easily?"

Cristella gave her a tense smile. "It just takes practice. I'll have some food brought up for you." She whisked the door closed behind her and was gone, her footsteps running down the hall.

Jaci went to the door and tried to open it. The door wouldn't budge. She turned to Liundur. "She locked us in."

Liundur examined the door. "Do you want me to break it down?"

Jaci thought for a moment. "No, let's leave that as a last resort, since we don't know if it's locked with a key or with magic. I just wish we knew what was going on. Whatever it is has frightened Cristella, so it can't be good." Jaci shivered in the chilly air and wished the room had windows to let in some warmth from the sun.

"I'll build a fire." Liundur crossed to the fireplace and stacked wood in the grate.

"Thank you. It is a little cold in here." Jaci paced the room. *What could have happened?* Surely Galenock must be involved to have caused such an uproar. She stopped short. What if it wasn't Galenock? What if it had something to do with Talan? Fear clutched at her. Was that why Cristella was so scared? *No, please let him be okay.* Jaci reached for her *druidainoch* stone and gripped it through her shirt, keys and all. A soothing warmth flowed through her, easing her anxiety. She breathed deeply, her mind thinking more clearly. Cristella had said someone would bring them food. As soon as that person showed up, they would get some answers.

*****

Galenock stood before the bespelled mirror in the royal bed-chamber of Castle d'Gaire, waiting impatiently. Before he'd slept, he'd used Keiresta's ring to scry her. The magic shield over Catir Enseidrinocha had prevented him from seeing her, but the twisted spell imbued in the ring had allowed him to see the room she was in, which at that time had been her bedroom. He'd cast one last spell to connect the mirror in this room with the one in hers, then collapsed and slept where he fell.

Now, refreshed from his rest and a bath, and dressed in royal attire, he awaited the High Enchantress. He'd had a trumpeter come and blast a few notes on his instrument to get the Enchant-resses' attention. The fear in their eyes when they'd seen him in Keiresta's bedroom mirror had been intensely satisfying.

A door opened in the mirrored room, and Keiresta marched in, followed closely by her retinue. She strode to the mirror, hatred flashing in her eyes. "How dare you befoul my mirror. Get out at once!"

Galenock smiled pleasantly. "My Lady Keiresta. Charming as always. I have a proposition for you — one that would be beneficial to us both."

"The only thing that would benefit me is your death. Now get out."

"It involves Talan d'Lochlann."

"What about him?"

"Quite simply, I want him. He has been a thorn in my side for far too many years. If you turn him over to me, I will make it well worth your effort. Name your price — other than my death, of course. I'm sure we can come to a mutually beneficial agreement."

If Keiresta was surprised Galenock knew Talan was with her, she didn't show it. Instead, she eyed him with the look of shrewd consideration he'd seen many times on her granddaughter, Soneira.

I've got you, he crowed inwardly. "You don't need to make a decision immediately. I'm willing to give you some time to think about it. Oh, and there's one other thing I want. Jacinda stole a key that goes to one of the rooms here in the castle. I'd like it back." He glanced out the window. "It's midmorning now. I will return in two hours to hear your terms. Until then, my lady." He bowed and walked away from the mirror. He chuckled to himself as he left the bedroom and headed down the hall. *This is going to be so easy.*

* * * * *

Jaci paced the room, her stomach growling loudly into the silence. Liundur stood at his usual post by the door. She wished she had a way to tell the passage of time. It had to have been at least an hour since Cristella had run from the room. Jaci wanted food and answers. *Now.*

Out in the hall, she heard footsteps approaching. Liundur tensed. The door opened, and a young girl in a plain dark dress with a white pinafore pushed a wheeled cart laden with a steaming pot of stew, thick slices of bread, and a pitcher of some spiced drink into the room. Jaci's mouth watered as savory aromas filled the chamber.

The girl curtsied nervously. "I'm to serve you, milady." She set out two bowls and ladled stew into them.

Jaci hastened forward. "Thank you. It smells delicious. But what I really need is to know what's going on out there. Can you tell me?"

"What do you mean, milady?"

"Keiresta — the High Enchantress — was testing my magic, and then she received a message and rushed out of the room. I need to know why. What happened?"

"I'm sorry, I don't know, milady. I only work in the kitchen."

"Do you know where she is, or where Cristella is?"

"No, milady, I'm sorry, I don't." The girl's hand shook, and she spilled a little of the fragrant drink as she poured it into the two cups on the cart. She hastily wiped it up with a cloth napkin. "I'm sorry, milady. Please don't be angry with me."

Jaci curbed her impatience. "It's okay. I'm not angry with you. What about the West Tower — do you know where that is? Can you take us there?"

The girl blanched. "Oh, no, I'm not allowed up there."

"What's up there?"

"The High Enchantress' private rooms."

"Well, can you at least take us to the tower? We can find her rooms from there."

"I could take you to the tower, but you wouldn't be able to get in. The door to the West Tower is magically hidden, and every day it moves. It could be anywhere in the castle. Only the Enchantresses know where it is." The girl backed away from the cart. "I'm sorry, I — I must get back to the kitchen." She made a quick curtsy, turned toward the door, then stopped as she saw Liundur blocking her way. She turned back toward Jaci, eyes wide with fear.

Jaci lifted her hands in a calming gesture. "Don't worry. We're not going to hurt you. We can let her go," she said to Liundur. "I don't want to get her into trouble. Now that the door's open, we can find out for ourselves what's going on."

Liundur stepped aside, and the girl bolted for the door. She stopped at the edge and looked back. "If you wait here a few minutes, I will find one of the Enchantresses and send them to you to answer your questions." She fled the room.

Jaci pushed the cart up against the door to keep it from magically shutting. She wasn't sure if the door could shut by itself or not, but she wasn't taking any chances. "All right, we'll give her a few minutes. But only a few." She handed Liundur a bowl of stew. "Let's eat while we have the chance."

She picked up the other bowl and downed half the stew before her mannerly side kicked in and made her eat more slowly. She finished the bowl and was reaching for the cup to take a drink when a sudden heavy tiredness swept over her, and her head spun. Her legs crumpled under her, and she found herself sitting on the floor.

Liundur fell to his knees beside her. "Must have... drugged the stew. I should have... tested it first... failed you..." He slumped to the floor and was still.

No! Jaci screamed silently. Then she knew no more.

CHAPTER 29

My time is nearly at hand! Galenock strode down the corridor, barely containing his glee at how the turn of events had swung in his favor. After so many, many years, he was finally going to win.

"What do you think the old bat will ask for?" Castellan Felgarth asked as he kept pace, a half step behind.

"She will demand the ancient spellbook, of course."

"How can you be sure?"

"Because I know how she thinks. All she wants is power and to have more of it than anyone else. That book is the only thing I have that contains more powerful spells than those she already knows."

"You're not going to give it to her, are you?"

Galenock shot him a look of disgust. "Of course not, you idiot. But I'm willing to negotiate access to a certain number of spells. There are many that can be shared without fear of her using them on me."

At the end of the corridor, Felgarth opened the stairwell door for his master, and they climbed the three flights that led to the north wing and the former rooms of the deceased royal family.

"So if she agrees to the trade of d'Lochlann for access to the spell book," Felgarth said, "that will be one thorn out of your side, but I don't understand how this will get you the key to Ridaur's crypt. You only asked for the key to Soneira's room."

"It's obvious," Galenock said impatiently. "Keiresta is nothing if not predictable. She never forgave Mirinesstra for her actions and will equally despise Miri's daughter. From the brief interaction I had with Jacinda, I can see she inherited her mother's recalcitrance. Jacinda will not want to give up d'Lochlann, especially since she considers him her 'rescuer.'" Galenock sneered the word. "She's not going to cooperate and hand over the key to Soneira's room, which means Keiresta will have to take it. When she does, she'll see the key to the crypt and take that too. And once she has that key in her hands, she won't be able to resist going to the crypt and casting the spell herself."

"But if she controls Ridaur's power —"

"She won't get that far. Once she leaves the safety of Catir Enseidrinocha, she will be vulnerable. And when she arrives at the crypt, she will find me there waiting for her. Her power is no match for mine. I will take the key and destroy her and her pitiful retinue. And once I have secured Ridaur's magic, I will wipe out the rest of the Enchantresses. All of Tarshane will finally be mine!"

"How do you know for certain she will go to the crypt? Will she dare to leave Enseidrinocha?"

"She doesn't know that I know about the key. She won't expect me to be there. She'll expect me to be here amusing myself with d'Lochlann. Even if Jacinda tells her that I've seen the key, the lure of Ridaur's power will be too great for her to pass up."

Felgarth nodded. "A brilliant plan, my lord."

A twitch of unease niggled at Galenock's confidence. "The only wildcard is Jacinda herself."

"Jacinda?" Felgarth scoffed. "How could she possibly be of any threat to you?"

"I don't know the extent of her magic. I underestimated her once. I will not do so again. However, I'm wagering that Keiresta will handle the problem of Jacinda for me, since the 'old bat,' as you call her, will not want to share any of Ridaur's power."

They reached the door to the royal bedroom.

"Stay out of sight of the mirror and keep quiet," Galenock ordered. A brief moment of doubt flitted through his mind. What if Keiresta didn't take the bait and refused further communication with him? If he stepped into the bedroom and found the mirror empty, all his plans would have been for naught. *No. She will be there. I know her too well.*

Calming his mind and stretching his lips into a pleasant smile, he opened the door and entered the bedroom, only to hear a tapping sound emanating from the direction of the mirror. As he crossed toward it, he could see the High Enchantress glaring out at him, her arms akimbo, her foot tapping with impatience. Behind her hovered her ever-present retinue.

Galenock had to work to keep the look of triumph off his face. "Good afternoon, Keiresta."

"Galenock. It's about time. You did say two hours and not two hours and half of another."

Galenock bowed his head contritely. "Please forgive my lateness. I was unavoidably detained. Have you considered my offer?"

"I want the ancient spellbook. Give it to me and I will give you Talan d'Lochlann."

Galenock ignored Castellan Felgarth's smirk. "Ah, yes, the spellbook. I might have guessed you would name such a price. Surely you understand that I can't just hand over something that would give you the means to destroy me." He steepled his fingers and assumed a thoughtful expression. "However, I would be willing to negotiate access to the book for a limited amount of time. I could bring the book here and have my castellan turn the pages for you, for say, two hours, restricting access only to a certain few spells. Would that suffice?"

Keiresta eyed him narrowly, considering. Then she raised her chin. "I will only agree under these terms: In regard to the turning of the pages, your castellan will follow my orders. If I see you have blocked access to too many spells, the agreement will be off. And if you manipulate the order of any of the letters or words of the spells to render them powerless, my truth spells will reveal it, and again, the agreement will be off. I will have Talan d'Lochlann taken to a location accessible to you. At the end of the two hours, if I am satisfied with what I have gotten from the spellbook, I will tell you where he is. Do you accept these terms?"

Galenock nodded. "Done. Give me an hour to prepare the book, and then the agreement will commence."

"Good." Keiresta turned and swept out of view of the mirror, followed by her retinue.

As Galenock watched them go, he suddenly noticed that there were only five Enchantresses in the retinue. There had always been six in the past. He wondered why the difference. *No matter. Soon, I will have the means to defeat them all.* He couldn't help but gloat as he turned to leave the bedroom. In a very short time, he would have his long-awaited victory.

Felgarth followed him out of the room and down the corridor. "Do you think she will keep her word about d'Lochlann?"

"I will give her enough so that she will. Now listen. Send word to that soldier, Vorstun. Tell him to take his best men and follow the Alladhainn River north toward Millianoch. When you find out where d'Lochlann is, send a message to him by way of carrier falcon, giving him the location. He is to bring d'Lochlann here. I don't care what he does to him, as long as he arrives alive and in one piece. I can't torture a dead man."

Felgarth smirked again.

"And tell the Riders to be ready to mount up in an hour's time," Galenock said. "Once I am done preparing the spellbook, I will ride with them to the crypt. The time Keiresta spends looking at the spellbook will give us enough of a head start to reach the crypt before she can." He clenched his fist. "At last, the endgame has begun."

*****

Talan d'Lochlann sat on the cold stone floor of the windowless cell with his arms circling his knees, listening to the faint noises around him, his vision still blinded by the cloth tied around his head. The smell of mold and the dampness of ages thickened the air. He heard whisperings of muted conversations. Solon, Nickalonis, and Owen were talking from their separate cells across the way, arguing about something, he couldn't tell what. It didn't matter anyway. There was no escape from the dungeons of Catir Enseidrinocha. When Aegis Nordrel had come for them at dawn, Talan hadn't known what to expect. He'd hoped they'd be escorted out of the city and released as Keiresta had ordered the previous night. Then they could find a place to camp and try to figure out a way to communicate with Jacinda. But when Nordrel and his soldiers had entered the barracks with weapons drawn, Talan knew his worst fears were about to be realized. He and his men had been taken down into the bowels of the palace and locked away.

Despair as heavy as the mountain of stone above him weighed on his heart. All that he had fought for, all the years of struggle and sacrifice in trying to free Tarshane from Galenock's iron grip, was now for naught. Keiresta's embittered pride and spitefulness would not let her forgive him for the death of her granddaughter. Nor, he realized, would she forgive Jacinda for her mother's abandonment of her duties and her homeland.

He clenched his fists. *No.* He could not lose hope. So many people were counting on him. Jacinda, his men, the people of Tarshane... *Jacinda...* Thoughts of her swirled in his head constantly. He felt again the touch of her lips on his cheek, the warmth of her in his arms. He'd memorized every word she'd said to him. And he'd promised her he would help her get home. He dipped his head against the ragged pain in his heart. No matter how much he loved her, he was honor bound to let her go.

She needs you! At least for a little while longer. Stop wallowing and start thinking. He roused himself from his despair and sat up straight. He had to find a way out of this deep hole in the mountains. But how? They'd all been locked in separate cells, and there was no way to get the keys.

The heavy tread of booted feet scuffed down the long corridor leading to their cells.

"Shhhhh, someone's coming," Solon said in a low voice.

Talan pushed himself to his feet and followed the damp stone wall of the cell around to the door. His fingers slid along the cold iron until he found the small barred opening near the top of the door. He listened to the approaching footsteps, apprehension tightening his gut. Three men — soldiers, from the sound of clinking chainmail and metal scabbards. Not enough men to be releasing all of them at once. He knew Aegis Nordrel wouldn't take such a risk. Either Carrick or Arnos could disarm and down three men in the space of a few moments. Unless Keiresta had had a change of heart and decided to free them. *That will never happen,* he thought bitterly.

The footsteps stopped in front of his cell. He heard a key rattle in the lock, and he stepped back, his apprehension ratcheting upward, caught between the overwhelming urge to rip off his blindfold and the need to prevent Galenock from seeing through his eyes. With a screech of rusty hinges, the door opened. Two sets of footsteps entered his cell.

"Don't move," said an unfamiliar gruff voice.

The sharp edge of a blade touched Talan's neck. He froze.

"Put your hands behind your back," the voice ordered.

Moving slowly and carefully so as not to appear threatening, Talan complied. The other soldier bound his hands with a length of rough rope. Talan could smell the man's sweat, the ale from his midday meal on his breath. Then the blade pulled away from Talan's neck, and the soldier gripped his arm and marched him out of the cell.

"Where are you taking him?" Solon demanded.

The soldiers didn't answer. Talan could think of nothing reassuring to say. He didn't know if he would live or die. Footsteps preceded him and followed after as the soldiers escorted him down the corridor.

"I said, where are you taking him?" Solon shouted after them. *"Talan!"*

Solon's voice faded in the distance as they turned down another long corridor and then climbed a seemingly endless spiral staircase up out of the dungeon. By the time they finally reached the top, Talan felt dizzy and a bit nauseous. He breathed in deeply the fresher air and tried to settle his stomach. They urged him forward, the sound of their boots on stone echoing in a vast space. Disoriented from his lack of sight, he had no idea of their direction or even where they were. His heart pounded as his mind conjured up visions as to where they might be taking him. Would they threaten to torture him to coerce Jacinda into some course of action she was refusing? Or would they stake him out in the elements to die of exposure, or simply toss him off the nearest cliff?

The soldier in front of him opened a door, and Talan was hit with a blast of freezing air. They were going outside. A modicum of relief eased his frantic thoughts. At least it didn't look like he was going to be used against Jacinda. The soldiers guided him none too gently down some stairs and across a courtyard, his boots crunching in a thin layer of snow. The sun warmed him, and he was struck with the sudden longing to see the beauty of the mountain sky.

After a few more minutes of walking, he heard another door open. This time warm, slightly humid air swept over him, carrying the strong odor of horses. *The stable? Why?* Where could they possibly be taking him? His feet slowed as comprehension dawned. *No!* Horror fueled his panic, and he fought the restraining hands, until a sharp crack on the back of his head sent pain crashing through his skull, and all went dark.

CHAPTER 30

"Wake up! *Please*, you must wake!"

The urgent words filtered through the buzzing in Jaci's head, prodding her awake. She became aware of a bitter taste on her tongue and wanted to spit it out, but she couldn't coordinate the proper muscles. More bitter liquid dripped on her tongue and down her throat. She coughed and almost retched.

"Jacinda? Jacinda, wake up!"

The cold dampness of a wet cloth brushed across her forehead, her cheeks. She knew that voice. She tried to get her sluggish mind to work. Cristella. The voice belonged to Cristella. Jaci opened her eyes and focused on the anxious face looking down at her. "What... where...?"

Cristella helped her into a sitting position. "You were given a sleeping potion. I've just given you the antidote. It will take a few minutes to fully neutralize the potion."

Jaci squeezed her temples. She felt like her head was stuck in a beehive. She tried to form questions, but all that would come out were single words. "Why? ...happened?" She turned her head and almost fell over. "Liundur?"

"I'll give him the antidote now." Cristella moved over beside the Black Bander.

Jaci put her head between her knees and waited for the buzzing to stop. Between the buzzing and Cristella's agitation rattling her nerves, it was hard to think.

After a few moments, Cristella forced a cup into her hands. "Drink this."

Jaci took a sip and barely resisted the urge to spit it back in the cup. "Yuck."

"Drink all of it. It will help clear your head."

Jaci held her nose and drank it down. She set the empty cup on the floor. "That... was disgusting."

Cristella gave her a strained smile. "I know, but it works."

Jaci rubbed her temples, awareness sharpening as the buzzing faded. She turned carefully to see Liundur. He was drinking the fluid mixture with a look of extreme distaste. "How long have we been asleep?"

"Several hours." Cristella met Jaci's eyes. "I'm so sorry. I had no idea Keiresta would do this."

"Why did she?"

"To get the key."

An icy dread settled in Jaci's stomach. She snatched forth the chain with her *druidainoch* stone. Both the key to Miri's room and the key to Ridaur's crypt were gone. "How did she know I had them?"

A swell of anxiety from Cristella, tinged with horror, crashed over Jaci like a storm wave.

"Galenock found a way to link a mirror in Castle d'Gaire with the mirror in Keiresta's bedroom in the West Tower," Cristella said. "When we went to the tower after the testing, we saw him in the mirror. He had a proposition for Keiresta." Cristella's anxiety spiked. "He said if she would hand over Talan, she could name her price."

Jaci's heart jammed into her throat. "Oh, no," she whispered.

Cristella nodded. "Then he said you had stolen a key from the castle and he wanted that back, too. He gave Keiresta two hours to think about it. I was horrified to see she was seriously considering it. We quarreled, and I pleaded with her not to do it, but she wouldn't listen. She sent Brenna to get the key from you, but then Brenna came back with two keys. Keiresta recognized one of them as the key to Ridaur's crypt."

Liundur sat forward. "Your Highness, you had the key to Ridaur's crypt?"

Jaci shifted so she wouldn't have to look over her shoulder at him. "Yes. It was in the clock along with the diary. I had put it in my pocket right before I was transported to Tarshane. Only Talan knew. He said the fewer that knew about it, the better, and asked me not to tell anyone. I'm sorry to have kept things from you."

"It is good that you kept it secret," Liundur said. "That key leads to a power better left untouched."

"The power it leads to is evil," Cristella said. "We argued about what to do with the key. Most of us wanted to hide it in the castle where Galenock would never be able to get his hands on it, but Keiresta disagreed. I could see she was thinking about taking the key and using it herself. And then I guessed that Galenock had known about the key but hadn't mentioned it, thinking she might take the chance to leave the castle and go to the crypt. I could clearly see how he could be setting a trap for her, but she still wouldn't listen. She said Ridaur's magic would give her the power to defeat Galenock without your help, and at the same time, she could get rid of Talan.

"I was frantic to save him, and begged her not to give him to Galenock. Then she suddenly backed away from me and looked at me with such revulsion and — and hatred. I knew she had discerned my secret. She hit me with a spell that stunned me, and I woke up locked in my room. I think the only reason I'm still alive is that my magic is useful to her."

Liundur gingerly rose to his feet. He swayed and caught himself on the wall, then stood straight.

"It looks like the effects of the potion are wearing off," Cristella said.

Jaci nodded, still a little dizzy. "I'm feeling better. Someone help me up."

Liundur lifted her onto her feet and steadied her.

Jaci grasped his arm to keep her balance, feeling stronger by the minute. "Where is Talan now?"

"I don't know." Cristella wrung her hands again. "Keiresta said Aegis Nordrel's men could leave him in one of the old outposts that the hunters and trappers use in the forest along the Alladhainn."

"The Alladhainn?" Jaci asked.

"The river that flows south out of the mountains."

"I know of it," Liundur said. "There are several cabin outposts along the river and throughout the forest."

"She was going to have him taken there," Cristella said, "but she wasn't going to tell Galenock until she was done with the spellbook."

Jacinda frowned. "What spellbook?"

"Elshaer's ancient spellbook. That was Keiresta's price for handing over Talan. I don't know whether she got what she wanted, but Keiresta and the rest of her retinue are gone. I fear that she and Galenock made their bargain, and Talan is now in Galenock's hands." Cristella wiped away the tears that had started to stream down her cheeks. "If only it hadn't taken me so long to wake and find the counterspell to the lock she'd placed on my room."

Jaci clutched her *druidainoch* stone and let it soothe away Cristella's anguish so she could think straight. That Keiresta was walking into a trap, Jaci had no doubt. She also had no doubt that the High Enchantress had sacrificed Talan for her own ends. Anger burned away the last vestiges of the potion's effects. "Where are the others who came here with me?"

"They're in the dungeon," Cristella said. "Keiresta found out they had stayed in the barracks overnight and was furious. She had them locked away down there. She gave Aegis Nordrel such a tongue-lashing, I was terrified she was going to lock him down there, too."

Jaci's anger burned deeper. "The first thing we have to do is get them out of the dungeon. Then we'll find Talan."

"But how can we do that? I can't cast attack spells. I can only boost the spells of others. And there are always at least a half-dozen guards down there when there are prisoners."

"Leave that to me," Liundur said, grim fury in his eyes.

"Can we get to the dungeon without being seen?" Jaci asked.

Cristella nodded. "The other Enchantresses are guarding the Great Stone that powers our shield, in case Galenock should attack. No one will hinder us. There is a back way into the dungeon. I can show you."

"We won't need a back way. We'll be going in the front door," Jaci said.

Confusion and distress flitted across Cristella's face. "But... the guards..."

"They won't be alarmed. I'll tell them that you brought me down there because I insisted on seeing my friends."

"Your Highness, I can't allow you to put yourself in danger," Liundur said.

"Don't worry, Liundur. I'll let you handle the guards." Jaci crossed to the fireplace and picked up a cast iron poker and an ash shovel. She handed the poker to Liundur.

He nodded his approval. "Thank you, Your Highness."

Jaci took a practice swing with the small shovel. "It'll do. Okay, let's go."

Cristella led them through countless empty corridors and down several flights of stairs, their way lit by softly glowing orbs. They saw no one. The entire palace seemed deserted. Worry for Talan tormented Jaci, quickening her steps. What if he was already in Galenock's clutches? What might they be doing to him right now? *Stop it*, she chided herself. *Don't borrow trouble. Concentrate on the problem at hand.*

They descended the last set of stairs into a small entryway that led to a dim corridor. Cristella gestured for them to stop and gather close.

"The guardroom is at the other end of the corridor," she whispered. "Then there's a long, narrow staircase down into the dungeon."

"Can you describe the guardroom?" Liundur asked.

"It's a fairly large room, with a long table and benches. They store weapons and armor along the walls on the left. The entrance to the dungeon is on the right."

"Cristella and I will go in first and say why we're there," Jaci said. "Liundur, you stay out of sight. When they tell us, 'No visitors allowed,' which I'm sure they will, we'll create a distraction, and then you take over. Cristella, when the action starts, get out of the way and stay back. Okay?"

The others nodded.

Slipping the ash shovel behind her back, Jaci stepped into the corridor. Cristella walked beside her, and Jaci sensed a new determination overriding her fear and anxiety. Liundur followed a few steps behind. About halfway down the corridor, Jaci heard the murmur of voices — she couldn't tell how many. She gripped the shovel with both hands and hoped she looked like she had her hands either clasped or tied behind her back. *Okay. Deep breath. Showtime.*

Jaci cleared her throat and called, "Hello!"

The murmur of voices ceased, replaced by an immediate scramble of movement.

Cristella and Jaci came into the guardroom and stopped at the sight of the guard coming toward them.

"My ladies," he said, obvious surprise on his face. He bowed, then his gaze flicked from Jaci to Cristella. "Do you need assistance?"

"Yes," Cristella said. "Jacinda wishes to see her friends and make certain they are all right."

The guard stepped closer, but maintained a respectful distance. "I'm sorry, my lady, but we have orders from the High Enchantress not to let anyone see the prisoners."

Jaci counted six other guards clustered behind him on both sides of a long table lined with benches. Along the walls on the far left side of the room hung an assortment of shields, swords, bows, arrow-filled quivers, and chainmail. On the far right stood a closed iron door.

Jaci took a step forward. "But there are seven of you and only two of us," she said for Liundur's benefit. "We wouldn't be any threat to you, so surely it wouldn't do any harm for us to see them, just for a few minutes."

"I'm sorry," the head guard repeated. "No one sees the prisoners."

Cristella drew herself up with convincing fury. "How dare you refuse us! I am one of the royal retinue. You will let us in!" She stalked toward the guard nearest the dungeon door, chanting and gesticulating as if she were preparing to cast a spell on him.

He shrank back, eyes widening. The other guards hesitated, and Jaci could see they had no idea how to handle a rampaging Enchantress.

The head guard started toward Cristella. "My lady —"

Jaci nailed him in the gut with the shovel. He doubled over with a groan. "Liundur!" she shouted, and whacked the guard over the head. He fell to the floor and was still.

Liundur charged into the room, jumped onto the bench, then the table, and took a flying leap onto three of the soldiers, flattening them. With a few well-placed punches and swings of the poker, they stayed down.

Cristella darted back into the corridor.

The three remaining guards whipped out their swords and attacked Liundur. He parried their blows with the poker and got in some jabs of his own. Jaci dashed up behind one of the soldiers and clobbered him with the shovel. He reeled against the table and Liundur punched him into oblivion. Liundur knocked another soldier over the table, then laid the last soldier out flat with the poker.

Jaci surveyed the soldiers sprawled on the floor, unmoving, and smiled at Liundur. "Nice work!"

He gave her a deferential nod. "I would say the same to you, Your Highness."

"That was a great acting job," Jaci said to Cristella as the Enchantress stepped back into the room. "You really had them scared."

Cristella flushed. "I was truly angry."

Liundur strode to the store of weapons and took down and buckled on a sword belt and knives. He swung the sword a few times to test its balance, then slipped it back into the scabbard. Jaci picked up an eighteen-inch-long mace. She had no experience with blades, but clubs she could wield. Liundur handed her a leather weapons belt, and she strapped on the mace. Then he found some rope and began disarming the unconscious guards and binding their hands and feet.

"I found the keys!" Cristella held up a metal circlet with numerous keys dangling from it that she had detached from the head guard's belt. She rushed to the dungeon door and began fitting keys into the lock.

Jaci hurried up beside her. The fifth key Cristella tried unlocked the door.

"Let me go first," Liundur said as he finished with the guards.

Jaci and Cristella stepped back and let him pull open the heavy door. A narrow, orb-lit staircase curled down into the depths of the mountain. Jaci wrinkled her nose at the rank smell.

Liundur drew one of his knives. "Stay close and keep watch behind us." He led the way down into the dungeon.

The air grew colder and more damp as they descended the winding staircase. A sheen of moisture blotched with mold coated the gray stone walls. Jaci cast nervous glances behind her every few steps, but no soldiers appeared.

Liundur signaled for a halt at the bottom of the staircase. Three passageways stretched out before them, to the right, to the left, and straight ahead. Not a sound broke the thick silence.

"Which way?" Cristella whispered.

"We don't have time to search every passage." Jaci cleared her throat and called as loudly as she dared. "Solon! Carrick! Where are you?"

The sudden scuffing of feet sounded from the right-hand passage. "Here! We're down here!"

Jaci ran down the passage, the others following. "Keep talking so we can find you!"

"Jaci, is that you?" Solon called out. "Great gods, it's good to hear your voice. I'm putting my hand through the bars near the top of the cell door. Do you see it?"

A hand appeared through one of the doors just ahead of Jaci. "Yes, I see it." She raced up to the door. "Cristella, the keys! Is everyone all right?"

"We're unharmed," Solon said, "but they took Talan. I don't know where. Are you all right?"

"I'm fine, and yes, I know about Talan. We think Keiresta made a deal with Galenock to trade him for Elshaer's spellbook."

"*What? No!*"

Cristella caught up to Jaci and gave her the ring of keys. Jaci heard Nickalonis' voice from the cell across from Solon's.

"That witch! How did you get away from her?"

"It doesn't matter how. Just be glad she's here," Owen said from the next cell down.

Liundur checked the nearby cells. "Carrick? Arnos?"

"Over here," Carrick called from a cell across the way.

Jaci stuck keys into the lock on Solon's cell as fast as she could until she found the right one. "Got it!" She turned to Nickalonis' cell as Solon emerged. "Cristella, tell them what you said earlier about Keiresta and Galenock."

Jaci flipped through the keys and unlocked the rest of the cells while Cristella related what had happened.

"So you did have the key to Ridaur's crypt," Solon said to Jaci when Cristella had finished. "When we read about the key in the diary, we wondered if that might be the one Deirdre had written about."

Jaci nodded. "Now Keiresta has it and Galenock is going to take it from her. We have to stop him."

"Ridaur's crypt is many leagues west of here," Carrick said, "and they have several hours' head start."

"First, we have to go south to find Talan," Solon said.

"We'll need horses," Nickalonis pointed out.

"We'll just have to borrow some." Jaci pocketed the key ring and headed back out of the dungeon, a thrill stealing through her as she envisioned herself aboard the horse with the beautiful feathery wings.

Nickalonis echoed her thoughts. "Let's take those winged ones. I'll bet they fly fast as the wind."

"They do," said Cristella.

"Wings?" Dread clouded Solon's features. "I'd forgotten about that."

"Don't worry, brother. We'll make sure you're strapped on."

"Are you afraid of heights?" Jaci asked Solon.

"I prefer to be firmly on the ground."

Nickalonis clapped him on the back. "If you fall off, Owen can fix you up."

"That's right, Solon." Owen grinned. "You've got nothing to worry about."

"Last I knew, you couldn't bring back the dead," Solon grumbled.

Jaci slowed as they reached the staircase to let the Black Banders go first. "Is anyone else afraid of heights?"

"We are not, Your Highness." Carrick stepped past, and he and Liundur started up the stairs. Arnos brought up the rear.

They stopped in the guardhouse long enough to arm themselves with swords and knives. The guards still lay on the floor, bound and unconscious.

Nickalonis slung a bow and full quiver over his shoulder. "So, what's our plan?"

"We borrow some horses, like Jaci said, and search the outposts." Solon turned to the Black Banders. "Liundur, you've traveled that area. You know where they are, don't you?"

Liundur stuck another dagger in his belt. "Most of them."

"But we can't just ignore Galenock," Jaci said, a plan forming in her head. "We're going to need help."

"Help? From where?" Nickalonis asked, eyebrows raised skeptically.

"I think we need to split up." Jaci turned to Cristella. "Can you convince the other Enchantresses to go with you to Ridaur's crypt to help Keiresta?"

"I can try," Cristella said with a troubled look. "Getting them to go against Keiresta's orders to stay and protect the Great Stone will be difficult. They won't want to provoke her wrath."

"It won't matter about the Great Stone if Galenock defeats Keiresta at the crypt," Jaci said. "She and her retinue will all be dead. And once Galenock controls Ridaur's power, he'll come here and kill everyone who's left."

"I will make them understand," Cristella vowed.

Jaci nodded. "Good. Go to the crypt, but stay hidden until you can see what's happening. Wait as long as you can for me to get there before you reveal yourselves. I'll try to protect you from Galenock's spells." She turned to the others. "Solon, can you and Nickalonis find your men and anyone else who's willing to fight and get them to the crypt to combat whatever troops Galenock brought with him?"

"We can do that, yes," Solon said, "but what about Talan? We can't just leave him out there."

Jaci gestured toward the Black Banders. "We'll rescue Talan. Owen, you'll come with us, in case Talan has been hurt." She swallowed the catch in her voice, her heart trembling at the thought. "Once we find him, we'll head for the crypt. We need everyone together if we're to have any hope of defeating Galenock. Is everyone agreed?"

Solon nodded reluctantly.

"Sounds good to me," Owen said.

"Agreed," Carrick said with a nod.

Nickalonis headed for the passageway. "Then let's go."

"Do you know how many guards there are between here and the stables?" Jaci asked Cristella as they hurried after Nickalonis.

"There are guards at all the palace entrances. Beyond that, I don't know."

"Can you get us past them?"

"I will try."

They rushed through the passageway, up the stairs, and through the remaining corridors to the cavernous foyer, their footsteps echoing softly in the rose-scented air. As they approached the palace door, two guards armed with spears snapped to attention.

"Stand aside," Cristella ordered as she neared the door.

The guards blocked the exit. "I'm sorry, my lady," said one, "but no one is to leave the palace until the High Enchantress returns."

"The High Enchantress is in grave danger. She will need our help. If you don't let us through, she will fall to Galenock. Now stand aside!"

The guards wavered, uncertainty in their eyes.

The harsh rasp of metal cleaved the air as the Black Banders drew their swords.

"We're going through that door, one way or another," Jaci said. "You can either get out of the way or deal with them." She hooked her thumb at the Black Banders. "Your choice."

The guards took one look at the grim-faced Black Banders advancing on them and stepped aside.

"Thank you," Cristella said. "Now tell the guards outside to do the same."

The guards opened the door, conferred a few moments with their counterparts, then all four stood down.

Jaci hugged Cristella. "Thank you for all you help. I'm so glad I met you."

"And I, you. Please be careful..."

"I will, and don't worry. I will find Talan and bring him back," Jaci said in answer to Cristella's unspoken plea.

"Thank you," Cristella whispered, her eyes glimmering with unshed tears. She gave Jaci one last quick hug, then turned and sped off into the palace.

Jaci faced the guards. "We need safe passage to the stables, and we'll need to borrow some horses. What Cristella said about Keiresta is true. Galenock has set a trap for her, and she may have already fallen into it. We're going to get help and try to save her, but we need your cooperation. I want two of you to come with us to the stables to see that no one interferes with us. Will you do that?"

One of the guards nodded. "As you wish, my lady."

Yes! Jaci stifled the urge to do a fist pump. "Good. Let's go."

CHAPTER 31

The frigid air burned Jaci's lungs as they dashed across the courtyard to the stables. She glanced worriedly at the sun inching downward toward the horizon of distant peaks.

"How much daylight do you think we have left?" she asked, as they crowded into the warmth of the stables.

"Two, maybe three hours," Carrick answered.

"Will that be enough time to..." Jaci paused, choosing her words carefully, "...get to where we need to go?" If the guards knew they were going to rescue Talan first, they might not be as cooperative.

"It depends on how fast these horses can fly," Liundur said in a low voice.

"Horace!" the guards shouted, leading them down a row of empty box stalls.

The old stable master met them at the end of the row, the other stable hands gathering behind him. "What in thunder... is all the hollering about... this time?" he puffed. He saw Jaci and bowed. "My lady."

"My lady and her companions need horses," one of the guards said.

"The flying ones," Jaci interjected. "The fastest ones you have."

Horace eyed them appraisingly as he caught his breath. "Have any of you ever ridden a winged horse before?"

"No," Jaci said, "but we're counting on you to tell us everything we need to know. Keiresta's life depends on it."

The blood drained from Horace's face. "Follow me." He shambled down the walkway, issuing orders to the stable boys, who ran on ahead, rounded a corner, and disappeared from view. "I knew she never should have left the palace," he muttered.

He led them to a large room filled with tall, freestanding frames made of metal pipes, where dark-colored fleece-lined coats and trousers in various sizes hung down to the floor. They reminded Jaci of costume racks she'd seen backstage at a play.

"If you're going to fly, you'll need these." Horace swept his arm toward the left. "Smaller sizes are on that end. Larger sizes are on the right. Boots, hats, scarves, and gloves are in those bins in the back. Find something that fits, then come to the south stable." He gestured to the guards. "They can show you the way." He bowed again to Jaci and hobbled out the door.

Jaci and the others rushed to the racks and bins and pulled on the warm outer clothing. They grabbed an extra set for Talan and stuffed it in a sack they found in another corner of the room.

"We're ready to go," Jaci said to the guards, as Owen slung the sack over his shoulder.

"This way, my lady." The guards hustled out the door and led the way down a wide path lined with empty box stalls. They ran through a short connecting passage and on through another empty stable. At the far end, the exiting passage hooked to the right and opened into a vast space filled with more box stalls, walls covered with tack, and huge mounds of straw and hay. Late afternoon sun poured in through several skylights.

Jaci breathed in the smells of horse, saddle leather, and hay as she followed the guards around to the right side of the stable. "Oh," she whispered, excitement shivering over her as she saw seven winged horses — four browns, two blacks, and a bay — tied to two long hitching posts. The stable boys were moving in and around between them, cinching down saddles and buckling on bridles.

Ears pricked forward, the horses turned toward the group as they came nearer, then turned away, snorting and shaking their manes and ruffling their wing feathers. Some of them nosed at the stable boys, as if looking for treats.

Nickalonis grinned. "This is going to be fun."

"No, it's not," Solon said, his face paling.

"The horses are almost ready." Horace moved from one mount to the next, rechecking cinches and straps.

Jaci stopped in front of the horses. She studied one of the saddles and its multitude of straps. "That looks complicated."

"Well, you don't want to be falling off in midair," Horace said, giving her a tight smile.

"Are they battle-trained?" Carrick asked.

"And will they stay put and not fly away if we get off?" Owen added.

"Yes, and yes," Horace answered.

"Will they hold two people?" Solon asked.

"No, you would need a special saddle to carry two," Horace said.

"But these horses can carry two people, can't they?" Jaci hesitated to ask for an extra horse, because she didn't want to explain why they needed one. If Talan was badly hurt or unconscious, he'd need to ride with one of them anyway.

Horace looked at her speculatively. "They can, but they wouldn't be able to fly as fast or as far. Why do you ask?"

Jaci improvised. "I just wanted to know in case... in case someone was injured or... or in case Solon here can't handle flying on his own because of his fear of heights."

Solon nodded. "Yes, good idea."

"Can we please have one of the horses tacked with a double saddle?" Jaci hoped she wouldn't have to pull rank as the High Enchantress' granddaughter and order him to do it.

Horace gave her a keen glance that told her he knew there was more to her request than she was letting on, but all he said was, "As you wish, my lady." He turned to one of the stable boys and commanded him to switch the saddle on one of the black horses.

"My lady, if you no longer have need of us, we will return to our post," one of the guards said.

Jaci nodded to them. "We should be fine. Thank you so much for your help."

"My lady." They bowed and left.

While the stable boys finished tacking the horses, Jaci gathered the others together a short distance away, so they wouldn't be overheard. "Okay, we all know what we're doing, right? Any last thoughts, suggestions, questions?"

The Black Banders shook their heads.

Owen shrugged. "Seems clear to me."

"Are you sure you can find him?" Solon asked, his face creased with worry. "What if she's wrong about where they took him?"

"I don't think Cristella is wrong," Jaci said, "but if we don't find him in the cabins, we'll keep searching until we do find him." She hugged Solon. "Be careful." She looked at Nickalonis as she stepped back. "Both of you."

"Talan loves you, you know," Nickalonis said.

Jaci's heart skipped a beat, then sped wildly as the irrational happy feeling bubbled up and overflowed. "He — he does?"

Solon cuffed his brother. "I gave my word I wouldn't tell her that."

Nickalonis lifted his hands. "What? You didn't tell her. I did." He winked at Jaci and walked over to the horses.

Solon rubbed his hand over his face. "I'm sorry, Jaci. Talan didn't want you to know, because he knows you want to go home. He doesn't want you to stay out of pity or a sense of obligation to him."

"The horses are ready now," Horace called.

Jaci didn't know what to say, her mind caught in a tug-of-war between joy and doubt. *He loves me. You don't belong in this world. But he loves me! But you're going home! Oh, God, what do I do?*

Wordlessly, she turned and went back to where Horace stood by the horses. The others followed.

Horace patted the horse next to him on the rump. "Mount up and we'll strap you in."

Jaci slipped in beside the black horse with the double saddle. The powerfully built gelding looked like he could carry two people easily. She held out her hand to him and stroked his neck, her fingers sinking into the thick softness of his black coat. He nosed her palm, then snuffled her coat pocket.

She laughed. "Sorry, there's nothing in there for you." He nuzzled her arm and shoulder. "Well, aren't you friendly." She patted his withers, then slid her hand over the velvety feathers of his wing. "I think we'll get along just fine."

Horace stepped in beside her. "Just like your mother. She had such a way with horses."

Jaci smiled. "Yes, she did. Did you know her well?"

Horace gave Jaci a leg up onto the gelding's back. "She came here every day to ride. I think she preferred the company of horses to people." He buckled the straps around Jaci's legs. "You're going after him, aren't you?"

Jaci looked down at him sharply. "Him? You mean Galenock?"

"No, I mean Talan. They flew him out of here several hours ago. He was unconscious."

Unconscious. What did they do to him? "Do you know where they took him?"

"No."

Jaci decided to level with Horace. "Yes, we're going after him. Some of us. The rest are going to get help for Keiresta. We'll join them as soon as we find him. Hopefully, Cristella will have convinced the other Enchantresses to help, and they'll be there, too. It's going to take all of us to overcome Galenock."

"You're a brave one," Horace said softly. "Just like your mother. May the gods of the wind and sky speed you on your journey and see you all safely home." He inclined his head. "My lady."

He patted her horse on the flank, then hobbled around in front of the hitching posts. Warmed by his words, Jaci listened carefully as he gave them a brief rundown on how to ride a flying horse and get in and out of the saddle straps quickly in an emergency. When he had answered all their questions, he called to the stable boys. "Open the doors!"

The stable boys pulled wide the tall double doors. Bright sunlight slanted in with a burst of icy cold air that made Jaci appreciate the warm clothing they'd been given. The doors opened onto a flat span of snow-dusted tundra that stretched about five hundred feet then dropped away into the deep blue autumn sky. The horses sidestepped and snorted and looked toward the sky, ears flicking back and forth, nostrils scenting the air.

"Easy, boy." Reins firmly in hand, Jaci stroked her mount's neck and took several deep breaths to calm her own rising jitters. She had expected the horses to lift into the air like an airplane taking off from a runway. The idea that they would be jumping off a cliff hadn't occurred to her. She'd never been afraid of heights, but cliff jumping was definitely not on her bucket list. She clutched her *druidainoch* stone and let it soothe her trepidation.

"Go in single file and let the horses choose their own pace when they launch," Horace said as he limped down the line, unhooking their mounts' lead ropes.

"Woo hoo! Let's go!" Nickalonis swung his bay horse around and headed out the door.

Solon, on one of the browns, reluctantly followed. Liundur, riding the other black horse, lined up next in the doorway. Jaci pulled her mount up beside him, watching as Nickalonis' horse galloped across the tundra, Solon about ten seconds behind him. The horse reached the edge of the cliff, spread its dark wings, and launched into the air. Moments later, Solon's horse did the same. Nickalonis' exhilarated whoops mingled with Solon's terrified screams as both horses rose into the sky, heading south.

Liundur turned to Jaci. "Are you ready, Your Highness?"

Jaci took another deep breath and nodded.

Liundur urged his mount out the door and into a gallop. Jaci counted to ten, then followed. Her horse took off across the tundra, gathering speed. Cold wind whipped her face, making her eyes water. Ahead of her, Liundur's horse launched into the sky and soared upward. Her black gelding surged forward. The edge of the cliff loomed, frighteningly close. Every muscle in her body clenched. She fought down her fear. *It'll be just like jumping over a fence,* she told herself fiercely. *A fence or a log or any other obstacle...* She tried not to think about the fact that this particular "obstacle" was several thousand feet in the air. The horse's muscles bunched beneath her, his black wings unfolding. She held her breath and concentrated on not interfering with his movements. The horse leaped upward; the cliff edge fell away. Powerful wingbeats caught the wind and lifted them up into the azure sky. Jaci gripped the black's mane and looked down at the misty emptiness of the canyon below them. She saw Carrick and Owen racing across the tundra, growing smaller and smaller as the black carried her higher. Lavender-gray mountains rose up on her left, their peaks dressed in thin clouds far above her. On her right, the sun shone in a dazzle of brightness. A gust of wind buffeted them, and her stomach lurched as her mount adjusted to the changing air currents, then leveled out. She eased her grip on his mane and, following Horace's instructions, used the reins and her legs to guide him toward Liundur, who was circling above, waiting for her and the others to catch up. The black responded, his great wings catching an updraft and carrying her upward.

She laughed for sheer joy. "Can you believe this?" she called to Liundur. "Woo hoo!"

He grinned.

Carrick, Owen, and Arnos joined them, high above the tundra.

"I never thought I'd be doing anything like this," Owen said with a laugh. "I think we need to relocate to the mountains."

"Fine with me," Liundur said.

"And me," Arnos agreed.

Carrick chuckled. "Don't tell Solon." He guided his horse up behind Liundur's. "You take point. Let's see how fast these horses can fly."

Liundur nodded and turned his mount toward the southwest.

Jaci looked down at the stable entrance and saw a tiny person waving — Horace. She waved back, then urged her horse after Liundur's.

The winged horses flew faster than any normal horse could run, soaring across the distances with what Horace had called "magically enhanced speed." He'd told them how the Enchantresses infused their magic into the foals when they were born, and how that magic bonded with the young animals and grew more powerful as they matured, giving them greatly increased speed and stamina. Jaci cast a worried glance at the sinking sun and gave fervent thanks for the extra speed. They'd need it if they were to have any chance of finding Talan before darkness fell.

He loves you, you know. Nickalonis' words slipped into her mind, reigniting the conflict within her. She resolutely set the thought aside. She couldn't afford to be distracted now. There was too much at stake.

They flew down out of the mountains, winging over crags and canyons, wind-whipped lakes, and small villages nestled in hidden valleys filled with scattered flocks of sheep. Jaci scanned the wild landscape, marveling at its beauty as she searched for any sign of Talan, on the outside chance he had been taken to some place other than the cabins. She understood why her mother had ridden every day. How could anyone resist the intoxicating freedom of the open sky? And it was so peaceful. The steady wingbeats of the horses and the occasional cry of a raptor were the only sounds she heard. She remembered the wistfulness in Talan's voice the previous night when she'd first seen the winged horses. She completely understood now.

The mountains gave way to scree and scrub land that broadened into a deep forest of mixed evergreens and hardwoods, their leaves blazing with autumn color. Jaci spotted the Alladhainn River meandering through the middle of the forest, its headwaters somewhere in the mountains behind them. Liundur signaled a descent and guided his mount downward toward one of the small clearings that dotted the forest canopy. Jaci and the others followed.

Jaci bit her lip, wondering how many cabins there were in this vast forest. Talan could be in any one of them. She shot another anxious glance at the western sky, now painted in deepening shades of pink, orange, and gold. Horace had said the winged horses could fly at night if there was enough moon- or starlight. But by then the forest would be pitch black and full of predators, and it would be too dangerous to land and search. They'd have to wait until morning. And she had the horrible feeling that such a delay would be disastrous.

Talan, where are you? She clasped her *druidainoch* stone and concentrated on him, picturing him in her mind and focusing on how she felt when his emotions stormed through her and his magic touched hers.

Pain and panic ripped through her and she cried out, her hand flying to her temple as she tried to control the raw emotion overpowering her senses. *Talan!* Her startled horse tensed and stopped his descent, jerking sideways and upward with rapid wingbeats as if trying to evade an unseen predator.

"Whoa, boy!" Jaci grabbed his mane with one hand to steady herself, thankful for the straps that held her tight to the saddle. She heard shouts from the others and saw them flying toward her.

"I'm okay," she called, then leaned over her horse's neck and spoke soothingly. "It's all right, boy, calm down. I'm sorry I scared you." She stroked his neck and guided him in a wide circle, murmuring to him until the spooked look faded from his eyes and his ears stopped swiveling.

Carrick paralleled her course. "Your Highness, what happened?"

"It's Talan. I felt a sudden burst of his emotions. He's terrified and in pain — somewhere that way." She pointed to the south.

"Do you still feel it?" Owen asked. "Can you find him?"

"Yes, though not as strongly, and yes, I think so."

Carrick gestured toward the south. "You lead, we'll follow."

CHAPTER 32

Jaci tried to keep her anxiety in check for her horse's sake as they flew south over the forest, following the Alladhainn. The intensity of Talan's pain and horror had lessened, though the emotions still clenched her chest. She could only imagine the terrible tortures Galenock's men might be inflicting on him.

The forest thinned into scattered clumps of trees, then ended in rocky, rolling pastureland. Jaci searched the green-brown expanse for any sign of horseback riders, but all she saw was a herd of red-and-white long-horned cattle grazing near the river.

The resonance of Talan's emotions faded into stillness. Jaci grasped her *druidainoch* stone and reached outward, searching for a trace of the emotional turmoil she had felt. Nothing. He must be either unconscious or... or... No. She refused to go there.

Not far in the distance, a flock of raucous crows burst into the air from behind a stony hill. A faint cloud of dust rose just beyond. Jaci waved to the others, who had spread out to cover as much ground as possible. She pointed toward the disturbance, and they urged their mounts forward.

As they flew over the hill, they saw a group of around twenty riders cantering southward. A long rope snaked back from one of the riders, pulling along a man with his arms tied behind his back. The rider dragged him over the dirt and rocks without a backward glance.

Talan! Jaci had to grit her teeth to keep from screaming his name.

Carrick veered toward her and waved to get her attention. He pointed to her and upward, then pointed to himself and the other Black Banders and swept his hand toward the riders.

Reluctantly, she nodded. She wanted more than anything to go to Talan, but she knew it would be foolhardy for her to land in the midst of the enemy soldiers. The Black Banders and Owen communicated with hand gestures, then started their descent. She held her breath as they arrowed down toward the riders. She thought if they could just grab Talan and go, they might all get out alive, but from the grim set of Carrick's face when he had told her to stay in the air, she knew they had no intention of taking the "easy" way out.

The horses glided in silently, their riders flicking off their straps as they neared the ground. The soldiers must have heard the wing-beats as the horses slowed up before landing, though, because they suddenly pulled up, their heads whipping around. Carrick and Liundur landed in front of them, their winged horses rearing and striking out with their hooves. Arnos and Owen landed in the back. Arnos leaned down and slashed the rope holding Talan. The front-line soldiers' horses reared, dumping two of the men. Some of the horses shied and tried to bolt. Owen slid off his horse, hooked his hands under Talan's shoulders, and pulled him away from the battle. His mount followed him and stood between them and the seething tangle of horses and men, kicking at any soldier that came near.

Jaci circled above and struggled to keep her horse in the air. The black gelding fought the reins, wanting to join the battle. She saw

Owen bending over Talan's unmoving form and wished desperately to know if he was alive. She looked back at the chaos below and saw Liundur decimating the soldiers around him, his sword slick with bright red blood. Carrick had taken down quite a few as well. She forced the black around in another circle. When she looked down again, she realized she couldn't see Arnos. His horse was trotting along the rear line of battle, lashing out with its hooves at the soldiers' horses, but Arnos was not in the saddle. She let her horse fly lower and spotted him in the midst of the fray, holding off three unhorsed Riders with a broken blade. She pulled the mace from her belt and flew down close to the battle. Just as she was about to fly over him, she yelled, "Arnos, catch!"

Arnos and the three soldiers looked up in surprise. Arnos lifted his hands as she swept overhead and dropped the mace. He caught it easily, and with a salute to Jaci, cracked his adversaries over the head before they could comprehend what had happened.

With powerful wing strokes, Jaci's mount reluctantly rose back into the air. She patted his neck. "I'm sorry, boy, but we're supposed to stay up here."

She looked down again just in time to see Carrick leap off his horse onto the back of one of the mounted soldiers' horses. He and the soldier tumbled off onto the ground. Jaci sucked in a breath, afraid he'd get trampled, but both he and the soldier rolled to their feet and fought into the clear, their swords clanging in a rapid beat. Carrick's horse blocked two mounted soldiers from pursuing them with vicious kicks and bites.

A soldier on foot slipped around the other side and moved up behind Carrick, a knife in his hand.

"Carrick, behind you!" Jaci screamed.

Carrick turned just as the soldier slashed downward. The knife cut deep into his upper arm instead of his back. Carrick grunted in pain, pulled one of his knives, and stabbed the soldier in the chest. As the soldier fell away, the blade of the first soldier cut across Carrick's side. Carrick staggered back, and the soldier kicked him to the ground.

"Down in the dirt, you Shiannoran dung heap! You are all going to die!"

Jaci gasped, recognizing the soldier's voice. *Vorstun!*

Vorstun hacked at Carrick with his sword. Carrick managed to parry the blows and regain his feet. They battled back and forth across the rough ground, moving away from the knot of fighting. Two riders broke away from the main battle and galloped toward Carrick, weapons bared.

"Oh, no," Jaci whispered. She released her tight hold on the black. "All right, boy, go!" The black swooped down and intercepted the riders, attacking the nearest one with his front hooves and teeth. The rider's horse swerved sideways with a frightened whinny and crashed into the second rider. Both horses fell in a tangle of legs, pinning their riders beneath them. The horses got up shakily and trotted off. The riders didn't move.

Jaci pulled the black around and scanned the battlefield. Carrick and Vorstun were still fighting. Riderless horses were cantering away across the torn ground. The only person still mounted was Liundur. He and Arnos took down the last two remaining soldiers, then Liundur turned and raced toward Carrick.

Jaci watched, her heart in her throat, as Carrick stumbled, recovered, blocked Vorstun's sword thrust, then stumbled again. Liundur slid off his horse just as Carrick parried another blow and drove his sword deep into Vorstun's gut. Vorstun uttered a hoarse cry as he fell to his knees, then sank to the ground and lay still. Carrick swayed and leaned on his sword.

Liundur stabbed his sword upright into the ground and lifted Carrick's good arm over his shoulder, supporting him while gesturing for Jaci to come forward.

Jaci cantered over and pulled up beside them. "How bad is it?"

"I'll live," Carrick said.

Liundur took Carrick's sword and stabbed it into the ground next to his. "Your Highness, can you take him to Owen?"

"Of course." Jaci held the black still while Liundur helped Carrick mount behind her. She looked Liundur over. "What about you? And Arnos?"

Liundur handed Carrick his sword, then retrieved his own blade. "I have no serious wounds." He glanced across at Arnos walking through the battlefield, Jaci's mace still in hand, examining the downed soldiers as if checking to see if they were alive or dead. "And Arnos is still standing. We will join you in a few minutes." He strode to where Vorstun lay and kicked him onto his back.

"Is he dead?" Jaci asked.

Liundur kicked him back over, leaving him face down in the dirt. "Yes."

Jaci exhaled in relief as she urged her horse forward, guiding him around the perimeter of the battlefield. *One major evil enemy down, one to go.*

Carrick shifted slightly in the saddle behind her and hissed in a breath.

She looked back at him over her shoulder. "Are you all right? Do you want me to stop?"

"You don't need to stop." He grimaced and reclamped his arm to his side to stem the bleeding. "Thank you, Your Highness, for your heroics during the battle. I owe you my life." He hesitated, then continued. "Your courage is an inspiration to us, but you must not put yourself at risk. You are the only member of the royal family and the last hope of our world. If you fall, all is lost."

The last hope of our world. That she had become such a pivotal player in the survival of these men and of the people of Tarshane still boggled her mind. But pivotal or not, she wouldn't think much of herself if she wasn't willing to risk as much as they were and do what was right. "You're welcome, Carrick. And I understand what you're saying, but I can't just sit by and let those I care about get hurt if there is some way I can prevent it."

"We are expendable."

"Not to me."

Carrick was silent for a few moments. Then he said softly, "It is truly an honor to serve you, Your Highness."

She smiled at him. "I am the one who is honored, that you and your men are willing to fight for me."

"We are yours to command," he said with a deferential nod.

A few minutes later, they reached the spot by the river where Owen had brought Talan. Talan lay still as death in the grass, but Owen had dressed him in the fleece-lined clothing they had brought from the stable, so Jaci clung to the hope that he was still alive.

Owen hurried over to them and helped Carrick dismount. He slipped Carrick's arm over his shoulder, supporting him as they crossed to where Talan lay. Jaci undid her leg straps and jumped down from the black. She rushed to Talan's side.

Owen eased Carrick to the ground. "I see blood on your arm and side. Anything else serious?"

"No." Carrick grimaced as Owen cut the cloth away from his wounds.

Jaci cupped Talan's cheek. His skin was clammy, and his dark hair lay plastered to his head as if he'd been caught in a deluge.

"How is he? And why is he so wet?" Her breath seized as she realized the answer. "They dragged him through the river, didn't they? That's why he was panicking. He was drowning."

"That would be my guess," Owen said grimly. "He has broken ribs and a broken arm and a lot of cuts and bruises that look like the result of being trampled."

Jaci remembered the long-horned cattle they'd flown over earlier. "That herd of cattle back there by the river?"

"Most likely." Owen finished cleaning Carrick's side wound, then pulled out a needle and some thread from his healer's pack. "But he's alive, and that's what counts. Now we just have to wait until he comes around to see if he has any lasting head injuries. Those gashes ran deep."

Jaci touched one of the neat lines of stitches along Talan's right temple. Horror welled up inside her again, and anger at Vorstun for what he and his cohorts had put Talan through. She bit her lip, wishing she could heal him the way Keiresta had healed Nickalonis. Fury hardened within her. This was all Keiresta's fault. *Why should we risk our lives to rescue her, after what she did?* Jaci looked around her, at Owen sewing up Carrick's wounds, at the dead bodies littering the battlefield, at Liundur and Arnos riding toward her, leading Carrick's horse. *Because life for the people of Tarshane can't go on this way, and we need Keiresta's power to defeat Galenock.* She set her jaw. Family or not, once Galenock was vanquished, she'd give Keiresta the tongue-lashing she deserved.

Liundur and Arnos dismounted close by. Liundur knelt next to Talan. Arnos came up beside him, two sets of saddlebags slung over his shoulder. Several water flasks dangled from his hand.

Jaci sat back. "He's alive, but hurt pretty badly." She repeated what Owen had said about Talan's injuries.

Owen finished sewing up the stab wound on Carrick's arm. "Arnos, you're next."

Arnos set the saddlebags and water flasks down. "There's food in the bags." Then he pulled the mace from his belt and held it out to Jaci. "Thank you, Your Highness."

She took it and slid it into her weapons belt. "You're welcome."

He bowed and went to trade places with Carrick. Jaci could see some gashes on Arnos' arms and legs, but nothing that bled profusely. As Owen began cleaning Arnos' wounds, she rose. "I want to tend to the horses."

Liundur nodded. "I'll go with you."

They checked the horses over and found no signs of injury. After watering them at the river, they adjusted the horses' bridles so they could graze freely. By the time Jaci and Liundur rejoined the others, Owen had finished bandaging Arnos, and they all sat together next to Carrick and Talan. Jaci looked at Talan as she settled beside him, wishing he would open his eyes. Owen checked Liundur's wounds while Carrick emptied the saddlebags and divided up the wax paper-wrapped bread, cheese, and dried meat, leaving some aside for Talan. The aroma of the chewy brown bread made Jaci's stomach rumble. She hadn't realized how famished she was, and had to restrain herself from bolting down her food.

"Tell me about Ridaur's crypt," she said between bites. "Talan said it was on the Isle of Lorn. How far is it? What's the land around it like? Can we get there without being seen?"

"The crypt is an ancient tomb of kings from a warrior race that died out centuries ago," Liundur said. "It's a few hours west of here, on the border between Hyanullis and the Wastelands. A few hours by normal horse travel, that is," he amended. "The winged horses should get us there faster."

"Hyanullis is the desert province, right?" Jaci recalled what Mandy had said about Hyanullis being the only other province not ruled by Galenock because the nomads that lived there were hard to pin down and had nothing of value to him.

"Yes. The Isle of Lorn is a large island in the Smoldering Lake. It's barren and mountainous, with no greenery. The spell Elsaesser cast to seal Ridaur in the crypt killed every living thing on the island and for miles around. The lake water turned red, and it churns and steams like a boiling pot, but it's not too hot to cross on foot, if necessary."

"So it's not deep?"

"Not on the end where the crypt is, but it drops off quickly once past that point. Legend has it that the lake itself is a burial ground. Warriors killed in battle were dropped to the bottom of the lake so their spirits could protect the souls of the dead kings entombed in the crypt as they made their way to the lands of the afterlife."

Jaci shivered. "Sounds creepy."

"We can fly in from the southwest and use the mountains for cover," Carrick said. "It will be dark, so we shouldn't be seen."

Jaci looked toward the west where the sun was just beginning to dip below the horizon. "Can we find our way in the dark?"

Carrick glanced up at the cloudless sky. "The stars will guide us."

"I'm about done here." Owen tied off a bandage on Liundur's thigh and gathered his medical supplies.

Arnos stood. "I'll get the horses."

Jaci looked down at Talan again and smoothed the sleeve of his coat. He lay so still. She clasped his gloved hand for a moment and prayed the long flight to the Isle of Lorn wouldn't worsen his injuries. Then she rose and followed after Arnos, anxious thoughts whirling in her head. Had Keiresta already fallen into Galenock's clutches, or was there still hope? Had Cristella convinced the other

Enchantresses to help? Would they get to the Isle of Lorn in time? Would Solon and Nickalonis and Talan's men? Would she?

They had to, or they'd all be dead.

CHAPTER 33

Galenock surveyed the rocky landscape before him and smiled with satisfaction. His men had hidden themselves well. He couldn't see a trace of them anywhere. They had arrived on the Isle of Lorn a scant hour ago, crossing the Smoldering Lake without mishap and easily traversing the winding dirt path that led to Ridaur's crypt. Keiresta had not yet arrived. His smile widened. He couldn't wait to see the look on her face when he took the key from her. He would make her watch while he opened the crypt and performed the ritual that would bind Ridaur's power to him. And then he would kill her.

Darkness was settling over the island, stretching deep shadows across the entrance to the crypt — an arched door in the side of a cliff, engraved with lettering from a lost language and flanked on either side by thirty-foot-tall statues of armored warriors, their up-raised shields and swords held at the ready. Above the door, a massive coat of arms with a snarling wolf's head had been carved into the stone. Centuries of wind and storm had eaten away at the statues, but most of the lettering remained intact, protected in part by Elsaesser's 150-year-old spell.

From his vantage point on a low bluff opposite the doorway, Ga-lenock could see the entirety of the open space in front of the crypt, where he imagined the ancient burial ceremonies of the lost warrior race had been performed. The space wasn't large enough to accommodate the landing of more than a few winged horses, and neither was the uneven strip of beach along the edge of the island, so the majority of however many soldiers Keiresta brought with her would have to land on the lakeshore. Likely the whole group would land there, with only a few riding across. His men, hidden in the rocks around the lakeshore and on the island, would be in perfect position to launch a surprise attack and subdue them.

Bright stars winked into being as night fell, the only sound a whisper of wind that carried the faint odor of brimstone from the roiling lake. The waning half-moon edged above the horizon, spilling silver light across the tips of the rocks. Galenock calmed his rising tension. He expected Keiresta to arrive after nightfall. He guessed she would opt for stealth and slip in under cover of darkness with a small group. So far, he had correctly anticipated her every move. She would be here, he was sure of it. The lure of Ridaur's magic would be too great for her to resist. He mentally rehearsed the newly twisted spell he had devised to render her and her retinue powerless. It would tire him a bit to cast it, but he should still have more than enough energy to open the crypt and cast the ritual spell. And once Ridaur's power was his, energy would no longer be an issue.

Soft footsteps sounded behind him, rushing up the path to the top of the bluff.

"Your Lordship, they're coming," one of his men said in hushed, breathless voice. "We can't tell yet how many, but it looks like thirty to forty."

"Very good. Resume your position. You know what to do."

"Yes, my lord." The man's footsteps faded as he raced away.

Galenock stepped back behind a tall boulder, out of sight, anticipation keying his nerves. He'd waited so long for this. Soon he would have the power to destroy all those who had stood against him. How he would savor crushing them. His eyes swept the night sky, searching for movement against the backdrop of stars. The half-moon had risen above the horizon, its glow painting a luminous path across the steaming lake. His lips thinned with impatience. *Where are you?*

There — small moving shapes blotting out the stars, growing larger as they neared the island. He studied the group, estimating their numbers to be around forty — no match for the two hundred he'd brought with him. A slow smile spread across his face as he watched the winged horses begin their descent, winged horses that would soon be his. He pictured himself flying across the length and breadth of Tarshane, lord of land and sky, exerting his kingship over all. Once he had dealt with Keiresta, he would find that wench Jacinda and wed her, making him king in both power and name. None would oppose him. A new dynasty — *his* dynasty — would begin.

Through breaks in the rocks, he watched them land along the lakeshore, heard the muffled thump of many hooves on the hard dirt. Torches with spheres instead of flames glowed to life, and a group of riders crossed the lake and dismounted on the rugged beach. He lost sight of them as they made their way on foot up the path toward the crypt. Then they reappeared, the glow from the spheres heralding their arrival in the open space. He counted twenty soldiers and archers surrounding Keiresta and her retinue, weapons bared and arrows nocked. There were still only five in the High Enchantress' retinue, instead of the usual six. Not that it mattered. He could render any number of them powerless with his new twisted spell.

One of the soldiers gestured to some of the others, who split from the group and disappeared into the rocks, presumably scouting the area. He had warned his men to watch for scouts and deal with them silently. The remaining dozen formed a loose circle around the Enchantresses, guarding the four entryways into the open space.

Keiresta strode forward between the giant feet of the statues, leaned the orb torch she'd been carrying against the door of the crypt, and traced her fingers over the ancient lettering. The five women in her retinue looked about nervously, poised to cast their attack spells. Galenock watched Keiresta closely. Any moment now she would pull out the copper-colored key and speak the words that would unlock the crypt. Or try to speak them. He grinned to himself.

The faint scrape of stealthy footsteps caught his ear. Someone was coming up the path, likely one of those cursed scouts. He stepped back into the deep shadows just as a soldier in the gray-and-blue uniform of Enseidrinocha topped the bluff. Galenock slipped a knife from his belt and waited for the man to come near. Then in a swift movement, he seized the soldier from behind, clamping his arm around the man's neck and thrusting his knife between his ribs. The soldier stiffened, then crumpled. Galenock eased him to the ground silently, curling his lip as he wiped the blood from his knife on the soldier's leather jerkin. Killing this way was so messy and barbaric. He much preferred the clean death dealt from a spell, but he couldn't afford to waste precious energy on such a casting.

Keiresta's voice intoning familiar words floated up to him, the vibrant hum of magic pulsing through the air. Shoving his knife into his belt, Galenock rushed back to his vantage point. Below him,

Keiresta stood with arms raised and palms pressed against the door, which was beginning to glow with magical light.

He shouted the words of the twisted spell, his voice echoing through the rocks. Keiresta's chanting ceased, replaced by choking sounds. The air turned brittle as the conflicting magics warred with each other, then Keiresta's magic shattered and she fell to her knees, clutching her throat. One of the Enchantresses raced to her side and helped her to her feet, while the other members of the retinue backed quickly toward her, heads swiveling as they searched for their unseen enemy. Keiresta's soldiers shouted for reinforcements and closed ranks around them, leaving room for the Enchantresses to cast their attack magic.

Right on cue, arrows flew from high up on the ridge to Galenock's right as his men took aim at the soldiers, downing half of them. Keiresta's remaining archers returned fire, releasing their arrows at unseen targets. The Enchantresses pointed toward the top of the ridge and opened their mouths to cast their spells, but no sounds came out. They coughed and choked, their hands flying to their throats. Two more soldiers fell, pierced by arrows. The last few soldiers put the Enchantresses behind them and squeezed as far back as they could into the space between the statues' feet.

Galenock's men filled the four entryways, the archers slipping through and training their arrows on Keiresta's soldiers. Galenock clenched his fist in triumph. The fact that no reinforcements had come to Keiresta's aid told him that his men on the lakeshore had carried out their orders and either killed or captured the rest of Keiresta's men. He gave an exultant laugh, his voice carrying into the open space as he stepped into view.

"My Lady Keiresta, such a pleasure to see you again. How do you like my new spell?"

"The pleasure is all yours, you horse's arse," Keiresta snapped. "Your perverted spell is as fiendish as you are."

Galenock chuckled. "I'd forgotten how much I enjoyed sparring with you. The Wizard's Guild was never the same after you left. And neither was Elshaer." He couldn't resist the dig.

Keiresta's eyes narrowed. "Get to the point."

"Ah, yes, you never did have time for idle chitchat. My point is that I have won and you have lost. You will tell your men to throw down their weapons or my archers will shoot them. I will be down from here momentarily, and then you will hand over the key to the crypt. Once I have the key, I will let you observe as I open the crypt and perform the ritual that will give me access to Ridaur's vast power. And don't worry. I will let you have a taste of the power that might have been yours if I hadn't outsmarted you. When I use it to kill you." He laughed again as he watched his men converge on his enemies. The four remaining soldiers guarding the Enchantresses dropped their weapons as directed by Keiresta and were marched out through one of the entryways, their hands on their heads. The Enchantresses were herded away from the crypt door and held at sword point against the base of the bluff. Gloating over his total victory, Galenock turned and strode down the path to the open space.

When he emerged at the foot of the bluff, he confronted Keiresta and held out his hand. "The key, if you please."

She glared at him. "You think I'm just going to hand it to you?"

He smirked. "Unless you would prefer I search you for it."

She gave him a withering look, then drew a cord from around her neck and threw it to the ground.

Never taking his eyes from hers, he gestured to one of his men. "Pick that up and give it to me."

The man complied.

Galenock backed away from Keiresta and looked down at the cord in his hand, at the two keys dangling from it — the key to Soneira's room in Castle d'Gaire and the key to Ridaur's crypt. *Yes, it was finally his!* He laughed again as he turned toward the crypt. He had only taken a few steps when he heard scuffling and choking sounds behind him. He whirled. Two of his men had forced Keiresta back up against the bluff. She coughed and held her throat, hatred in her eyes.

Galenock shook his head. "Tsk, tsk, my lady. In case you didn't figure it out the first time, my new spell will prevent you from speaking any words of magic. You are completely helpless." He grinned as he turned his back on her and crossed the open space to the crypt door. Slowly, he lifted his hands and touched the cold stone, tracing the unknown lettering as Keiresta had done. So many years he had waited for this. He took a few moments to savor his victory, then he flattened his palms against the stone and intoned the words of the spell that would break the seal that had locked the crypt for so long. His fingers tingled as the door began to glow. The ground and the whole cliff face shook faintly as ancient magic strained against the spell like a mesh wall, stretching, resisting penetration. Galenock repeated the spell, his voice sharply inflecting the syllables as he exerted his power. A rune appeared, etched into the right side of the door about halfway up. It resembled the letter E entwined with a backwards R in a continuous circle. In the center of the rune was a small keyhole. Keeping his left hand flat against the door, he grasped the copper-colored key with the thin ribbon of black metal twisted around it and inserted it into the keyhole. As he did so, the ribbon of metal uncoiled itself, twisting and extending until it filled the grooves of the etched rune. He turned the key, and a bright light flashed. The ancient magic snapped with an audible crackle, and the glow faded from the door.

Both rune and key vanished. The door swung inward with an exhale of stale air.

Galenock stumbled forward and nearly fell, his whole body trembling. It had taken much more energy than he'd expected to break the ancient spell. *Curse you, Elsaesser.* Now he would have to rest before performing the ritual.

With shaking fingers, he picked up Keiresta's glowing orb torch and shone it into the crypt. Deep shadows filled the vast space.

"Bring more light," he barked at his men.

His soldiers lit some torches and brought them forward.

With his soldiers flanking him on either side, Galenock entered the crypt. Two rows of sarcophagi stretched into the depths of the crypt with a ten-foot-wide path between them. The lids had been carved in the likenesses of the kings whose remains they held, while the sides showed scenes chronicling their exploits. After a cursory glance at the sarcophagi, Galenock swept his orb torch low to the ground, searching for the remains of Ridaur and Elsaesser. Along the base of the wall on his left, he spotted what looked like scattered bones. Gathering his strength, he crossed to the wall and knelt. Pieces of bone lay all around him, half buried in the dirt. Gingerly, he picked up a dismembered skeletal hand. A gold ring crafted in the shape of intertwined branches with green leaf-shaped gems encircled the third finger. He recognized the ring from Elsaesser's portrait in the Wizard's Guildhall. He looked again at the scattered bones. Ridaur, in his fury, must have used one of the most impressive spells in the spellbook, one that would tear a man to pieces. Galenock had never mastered that spell, had never been able to generate enough power. *But soon, I will have more than enough.* He twisted the ring, and the finger bone cracked and crumbled away.

Tossing the skeletal hand aside, he slid the ring onto his own finger and heaved himself to his feet. "Look for more bones."

His men searched along the wall to the right of the door and around the sarcophagi.

"My lord, there are piles of gold and jeweled weapons between all these coffins," one of them said.

"Take it. The dead have no need of it."

The man saluted and ordered one of the others to find something in which to pack the treasure.

"My lord, over here." One of his men was looking behind the door.

Galenock hurried across, and the man stepped back out of the way. Another skeleton lay on the ground in the shadow of the door, this one fully intact. The wall beside it was scorched black, likely from Ridaur attempting to blast through it. A dagger lay in the dirt next to the wall, and Galenock could see deep gouges in the blackened stone. The most powerful wizard ever known reduced to scratching at the stone wall like a common dungeon dweller. How pathetic.

Galenock handed the orb torch to the man nearest him and knelt beside the skeleton. Carefully, he cupped the skull with both hands and closed his eyes. He stiffened as the pulse of Ridaur's aura prickled his fingertips, stronger than expected. Excitement shivered through him. So much power, his for the taking. He cursed his current weakness, then drew a calming breath. With a couple of hours rest, he would have more than enough strength to cast the spell and bind Ridaur's vast power to him. All he needed was a single bone to work the spell, and he knew exactly which one he would take. He tightened his grip on the skull and gave it a sharp twist. The skull snapped off the neck bone. Cradling it against him with one hand, he levered himself up and strode from the crypt.

The moment he stepped through the door, Keiresta straightened and pressed forward, the guards restraining her with ease. Her eyes fastened on the skull, and her face paled.

Galenock lifted the skull up to give her a plain view. "Here it is — the bone from Ridaur that I will use to crush you." He laughed at the mix of fear, anger, and jealousy in her eyes. "I need to rest for a bit, and then you will have the honor of witnessing my binding spell in action."

CHAPTER 34

Jaci adjusted her hold on the black horse's reins to ease the cramping in her gloved fingers and leaned forward once more over Talan's back to give what warmth she could. The Black Banders had strapped him into the front saddle and rigged a harness to hold his unconscious form in position as he lay over the horse's withers and neck. They'd flown through the moonlit sky at a high altitude for hours over barren, mountainous desert straight out of the Badlands of New Mexico, and still he hadn't awakened. She'd been tempted to try the healing spell, but knew it would drain her too much and do little good.

She shivered in the frigid air, thanking Horace again for the fleece-lined clothing that had, up to this point, kept her relatively warm. But now a chill was beginning to steal through her body, deepening the ache in her tired muscles. Shifting the reins to one hand, she readjusted the ice-crystaled scarf protecting her face and shot a worried glance at Carrick, a few wingspans away on her left. He sat hunched in the saddle, leaning farther over his mount's neck than he had been the last time she'd looked. Owen flew to her right, with Arnos at rear guard and Liundur leading. She reached around Talan and stroked the black's withers, sensing her mount's fatigue.

Though his wingbeats were still strong, he needed to rest. She urged the black up beside Liundur, pointed to her horse, then laid her cheek on her hand to mime sleep and pointed at the ground.

Liundur pointed to a group of low mountains just ahead, then held up his hand with his finger and thumb about an inch apart, which Jaci interpreted to mean they didn't have far to go. She nodded and let the black drop back behind him.

A short time later, they began their descent toward the Isle of Lorn, swinging around behind the mountains and flying over a roiling, steaming, moon-silvered lake before dropping down, single file, into a twenty-foot-wide canyon. It was dark in the canyon, but the air channeled in from the lake was warm and smelled faintly of sulfur.

Jaci undid her straps and carefully slid from the saddle to avoid jostling Talan. She leaned on her horse for a moment to let her wobbly legs get used to standing again while her eyes adjusted to the deeper darkness. The others dismounted. Liundur and Arnos handed their horses' reins to Carrick, then circled the group, reconnoitering.

"Are you all right, Your Highness?" Carrick asked in a barely audible whisper.

Jaci straightened. "Yes. Are you?"

"I am still standing, as Liundur says."

Owen checked Talan. "He's still out. Did he come to at all?"

"No." Jaci bit her lip and tried to calm her worry.

Soft light flared by the canyon wall about ten yards ahead on the left. The light held steady, not flickering like a flame torch.

"That looks like one of the Enchantresses' orbs," Jaci whispered.

The light bobbed slightly as whoever carried it walked toward them.

Jaci heard the hiss of metal as the three Black Banders drew their weapons and blocked the path of the advancing light.

The light-bearer slowed. A male voice called softly, "Hold there. I am Svared of the Hawkflight Vanguard, from Enseidrinocha." He moved the light closer to his body to illuminate his gray and blue uniform. "I saw you fly in. Is My Lady Jacinda with you?"

Jaci stepped up beside the Black Banders. "I'm Jacinda, and this is Carrick, Liundur, and Arnos. Are the Enchantresses here?"

Svared swept her a bow. "Yes, as many as could be spared from guarding the Great Stone. We arrived about two hours ago."

"The Enchantresses — how many?"

"Twelve. They've gone to the crypt, along with fifty men from my vanguard."

"Have you heard anything from them? Do you have any idea what their situation is?"

"No, I've had no word."

Everything that could possibly have gone wrong flitted through Jaci's mind. "How far is the crypt from here?"

"About an hour's hike," Liundur said.

"You can leave your horses with ours. There's a large cavern over there." Svared gestured toward the left side of the canyon.

Carrick turned to Owen, who had come up behind them, leading the horses. "Owen, you can take Talan and the horses to the cavern."

Liundur put his hand on Carrick's shoulder. "You should stay and guard them. With your wounds, you cannot travel quickly and will slow us down."

They held each other's gaze for a few moments, then Carrick nodded.

Jaci released the breath she'd been holding, relieved that Carrick would be out of the fighting, at least for now. She only hoped the Enchantresses were still safe. If they'd been captured...

Gathering her courage, she faced Liundur and Arnos. "Shall we go?"

*****

Galenock woke to the sound of heated whispers outside his tent. *Idiots!* If they'd roused him before his magical strength had been completely restored, he'd have them skewered. He shoved aside his blankets and sat up, stilling his anger so he could accurately measure his energy levels. The magic within him thrummed in readiness. An anticipatory smile played over his lips as he picked up Ridaur's skull and cradled it in his hands. Soon, he would become the most powerful wizard ever known. Ridaur, Elsaesser, Elshaer — all would be forgotten, their magical abilities miniscule compared to his. How he would bask in the gloriousness of his triumph —

More urgent whispers filtered through the fabric wall of his tent, interrupting his thoughts. Scowling, he rose, threw back the tent flap, and stalked out into the open space in front of the crypt. *"Silence!"*

The whispering ceased as the half-dozen arguing soldiers momentarily froze, then whipped into a straight line, left fists crossing to right shoulders in salute.

Galenock strode up to them. "What is so important that you would dare disturb my sleep?"

One of the men lifted a shaking hand and pointed at the cliff face above and behind Galenock. "It's the wolf's head, my lord. When we were in the crypt collecting the treasure, it started glowing. The guardian spirits have been awakened. We must put the treasure back, or they will kill us!"

Galenock turned and looked back at the crypt. In the center of the coat of arms carved above the door, a dull yellowish glow outlined the snarling wolf's head. He hid his surprise. He'd never heard or read of such a thing happening in the past, though he did know the legend of the dead warriors "buried" in the lake.

The last thing he needed at this critical juncture was for his men to panic and disrupt the ritual he was about to begin. He glared at them. "Nonsense! There are no such things as guardian spirits. That is just a myth. The wolf's head is glowing to signify my breaking the spell and opening the tomb, nothing more. Now get back to your duties. It is time for the ritual!"

*****

Jaci sank down onto a flat rock and wiped the sweat from her forehead with her sleeve as she caught her breath. Liundur stood guard beside her. Arnos had vanished into the rocks to scout ahead. They'd been climbing over the island's rough terrain for what she estimated to be the better part of an hour without seeing or hearing anyone. She wished for the hundredth time that she knew what was happening at the crypt. Worry for Cristella and the other Enchantresses knotted her stomach. What if the silence meant she was already too late?

A warm breeze blew through the rocks, the air slightly humid and smelling more strongly of sulfur. Somewhere off to her right the bubbling and steaming of the lake rose in volume, as if someone had turned up the heat under a simmering pot. A twitch of unease shivered over her skin, and she glanced back at Liundur to reassure herself that he was still close by. Liundur was looking in the direction of the lake as if he, too, had noted the increased roiling. She waved to get his attention, then cupped her ear and pointed to the lake. He nodded and lifted his hands in a shrug.

A darker shadow slipped out of a nearby chasm, and she stifled a startled cry as Arnos rejoined them. He gestured for them to follow. Liundur gave Jaci a hand up, and they hurried after him. They groped their way through the chasm, climbed over a rugged pile of rocks, then wended through another twisting gorge that opened into a rock-strewn canyon. At the edge of the gorge, Arnos stopped and pointed to a wind-carved tower of rock partway down the canyon. Jaci squinted into the moonlit darkness and thought she saw movement at the base of the rock. *The Enchantresses?* She pointed at the area of the movement, showed her *druidainoch* stone, and looked at Arnos questioningly. Relief and hope swelled within her when he nodded. Then Arnos indicated three other rock formations between the rock tower and where they stood and patted his weapons belt. *Soldiers on watch.* She nodded her understanding.

Taking a deep breath, Jaci lifted her hands in a gesture of peace and walked into the canyon. Liundur and Arnos flanked her and did the same. The soldiers intercepted them, then lowered their weapons and bowed to Jaci. One of the soldiers escorted them to the base of the towering rock, while the others resumed their positions. The Enchantresses stood in a group by the rock with a few of the vanguard soldiers. A murmur of voices reached Jaci's ears as she approached them. Then silence fell, and all eyes turned toward her and the Black Banders.

Cristella rushed forward and hugged Jaci. "I was so afraid you wouldn't get here in time," she whispered in Jaci's ear. "Did you find him?"

Jaci steeled herself against Cristella's overpowering anxiety. "Yes. He's hurt, but alive." She stepped back as the other Enchantresses encircled them. "Where are Keiresta and Galenock? Have you seen them?"

Cristella nodded. "Keiresta and the others are being held prisoner by Galenock's men. Galenock has opened the crypt. He has Ridaur's skull. He's going to perform the binding ritual, and then he's going to kill them. I don't know how we're going to rescue them. We can't use our magic!"

"What? Why not?"

"We can't speak the words. Another one of Galenock's twisted spells."

"My protective bubble doesn't require words, so hopefully that should still work. We just have to find a way to get to Keiresta. Where exactly is she?"

Cristella described the open space in front of the crypt and the relative positions of everyone within. "And Galenock has soldiers and archers stationed in the rocks all around the crypt," she continued. "One of our vanguard was able to remove one of them and take his place. He's been giving us information by way of messengers."

"How far is the crypt from here?" Arnos asked.

"A mile or so. It's just beyond the end of the canyon," Liundur said. "If we can get to the top of the low bluff across from the crypt, there's a path that leads down to the floor of the open space, right next to where you say Keiresta is being held."

Running footsteps pounded across the canyon floor, approaching the tower rock. Liundur and Arnos reached for their weapons.

"It's one of our messengers!" Cristella's anxiety spiked as she and the rest of the group hastened to the edge of the tower rock wall to meet him.

"Starting... ritual," the messenger gasped out. "In front of... the crypt..." He bent over and braced his hands on his knees, breathing hard.

Cristella's hand flew to her mouth. "Oh, no! How do we stop him?"

"We'll figure that out when we get there," Jaci said. "Come on!"

CHAPTER 35

Jaci and the Black Banders raced to the end of the canyon, the Enchantresses and the vanguard soldiers right behind them. They veered northeast into a maze of weather-beaten rock formations to avoid detection by Galenock's men, eventually emerging onto a winding trail that led upward to the top of a high ridge. Jaci, Liundur, and Arnos followed one of the vanguard soldiers up onto the ridge where their spy lay hidden behind some small boulders. He raised his head at their approach before looking down again on the area in front of the crypt.

Galenock's voice rose into the night, sharply inflecting the words of a spell. The hairs on the back of Jaci's neck stood on end, and she shuddered, sensing an evil aura permeating the air. Liundur touched her arm in concern. She took a deep breath and forced down her fear. She had to stay strong for Talan and for Tarshane.

The spy waved them forward and slid sideways to give them room. Jaci nodded to Liundur, then she and the Black Banders crawled on their bellies and peered over the edge. A large circle of both orb and flame torches placed in thin metal stands illuminated the open space below. Inside the circle, an octagram had been drawn with white paint. Small glass globes filled with dark substances and set on similar metal stands marked seven of the octagram's eight points. Galenock stood in the center of the shape, chanting his spell while rubbing what looked like blood over a human skull.

Off to the left, at the base of a low bluff, Keiresta leaned forward, nearly pressing up against the intervening crossed swords held by Galenock's guards, avidly watching Galenock. Her retinue huddled behind her. Aegis Nordrel and his soldiers were nowhere to be seen. *They're probably all dead,* Jaci thought with a pang of sorrow.

Giant stone warriors towered directly across from the captives, and Jaci could see an open door in the cliff between their massive feet, which had to be the door to the crypt. On the rock wall above the door, a carved wolf's head glowed yellow.

She pointed toward the glow and raised her eyebrows at the vanguard spy, but he just shrugged and looked mystified.

Liundur gestured toward the top of the low bluff. The spy pointed at Galenock's men and held up six fingers. He whipped a piece of charcoal out of his pocket and hastily sketched a map showing their positions.

Liundur nodded, then started crawling back the way they had come. Jaci followed with Arnos behind her. Crouching low, they dashed back down the trail to where the others waited. Arnos took two of the vanguard soldiers and set off with them down a side path. Liundur sent half of the remaining soldiers in the opposite direction to take out as many of Galenock's men as they could along the higher ground. He gave Arnos about a thirty-second head start, then waved the Enchantresses and the rest of the soldiers forward and raced after him. Jaci ran behind Liundur, her ears straining for any sounds of combat that could give them away. She heard nothing but the soft tread of their swiftly running feet and Galenock's muffled chanting. *Keep talking, Galenock*, she urged silently. The longer it took him to cast the binding spell, the more time they would have to get into position to do... something.

They caught up with Arnos and the two vanguard soldiers at the top of the bluff. The bodies of two of Galenock's men lay off to the side, half-hidden behind some rocks.

Galenock ceased chanting and laughed triumphantly.

Jaci rushed forward and peeked around a massive boulder. Liundur moved up behind her, and the others squeezed into any available spot where they could see what was happening. Galenock stood facing them with arms upraised in the center of the octagram. He had set the skull on the ground on the empty point. Red lightning flared between his hands, the skull, and the seven globes, traveling along the lines of the octagram in a continuous circuit. The globes shattered, spewing dark liquid that hissed as it touched the ground and burned holes in the rock floor. The red lightning zapped into the skull, and it exploded. The ground shook as fragments of bone flew everywhere. Then the lightning crackled and disappeared, leaving only a fiery red outline around Galenock's hands. He laughed again and took a step toward Keiresta.

Jaci pushed away from the boulder and bolted down the path toward the open space. The others followed, as Galenock's taunting voice said, "See the magic that is mine and not yours. And now I will show you just how powerful it is!"

As Jaci reached the bottom of the path, Galenock stretched his arms out in front of him, glowing red fingers aimed straight at Keiresta. The guards scrambled out of the way. Keiresta's eyes widened, and she took a step backward. Her retinue pulled her behind them. They lifted their hands and tried to speak the words of their spells but none came. They coughed and choked, their arms still held out in front of them as if they would ward off Galenock's spell with their bare hands. Jaci darted past the fleeing guards and flung herself in front of the retinue just as red lightning shot from Galenock's fingers. White light blazed from her *druidainoch* stone and encased her in the iridescent, translucent bubble. Heat like molten fire seared through her. The red lightning struck the bubble, knocking her backward into the retinue. The bubble held, but the concussive force of the blow stunned her.

"Jacinda!"

She heard the sharp emotion in the voices that called out her name — surprise from the retinue, horror from Cristella, fury from Galenock. The retinue got her back on her feet, and the bubble faded. The clash of nearby sword battles rang in her ears. She rubbed her temples to ease the pounding in her head and tried to focus on Galenock.

Another blast of red lightning streaked toward her and slammed into a new bubble. She would have been knocked her off her feet again if the retinue hadn't caught her.

"Hold on, Jacinda, I'll help you!" Cristella appeared on her left. She gripped Jaci's shoulder. An influx of magical energy, similar to Talan's though not as strong, bolstered her, helped clear her head.

Galenock chortled. "You think you can stand against *me?*"

"All in formation!" Keiresta thundered from Jaci's right.

A hand, not Keiresta's, gripped Jaci's other shoulder, and she caught a glimpse out of the corner of her eye of all the Enchantresses lined up in offset rows, connected with similar hand-to-shoulder links. Jaci's bubble blazed forth in a flash of white light, surrounding the Enchantresses and blocking the twisted spell that had kept them from casting. Lifting their hands, they chanted in unison. Their *druidainoch* stones glowed as blue lightning shot through the bubble and flew toward Galenock.

Galenock shouted a spell, and a wall of red flames appeared in front of him. The blue lightning hit the flaming wall and fizzled out. The wall dissipated, and Galenock struck back with another blast of red lightning.

Jaci braced herself as the lightning smashed against the bubble. The Enchantresses held firm behind her and helped absorb the impact. The bubble thinned, but it didn't break.

Galenock growled in anger and altered his spell. Continuous bolts of red lightning bombarded the Enchantresses, each blast striking the protective bubble with the force of exploding dynamite. Jaci staggered under the relentless onslaught. The light from her *druidainoch* stone dimmed as she fought to stay conscious. The Enchantresses were reeling back against the bluff, just managing to keep their grip on each other and stay within the weakening bubble.

Cristella steadied Jaci, then they both cried out as another bolt knocked them sideways. Cristella and the other Enchantress that had gripped Jaci's shoulder lost their hold on her, and they all stumbled to their knees. The bubble faded.

Something whizzed out of the dark right through the space where Jaci had been standing and hit the Enchantress behind her. The Enchantress screamed and fell. Jaci whirled at the sound. The Enchantress lay on the ground, clutching at an arrow sticking out of her upper arm. Another arrow from high up in the rocks on the left shot past Jaci, narrowly missing her. She heard running footsteps, then Liundur leaped in front her, swinging his sword and deflecting a third arrow, while Arnos raced off in the direction the arrows were coming from.

Jaci scrambled to her feet as red lightning streaked toward Liundur. She caught the back of his leather jerkin just before it hit him. The iridescent bubble swallowed them both and blocked the lightning, but the impact drove them backward, and the bubble winked out. An arrow thunked into Liundur's ribs. He grunted and recoiled into Jaci. Another arrow struck deep into his left shoulder.

"No! Liundur!" Jaci cried, as he staggered back and fell to one knee.

Liundur heaved himself to his feet, blood darkening his front. "Stay… behind me."

"Jacinda, take my hand!" Cristella called out.

Jaci spun around and grasped the hand reaching toward her. Backed up against the bluff, the Enchantresses had rallied and re-connected. The bubble blazed forth and blocked another of Galenock's rapid-fire attacks. The blasts slammed Jaci to the ground. The bubble faltered as she struggled to rise.

A fierce wave of terror and fury swept over her, shocking her. *Talan!* He was awake, and close by. Joy and fear for him warred within her as Cristella and Liundur pulled her to her feet. She let go of them and let the bubble fade for a second so she could see clearly. High in the sky, a dark shape winged toward them.

They had to distract Galenock so he wouldn't see Talan coming. Not that keeping Galenock's attention would be difficult. Jaci grabbed Cristella's hand and Liundur's jerkin just as Galenock shot more blasts of red lightning. A new bubble stopped the blasts, but the impact flattened them.

"Had enough yet?" Galenock taunted.

Dazed, Jaci swung up onto her knees, one hand holding her throbbing head. Cristella sat up slowly beside her. Behind Cristella, the other Enchantresses were regaining their feet. Liundur lay un-moving, eyes closed, his breathing harsh and shallow, his chest and side covered in blood. *Liundur!*

Jaci clenched her fists, anguish hardening into anger. She lurched upright, pointed at Galenock, and let fly the blue lightning spell, pronouncing it exactly as she had heard Keiresta speak it. Jagged blue light streaked from her finger straight toward Galenock. She felt Cristella's surprise mix with her own elation at her success in working the spell. Cristella clasped her shoulder, and then the Enchantresses echoed her words, sending bolts of blue lightning at Galenock. The lightning struck his summoned wall of red fire, driving him back a few steps instead of fizzling harmlessly.

Jaci stepped forward and glared at Galenock. "Take that, you overblown sack of crap!" She glimpsed the winged horse dropping down out of the night sky behind him and prayed none of his men would see it and give the alarm. "We're going to take you down, do you hear me?" She shouted the blue lightning spell again. The others reconnected and joined in, their voices echoing into the night.

Galenock braced himself, and his defensive wall held, though a bluish tint burned through the red flames before they dissipated.

Jaci stuck her hands on her hips. "Had enough?"

Before Galenock could speak, the winged horse — the black she had ridden — swooped to the ground behind him. Carrick and Owen leaped from the saddle and tackled Galenock. Another winged horse flew in from the side and landed near the Enchantresses. Talan slid from the saddle and sank to his knees.

"Talan!" Jaci and Cristella cried, running to him as both horses launched back into the air.

"Jacinda..." he whispered. "Can boost... your power..."

Galenock roared out a spell. He swung his hand wide and sent Carrick and Owen flying through the air. They crashed into the feet of the stone warriors behind him and lay still. Then he turned on Jaci. "I will break you with my own hand!" He stalked toward her.

Keiresta and the Enchantresses rushed to Jaci's side. Jaci clasped Talan's hand as Cristella gripped her shoulder. The iridescent bubble enveloped them all, and they screamed out the blue lightning spell. A weak influx of power flowed from Talan into Jaci, his dire injuries hampering his ability to channel energy.

Galenock snarled the words of his defensive spell. The wall of red flames burst to life in front of him. The blue lightning hit the wall and burned, slowing him down but not stopping him before it died.

Through the milky translucence of the bubble, Jaci saw the flaming wall fading and Galenock lunging toward her. "Keiresta heal Talan! We need his power —" was all she got out before Galenock broke through the bubble and grabbed her. He pulled her back against him, his arm wrapped around her, pinning her. Then he kicked Talan in his broken ribs and knocked aside Cristella. The moment the connection between Jaci and the Enchantresses was broken, the bubble faded. Galenock rattled off the words of another spell, and with a sweep of his hand, flung the Enchantresses and Talan across the open space into the cliff. They dropped to the ground, groaning and barely moving.

Jaci elbowed Galenock hard in the gut and twisted out of his grasp. Before she could get away, he caught her arm and backhanded her across the face. Pain exploded in her skull, and her head swam. He shoved her roughly up against the bluff. She cried out as the back of her head hit the rock. Pain clouded her mind.

He pressed his forearm against her throat. "You little wench! I was going to let you live, but I've changed my mind." He pressed harder, cutting off her air.

She struggled wildly, clawing at his arm, panic scattering her thoughts.

He flattened her against the rock wall with the side of his body. "Die, wench."

Her mind grew fuzzy; her movements slowed, her hands falling to her sides as awareness dimmed. Her right hand touched something sharp. *Mace.* With the last of her strength, she pulled the mace from her belt and whacked Galenock in the head.

He staggered and fell, blood pouring down the side of his face. Jaci dropped the mace and collapsed, gasping for air, her breath rasping painfully in her throat.

"Jacinda!" Talan was beside her, lifting her. He carried her over to where the Enchantresses were gathering. Keiresta rose from the side of the Enchantress she had just healed, and without a word, glided her hand in the air above Jaci's head and throat. The pain disappeared, and Jaci could breathe freely again. Keiresta met her gaze briefly before turning away and kneeling beside another injured Enchantress. The icy, jealous anger in Keiresta's eyes froze the words of gratitude Jaci had been about to speak.

"Jacinda?" Talan's anxious voice roused her. "Jacinda, are you all right?"

She blinked and tried to shrug off Keiresta's animosity. "Yes, I think so. Are you?"

He let out a long breath, his relief palpable. "Yes."

He set her on her feet and stepped back, shuttering his emotions. She would have thrown her arms around him, but Cristella hugged her first. Jaci hugged her back, rejoicing that Cristella had survived and that Keiresta had healed Talan despite her hatred of him. Then fear surged through her, and she pulled away and looked back toward the bluff. "Is Galenock dead?"

"If he isn't, he will be," Talan said to her over his shoulder. He had drawn a knife from his belt and was headed across the open space toward where Galenock lay.

"Wait!" Jaci raced forward and caught his arm. She whirled on Cristella, who had followed her. "Try to cast a spell. Any spell."

Cristella opened her mouth and choked.

Jaci's gut turned to ice. "He's not dead."

Jaci's *druidainoch* stone suddenly blazed, and a bubble encased her and Talan.

"What...?" Jaci gasped as Talan tensed beside her.

The bubble vanished.

"What happened?" Keiresta demanded, coming up beside them.

"I don't know," Jaci said, shaking with reaction.

The rest of the Enchantresses clustered around them.

Something moved at the base of the bluff.

"Oh, no," Jaci whispered.

Galenock heaved himself up and staggered to his feet. Blood oozed from his wound and plastered the whole left side of his face, neck, and shoulder. His hands glowed red.

Keiresta's eyes narrowed. "All in formation!"

The Enchantresses rushed to form their interconnected lines. Jaci stood between Keiresta and Talan, with Cristella gripping Jaci's and Keiresta's shoulders from behind. Jaci clasped Talan's hand as he moved close. Surrounded by an iridescent bubble, Jaci and the others shouted their attack spell. Blue lightning streaked across the open space toward Galenock. Jaci drank in the full force of Talan's power and channeled it into the spell. The lightning grew white hot.

Galenock's fiery wall appeared in front of him. The lightning hit the wall and burned through it, engulfing Galenock in white flames. He screamed.

Bile rose in Jaci's throat as his flesh melted before her eyes. Then his screams changed, and she suddenly realized he was screaming out words. The hairs on the back of her neck stood on end as a red glow suffused his body. The white flames snuffed out. An aura of malevolence sent chills crawling over Jaci's skin.

Still glowing, Galenock sprinted across the open space toward Jaci. Knife in hand, Talan leaped in front of her. Keiresta and the Enchantresses invoked the blue lightning spell again, but it couldn't penetrate the red glow. Galenock launched himself at Talan. The impact ripped Talan from Jaci's hold, and the two men rolled around on the ground, grappling with each other.

"Talan!" Jaci ran toward them, horror squeezing her heart as she realized why her protective bubble had enveloped them earlier.

Talan screamed as Galenock chanted the wound transfer spell. Blood spilled from the side of Talan's head, and his skin burned down to red, oozing flesh. He lay on the ground, moaning. Jaci skidded to a stop as Galenock rolled to his feet between her and Talan, completely whole.

"Now, wench, it's time for you to die." He called out a spell and flung his arm outward. Keiresta and the Enchantresses flew backward and crashed into the cliff wall. "It's time for all of you to die." He shouted more words, and Jaci recognized the red lightning spell.

"No!" She dashed to the side to get between Galenock and the Enchantresses, who were floundering at the base of the cliff.

Before she could get there, red lightning streaked across and struck the Enchantresses. They shrieked as it burned into them. Galenock strode toward them, repeating the spell. Jaci blocked it, but the impact rammed her to the ground. Stunned, she crawled onto her knees. Galenock advanced on her. The words of the spell rang out like a death knell. She tried to get to her feet, but her legs wouldn't hold her.

A flash of metal flicked through the air. Galenock froze in midstride, his spell silenced by the knife lodged in his throat. Clawing at the hilt, he toppled to the ground, twitched for a few moments, then lay still.

Jaci stared in shock, uncomprehending, until a winged horse landed nearby and Katar jumped to the ground. Another winged horse glided in behind him, and Nickalonis leaped down. Both men rushed to Jaci's side.

"Jaci!" Nickalonis slung his bow over his shoulder and lifted her to her feet. "Are you all right?"

"I — I think… I'm okay. Katar… th—thank you," she stammered, her mind still hazy. She was vaguely aware of more sword battles in the distance. Her eyes fell on Talan's burned body across the way, and a sob escaped her. Was he even still alive? "Keiresta — where is she? I need her." She took a step toward the Enchantresses and nearly fell.

Nickalonis steadied her. "Easy, there. Lean on my arm. We'll find her."

Jaci gestured toward Galenock. "Someone make sure he's dead."

"With pleasure." Katar retrieved his knife, then drew his sword, lifted it high, and sliced downward, cleaving Galenock's head from his body.

Nausea twisted Jaci's stomach, and she turned away from the grisly sight.

Nickalonis shifted his position, blocking her view of the corpse. "Is Talan here? Where's Carrick and Liundur and —"

"Dying or dead, I don't know. That's why I need Keiresta." Jaci wiped at the tears sliding down her face. Leaning on Nickalonis, she stumbled over to the cliff face where the Enchantresses huddled. The fact that several of them were sitting up and appeared not to be in any distress gave her hope that Keiresta hadn't been killed by the red lightning blast.

They found Keiresta healing an Enchantress with raw, oozing skin on her arm and side. The other Enchantresses were supporting those still injured. Jaci saw second- and third-degree burns, but nothing life threatening. Cristella, her back red and blistered, was kneeling across from Keiresta, alternately berating her and begging her to heal Talan. Keiresta was ignoring her.

Jaci's anger flared. She let go of Nickalonis and crossed the last few steps on her own. "Keiresta! Talan is dying. You need to heal him."

Keiresta rose and moved toward the next wounded Enchantress. "I need do nothing of the sort. I healed him once. That's all he'll ever get from me."

Jaci lunged forward into Keiresta's path. "Hasn't he suffered enough? All he did was have the impudence to love your granddaughter. She said she loved him, and then slept with every Tom, Dick, and Harry around, including Galenock." Jaci stabbed her finger back toward the dead wizard. "She died because of her own bad choices, not because of anything Talan did. Talan has spent his life trying to free Tarshane from Galenock's rule. What did you do all that time? Hide in your castle like a coward. He deserves to live more than you do. Now heal him *and* his men, or so help me, I'll use that blue lightning spell on *you!*"

Ire burned through the ice in Keiresta's eyes. "How dare you speak to me that way. If anyone was a coward, it was your mother, running away like she did."

"My mother left because she didn't want her life dictated by others. Tarshane was at peace when she left, so don't you dare call her a coward! And you can hate Talan's father all you want for whatever he did to you, but you have no right to take that hatred out on him." She pointed at Talan. "He sacrificed everything to atone for something that wasn't his fault. Something you wrongly blamed him for. You owe him. Now give him his life back. And I mean *now.*"

Jaci and Keiresta glared at each other. None of the Enchantresses spoke. Cristella was still kneeling by the Enchantress Keiresta had healed, her expression a mixture of anguish, desperation, and hope. Nickalonis stood a few steps to Jaci's left, tense and silent. Sword clashes still rang in the distance, but Jaci barely heard them.

Keiresta gave Jaci the same inscrutable look she'd given her once before, then turned and stalked to where Talan lay. She looked down at him for a long moment. Jaci held her breath, praying he was still alive. Keiresta knelt and glided her hand above his body, healing his burns and the mace wound. Jaci closed her eyes and exhaled a long breath. She forced herself to stay where she was, not wanting to get in the way or do anything to make Keiresta change her mind. Cristella slipped to Jaci's side and squeezed Jaci's hand, tears dripping down her cheeks.

When Keiresta had finished, Talan lay with his eyes closed, his chest rising and falling slowly as if in deep sleep. Keiresta performed the same motion with Liundur, who now lay beside Talan, along with Carrick. When she had finished with Liundur, she tossed aside the arrows that had pierced his ribs and shoulder. As she was healing Carrick, Katar dragged Owen by the shoulders over beside them. Blood covered Owen's forehead.

"Where is Arnos?" Nickalonis whispered.

"I don't know. I saw him running up toward that ridge a while ago." Jaci indicated the high cliff to the left of the bluff. "An archer was shooting at us."

"Are you all right here if I go find him?"

Jaci nodded.

Nickalonis started toward the path beside the bluff, then stopped as two bloodied vanguard soldiers limped down the path, carrying an equally bloody Arnos.

"Oh, no," Jaci whispered. "Please tell me he's not dead."

Nickalonis ran across and spoke to the soldiers. "He's alive!" he called to Jaci. He helped carry Arnos over to where the others lay. They set Arnos down, and the soldiers collapsed beside him.

Keiresta healed all of them, then rose and strode back to where Jaci and Cristella waited.

"Thank you," Jaci said.

"Yes, thank you for saving his life," Cristella added.

Keiresta faced Jaci, her eyes and voice cold as deep winter. "Don't ever ask me for anything again." She brushed past them and knelt next to one of the wounded Enchantresses.

Jaci and Cristella rushed to where Talan lay and dropped to their knees beside him.

Jaci cupped his cheek. "Talan? Talan, wake up!"

Talan stirred and opened his eyes. "Jacinda?"

"I'm here." Jaci helped him to sit up.

He tensed and looked around. "What happened? Where's Galenock?"

She caught his face between her hands and smiled, her eyes filling with joyful tears. "He's dead. We've won!"

"He's dead? Truly?"

Jaci nodded. "Katar made certain of it."

The Black Banders and Owen had risen, and they gave Talan, Jaci, and Cristella a hand up.

"But how?" Talan asked. "Last I knew, he had this red glow around him and he was running toward me. I don't remember anything after that."

Jaci put her hand on his arm. "He transferred his wounds to you. And then he attacked the Enchantresses and he was about to attack me. Katar saved the day with his knife-throwing skills. If not for him, we'd all be dead." She shuddered at the memory.

Talan pulled her into his arms and held her close. "I'm so sorry you had to go through this," he whispered.

Jaci closed her eyes as the intensity of his love enfolded her, electrifying her whole being. Breathless and trembling, she drew back a bit and looked up at him. "I'd do it again, for you."

His eyes darkened with a deep yearning. He brushed back a stray lock of her hair, his fingers caressing her cheek and slipping to the nape of her neck as he lowered his head and kissed her.

For a few precious moments, the world stopped, and everything around them fell away. The songs of wind and water and mountain swelled in Jaci's heart and soul in exquisite harmony. Talan's arms tightened around her, his kiss strong and wanting, yet tender. She slid her arms up around his neck and leaned into him.

He abruptly let go and stepped back. "I'm sorry, I should not have —"

She grasped his shirt front, pulled him back down to her, and kissed him with all her pent-up passion. He crushed her close again, returning her kiss with equal passion.

Terrified screams pierced the night, coming from the direction of the lake. The pungent smell of sulfur thickened the air.

They broke apart and looked toward the sounds.

"What was that?" Jaci asked.

More shouts echoed through the open space. Fear curdled her blood as she recognized one of the voices.

"Solon!" Nickalonis raced out through one of the openings toward the lake.

Surrounded by Black Banders, Jaci and Talan followed. They ran down the path to the narrow, rocky beach, the Enchantresses behind them.

A chaotic battle between Galenock's troops, Talan's men, and mysterious fighters in some kind of desert-badlands camouflage clothing raged along the opposite shore.

Solon appeared from the midst of the battle. "Get back!" He waved frantically at them. "Stay out of the water!"

Nickalonis, who had taken a few steps into the lake, reversed course and splashed back out. Carrick and Arnos pulled him up onto the shore just as something rippled through the thigh-deep water near his feet.

The camouflaged fighters forced a group of Galenock's soldiers off the edge of the shore into the lake. The soldiers screamed and flailed as they tried to swim back to shore. Jaci gasped as skeletal warriors in tattered clothing, their scimitars gleaming dully in the moonlight, rose up out of the water, hacked at the soldiers, and dragged them under. More skeletal warriors climbed up onto the far shore and attacked Galenock's troops, their eerie battle cries echoing through the mountains.

"The legend is true," she whispered. Then she cried out as a group of skeletal warriors emerged from the roiling lake right in front of her. Pinpoints of yellow light glowed in their empty eye sockets, and water dripped from the few strands of hair still attached to their skulls.

Talan thrust Jaci behind him. "Everyone get back!" he called as the Black Banders leaped to the forefront.

But the dead warriors walked past them as if they weren't there. Jaci stared in surprise as they creaked up the path toward the open space and disappeared around a bend. "What are they doing?"

"I don't know. Stay close." Talan took Jaci's hand and headed up the path behind Carrick and Liundur, who were following the dead warriors.

When they reached the open space, Jaci and the others watched as the warriors went straight to a shadowed area to the left of the bluff and picked up some objects from the ground. Moonlight glinted off bright metal and gemstones as the skeletal warriors carried the stolen treasure back into the crypt.

Moments later, one of the warriors closed the crypt door, then placed its bony hands flat against the stone and uttered a strange screeching sound that grated Jaci's nerves like fingernails on slate. The door glowed with a yellow light that matched the glow of the wolf's head. The other warriors threw back their heads and joined in the screeching until the entire island reverberated with the sound.

Jaci cringed and covered her ears as the piercing screech rattled her brain. Her whole body began to shake, the world spinning around her in dizzy circles.

Talan lowered his hands from his ears and slipped his arm around her. He cupped her cheek in concern. "Jacinda?"

She clung to him, barely hearing his voice. "Whoa... don't feel so well..." Her vision grayed as her head spun, and all went black.

CHAPTER 36

Soft lips nipping at her cheek tickled Jaci back to awareness. She blinked her eyes open and found a large black nose gently bumping the side of her head and snuffling in her ear.

She laughed and stroked the black winged horse's face. "Hello, boy. You'd make a great alarm clock."

The horse snorted as Jaci sat up slowly and looked around. She was lying near the base of the bluff in a nest of fur-lined coats and blankets. The Enchantresses and vanguard soldiers had gathered on the opposite side near the stone statues. Some of the soldiers were helping Talan's men scrub away the octagram and remove the ritual paraphernalia.

"Your Highness." Liundur shooed the black away. "Are you well?"

She considered. "I seem to be. I don't hurt anywhere, anyway." She glanced up at the pale pink clouds feathering across the dawn sky. "Have I been out long? What happened? I don't hear any sword fighting."

"A couple of hours." Liundur turned to the side and called out, "Talan!" Then he helped her up. "The battle is over. Galenock's men have been dealt with."

She shuddered inwardly at the finality in his voice. "What about the dead warriors?"

"They went back into the lake."

Talan rushed up. "Jacinda!" He gently caught her shoulders. "Are you all right?"

She nodded and stepped into his arms. They held each other tight. She felt his lips brush her hair, then he eased back and gave her a faint smile.

"You scared me half to death."

"I'm sorry." She smiled ruefully. "I guess my brain decided it'd had enough."

"Jaci!" Solon jogged over from one of the entrances to the open space. "Perfect timing. I'm glad to see you're all right. You had us worried." He turned to Talan. "I think everything is ready."

"Ready for what?" Jaci asked.

"To destroy Galenock and Ridaur for good," Talan said. "The Enchantresses have agreed to use their blue lightning spell. With their power, and yours and mine, we'll burn them to dust."

"What do you want to do with the rings?" Solon asked.

Talan frowned. "What rings?"

"Galenock had two rings. One with green stones on his finger, and a small one with a purple stone in his pocket. They look valuable."

Talan raised his eyebrows. "You searched Galenock's pockets?"

Solon flushed. "I didn't. Nick did. And there was a key, too." He produced the items and held them out.

Jaci nodded toward the key. "That goes to" — she caught herself before she said Soneira's name — "one of the rooms in Castle d'Gaire. Keiresta stole it from me, and Galenock must have taken it from her."

"It's yours, then." Talan picked up the key and handed it to her. "As heir to the throne, Castle d'Gaire belongs to you."

She hesitated before taking the key and sticking it in her pocket. *That huge castle is mine.* She couldn't get her head around the idea.

Talan examined the rings in the dawn light. "I've seen these before. Elshaer used to wear the one with the purple stone on a chain around his neck, and Elsaesser is wearing this green one in his portrait in the Wizard's Guildhall. Galenock must have stolen it from his body in the crypt."

"Those rings should be yours, Talan," Jaci said.

Talan looked at her in surprise. "Why do you say that?"

"Because Elsaesser is your great-great-however-many-times-removed grandfather. Elshaer was your father."

Solon gaped.

Talan stared, stunned. "What? How — how do you know this?"

"There's someone you need to meet." Jaci smiled at the look on Talan's face. "Stay here. I'll be right back."

Jaci trotted over to where Cristella sat on a low rock apart from the other Enchantresses. Cristella looked up when Jaci stopped beside her, and her lonely, troubled expression slid into one of relief.

"Jacinda, you're awake!" Cristella jumped up and hugged her.

"Yes, and I'm fine." Jaci took Cristella by the hand. "I need you to come with me so I can introduce you to someone." She led Cristella back across the open space to where Talan and Solon waited.

"Is this a good idea?" Cristella whispered. "Perhaps it would be better if he didn't know."

"He needs to know," Jaci said firmly.

"But what if he hates me because I'm an Enchantress? After the way Keiresta treated him —"

"He won't."

Jaci halted in front of the two men and drew Cristella up beside her. "Talan, I would like you to meet Cristella. Your mother."

Solon's jaw dropped even farther.

Talan met Cristella's eyes, and Jaci noted again the strong resemblance. She sensed that Talan recognized it, too.

"My... mother?" he said softly.

Cristella's eyes filled with tears and she whispered, "My son."

Tentatively, he embraced her.

She wept on his shoulder. "I've wished for so long that I could tell you."

He comforted her wordlessly. The poignant mix of shock and emotion from the two of them wrung Jaci's heart. She wiped tears from the corners of her eyes. So did Solon, surreptitiously.

Jaci squeezed Talan's arm, then stepped over beside Solon and drew him a short distance away. "Solon, what happened with those dead warriors? Liundur said they went back into the lake. Did they hurt any of your men?"

"No. They only attacked Galenock's men. I don't know how they knew that it was his soldiers who had violated the crypt, but somehow they must have because they didn't harm anyone else. While they were fighting, we heard this horrible shrieking coming from the area of the crypt, and all the spirit warriors on the battlefield started shrieking too. Great gods, I'd never heard such a hideous sound. I'm glad it only lasted a few moments, because otherwise, I think I'd be deaf." He rubbed his ears.

"Did Talan tell you about the warriors putting the stolen treasure back into the crypt?"

"Yes. He said once the door was resealed, the wolf's head stopped glowing, and the warriors ceased their shrieking. And when all of Galenock's men were dead, the warriors returned to the water, and the lake calmed to its usual bubbling. We figured they'd gone back to their rest."

Jaci looked up at the wolf's head, remembering the glow she'd seen earlier. Now it was completely dark, hidden in the shadow of the stone warriors. "Who were those camouflaged fighters?"

"The nomads of Hyanullis. When we first got here, we were so far outnumbered by Galenock's troops I thought we were done for, but then the nomads appeared out of nowhere and saved us." Solon gestured toward the lake. "They're camped on the lakeshore. They want to meet you."

Jaci's stomach knotted. "They do?"

"You are our princess, heir to the throne of Tarshane. They don't usually have much to do with the rest of the world, but they are curious about you."

"I see." Jaci bit her lip. The sudden mental image of herself wearing a crown and sitting on a throne made her queasy.

Talan and Cristella walked over to them.

Talan touched Jaci's arm. "Do you feel well enough to use your magic?"

She nodded. "Let's get it over with."

"I'll get everyone else out of the way." Solon headed off across the open space.

Jaci took a deep breath, then led the way toward where the Enchantresses had grouped together by the feet of the stone statues. Keiresta stood with her back to Jaci, addressing the other Enchantresses in low tones. The vanguard soldiers guarding them bowed respectfully. Jaci nodded back as she stopped in front of them.

A soldier stepped forward, and Jaci recognized him immediately. "Aegis Nordrel."

He bowed. "My lady."

Jaci smiled, her heart lightened. "I didn't see you earlier and was afraid you'd been killed."

"I was shot by Galenock's archers and left for dead. My Lady Keiresta found and healed me."

"We're ready," Talan said.

Aegis Nordrel nodded. "I will tell my lady." He turned and made his way toward Keiresta.

Jaci gave an inward sigh of relief, glad she didn't have to talk to her directly.

Jaci, Talan, and Cristella walked back to the middle of the open space. The octagram had been cleaned away, and all that remained from the ritual were the small hollows burned into the rock floor.

"Where is Galenock's body?" Jaci asked.

Talan pointed to the base of the high ridge. "It's there, along with what was left of Ridaur. We collected Elsaesser's bones to bring back for a proper burial."

Keiresta and the other Enchantresses joined them. Silently, they stepped into their formation. Cristella moved behind Jaci and Keiresta and put a hand on each of their shoulders. Talan stood on Jaci's left. He clasped her hand tightly. Jaci and the Enchantresses lifted their hands and chanted the spell. Blue lightning shot forth, intensifying into a white-hot blaze as it incinerated Galenock's corpse and Ridaur's remains.

They stood for a moment, watching the breeze swirl through the pile of dark ash. Then whoops and cheering rose into the air. Talan's men swarmed around him and clapped him on the back. The Enchantresses embraced each other.

Nickalonis seized Talan's arm. "Those spells — the seeing through others' eyes and transferring wounds — those are gone now, right? Because Galenock is dead?"

Talan nodded, his intense relief flooding Jaci's senses. Jaci threw her arms around him, and they held each other close, thankful to be free of the horrific spells. Cristella hugged them both as Nickalonis celebrated.

Solon, his eyes reddening with tears, hugged Talan, then Jaci.

"You did it!" he cried, and hugged her again.

Jaci laughed. "You mean we did it."

Solon shook his head. "No, I mean *you* did it. Yes, you had help, but this would never have happened if not for you."

He turned to hug his brother again.

Keiresta, who had been standing stiffly while the others celebrated, turned without a word and strode away.

Jaci ran after her. "Keiresta, wait!" She caught up with her and stepped in front of her so she had to stop. "I want to thank you for your help. We would not have defeated Galenock without you."

Keiresta eyed her with her usual iciness edged with jealousy. "Are you through?"

Jaci clamped down on her temper. "No, I'm not. I want you to know that no matter how much you hate me, I will not hate you back. That's not my way. If you ever decide you want to be a family again, let me know." She caught Talan's hand as he came up beside her, her heart fluttering at the love in his eyes. She smiled, her decision made. "I'm going to be around a while."

Talan's sudden surge of joy stole Jaci's breath.

He squeezed her hand, then he drew Soneira's blue spellbook and the ring with the purple stone out of his belt pouch and held them out to Keiresta. "Thank you for healing me."

Keiresta stared at the ring, and Jaci heard a faint catch in her breath.

"He never took it off," Talan said quietly.

Keiresta's eyes misted. She snatched the ring and the book and rushed away.

As they watched her go, Jaci wondered what Talan had done with Soneira's letter. She hoped he'd destroyed it. "How did you know the ring was hers?"

"Elshaer had many sketches of her from when she was much younger scattered around his chambers. He was as good an artist as he was a spellcaster. In some of the more detailed drawings, she wore a purple ring." Talan cupped Jaci's shoulders. "Did you mean what you said about staying around?"

She smiled and curled her arms around his neck. "I always mean what I say."

He pulled her to him. Their lips met in a hungry kiss.

Someone cleared his throat, and Jaci vaguely heard Solon's voice.

"Ummm... I'm sorry to interrupt..."

They drew apart reluctantly.

"The Enchantresses are getting ready to leave," Solon continued, "and the nomads are asking to meet Jaci."

Jaci sighed. "Then we must say goodbye and go meet our new friends."

They followed Solon out of the open space and down the path to the lake.

Keiresta and the Enchantresses had gathered along the narrow strip of land at the water's edge. The winged horses had been retrieved from the cavern on the other end of the island and brought to the far shore. Mounted vanguard soldiers were leading some of the horses across the lake to the Enchantresses, while others on foot strapped the dead onto the remaining horses to take them home for burial.

Jaci hugged each one of the Enchantresses, and they exchanged thank yous.

When she came to Cristella, she embraced her fervently and said, "Do you have to go? Why don't you stay here with us? We need time to get to know each other."

Talan nodded. "Yes, please stay."

Cristella's eyes brightened with tears. "I would love to, but... Keiresta... I don't know if she would allow it."

"Why don't you ask her?" Jaci said.

Cristella looked at Talan again, then nodded resolutely. "I will."

Jaci caught Cristella's hand, and they made their way over to where Keiresta was mounting her winged horse. Aegis Nordrel held the horse's bridle until she was fully strapped in.

Jaci and Cristella stopped beside her. Cristella stepped forward. "Keiresta, I would like to stay with Talan and Jacinda for a while so we can get better acquainted. I need time to get to know my son. Is this all right with you?"

"Family is important to us," Jaci added.

Keiresta regarded them silently.

Jaci felt Cristella's tension rising, and braced herself for a backlash from Keiresta, but none came.

"Very well," Keiresta said, gathering up her reins. Jaci noted that the ring with the purple stone was on her finger. "Permission is granted."

Keiresta swung her horse around and headed across the bubbling lake, the other Enchantresses following her. When she reached the opposite side, she spoke to one of the vanguard soldiers, who Jaci recognized as Svared, the soldier they had met when they'd first landed on the island. After a brief conversation, Keiresta rode on to where the horses with the dead soldiers had been corralled.

Aegis Nordrel watched her for a moment, then turned back to Jaci, a surprised and thoughtful expression on his face. "Thank you for saving their lives, and for helping us to defeat Galenock. We, and all of Tarshane, are greatly in your debt."

Talan had come up beside them, and Aegis Nordrel shook his hand. "Yours, too. Please give our profound thanks to your men. I hope we get to see you both again. Soon." He bowed to Jaci and Cristella. "My ladies."

He mounted his horse and crossed the lake.

Cristella hugged Jaci. "Thank you so much! I never thought she would agree to it."

"Looks like they're leaving a horse for you," Talan said.

Svared was riding across the lake toward them, leading a dark chestnut horse with pale wings.

He handed Cristella the reins, then patted the horse on the flank. "My lady said he could stay with the others."

He gave a half-bow to Cristella and Jaci. "My ladies." Then he rode back across the lake.

"The others?" Jaci looked at Talan and Cristella.

Cristella lifted her shoulders and shook her head.

"I thought they had collected all of them," Talan said.

Solon, Nickalonis, Owen, and the Black Banders gathered around them, now that the strip of land was empty. The rest of Talan's men had camped on the far shore.

Talan and Jaci slipped their arms around each other and watched as the winged horses galloped across the hard ground and launched into the sky, heading northeast. Higher and higher they flew, dark shapes against the rosy mauve of the sunrise.

A piercing whinny from behind startled them and had the Black Banders reaching for their weapons.

They whirled to see the black gelding and the bay Nickalonis had ridden clatter down the path toward them. Jaci and Nickalonis rushed forward and caught them.

"Whoa, easy, boy." Jaci stroked the black's neck as he stood, ears pricked forward, every muscle rigid as he watched the other horses flying away. "What are you still doing here?"

The bay whinnied, and the chestnut Cristella held sidestepped and snorted, his ears flicking back and forth.

Jaci let go of the black and stepped back. "Do you want to go with them? Go ahead."

The black shook his mane, looked toward the horses growing smaller in the distance, then turned back to Jaci and snuffled her pocket.

"I can see I've got to start carrying some sugar," she said with a grin.

The others laughed.

She looked up at the sky again, just able to see a few tiny shapes. "Thank you, Keiresta." Maybe in time, her grandmother might come to accept her after all. Though she didn't hold out a lot of hope.

A crowd had begun to gather on the opposite shore of the lake. Figures in loose-fitting clothes in varying shades of brown, black, and gray were watching them silently. Similarly colored headcloths covered all but their eyes.

Jaci took a deep breath. "Okay. The nomads."

"Officially, they're called Hyans," Solon said in a low voice.

"They are fierce warriors." Talan boosted Jaci and Cristella up onto their mounts. "But you needn't fear them. They just want to meet you."

Talan's men joined them when they reached the far shore. Jaci dismounted. Talan and the Black Banders stood close beside her as two of the Hyans stepped forward, the rest massing behind them. The two Hyans removed their facecloths, and Jaci was surprised to see that one was a woman. Both were dark-skinned and had deep brown eyes. The man's weather-beaten face marked him as middle-aged, while the woman looked to be about twenty years younger.

The man's eyes widened as he looked at Jaci, and he spoke in a language full of r's and k's and other hard sounds. The only word Jaci recognized was "Deirdre."

The woman said something back to him in the same language, then spoke to Jaci in heavily accented words she could understand. "I am Halindrika, and this is my father, Dakarrtrik. It is our honor to meet you, Lady of the Royal Family."

Jaci cleared her throat. "Thank you, Halindrika. I am Jacinda, daughter of Mirinesstra. I am honored to meet you as well. And thank you for helping us defeat Galenock's men. We are very grateful."

"You are welcome. They were like a plague on our land, sickening it." She spat. "They will befoul the land no more."

"Neither will Galenock. We have made sure of it."

"For that, we thank *you*," Dakarrtrik said in an even thicker accent.

Jaci smiled. "We have to go back to Shiannora now, but I would love to learn more about your people and your culture and become better friends. May we visit you sometime?"

Halindrika looked pleased. "I would like that. What say you, Father?" she asked Dakarrtrik.

He nodded. "You will always be welcome in our lands."

Jaci nodded back. "Thank you. You honor me."

Dakarrtrik and Halindrika touched their fingertips to their foreheads, then their hearts, and bowed their heads.

Then Halindrika spoke. "We will take our leave now, Your Highness. May the gods always guide you along safe paths."

They dipped their heads again and then readjusted their face-cloths. They strode away to the south, en masse, and disappeared into the desert canyons.

Talan shook his head in amazement. "Jacinda, do you realize what you've just done? You've made allies out of the most fiercely independent and solitary people in Tarshane. Not even King Brannad, as well liked as he was, could do that. You're a natural-born leader."

Jaci blushed. "Thank you."

The harsh cry of a hawk sounded high above them.

Jaci shaded her eyes against the rising sun. "Is that Sharrow?"

Talan nodded. "Yes, and another hawk, one of Cranton's, I think."

Jaci felt the tension and worry building inside him as he slipped on his heavy glove and lifted his arm. A small brown-and-white hawk flew down and landed on the glove. He undid the message capsule and gave it to Jaci.

Jaci pried open the tiny capsule and uncurled the message. "It says, 'It is safe to come home.'" She looked at Talan. "What does that mean?"

Talan let out a long breath. "I'm not sure, but at least it's good news and not bad." He had Jaci write 'MR' on the back of the note, then reattached the capsule and sent the hawk on its way. Sharrow followed the hawk for a short distance, then circled in the sky.

"Home." Solon brushed at his misty eyes. "We've not had a home in nineteen years."

Talan squeezed his shoulder. Jaci clasped Talan's hand tightly, sharing his emotional upheaval as the staggering reality of Galenock's death finally sank in.

"We're free," Nickalonis said softly, wiping away tears of his own. Then he whooped and shouted it out. "We're free!"

Talan's men echoed the shout, and whooping and hollering filled the air amid much hugging, backslapping, and celebration.

Eventually, they began packing up their gear and making ready to leave. They'd worked out tentative plans for fighting the remainder of Galenock's troops, both out in the open and in the retaking of Castle d'Gaire. With the Black Banders scouting ahead, they'd have ample warning of any approaching danger.

Jaci and Cristella sat on a flat rock by the lake and watched as Talan and his men finished breaking camp. Liundur leaned against a boulder close by, sharpening his knife.

Cristella couldn't stop smiling. "I'm so glad to be coming with you. Thank you again for everything you've done, but thank you most of all for giving me back my son."

Jaci smiled back. "You're welcome. I'm excited, too, not just because I can get to know you better, but because you can teach me more spells."

Cristella laughed. "I will do my best. You definitely have magical talent, judging by the way you cast the blue lightning spell."

"I was thrilled that I could do it. Funny thing about that spell, though. It didn't exhaust me like the healing spell did, and I noticed it didn't tire out the Enchantresses, either. I thought at first that it was because it's Enchantress magic. But then I remembered reading in Deirdre's diary that Elshaer and Galenock used the spell, too, in their battle, and I didn't think anyone but Enchantresses could use their type of magic."

"Actually, it's not Enchantress magic. It's nowhere in the *drinoch arcantus*. I looked. Keiresta taught us the spell, but she would never say where she learned it. I think Elshaer created it, perhaps just for her. They obviously had some kind of relationship when she studied with the Wizard's Guild. Galenock likely stole the spell. I'm sure Elshaer would never have given it to him."

Jaci's gaze shifted to the northeast toward Millianoch as she thought about Keiresta and Elshaer, pondering what might have happened between them to have left Keiresta so embittered. Was it his roving eye, or had something else driven a wedge between them? Whatever it was, she hoped Keiresta could find some small sense of peace in the knowledge that he'd cared for her to the very end.

CHAPTER 37

It was midmorning when they rode away from the Isle of Lorn. They traveled at a comfortable pace down out of the rocky wastelands and along the arid edge of Hyanullis, crossing the border into Shiannora by midafternoon. Villagers and townspeople lined the roads as they came through, first out of curiosity, then in celebration as Jaci introduced herself and told them of Galenock's death. Word of the wizard's demise spread with the shock and impact of a lightning storm. Crowds gathered from all the neighboring towns. Everyone wanted to meet the new princess with the winged horse and hear the story of how Galenock had been defeated.

By nightfall, Jaci was exhausted. They were still hours away from Catir Coronin, so they accepted the hospitality of a village innkeeper, who was more than happy to host a member of the royal family. After a hearty meal, Jaci crawled into her bed and slept soundly.

The next day mirrored the day before, but on a much grander scale. People came in droves to see Jaci, pay their respects, and celebrate. Many followed along with her as she traveled. Jaci did her best not to quail at the multitudes and to speak to as many as she could. Talan and the Black Banders kept their eyes on the crowds, but all those Jaci encountered had smiles and kind words.

It was late afternoon when Jaci and her now huge entourage crossed the grassy plain to the walled city of Catir Coronin. The massive gates had been thrown open, and more cheering crowds spilled out onto the plain. There were no signs of any red-cloaked Riders or other Ruusitaran soldiers. *Had they been defeated?* Jaci wondered. *And if so, by whom?*

They entered the city, and Jaci was struck again by the beauty of the ornate and brightly painted houses and shops. People lined the cobblestone streets, wildly cheering and bowing to Jaci as she rode by. She waved to them, completely overwhelmed by the outpouring of support. At least she wasn't the only one receiving stares this time. Cristella drew many awestruck looks, as did Talan and the Black Banders.

Just beyond the marketplace, Cranton and Zaiya waved to her from the steps of their house, broad smiles on their faces.

Jaci reined in and jumped down from her horse, along with Talan and some of his men. They made a path for her through the crowd to the doorstep.

Jaci and Talan embraced their friends.

"We're so glad you're safe," Zaiya cried, tears in her eyes. "We've been so worried."

Jaci hugged her again. "Thank you so much for your help."

"Of course, dear. Anything for the two of you. Please come visit us when you can."

Cranton grinned. "Yes, you are welcome to appear in our closet any time you wish."

Jaci laughed. "Thank you. Don't be surprised to see me there sometime soon."

Talan put his hand on Cranton's shoulder. "And thank you for the message about..." His voice roughened, and he trailed off.

Jaci caught his other hand and squeezed it.

Cranton clasped Talan's arm. "It's way past time for you to come home."

They embraced once more, and loud cheers and applause filled the air.

Jaci glanced around at all the smiling faces and wondered again at the disappearance of the enemy soldiers. She turned to Zaiya. "What happened to all the Ruusitarans? I haven't seen a single one."

Zaiya spread her arms wide. "Isn't it lovely? We can breathe freely again!" Jaci looked at her questioningly, and Zaiya laughed, then gave her a mysterious smile. "You'll see."

"Now I'm really curious." Jaci hugged her one last time, then she and Talan and the others made their way back through the crowd and remounted their horses.

They rode on through the city, winding through the packed cobblestone streets. Jaci looked ahead to Castle d'Gaire, illuminated in the warm rays of the setting sun, and thought about how menacing it had looked when she'd first seen it. It didn't look half so frightening now. She only hoped Mandy and Allina and the others who had helped her escape were still safe.

They reached the guard tower, passed through the open portcullis, and clattered over the bridge across the moat to the curtain wall. Here, too, the gates stood wide open, and they rode on across the courtyard to the castle. As they pulled up at the bottom of the imposing staircase, a large group of men led by a familiar burly figure burst out through the castle entrance and down the stairs.

"Welcome to Castle d'Gaire, Your Highness," the figure said with a bow. "I can't tell you how happy we are to see you."

"Willem!" Jaci slipped down off her mount as the others dismounted behind her. "Not nearly as happy as I am to see you. I'm terribly sorry for the loss of your mill, but I'm so glad you all weren't lost with it."

"I told them they would pay for burning my mill. They deprived me of my livelihood, so we deprived them of theirs." He grinned and jerked his thumb back toward the castle. "It's all yours, Your Highness."

Jaci craned her neck upward, taking in the high walls, the lofty towers and turrets. This enormous castle — hers? The thought still staggered her.

Talan clasped Willem's arm and clapped him on the back. "So you're the ones responsible for freeing the castle. Well done, my friend!" He swept his gaze over the men behind Willem. "Well done, all of you!"

"Well, it was us and half the people of Shiannora." Willem nodded to Jaci. "You started one colossal rebellion up there in Garsondale."

Talan smiled at Jaci. "Like I said before, you have a knack for making people rise above themselves."

Jaci blushed. "Thank you."

"Now I only have one more thing to do before I start rebuilding my mill." Willem's expression darkened. "Track down that son of an arse Vorstun and feed him my sword."

"You don't have to," Jaci said. "Vorstun is dead, thanks to Carrick." She gestured toward the Black Bander.

Willem strode over to Carrick. "You killed him? Let me shake your hand. I can't tell you how happy that makes me. That whoreson terrorized more people than Galenock himself. Many, many thanks to you for ridding us of that scum."

"It was my pleasure," Carrick said.

Willem grinned. "I'll bet it was."

Jaci smiled. "And many, many thanks to you, Willem, for all you've done." She turned and spread her arms wide, encompassing everyone around her. "Thank you all!"

Willem went down on one knee. "It is my honor to serve the Royal Family."

Willem's men and Talan and the Black Banders did the same.

Jaci held her breath as every person around her, even Cristella, dropped to one knee. Looking over the sea of bowed heads, she swallowed the lump in her throat and tried to find her voice. "Th— thank you." She cleared her throat and took a deep breath to settle her nerves. "Thank you for your faith in me. Please rise and know that I will do my best to uphold the name and honor of the Royal Family."

As everyone was rising, a female voice called out from the top of the staircase.

"Your Highness?"

Jaci looked up to see one of the castle maids waving to get her attention.

The maid curtsied. "The feast is ready if you would like to come inside."

"Feast?" Jaci suddenly realized she was famished.

Willem smiled. "Ever since we got word of your victory, they've been preparing a feast. They've got enough food down there in the kitchens to feed ten armies."

"That sounds perfect." Jaci turned to the crowd. "Please come in and join me in celebrating our victory!"

A roar of approval went up, and everyone applauded.

Jaci caught a frisson of unease and apprehension from Talan before he suppressed it. She curled her fingers around his. "Is something wrong?"

"No." He met her eyes, then looked up at the castle. "It's been so long. The last memories I have of this place are not good ones."

Jaci saw similar expressions on the faces of Solon, Nickalonis, and the Black Banders.

She nodded. "I understand. But you once said to me that what's happened has happened and can't be undone. We have to move on and look forward. It's time to make new memories." She raised her eyebrows and looked at the others. "Are you ready to sweep out the old and start anew?"

Solon didn't speak, but his expression grew resolute.

Nickalonis threw his arm around his brother's shoulder. "We are."

The Black Banders stepped forward, and Carrick spoke. "Nineteen years ago, we failed the Royal Family. We will not fail you."

Jaci choked down another lump in her throat. "Thank you. I have total faith in you."

They bowed their heads in acknowledgment.

Jaci gave Talan's hand a squeeze. "Shall we go in before Bessa comes out and yells at me for taking too long and ruining her feast?"

Talan smiled. "Yes, we should avoid that at all costs."

"I agree," said Willem. "She's an excellent cook, but my, what a sharp tongue she has."

"That she does," Jaci said, as she and Talan headed up the stairs and led the way into the castle.

For the next few hours, they feasted, shared stories of their adventures, and celebrated their victory over Galenock and the Ruusitarans. Jaci met so many new people that she gave up trying to remember all their names. By the time the ten o'clock bell chimed, she was so tired she could barely keep her eyes open. The city dwellers bid her goodnight and went back to their homes,

Those that had followed Jaci in from other towns and villages filled the inns and barracks or camped out on the plains.

Jaci had her choice of rooms, but when asked if she wanted the royal suite, she politely declined. For now, she wanted the familiarity of the room she'd stayed in previously. Mandy and Allina joyously welcomed her. Talan and the Black Banders took up rooms nearby, with Liundur assuming guard duty by Jaci's door.

It was nearly midnight by the time everyone was settled in. Jaci had just finished changing into a soft blue sleeping gown when someone knocked on her door.

She looked toward the door in surprise. "Now who could that be?"

"I'll get it, miss — I mean, Your Highness," Mandy said.

Jaci threw on the matching blue robe Allina handed her, while Mandy went to the door and opened it.

Talan stood in the doorway. "Jacinda, may I speak with you for a moment? I'm sorry, I know it's late, but I... well... there's something I want you to see."

Jaci's heart fluttered, her cheeks flushing pink at her sudden desire for him to stay a lot longer than a moment. *Behave yourself. That's not why he's here.* "Of course. Come in." She crossed to his side as he stepped in the door. "Is everything all right?"

"Yes, everything is fine..."

He hesitated, and Jaci noticed he had a crumpled piece of paper in his hand.

"Allina and I will go to the linen closets for some more blankets," Mandy said quickly. "It's going to be a chilly night."

She gestured to Allina, who looked momentarily surprised, then comprehended and hastened out the door. Mandy followed, closing the door behind her.

Jaci touched Talan's arm. "What did you want me to see?"

Talan took her hand and led her over to the fireplace. Jaci breathed in the scent of burning pine and tried to calm the heat rushing through her.

"I wanted you to see this." He opened up and flattened out the scrunched piece of paper in his hand.

Jaci recognized it with a pang. Soneira's letter.

"I didn't mean I wanted you to see the letter," he amended. "What I meant was, I wanted you to see *this*." He crumpled it up again and threw it into the fire. The flames curled around it, blackened it, burned it to ash.

Jaci's heart leaped. *He did it! He finally destroyed the letter!*

He slid his arms around her. "Jacinda, I love you. I thought I loved her, back then. But what I believed her to be was not the truth of what she was. My heart saw what it wanted to and not what was truly there. I came to realize that after meeting you. You, with your strength and courage and openness, your genuineness of feeling and honest concern for others — you were everything she was not. You are everything..." He caressed her cheek. "My heart will forever be yours."

She smiled, joy effervescing through her, and cupped his face with her hand. "I love you, too. And I will be here with you, forever."

He smiled back and kissed her.

The moment his lips touched hers, a wild influx of happiness dizzied her, and she clutched his shirt to steady herself. "Whoa, that's one potent kiss you have there."

"Sorry." He tamped down his emotions.

"No, don't." She gave him a mischievous grin. "Bring it on." She slipped her arms around his neck. "Just don't let me fall," she said softly.

"Never." His arms tightened around her as their lips met in another passionate kiss.

A short time later, Jaci heard a loud knock.

Mandy's raised voice projected through the door. "We're back with some blankets!"

They reluctantly let go of each other as the door opened to admit Mandy and Allina, who both had their hands full. Mandy was carrying an armload of blankets, while Allina bore a tray with two cups of amber liquid, which she set on the low table. Liundur closed the door behind them.

Mandy dropped the blankets onto the loveseat. "We went down to the kitchens for some of Bessa's warm honey apple cider. We thought you might like some."

Allina brought the cups to Jaci and Talan and handed them over shyly. Then she hurried to the loveseat, picked up the blankets, and scurried into the bedroom.

"Everyone is so excited," Mandy continued. "They're saying how wonderful it is to have a member of the Royal Family back in the castle and how everything will be right again with Tarshane once you become queen."

Jaci nearly choked on her cider. *Queen.*

Talan put his hand on her back. "Jacinda?"

"I'm okay." She wiped her watering eyes. "It's just the thought of being queen is... well... a little frightening."

"You'll be the perfect queen," Mandy said. "I just know it."

"But I don't know the first thing about running a country," Jaci protested. All she could think of was how complicated and contentious politics were in her world. How would she deal with wars and taxes and infrastructure and keeping the diverse provinces happy, or at least on speaking terms?

Talan slipped his arm around her shoulder. "I agree with Mandy. You will be a great queen. And you won't be alone. We'll be there to help you. All you have to do is be yourself and everyone will come to love and respect you."

Jaci forced a smile. "I hope you're right."

"I am." He drained his cider and handed the cup to Mandy. "Thank you." He squeezed Jaci's shoulder, then stepped away. "I'll leave now so you can get some sleep."

Jaci walked with him to the door. "I'm glad you came."

He smiled. The look in his eyes sent the heat rushing through her again, and the intensity of his joy filled her soul. "So am I. I'll see you in the morning."

She closed the door behind him and leaned against it, giving her racing heart a moment to settle down.

"I can take your cup if you are done with it," Mandy said.

"What... oh, yes, thanks." Jaci swallowed the last of the cider and gave Mandy her cup.

"He's very handsome," Mandy observed, then clapped her hand over her mouth. "That was impertinent of me. Please forgive me, mi — Your Highness."

Jaci smiled. "He is, isn't he? And you don't need to apologize. Please speak up whenever you like. I value your thoughts and opinions."

Mandy looked relieved. "Thank you for not being angry, Your Highness. And if I may say so, your willingness to listen to everyone and not just the nobility is one of your queenly qualities." She blushed and headed for the bedroom. "I will help Allina turn your bed down."

Jaci went into the washroom and took a good look at herself in the small mirror tacked on the wall above the pitcher and basin. Her cheeks were flushed a deep rose, and her eyes shone with happiness edged with doubt. *Queen. Do I have what it takes to be a queen?*

She took a deep breath and let it out slowly. "I guess we'll find out."

CHAPTER 38

Talan paced the edge of the forest along Wolf Run, pausing near the twisted pine to listen for the stealthy step of a wolf pack. So far, he'd seen no sign of any wolves, but the sky was darkening into evening, and he knew they would soon be on the prowl.

He glanced at the horses nibbling unconcernedly at the frosted grass and felt some measure of reassurance that there were no predators close by. Resuming his course, he inhaled deeply the scent of evergreens and tried to calm the anxiety that tightened his chest and imprisoned his heart.

"Talan, you are going to dig a ditch in the meadow with your pacing," Nickalonis said. He sat with his back against a tree, twisting a piece of tall grass in his fingers, his bow and quiver by his side. "Why don't you sit down and relax? You're tiring me out just watching you."

"I can't relax." *Not when she's in a place where I can't be.*

"She said she would be here, and she will be."

Talan turned on Nickalonis. "What if she doesn't come back through? What if she changes her mind and decides to stay in her world? Or what if something happens to prevent her from using the portal?"

Nickalonis gave a short laugh. "This is Jaci we're talking about here — the woman who threw me flat on my back, knocked Galenock into a fireplace, and cowed the witch of the Enchantresses into submission. I pity anyone who tries to prevent her from doing anything." He grinned. "Remember the look on Governor Misaldt's face when she blasted the hat off his head after he questioned her authority?"

Talan heard Liundur chuckling from his post by their horses and cracked a smile in spite of his worry. He had to agree that her response to the governor's rudeness had been highly amusing.

Nickalonis tossed aside the piece of grass. "Why don't you think she'll come back?"

Talan's smile faded as he thought about some of the other difficult situations that had arisen over the past few weeks, generally revolving around the provinces wanting back some of the heavy tax money Galenock had taken from them. Jaci had handled everything with fairness and grace and only the occasional loss of temper. She had earned a great deal of respect, and the majority of the governors had already pledged their fealty to her, even though she had not yet been crowned queen. Even Keiresta had begrudgingly acknowledged her as heir to the throne, much to their surprise. But it had not been an easy process.

When Jaci had initially broached the subject to him about going back to her world to say goodbye to everyone there and settle her accounts, his first thought was that she wanted to escape the intolerable pressure of her royal duties and go home. He'd been terrified ever since that he would lose her. But he wouldn't try to stop her.

He sighed heavily. "I fear that now she is in her own world, she will realize how much she missed her friends and the ease of her old life, and will want to stay there."

"She said she was only going back to settle her affairs. She will be back. I'm sure of it."

"I hope you're right." He looked down at his boots and closed his eyes. *Please come back. I can't live without you.*

A flock of crows in the nearby trees cawed in alarm and rose into the deepening twilight. Sharrow shrieked as she circled high above.

Talan sucked in his breath as the familiar aura of magic charged the air.

"Talan." Liundur nodded toward the meadow.

Talan turned and saw the woman who had stolen his heart standing in the meadow. She shoved back her unruly curls and looked around. The anxiety that had bound and tortured him melted away. He gave a jubilant cry and started off through the tall grass. "Jacinda!"

*****

Jaci whirled at the sound of her name, nearly floored by Talan's euphoria.

"Whoa!" She laughed and ran toward him.

They met halfway across the meadow. Talan swept her into his arms and lifted her off her feet. Then his lips were on hers in a kiss of shared ecstasy.

"You came back to me," he said softly after a few minutes.

"Well, of course I did." She brushed his hair back from his temple. "I love you."

He kissed her again, and no more words were spoken for a very long time.

A wolf howl, not too far away, finally broke them apart.

Liundur and Nickalonis led the skittish horses over to where they stood.

"I think it's time we left," Nickalonis said with a glance at the forest behind them. He handed Jaci a warm coat. "We're very glad to see you back."

"Yes, welcome home, Your Highness," Liundur said.

Home. Jaci slipped on the coat and smiled. This world did indeed feel like home now. In the entire two weeks she'd spent in her old world, she hadn't once been tempted to stay. All she'd been able to think about was who waited for her on the other side of the portal.

She'd needed to go back to her old world, though. She'd had to let Courtney and her other friends know she was all right.

When she'd returned through the clock portal, she'd found the Brunswick house abandoned with a for sale sign stuck out by the road. She'd retrieved her car and her belongings from the police impound office (once she'd managed to convince them that no foul play had occurred) and driven out to Courtney's house. Courtney had wept with joy and relief, and Jaci had told her everything, swearing her to secrecy. Jaci had then arranged to buy the grandfather clock from the Brunswick estate and have it transported to Courtney's for safekeeping. She'd sold her apartment in White Plains and said goodbye to all her other friends, telling them that she would be doing some traveling and it would be a long time before she'd be around again.

While she was at Courtney's, she saw on the news that the deputy sheriff that had questioned her about Deirdre's accident had been arrested for drug dealing and murder, along with Tom, the station attendant, and some other Marston locals. According to the story, the Brunswicks had returned from months abroad to find that their home had been turned into a drug den. Not long afterward, they'd died in a car accident under suspicious circumstances. Then when Deirdre had shown up, the local thugs had tried to scare her off. After Jaci's disappearance, the state police, spurred on by

Courtney's repeated phone calls, had descended on Marston and uncovered the criminal activity. From what Jaci read about the investigation, it appeared Deirdre's car had been tampered with, too. The news both angered and saddened Jaci, but at least those responsible had been brought to justice.

When the time came for Jaci to go back to Tarshane, she was more than ready. She and Courtney shared tearful goodbyes, then Jaci climbed into the clock and spoke the magic word. The sudden crackle in the air told her the spell was working. She'd never in her life been so happy to see a field full of tall grass.

Jaci smiled again and nodded to Liundur and Nickalonis. "Thank you for your wonderful welcome. I'm very happy to be back." She looked at Talan and saw everything she was feeling mirrored in his eyes.

They mounted their winged horses, with Jaci and Talan on the black, Nickalonis on his bay, and Liundur on Cristella's chestnut.

Jaci patted the black's neck before urging him forward. "Let's go, boy."

The horses galloped across the meadow and lifted into the air.

"Woo hoo!" Jaci grinned as they climbed higher into the twilight. "They don't have these back in my old world."

"Good," Talan said, his lips by her ear. "At least this world has one advantage."

"Oh, I can think of another advantage that's much more important."

"What's that?"

"You." She settled back against him, his arms close around her, and listened to the song of the stars as she flew toward home.

THE END

ABOUT THE AUTHOR

Lori L. MacLaughlin traces her love of fantasy adventure to Tolkien and Terry Brooks, finding *The Lord of the Rings* and *The Sword of Shannara* particularly inspirational. She's been writing stories in her head since she was old enough to run wild through the forests on the farm on which she grew up.

She has been many things over the years – tree climber, dairy farmer, clothing salesperson, kids' shoe fitter, retail manager, medical transcriptionist, journalist, private pilot, traveler, wife and mother, Red Sox and New York Giants fan, muscle car enthusiast and NASCAR fan, and a lover of all things Scottish and Irish.

When she's not writing (or working), she can be found curled up somewhere dreaming up more story ideas, taking long walks in the countryside, or spending time with her kids. She lives with her family in northern Vermont.

www.ingramcontent.com/pod-product-compliance
Lightning Source LLC
Chambersburg PA
CBHW032156180726
48284CB00001B/64